A PLACE FOR MY HEART

Encounters of the Heart Series - Book 3

I0687002

BESTSELLING AUTHOR
Ann Marie Bryan

Victorious By Design
Tallahassee, FL

To order copies of this book, please contact:
Victorious By Design, LLC
P.O. Box 6141
Tallahassee, FL 32314
Lighting the path to your next level

Visit our website at: www.victoriousbydesign.com
Email us at: orders@victoriousbydesign.com

Book cover created by Humbird Media Company

ISBN-13: 978-0985146887
ISBN-10: 0985146885

ENCOUNTERS OF THE HEART SERIES
#1 AMAZON BESTSELLING SERIES
(AFRICAN AMERICAN CHRISTIAN FICTION)

PRAISE FOR BOOK 1

SHADES OF THE HEART

"This book in one word: POWERFUL! As a married woman, this book ministered to my soul. I loved how the author took us through every emotion of dealing with the extreme lows in crisis to the extreme highs. The personal battle to move towards forgiveness, restoring, rebuilding and ultimately the true meaning of love were all brought in full circle showcasing that love truly endures all things. This is an excellent display of how our faith and relationship with God can develop and the importance of having strong and true supporters in your corner. I loved Blake and Gabby together but what I loved most was their individual story of growth. Excellent job and excellent read!" *Author Untamed*

"I loved this fabulously written Christian romance novel centered on a married couple dealing with infidelity by the wife. Although it contained prayers, Scriptures, and a few short sermons, it wasn't preachy but right on time for me. I loved reading about the trials and tribulations of Christian marriages and this one covered all of the emotional basis to draw me in and keep me turning the pages. I couldn't wait to read the beautiful ending. Just a fabulous story that pulled on all the heartstrings!" *Author Barbara Joe Williams*

PRAISE FOR BOOK 2

MIRRORED HEARTS: SEALED BY FIRE

"...I found this novel to be particularly meaningful, because it urged me to look at myself—a Christian, a wife, a mother, a writer, a teacher—in a different light. I can honestly say it caused me to enter into some deep self-examination as it relates to being judgmental of the sins of others while carrying around sin that is no more or less 'sinful' than theirs. I love a book that makes me think. This novel did more than that—it made me pray... A true wordsmith, she has the ability to transport you 'smack-dab' into the middle of a scene. There were times I felt as if I was in the room watching the characters interact with each other. I could hear the emotion in their voices and feel the tension in the air... I was amazed that by simply shifting perspectives, the writer was able to get me to feel sympathetic towards a character... whom I absolutely did not like... You absolutely ROCK, Ms. Bryan!" *Amazon Customer*

"Ann Marie Bryan's second installment in the Encounters of the Hearts series is [a] powerful story of one married couple's struggle to overcome the double betrayal of their wedding vows... Bryan makes it very clear throughout this moving story that love and faith are keeping this marriage afloat as Larry and Rozene navigate these turbulent waters. The characters constantly turn to their faith to guide them in their darkest moments and to give them the strength to persevere, to find the sun waiting for them just over the horizon. This is a beautifully written and powerful story! I highly recommend it!" *Amazon Customer*

DEDICATION

I dedicate this book to Mr. Shirley (Dada) Bryan, a wonderful man of God whom I have the privilege of calling father-in-law.

Dada, I enjoy being in your presence and I am a better woman of God because of the wisdom that consistently proceeds from your mouth. May God continue to bless and keep you. Stay victorious.

CONTENTS

ACKNOWLEDGEMENTS

As always, I am grateful to the many persons who contributed to the completion of this book. Surely, God made each of you special. Thank you.

My Heavenly Father – I cannot thank You enough for Your love. It is a joy to live in Your presence. I love You. You are God and in You I am well-satisfied.

Orville, my husband, my beloved – Your love means everything to me. I love our conversations and the intellect you bring to the table. All I can say is, "Oh, what a man!" I love every moment spent with you. I will love you always and forever.

Estrina Johnson, my mom – I love you. God made you special. I am glad you are my mother. Thanks for being the awesome woman of God that you are.

I love my ten siblings – Six sisters and four brothers. Gosh, I enjoy meeting up with all of you. I'm so grateful that God gave me each of you.

A big thank you to my sister and second mom, Mrs. Icylin Morgan. I love it when we discuss the characters in this book. Keep being the wonderful person that you are. I love you.

Thank you to my pastor, Bishop John E. Baker, and his wonderful, spirit-filled wife, First Lady Elder Ann-Marie Baker, for continuing to impart God's word into my life. Thanks to my church family, New Hope International Outreach Ministries.

Extra-special thanks to Paula Owen, for selecting the title of this book, and to Shauna-Kay Battick of Humbird Media, for designing the cover.

Heartfelt thanks to my literary sisters – Authors J.L. Campbell, W. Mason Dunn, Tesa Erven, Angela Hodge, M.A. Malcolm, Melissa Mallory, Melinda Michelle, Ramona Poole, Danyelle Scroggins, Lorine Thomas, Untamed, and Genevieve Woods, for your support and encouragement. You are all amazing and I thank God for each of you.

I love my sisters who are my beta readers and first round editors – Millicent Battick, Melissa Mallory, Yamecike McMillan, Henritta Stewart, and Julianne Veira. Thanks for your prayers, critiques, words of encouragement, wisdom, and attention to detail. You all rock!

I am grateful for my official editors – Author J.L. Campbell of The Writers' Suite and Author M. A. Malcolm of Nitpicking with a Purpose. Thank you for helping me bring life-changing books to the world.

9

ABOUT LOVE

"Love suffers long and is kind; love does not envy; love does not parade itself, is not puffed up; does not behave rudely, does not seek its own, is not provoked, thinks no evil; does not rejoice in iniquity, but rejoices in the truth;"
(1 Corinthians 13:4-6)

PROLOGUE

Chandler clutched the windowsill like a lifeline as his stomach plunged to his feet. That was not the way he had seen the evening going. By now, his lips should have been hot on Rozene's and she should be pleading for more of him. She was pleading all right, but not exactly in the way he had thought she would.

Peering blindly through his living room window, he tried desperately to compose himself, yet, he couldn't. It was hard enough for him to think she didn't want to be with him, but to actually hear her say it...

No. He didn't want to hear any more of her speeches about him finding someone else. And about the good Lord providing a wife for him. *Yada. Yada. Yada.* Enough. She was a cosmic killjoy, sucking away the very breath he needed to stay alive.

He had begged her on bended knees to be with him, but she remained resolute. She gave him no wriggle room. She wanted her husband. *She chose him... over me.* And just like that, she had stripped away his confidence and unraveled his universe with two words—'It's over!' Her voice echoed in his sanctuary, in the very place where everything was supposed to be safe and secure for him.

Not realizing he had closed his eyes, he opened them and squared his shoulders. *Maybe if I begged one last time... just one last time.* He needed to fight for what he believed in, right? Frustrated by his own lack of self-control, he used the back of his hand to swiftly brush away the single tear that had rushed down his cheek.

As the pampered child of overprotective, even though absent parents, he had wanted for little in his life. Yet, for the second time in his life, what he desired—what he longed for and consistently dreamed about—was seemingly

11

impossible to attain. She had not given him a single thread of hope. Yet, he had to hope.

His love for her had changed him. With Rozene it was not about sex; he actually loved her. Until today, he hadn't realized how difficult it was to love someone when the love was not reciprocated. Now, he fully understood why some of the women he'd dated ended up hating him when he didn't respond in like terms to their confessions of love in the relationship that they had orchestrated in their minds.

Not that he was into breaking women's heart on a whim. Before he engaged in relationships with them, he'd always been upfront about what he needed. No strings attached. No emotional baggage to complicate the situation. Nothing permanent. Only sex… and definitely, no hassle. Yes, he had been upfront.

In any case, women might grumble about him being a Casanova, but that had never deterred any of them from hopping into his bed. And if they agreed to his terms, he would hop right in with them.

Rozene gazed at Chandler's back as she stood behind him. She knew she had 'knocked the wind out of his sail,' but, she had to. He was head strong and determined, but so was she. She wanted to be left alone. However, she hoped she hadn't pushed him too far over the edge, causing him to do something outlandish. Lord knows, he seemed desperate enough.

She stepped back. She didn't like how he was making her feel. More than ever, the only thing she wanted was to be left alone so she could pull her marriage back together again. She sent up silent prayers as she moved further away from him and sat at the edge of the sofa.

Chandler turned to face Rozene, his demeanor resolute. He had tasted heaven, and no way was he giving it up, not without a fight. He moved to sit next to her.

12

I can take him down. Rozene adopted a ready-to-charge posture, in case Chandler made any surprise moves.

"Give me your hand," he said.

Her bravado flew out the window. Her heart was beating so hard she was sure he could hear it. "Why do you—?"

"What do you think I'm going to do? Break it?" He dropped his gaze to the floor. "I need… I need a little of your strength to share something with you."

Seriously? Rozene wanted to beat her head against something. Anything.

"I won't hurt you, if that's your concern." His voice broke. "I-I…"

Rozene gazed at him, wishing she was not in her current position. Nevertheless, she extended her hand to him, and he placed it on his knee and covered it with his own.

"I love you," he told her earnestly. He held up a hand as she began to protest. "I didn't know I was capable of loving anyone. The last time I thought I was in love was around sixteen years ago. Her name was Alana." He smiled to himself. "She made my days worth living, and live we did. Every minute we spent together, I fell deeper in love with her. I was almost twenty-two years old but I knew I wanted to spend the rest of my life with her." He let out a hollow laugh. "Of course, I proposed. Why wouldn't I? Everyone thought we would get married anyway."

He shifted a bit to settle against the sofa. "We planned a lavish wedding—over-the-top, in my estimation. My parents wanted a grand occasion, so they threw us the 'wedding of the century' as Mother dubbed it."

He sat up to make sure Rozene was paying attention.

She was. *Left that poor girl at the altar, didn't you?*

He sighed at her expression. "You think you know me, huh? I did not leave her at the altar, Ro. She left me at the altar," he said, casting an accusatory glance her way. "She did not show up and neither did the best man."

Rozene felt a tug on her heart strings. "That must have been hard for you to deal with. I'm sorry that happened to you. When you extend your love to someone, there is never any assurance that it will be reciprocated."

"Sorry?" He looked at her with slight disdain. "But you're doing the same thing. You threw the love I have for you back in my face."

"Chandler, I'm married, and I have a family. What I felt for you was lust. That's not love. First Corinthians 13:4-7 describes exactly what love is: It is patient and kind and—"

"Whatever, Ro." Anger rushed through him. "You can pretend all day long but you cannot deny that what you feel for me is real."

Her eyes narrowed defensively as she decided to be frank with him. "I'm not saying that I didn't feel some sort of... passion for you but that's not love. Yes, passion is a part of love; but love takes time. It's intimate and—"

Chandler chuckled loudly. "After all that whooping you do when we're together... you say that's not love. You had me fooled. You don't look like the type to fake it," he said sarcastically. "Just so you know, all my moans and groans were for real."

"Why do you have to take it to that level?" Displeasure laced each word.

"What level? I'm speaking the truth."

She watched him keenly. He'd never been angry with her but now he was. "Look, Chandler, I'm not here to fight with you. I'm sorry that I led you to believe I was in love with you. I have never been in this situation before—"

"Situation?" He thundered incredulously. "Situation? Is that how you plan to remember our relationship?" He watched as guilt spread across her face. "Yes, I said

14

relationship. We had a relationship." His gaze ripped into her. "While you are busy putting our situation in File Thirteen, this is how I'll remember it—I loved you, but you used me. Yes, Ro. You used me. It took me years to build up the courage to love someone, to trust someone. I thought we were going somewhere with our relationship. You led me on and made me love you. I trusted you and within a few seconds, you've crushed my heart like it was nothing."

The painful memory he would carry because of their situation gave Rozene more than a few anxious moments. She studied him, torn between wanting to comfort him and wanting to slap him. She angled her head and met his gaze with a challenge of her own. "Chandler, aren't you tired of playing the blame game?"

She stood and looked down at him. "From day one, you knew I was married. I never told you, ever, not one time, that I intended to leave my husband." She held his gaze and her eyes filled with tears. "Chandler, please try to understand. I cannot give you what you want."

Frustration mounting, Chandler stood abruptly, folding his arms across his chest, hostility in his gaze. "Say what you want, but you and I both know that our relationship evolved into something beautiful." Cold laughter rolled from his mouth. "Silly of me to even think that thought. How dare me? What would possess me to think that Mrs. Mighty Prayer Warrior would want to stay in my chamber forever? You sure had me fooled. You had one intention— to satisfy your needs and get back to your ready-made family and holy living. Didn't you read where the good book said, 'Do not commit adultery'? His jaw tightened as the words erupted from his mouth.

Instinctively, Rozene stepped back, speechless for a moment. He might as well have slapped her. She allowed her tears to fall as a pang of guilt hit her in the stomach.

15

"I'm sorry. I had no intention of hurting you, but, I can't love you the way—"

"Right." He glowered at her. "So you're just going to grovel, begging him to take you back?"

Reeling from his words—because she knew that was exactly what she had to do—more tears spilled from Rozene's eyes. Larry was hard, unapologetically so, but she would never stop trying. She intended to use every avenue to win back his love.

"Yes. If that's what it takes," she croaked, the tension in her chest almost stopping her breathing.

"How the mighty has fallen." The hiss in his voice was a firm reminder of his feeling towards her.

Fury rose within her and she grabbed her bag from the sofa, and swung past him towards the front door.

He caught her by the arm and turned her to face him. "Don't leave here like—"

"Let go of my arm," she insisted, threatening him with her eyes.

"What can I do to make it up to you?" he implored, releasing her. "Don't leave here like this."

His suave, velvety voice would make any woman swoon, but Rozene did not utter a word. She steeled herself from becoming putty before him as his eyes twinkled seductively at her. She took it all in—his smoky bedroom eyes, his easy-going, gorgeous smile, his fit physique… *Just sinful.*

"Ro," he attempted to engage her heart once more, soft and beseeching. "Make love with me one last time." His eyes were dark with desire as they met hers.

Her heart jolted in her chest and her purse fell to the floor with a loud thud.

In the commotion, he pulled her to him.

"Don't," she pleaded with him, pressing her palms against his chest.

16

Ignoring her protest, he rubbed against her, reveling in the warmth their bodies created. "I know you want me."

"Chandler, stop," she said firmly, pushing him away, but he yanked her back, holding her firmly against him. She wriggled, attempting to get away from him, but instead of being turned off, it turned him on.

"Tell me you want me." His voice was deep with need.

Fear tightened her chest. "Stop it."

"Stop struggling," he told her, annoyance then disappointment washing over him as he released her. "You never struggled before."

She backed away from him. "I can't, Chandler."

"Can't? Or won't?"

His eyes rested on her supple bosom, which rose and fell with each breath she took. Eventually his eyes pierced hers and the raw desire was like an intimate touch, causing her breath to quicken. She closed her eyes to prevent herself from being sucked in. In that moment, Chandler scooped her up and they fell in a heap on the sofa.

Her breath halted in her throat. "Get off me!"

"Shhh," he murmured, raining kisses over her face. "I know you want me." He dragged his mouth down her neck.

"Don't," she said, her breathing panicky, as she moved her neck out of his reach. However, her sharp gasps and movements against him only served to heighten his excitement. He gazed at her lips ready to partake, and definitely ready to tame her.

"Don't do this," she begged, her voice choked with fear.

He noticed the fear in her eyes and the desire in his own faded into oblivion. He laughed for a few seconds, and then became silent. *When have I ever had to beg for sex? Never. Not in this life.* He rolled off her and rested his head next to her shoulder. "Let me hold you for a minute." He wrapped an arm around her waist and lay motionless.

17

Rozene's body felt numb, several emotions spiraling in her head. She didn't even realize she was crying until she wiped the tears.

Soon, he heaved his body from hers. He watched as she quickly gathered her purse, knowing he'd traumatized her, but he didn't care.

"Take care of yourself, Chandler." Her voice was uneven, and her hands were shaking as she smoothed her hair.

"You're lying to yourself, you know," he muttered, his eyes stark with pain.

"I'm done fighting with you." Yes, all the fight had gone out of her. She was even planning to stop fighting herself for her stupid mistake. "I wish you the best. Bye."

But he didn't move, he sat gazing straight ahead.

Hurrying away before he started another unwanted conversation, Rozene walked through the front door, and closed it behind her.

Half an hour later, Chandler left his townhouse. He straightened, welcoming the cool evening breeze that hit his swollen eyes. He couldn't think about her anymore.

Willing the throbbing in his head to go away, he pulled the hood of his sweatshirt over his head and scurried the distance to the main entrance gate of the subdivision while allowing his vision to adjust. The second he exited the gate, he started running. That seemed to set him free.

He ran hard, with his head and shoulders thrust forward. His breath came out in short pants, tearing at his throat, but that was not enough to stop him. Sweat, mixed with tears, ran down his face. For miles he ran, with no particular destination in mind; seeing nothing, feeling nothing, hearing nothing except the pounding of his feet in sync with the pounding of his heart... nothing mattered anymore. Running was sufficient in itself. Hopefully, his run would halt the madness closing in on him.

18

CHAPTER 1

Six months later

Inside, Chandler was screaming. This place was both a memory he would like to forget and a portal to the life he'd thought he had.

He tensed as the desire to flee whipped through him. He'd driven fifty minutes to get there. *Why run now?* He eased away from the door of his black sports BMW and planted his feet firmly on the ground. He had to stop running. Had to push forward. He was dying a slow death on the path he was currently traveling.

A wary sigh escaped his tired soul as he stared blindly at the sturdy young woman before him, hoping this would be a wild goose chase. But no! Here he was, again. It seemed life had other plans for him.

"Please don't leave," the woman, who had a few minutes ago introduced herself as Amber pleaded. "I will get her for you."

After a few anxious glances to confirm he would stay, Amber hurried away, disappearing through the oak double doors of Zion Apostolic Church. A few people were still milling about the church yard on that cool, slightly windy Sunday afternoon.

Folding his hands across his brawny chest, Chandler leaned against his car. *This must be done, plain and simple. It is the right thing to do.* He had to stop living in the shadows and move beyond his waking nightmares.

Inside the church, Amber barreled through the aisle towards Sabrina. "Rina! Rina!" she yelled, her mind reeling. She almost had to scrape her bottom jaw off the ground when the fine, caramel-colored man had asked for Sabrina. He couldn't recall her last name, but Amber was oh-so-thankful she was on hand to assist him.

Divinely orchestrated—that was how Amber pegged this encounter. And no way was she going to let Sabrina miss this golden opportunity. He was perfect for her. *Just perfect!*

What now? Sabrina glanced up from where she'd squatted down at the edge of the first row of burgundy chairs. She zipped her purse, rose and swung it on her shoulder. "Thought you would be wearing out the road by now," she said to Amber. "What's up?"

Amber grabbed Sabrina by the wrist, pulling her down the aisle. "Let's go!"

"What on earth?" Sabrina stopped, snatching her hand back. "What is wrong with you?"

Amber flashed a wide grin. "I'm proud of you, cousin. I'm so proud right now."

"Stop creating a scene, Amber Shaffer."

Anxiety creased Amber's face. "You've got to come. Someone is…" She paused to smooth Sabrina's hair.

"Stop that!" Sabrina slapped her hands away.

Amber squeezed her hands at her chest. "Rina, your man is here." She playfully wagged a finger at Sabrina. "I forgive you for keeping him a secret."

Sabrina all but rolled her eyes. *Here we go again.* "What you need to do is go home to your husband and child."

Amber gripped her hand, tugging her at a slower pace down the aisle. "Come, he's waiting outside." She lifted Sabrina's hand and attempted to high-five her. "God has been good to you."

Sabrina dragged her hand away. "Yes, He has, but stop this foolishness."

Amber grinned at her before rushing them through the door to the foyer. "I want to be on your bridal party," Amber told her. Before Sabrina could respond, she burst through the front door.

20

Lord, help her! Sabrina rolled her eyes and followed her.

"There he is." Amber pointed at Chandler's back, her hand trembling with excitement.

Sabrina's brows furrowed. "I don't know who that is."

"He asked for you by name," Amber hissed under her breath as Chandler turned towards them. "Get it, girl! Go get that fine thang."

"I told you I don't know that man," Sabrina insisted under her breath, looking in Chandler's direction.

Chandler attempted a smile.

"See, he knows you." Amber all but pushed Sabrina towards Chandler. "Now is a great time to get to know him. I'll wait in my car."

Amber waved joyfully at Chandler who lifted his hand in acknowledgement. She walked slowly away, but not before stealing another glance at him. He was well over six feet, she noticed. Everything about him conveyed vigor and all that was wonderful about life. *He is perfect for Rina. Lord knows someone needs to light a fire under her always cool exterior.*

Chandler gazed at Sabrina, the woman who had saved him the night he was drowning in a sea of reality. He hadn't realized she was so strikingly beautiful. *An angelic beauty!* He watched as her slender, yet curvy, five-foot-seven frame glided towards him. Her shoulder-length black hair blew slightly in the wind, away from her oval-shaped face. But what struck him most about her as she stood before him was the flawlessness of her golden-brown complexion.

Her wide, dark eyes stared intently at him under naturally arched eyebrows. "Hello. How can I help?" she asked.

21

Chandler gave her what he hoped was a genuine smile, pulling his gaze from her beautiful, bow-shaped lips. "Hi, I'm Chandler."

Her eyes registered confusion, and as she opened her mouth to speak, Chandler decided to put her at ease. "I see you don't remember me."

An apologetic smile covered her face. "I can't recall that we've met," she said softly.

"I came here one night bawling my eyes out and—"

"Oh my God!" Sabrina shrieked, bear-hugging a stunned Chandler. "Thank You, Jesus!" She released him and held him at arms-length before hugging him again.

That was unexpected. Chandler's hands remained stiff at his side before loosely holding her so they wouldn't topple.

Sabrina slid out of his arms and smiled up at him, exposing even, white teeth. "You have no idea how much I've prayed for you. God is so good. You look great."

"Thanks," Chandler responded slowly, unsure what else to say. He hadn't seen such unadulterated genuineness in a long time.

"Wow!" Sabrina threw her hands in the air, and then stopped abruptly, knitting her brows. "You disappeared. Pastor told me you'd asked him to leave you on the street that night. My only consolation was he gave you his card. We were hoping you would come back to us."

His gaze brushed across her face. "I'm much better now. Swinging by to say thanks. I was hoping to see your pastor, too, but Am..."

"Amber," Sabrina filled in.

"Right. Amber told me he'd already left."

"Yes, he has. But I'm sure he would like to see you."

"I'll try and swing by again," Chandler said, knowing he wouldn't.

22

She smiled joyfully at him. "That would be wonderful."

"Can I take you to lunch?" Chandler heard himself ask, then almost slapped himself.

She looked at him, puzzled.

"I promise I won't kidnap you. We can meet in a public place." And when she still couldn't make up her mind, he added quietly, "I'm leaving town and just want to—"

"Sure. I'd love to."

"Great. Would mid-week be okay for you? I'm leaving on Friday."

"Yes, Wednesday is fine. I know this really cool place."

Miss Take-Charge. He shot her a glance, a tiny smile playing on his lips. "Where's that?"

She cocked her head, knowing exactly what he was thinking. "Meet me in front of Macy's at the Cordova Mall, and we'll walk there. It's outdoor, so dress casual."

"Okay. Twelve-thirty good?"

"Perfect."

He stared at her, his smile widening somewhat. "Take my number in case something comes up and you can't make it."

"Okay." Sabrina took her phone from her purse and entered the digits as Chandler said them. She smiled at him. "Got it."

Her smile had a calming effect on him. Strangely, it made him feel hopeful. "Last name is Peynard. Call me so I'll have your number."

"Okay." She dialed his number. "My last name is Benjamin."

"Got it," he mimicked her, entering her name into his phone.

23

She couldn't help but smile. "See you on Wednesday, Chandler Peynard."

"Wednesday it is, Sabrina Benjamin. Have a great evening."

"Thanks. You, too."

As Sabrina walked towards her navy-blue Acura, she heard him pull away. Still deep in thought, she gasped when she came face-to-face with a smiling Amber.

"You don't know him, huh?" Amber bumped her shoulder, playfully. "I saw when you climbed on his chest. Naughty, girl."

Sabrina stared at her, stunned. "Oh, I don't know him."

Amber wagged her eyebrows. "Uh-huh."

"He's the guy I was telling you about who rushed into the church around six months ago, crying his heart out."

"What?" Amber shrieked. "You didn't tell me he was handsome. He looks like an upgrade to Shemar Moore. Look at me, I'm drooling."

Sabrina chuckled. "So I see."

"Yum! Yum! He's insanely gorgeous. I can only imagine how many male egos he destroys every time he walks into a room. And I bet women are throwing themselves at him. I can't believe you didn't realize he was fine."

"He was wearing a hoodie and hollering, remember?"

"So you're not denying he's handsome," Amber railed on. "Even dream-worthy."

"Dream-worthy!" Sabrina pulled back, laughing. "I can't win."

Amber frowned at her. "Don't tell me he didn't have you doing a double-take. Square-shaped face that is flawlessly proportioned with slightly high cheek bones, chiseled jawlines, full symmetrical lips, and a prominent chin." Amber pranced around in circles. "His hair is nice, too—slightly curly, jet-black. And how could you resist stroking his neatly trimmed beard. Love, love his thin mustache." She edged nearer to Sabrina's car with hands akimbo. "I don't care what you say. He's very handsome."

Sabrina eyed her, pursing her lips. "I'm glad you noticed, Mrs. Shaffer." Pulling her car keys from her purse, Sabrina unlocked the doors. "Please remember, the man is recovering from whatever was ailing him."

"Rina, that was six months ago. I'm sure he's okay now." She eyed Sabrina suspiciously, leaning against the car door so she couldn't open it. "You are not about to turn this man into one of your pet projects, okay?" Frustrated, Amber threw a hand in the air. "Why do you always do that? Everyone doesn't need your help. You need to help yourself to some of him."

Inwardly, Sabrina cringed. "I told you the man has issues, Amber. You need to be praying for him."

"Wonderful!" Amber clapped her hands excitedly. "Help him take his issues to Jesus."

Sabrina knitted her brow, tugging on her car door. "I can't deal with you and this craziness."

Amber eased away from the door. "Don't turn him into a pet project, Rina," she warned again. "Now here's a better idea—turn him into a real project for yourself. I hope you're seeing him again."

"I'm seeing him again, but it's not like that."

Amber threw her hands in the air. "A date! Yesssss!

"You need prayer," Sabrina told her. "It's not a date. He invited me to lunch. A thank you lunch. He's leaving town for a while."

A joyful expression covered Amber's face. "I have a great feeling about this. We need to make sure you're all dolled up. I want you to be the only star in his universe."

Sabrina pursed her lips, pushing out a long breath. "The man is giving me a thank you lunch. This is not a date, so stop thinking like that."

25

Amber feigned indignation. "Come on, Rina, you're acting nonchalant. Skip a little. Pretend to be inspired."

This is a no-win situation. "I've got to run." Sabrina opened her car door. "I have to take care of one of my," she air quoted, "pet projects. Then, I'm going to pop by and see Aunt Connie."

Amber shook her head in disbelief. "You're going to read to Mother Rogers again? Thought you went last Sunday?"

"I'm filling in for Jenay. She and Brandon needed to have some me-time with the twins."

"Okay, I'm right behind you. Mother Rogers is a sweetheart."

"Shouldn't you be heading home? I'm sure Paul must be wondering where you are."

"Husband will be fine. He's having me-time with baby girl."

Sabrina smiled at her. Four-year-old Kayla had Paul wrapped around her fingers—all ten of them. "Let's go, but promise me, no more crazy talk about Chandler."

"Ohhh, Chandler! What are you going to call him? Chand?" Amber chuckled loudly.

Stone-faced, Sabrina told her, "If you're done carrying on, I'll see you at Mother Rogers'."

"Not done yet." Amber grinned, walking away. Suddenly, she stopped and turned towards Sabrina. "Didn't you see Aunt Connie at church? You know you'll have to answer all her questions about the internet." Her eyebrows landed at the top of her forehead before she burst out laughing. "You're a sucker for punishment, aren't you?"

Sabrina grinned at her. "Stop it!"

Amber shook her head and walked away.

"She's family." Sabrina threw at her back before hopping into her car.

26

CHAPTER 2

Chandler let out a sigh of relief when he pulled into the garage of his townhouse in the exclusive gated community of Baladere Estate. He was glad he'd stepped out, but he was equally glad to be back in his safety zone. Soon, he kicked off his shoes in the living room, reached for the TV remote then paused, deciding not to watch TV. He walked to the kitchen and grabbed an apple from the counter.

Next, he slid down into the easy chair on the terrace. He bit into the apple and felt the sweet nectar run down his throat. He'd hardly closed his eyes when memories of Rozene Kanate rushed in.

Her soft, full lips.

Vivid, hazel-colored eyes.

Straight nose, perfectly placed on her beautiful oval-shaped face.

Tall and well-proportioned body.

Flawless caramel complexion.

Long, curly, light-brown hair, which he couldn't resist pulling on.

Strangely, all of that paled in comparison to what he found most fascinating about her—she was a Christian, in full-blown ministry for God.

He smiled inwardly because he didn't really believe in all this God stuff, but she'd almost made a believer out of him.

Rocky. That's how their relationship had been.

Tears weighed on his lashes. For him it had been a relationship, but for her a passing fling, a 'situation' she could no longer afford in her life.

His heart pounded as he recalled when the inevitable had occurred. God, running was all he could think of doing.

Running away from the situation. Running away from himself.

27

He remembered falling to his knees, sobbing.

And sobbing.

Harsh, broken sobs, just ripping out of his soul.

He didn't know how long he had wailed but when he'd stopped, he heard music... a welcome distraction from the coldness that enveloped his soul.

When his eyes focused, he realized he was across the road from a church. It had to be, because the huge lighted cross mounted on the roof stood out like a beacon of hope against the dark sky. The cross beckoned to him, and he staggered to his feet.

His lungs on fire, he looked around wildly, desperately needing to escape the looming darkness that was choking life out of him. His eyes locked on the double doors of the church and he knew he had to get inside.

That night, as the Host of Heaven prepared to snatch him from the gates of hell, he felt compelled to participate in his own triumph.

Fresh wind from on high propelled him across the road, and he leaped, bursting through the doors of Zion Apostolic Church.

That evening, he came face-to-face with Sabrina Benjamin, who was standing behind the last pew. He fell on his knees before her, clutched her feet and wept bitterly. He felt her hand on his shoulder and she began to utter words of encouragement.

Soon, he heard many voices praying for him. Those voices didn't stop until he stopped weeping. When his tears subsided, two men took him into what he assumed was the Pastor's office. He was distraught, bowed over on the chair, but he knew Sabrina had accompanied them, because he heard her praying.

By the time he was able to speak, Sabrina had left. The taller man introduced himself as Pastor Anthony Jackson, and the younger man as Deacon Walter Tucker.

28

Chandler did not divulge what had taken him over the edge, and neither did the men pressure him to share it. When his breathing returned to normal, Chandler thanked the men, and then told them he needed to leave. They prayed with him again, and Pastor Jackson offered to drive him home.

He was quiet all the way, only asking Pastor Jackson for the name of the lady who was praying along with them. He was sure Pastor Jackson had mentioned Sabrina's last name but with all that was taking place, Sabrina's first name was all he remembered.

That night, he was too embarrassed to let Pastor Jackson know where he was living, so he asked Pastor Jackson to leave him about half a mile from his subdivision. He was sure Pastor Jackson wanted to insist on taking him home but the dogged determination in Chandler's eyes stopped him in his tracks. He gave Chandler his card and told him to call anytime.

The reality of what had happened back then hit Chandler and an extra dose of sadness blanketed him. Looking back, he should have protected himself from Rozene; all the signs were there, but he'd chosen to disregard them.

Even when she'd entered his home that fateful Wednesday evening in August, the determination in her gaze should have told him she was out for blood.

He could still see her.

The knife in her hand.

She didn't bother to kill him slowly. You know, break his legs one at a time. Instead, with swift moves, her words had cut him over and over again, like a knife plunging into the same spot. She'd swiftly brought him to his knees.

Chandler reined in his emotions by shifting his gaze from the greenery before him. Of course, that didn't work because he remembered all too well.

Her words of endearment.

Her scent…

Tension hit his frame. For he remembered, too—his fears. His pleading. And no matter how many times he replayed their romantic tryst in his mind… it never ended well.

CHAPTER 3

Why am I doing this? Sabrina shook her head and then stared at her cell phone. "Because you want to make sure he'll turn up," she said out loud.

It was Tuesday evening and she hadn't heard a word from Chandler. The least he could do was call to say their lunch 'date' was still on.

Pouting, she flopped down on the pretty, cream-colored, modular sofa in her living room. *I'll give him another half hour. He should be home by eight.*

Her gaze wandered around the spacious, elegant living room of her three-bedroom, two-car garage, single-family home. She'd purchased it three years ago and decorated its interior with stylish mahogany furniture that contrasted with its cream-colored walls. Thanks to Amber, the touches of red accents were more vibrant than Sabrina would like, but not withstanding, her personality shone through.

Enough of this waiting around, Sabrina thought, dialing Chandler's number.

"Hello, Sabrina," Chandler answered.

His voice made her glad she'd called. "Chandler, how are you?"

"I'm doing good. How about you? Great, right?" he teased.

Sabrina stared at her phone for a second, catching herself as a tiny smile escaped. "Yes, I'm doing great."

"I can tell." He chuckled, well aware he'd caught her off guard. "Calling to check on your pet project?"

This time Sabrina stared hard at her phone. This was not the conversation she was expecting to have. "Pet project?"

"Come on, admit it, you've been thinking about me. Wondering if I'm okay," Chandler responded playfully. "Wondering how you can nurse me back to health." He

31

spread out on the black leather sofa in his living room. He had to tease her a bit, for he'd seen the hint of worry in her eyes on Sunday.

She hesitated a second. "Chand—"

"I know you've been praying for me. At least that," he said with mock sternness.

"Do I get a chance to respond?" she countered.

"Yes, ma'am," he said dramatically.

"You're not my pet project, but I do pray for you," Sabrina declared.

"Why do you pray for me?" he asked quietly.

Sabrina knitted her brows, still trying to figure out how their conversation had turned into this discussion. "I believe that prayer changes things. And I'm trusting God to see you through, whatever your situation is."

He was quiet for a moment, and a smile tugged at his lips. "Thanks."

"You're welcome. How have you been?"

"Better," he admitted soberly. "Much better, but some days are hard."

She heard him sigh, so she hastened to encourage him. "I'm glad you're improving. So glad. You have no idea how concerned I was about you. I even spoke to Pastor Jackson about it, but he said you hadn't called."

"Thank you. I was a basket case when we met. Hope I didn't destroy your dress with my tears."

"Actually, you did," she said, lightening the moment. "You owe me big time."

Chandler relaxed and chuckled softly. "I'll pay up. I'll get you a replacement." He was enjoying their light, happy chatter. "Apart from praying, what have you been doing?"

What? We're like that now? "Working and doing whatsoever else is required. Thanks for asking."

"Really? All I heard was—mind your own business, Chandler."

A slight chuckle escaped her. "I'm not going there with you."

"I know you consider me to be a man on the run, but I'm not fragile."

"Far from it," she hastily told him. "Even though you disappeared the last time."

"So, I'm a runner now?"

"You tell me." She knitted her brows, then remembered he couldn't see her. "Why are we going down this road?"

"Because that's the reason you called, to find out if we're actually doing lunch tomorrow. Admit it."

She relented. "You're right. I wanted to make sure."

"I plan to be at the appointed spot, 11:45 a.m. sharp, but under one condition."

"Just when I thought things couldn't get any better," she said with a smile.

He let that slide. "Don't treat me like a basket case. You know—frail."

"Oh gosh, Chandler. No, I will not. I promise."

"We're good then," he drawled.

"Okay, great. I'll try and make it," she said.

"You have jokes, Sabrina Benjamin." He chuckled loudly. *Oh God, that felt good.* His mood lifted.

She chuckled, too, pulled in by his deep baritone. "Why don't you just say my full name?"

"I would if you'd told me your middle name from the get-go. Mine is John. Most people call me C.J. and I'm okay with that. What's yours?"

"I'm not saying. At least, I would say if I thought you were really interested in knowing."

He smiled to himself. He liked her wittiness. "You're reading my mind?"

She heard the smile he was trying hard to hold back.

33

"My special gift, straight from the Lord. And, speaking of gifts, your voice is incredible. Do you do public speaking? Just curious." His distinct timbre would definitely keep a crowd interested.

"Work-related presentations." His voice sounded tight in his ears. "Thanks."

Sabrina sensed she shouldn't ask anything else. "It's Abigail," she told him.

"Sabrina Abigail Benjamin. It's beautiful, S-A-B."

She beamed. "You're quick. Yes, the first three letters of my first name."

"I've been described in many other ways, so I'll gladly add quick to the top of the list."

"Yes, you may quote me on that," she teased.

"Mos' def."

A carefree chuckle slipped from her. "I will see you tomorrow, Chandler."

"Mos' def."

Now she was chuckling hard. "Bye," she managed to say, before disconnecting the call.

Rising from the sofa, Sabrina found herself still grinning as she headed for her bedroom. *He may be down, but definitely not out.*

CHAPTER 4

Wednesday came way too quickly, Chandler thought. He rolled his shoulders a few times before exhaling a cleansing breath.

After several attempts to dial Sabrina's number and put off their lunch meeting, he finally dropped his cell phone on the bed and donned a pair of khaki-colored Ralph Lauren cargo shorts and a navy polo shirt.

Glancing at his watch, he knitted his brow. He had to hurry or he'd be late. He quickly brushed his hair in place, and then used his hand to smooth his beard and mustache. After another cursory glance in the dresser mirror, he picked up his watch and clasped it on his wrist, slipped on a pair of tumbled leather boat shoes, and was out the door.

Forty minutes later, having kept the pressure on the gas pedal, Chandler stepped out of his car at the Cordova Mall and headed towards Macy's.

He didn't have to look for Sabrina; she was waiting for him near the front doors, all decked out in a yellow, scoop-neckline dress with a handkerchief-hem. Pretty black gladiator sandals and sunglasses completed her outfit.

As soon as she spotted Chandler, her eyes sparkled as if she was glad to see him. She smiled, opening her arms, and he walked right into them.

"Hey, Sab." *A hugger?* He would have to make some adjustments to accommodate her.

She let out a throaty laugh, remembering their conversation the previous evening. "Hey, you!"

She released him from their embrace, paying no attention to the stiffness in his arms.

"Did you find here easily? I know this is not your side of town." Her assessing gaze never left his face as she rested her sunglasses on top of her head. *He didn't suffer from any deficiency in looks,* she noted. She tried not to

35

stare at the soft strands of hair that dusted his muscular arms.

"I found it okay," he managed to say, under her laser-sharp gaze.

"Good," she said.

"Where are we going?"

"Now you ask." She sent him an eyebrow lift before moving off, her ponytail dangling behind her. "Afraid I'll abduct you?"

A slight smile curved his lips as he took in her shapely form ahead of him. Her small black purse hung across her shoulder and rested near her hip.

"I think the lady is having too much fun at my expense," he said, catching up with her. "Thought you did enough last night."

Her eyes narrowed playfully. "Me? I called in peace, and you terrorized me."

"I did?" He feigned innocence. "It was a friendly banter."

"Friendly, huh? I'll have to take your word for it. We're going to eat at Vicky, the best hot dog and burger joint in the whole world."

"Is that so?" His brows shifted upward.

She didn't miss a beat. "It's really good. I promise."

Half an hour later, he had to agree with her as they sat across from each other outside the quaint, local diner. He savored the last mouthful of seasoned, grilled beef. "This was really good."

"I told you so. Vicky is the best."

"You're not supposed to say that."

"Why not?" She grinned at him. "I did tell you so."

His mood visibly lightened, and he peered at her. "Why do I get the feeling you're having fun at my expense? Again."

"No. Noooo." She tried to convince him.

36

"Keep doing that and I won't be hanging out with you anymore."

She tilted her head, a smile curling her lips. "We can't be hanging out here anyway. Don't want to be packing on the pounds. I can't believe you gave me your red velvet muffin." She gave him the side-eye. "And watched while I ate it."

"Come on now," he chuckled softly, leaning against the wicker chair while keeping his gaze on her. "It would be a long time before the pounds start showing."

"I just can't afford to be the biggest girl on the dance floor."

"Dance floor?"

"Yes. Sometimes, I teach praise dance at church, but mostly sing with the praise and worship team."

Chandler's eyes stretched a little with curiosity. "Is that right?"

"Yes, love to dance." She chuckled softly. "Amber would say my first love is red velvet cake and muffins, but not so. Dancing is my first love, and then singing. I enjoy the performing arts."

He laughed softly, delighted by her enthusiasm. "I see."

"In a couple of months, we'll start rehearsing for our summer production at church."

"You sound excited." Chandler gazed at her, the sweetness in her voice consistently drew his attention.

"I am. Have you seen any praise dancing?"

He looked away, fixing his expression before responding. On TV, he recalled seeing dancers from Rozene's praise dance academy minister before some of her teaching sessions.

"Only on TV," he mentioned casually, but something in Sabrina's glance told him he didn't sound as casual as he thought. He tried harder. "Is that what you do for a living?"

37

"I wish. I'm a professor at William J. Cordova University, half an hour from here."

He smiled at her. "One of the best in this region, especially in terms of medical research. I have definitely seen your marching band. Phenomenal. What do you teach, Dr. Benjamin? Or is it Dr. B?"

Laughter burst from Sabrina. "Mostly Dr. Benjamin, but some students do refer to me as Dr. B. I teach MBA classes for International Financial Markets, and my all-time favorite just because I get to travel the world in this class— Cross-Cultural Management."

"You enjoy different cultures, huh?"

"Ohhh, yeah! What kind of work do you do?" *Apart from body building, that is.*

"What's so funny?"

She didn't realize she'd chuckled. "Nothing. That's my bad." She used her fingers to zip her lips.

"Not forgiven. You're not taken to outbursts of giggles, are you?"

"No, not at all. I had a moment there. Please ignore." She mashed her lips together.

Chandler looked skeptical. "If you say so. I do engineering at Rinauto Aeronautical and Design Corporation."

"Rinauto? I know the location, here in Orlando, but the main headquarters is in Chicago."

"Correct. Chicago is where I'm heading on Friday."

"Is that where you work most of the time?"

He looked away, wishing he didn't have to return to Orlando. Ever. When he looked at Sabrina again, he saw concern in her eyes. He hastened to fix it. "I spend most of my time running between here and Chicago. I go wherever the job needs me."

"Isn't it unsettling jetting around all the time? What about your family?"

38

His lips thinned and he rubbed the back of his head, looking away from her.

"Sorry, you don't have to answer," she said hastily. "Chandler, I didn't mean to get into your—"

"That's okay," he remarked quietly.

Uneasiness splattered her heart as she caught a glimpse of the pain in his eyes. She had no desire to remind him of whatever burden he was trying to let go.

He shot her a look. "I need to go."

Her mouth hung open for a moment, then she gathered herself. "I'm sorry. I…" She stopped short because he was already pushing back his chair. She grabbed her purse and followed suit.

The silence was like a heavy weight between them as their feet hit the pavement, moving them away from Vicky.

For the life of her, Sabrina couldn't come up with a suitable line of conversation to ease the weird tension between them. Clearly, she'd hit a nerve asking about his family. Did some woman hurt him? A man of his caliber wouldn't have any difficulty attracting women. She hadn't failed to see the many female heads that pivoted in his direction while they were at Vicky.

"Okay. We're here," she announced hesitantly when they'd arrived near Macy's. "Have a safe trip."

"I'll walk you to your car," Chandler said.

"Thanks, I'm three rows away." She tried to sound nonchalant, leading the way. "Sorry if I brought up unwelcome memories."

"We're good."

"Okay," she responded, opening her car door with a quiet pop, and throwing her purse on the passenger seat. She turned to face him and prepared to hop in. "Thanks for lunch. Take care of yourself."

"You're welcome," he said, holding on to the door. "Aren't you going to ask me?"

His eyes rooted her in place. She was slow to speak, not wanting to make the situation between them any more uncomfortable. "I figured you would tell me if you wanted to, or when you wanted to."

"Thanks for not asking."

"Okay." What else could she say? "Let me know when you're back in town," she said, then wanted to kick herself. *He's trying to get as far away from you as possible.*

"I will," he promised. "Sorry about lunch."

Despite the tremor in her belly, Sabrina touched his hand where it rested on her car door. "No problem. Always tell me when I have overstepped my bounds."

She was sure she saw tears in his eyes. She opened her arms and he fell into them.

His touch was gentle, like he was afraid of hugging her too closely.

"Thank you for everything," he whispered, trying to control the erratic beating of his heart. He pulled out of their embrace and ran a hand over his hair. "Please continue to pray for me."

"I will."

Sabrina watched him until he was out of sight, then she hopped into her car. Mindlessly, she turned on the ignition then found herself hoping he would be alright. He had to be. She was trusting in God.

CHAPTER 5

Chandler pressed his hand against the cool window of the private jet as he stared out at Orlando beneath. He took a calming breath and his thoughts wandered to Sabrina. A tiny smile escaped. *So serene.*

She'd called and met him at the airport with a gift, which she'd asked him not to open until he was in Chicago.

"God loves you," she told him confidently, hugging him.

He had no response to that, so he mumbled something incoherent during their embrace.

As soon as he was seated, he tore away the wrapping paper. Nothing had prepared him for her gift. *A Bible.* He sighed, thinking he should leave it on the jet; however, Sabrina's thoughtfulness caused him to place the Bible in his work bag.

God loves you, he recalled Sabrina's words. *Strange, how I can't find a soul on earth who loves me.*

Suddenly, he wanted to kick something. Love had eluded him—not once but twice… taking all the excitement of living with it. Still, he had never imagined the relationship between himself and Rozene would fail.

Their connection had been strong.

He saw it as clear as day—win-win, all the way.

The bitter taste of resentment rose in his mouth and he tried to quell it. He had no one to blame but himself. Going in, he knew Rozene was married. What he wasn't prepared for was his growing attachment to her.

Explosive! That was how he recalled the first time their eyes met during the lunch break at her three-day writers' conference and book tour in Washington, D.C. last fall. All he could think was, *Wow! She is beautiful!*

41

She couldn't have enough of him either, because she was staring at him like her favorite cupcake with a cherry on top.

The blast of desire between them was the craziest experience he'd had in a long while. He flashed a hello-beautiful smile while moving in her direction, but was disappointed when she hastily moved to the podium to announce that fifteen minutes remained until the end of lunch break.

Resistant, huh? That did not deter him.

Hunter! That should have been his middle name. He loved a great chase. He would not be denied. Anyway, he could tell he'd sparked a flame in her.

After lunch, he sat at a table directly in front of the platform to check her out from head to toe. She tried to ignore his undisguised admiration during her presentation, but he could sense her growing curiosity. He held up a hand and waited for her to respond.

Armed with a microphone in hand, poised and controlled, her gaze shifted to him. "Yes, sir."

He stood up, reached for the microphone on the table, and lifted it to his mouth. "I have a question," he said, dazzling her with a blinding smile.

"Please go ahead," she responded, remaining unmoved by his blatant admiration.

Of course he was going ahead, but not before letting his eyes do the talking, *Was there a possibility?* His chest bubbled at the defiance in her eyes.

"Thanks for taking my question," he began. "You've been talking about love. Love is an intoxicating emotion. It's all-consuming. It's addictive."

Rozene's gaze bounced around the room before returning to his.

42

BAM! He had scored. His words were shifting her senses, and she was struggling to remain neutral under his laser beam gaze.

"Someone mentioned love at first sight, but I don't believe you addressed it," he continued. "Do you believe in love at first sight?"

The conference room had become remarkably quiet and he sensed the audience eagerly awaiting her response.

Sensing her mental deliberations, he shot a laugh in the air, telling her, "From what I've read of your life story, you should understand what I'm talking about."

It could have been his imagination but he was sure he saw the muscles in her jaw twitching.

Moving to stand behind the podium, Rozene lifted the microphone to her mouth, an awkward smile playing on her lips. "Sir, as I already stated, I do not believe in love at first sight."

From the increase in the volume of her voice, he could tell she was annoyed. She looked into the audience. "Any two persons can experience an instant attraction towards each other - an attraction that is intense and overpowering… even an intimate connection. Your eyes meet across the room, your hearts begin to pound in sync, and," she covered her heart with her hand, "suddenly you know, you've found the one." Her eyes widened, before she playfully added, "So in essence, you are saying, Cupid—for it had to be Cupid—aimed for your heart and shot his arrow right through it."

Pockets of snickering broke out in the audience.

She tilted her chin. "Seriously," she said, stifling a laugh, "can you decide in a few minutes that you're in love?"

Fixing me with a question, huh? He blinked in surprise before moving the microphone to his mouth. "Yes, I can," he responded charmingly, flashing even white teeth

43

that drew female interest. *Got something else for you.* He couldn't help it. His lips blossomed into a full eat-your-heart-out smile.

That day, they argued back and forth, but in the end, he had to bow out gracefully. Still, the spark in her eyes was a dead giveaway—she wanted him. He dared not deny her...or himself. Unfortunately, a call from work canceled his plan.

Three weeks later, he was back, staring at Rozene during her *Letters to Husbands* book tour in Chicago. All week, during the events, he'd stared at her. Gosh, he loved looking at her bed-me-now body... and her hazel-colored eyes caused his body to be on full alert, all day.

At the end of the conference, his joy was complete when Don, his half-brother introduced them. Don was in charge of promoting, marketing and handling all matters pertaining to her books and ministry.

"This is Chandler Peynard, my half-brother on my father's side of the family," Don said. "I may have mentioned him but I don't believe you've been formally introduced. Meet my little brother."

Don was a mere five years older, but he took pleasure in pointing out that Chandler was his little brother. They were the spitting image of each other, but Don was lean and a tinge of gray shot off at the edges of his hair.

Rozene had no choice but to look in Chandler's direction. "Yes, I remember his name. I also remember him trying to stir up controversy at my book tour in D.C. Nice to meet you, Mr. Peynard." She gave him a tight smile, extending her hand.

"The pleasure is mine, Mrs. Kanate." His voice was sincere and smooth. Way too smooth. "No controversy. I am a fan." He lightly caressed her hand and she quickly withdrew it.

44

The highlight of Chandler's evening was taking Rozene back to the hotel. Thanks to Don, he'd booked at the same hotel deliberately, just for this opportunity.

He allowed her to step into the elevator before entering and punching the button to the ground floor. He stood beside her, way too close, but she refused to look at him. When he fixed his eyes on her chest, her lips quivered as if breathing was becoming a chore.

Every muscle in his body was taut as he watched her. He loved being in her presence. She was like a breath of fresh air. He had watched her sizing him up outside the elevator without making a comment. Now it was his turn and he intended to feast on her.

He'd heard Don on numerous occasions bragging about her and her achievements. Admittedly, he was remotely curious, but he was not into this God thing. However, one night he was finding it difficult to sleep, so he'd decided to channel-hop, and that was when he discovered her. The more he listened to her TV program, the more he liked her, and before long, watching her program had become a weekly routine... his little dirty secret, fueling his passion.

At the hotel, he was only too happy to escort her to her room to collect the box of books she had for Don. Her hands trembled as she opened her room door.

"Wait here," she told him before stepping into her lavish suite. She turned when she heard the door close behind her.

He held up a hand to stop her from commenting. "I'm coming in to get the box of books. Why do you want me to hang out at the door? Can't handle what you're feeling?"

"Chandler," she spoke quickly. "Thanks again for all you did and for taking me here." She pointed to the box of books next to the desk. "Thanks for giving that to Don for me. I do appreciate your kindness."

45

He gently took her hand in his, and brought it to his lips. His arresting gaze was filled with desire… all-consuming desire.

"Wha-what are…?" She held her breath.

Triumph flared in his eyes and he all but took a victory lap.

"You were leaving," she said breathlessly, pulling away her hand.

"It's a matter of timing," he said, ignoring her comment.

Momentarily thrown off guard, she stared wide-eyed at him for a couple of seconds. "More like never."

He smiled wickedly at her. "Never?"

"That's what I said."

His eyes etched in ruthlessness, he moved to retrieve the box of books, and left her room.

Later that evening, he had to lift his bottom jaw off the ground when Rozene entered the not-so-crowded hotel lounge. He admired her for almost an hour as she sipped non-alcoholic wine at a table in the corner while gazing at the television.

She was yawning when her eyes caught his.

Shocked! Yes, she was. Her eyes registering, *How did I miss him?*

He wasted no time. The heat between them was short-circuiting his brain. He was prepared to die for a worthy cause. He flashed a smile, moving in her direction. *Ooh wee!* Mission accomplished! She was swooning like a teenage girl.

"I-I was just leaving," she told him, leaning across the table to grab her purse.

He sized up her body, flashed a disarming smile, and offered his arm. "Me, too."

He saw her trying to work up an excuse before begrudgingly tucking her hand in the crook of his arm, murmuring, "You don't have to."

"I want to," he told her as they moved off.

Soon, she swiped her key at her room door. "Thanks for the company," she said, entering her room. "Have a good night." She turned to close the door and bumped into him. "Ouch!" she gasped, gazing at his solid chest.

He closed the door, and scooped her into his arms. "Did I hurt you?"

Her body trembled as his fingers tipped her chin and forced her gaze towards him. "Tell me you want me as much as I want you," he said, running his hands down her back.

She closed her eyes, and no words came from her lips.

"Hmm," he purred, enjoying the deliciousness of the warmth emanating from their bodies. "Don't be afraid, Sweetheart."

Her body shuddered against his. "Chandler, I-I-"

"You won't regret it," he told her softly, his hands tightened against the soft skin at her waist. He gently swayed her in a slow intimate dance, brushing his lips along the curve of her jaw, slowly making his way to her lips.

A satisfied "Yes!" issued from the back of her throat when his lips finally found hers. He parted her lips and began delivering slow, long kisses designed to drug her. It was as if he was sampling his favorite meal, and couldn't get enough. Her moans of delight only served to fuel his hunger. He lifted his lips from hers, feeling elated. No… more like ecstatic. Had he died and gone to heaven? Maybe he had, her languid expression indicated pure bliss, but in a matter of seconds, changed to one of wide-eyed astonishment.

47

Chandler dotted her lips with butterfly kisses, but he still noticed her lips were tense against his. "It's okay, Sweetheart," he said softly between kisses, "it's okay."

But Rozene couldn't relax. "N-nooo." She tore her lips away from his and dropped her forehead on his chest. "I can't."

He slipped a hand up the small of her back while the other hugged her waist. "Hey. Hey. It's going to be all right," he said, kissing the top of her head. He lifted her chin with his hand and she looked at him. "Let's have a little fun. You can tell me when to stop."

When she nodded, he wasted no time. His mouth found hers again, teasing her with desire.

She moaned softly, clenching his shirt and pressing her body against his as he cupped the back of her head and kissed her deeply, thirstily.

When he scooped her up in his arms, she curled against him like her life depended on him. His eyes lit up and a slow smile spread across his face as he headed for her bedroom.

Severe air turbulence pulled Chandler back to the present. Clinging to the armrests, he stared out the window. He was glad to be leaving Orlando… to leave his situation behind.

CHAPTER 6

"Are you trying to avoid me?" Amber eyed Sabrina suspiciously in the doorway. Her deeply-tanned, five-foot-seven frame was covered in a white camisole and a pair of knee-length jean shorts.

"Of course I am. Happy Saturday!"

Sabrina stepped back so Amber could enter her home.

Amber's dark brown eyes penetrated hers before she stepped through the door. "And she has the nerve to say it," she muttered, throwing her long, chemically-processed hair behind her. "Don't think I didn't see you slipping out of church on Wednesday after Bible study. You knew I wanted to hear about your date," she accused.

"Didn't we have a telephone conversation Wednesday night?" Sabrina couldn't help but shake her head before closing the door. She stared at Amber's back. "If you were me, you would have avoided you, too."

"I'm going to ignore that." Amber walked towards the living room and dropped her purse on the sofa before turning to face Sabrina. "I'm here to talk business."

"Now, that's a first. This I've got—"

"I hope you're not over here praying away the hunk… with Jenay. She's happily married to Brandon and she has Ariel and Alina, so don't let her convince you to do otherwise."

Sabrina forced away the irritation that was building in her chest, before heading to the kitchen. "You clearly don't know Jenay."

Sabrina and Jenay, who was also a professor, had hit it off when Sabrina had started working at the School of Business and Industry at the university. They were around the same age and realized they had a lot in common, beginning with their love for the performing arts. That was how Sabrina had started to attend Zion Apostolic Church

49

seven years ago, since Jenay was in charge of the Praise Dance Ministry. Two year later, Sabrina became the director of the Worship and Arts Ministry, which included dance, drama, and music.

Amber followed Sabrina into the kitchen. "I know Jenay, all right. I'm aware she has your back. All I'm saying is, I need you to put a little action behind your faith or you'll be single, all the days of your life... forever!"

"Forever." Sabrina chuckled at the seriousness of Amber's expression. "Is that a bad thing?" she teased, standing near the sink.

"Rina," Amber leaned against the cupboard adjacent to the sink, "give this man a chance."

Sabrina decided to humor her. "You only met the man for a few minutes, and you've drawn that kind of conclusion?"

She took up the sponge and squirted dishwashing liquid on it.

"Yes, a few minutes, but I have a good feeling about him. Why do you think he came back? It's a sign from God. And I can't thank God enough for sending him back to you. I'm so glad you went out with him, even though you refused to share the details."

Sabrina watched her in disbelief before starting to wash the plates she'd used for breakfast. "You are delusional. I'm not even sure why we are having this conversation."

"See, that's what you always do. Kill the plant before it starts to germinate. You are your worst enemy." Her grim expression was not lost on Sabrina.

Sabrina's back went ramrod straight. "Amber, how many times have I told you, if the Lord wants me to get married, He'll provide someone?"

"He's making a way and you're missing it. You know those female vultures are trying to get their claws on him

50

every day. A man can take so much and no more. Don't let him slip away."

Sabrina paused to stare at her. "Slip away! Okay, time to check your temperature."

She may not have been on a date in a while—okay, a long while—but that didn't mean she was going to be delusional. *This is crazy!* In any case, she was not accepting relationship advice from Amber who was a year younger, albeit, more experienced concerning men.

"Look, Amber, let the Lord have His way in my life."

Amber raised both eyebrows, clearly unconvinced. "Yes, the Lord is working in your life, but you have to admit He's taking His time in that area. Thirty-five is around the corner."

No filter. Sabrina sighed, stacking the last plate in the dishwasher. "Thirty-five is not around the corner. It is three and a half years away, so quit wielding that ticking clock. I'm not buying it."

"Seriously, Rina," Amber pleaded. "I think he'd be good for you. If the opportunity presents itself, say yes. I'm adding you both to my prayer list."

If the situation wasn't so serious, Sabrina would have laughed aloud. Instead, she attempted diversion. "Where are you off to this morning?"

Amber grinned at her. "The love I have for you, cousin, caused me to pop by. I'm actually on my way to the mall. And I'm off and running."

"As usual," Sabrina quipped, drying her hands with a paper towel.

"Hey, every day is a sale day at Macy's," Amber said as they walked to the living room. She gave Sabrina a winning smile before picking up her purse. "I have to catch the sale while it's on." In a flash, she wrapped Sabrina in a tight embrace. "I'm just looking out for you, you know."

"I know." Sabrina squeezed her tightly.

51

They had been in each other's lives since forever. They had gone to the same elementary, middle, and high school. In college, they'd had each other's back, and when Sabrina took a job at William J. Cordova University, Amber also took up a nursing position at William J. Cordova Hospital a year later. It was there, six years ago that Amber had met Dr. Paul Shaffer, the love of her life, and they were married a year later.

On the patio, Amber's eyes searched Sabrina's for the promise of hope that she would consider their conversation positively. She found nothing, so she had to try again.

"Rina, please don't let what happened between you and Cal keep you from what God is doing now. And on that note, I hope you've changed your mind about attending his wedding. He's got some nerves."

Sabrina's gaze darted outside so that Amber couldn't see the disgust in them.

Calvin Token was a piece of work. With his father, a prominent, up-and-coming senator, and his mother, a lawyer, the world was his oyster, and his attitude said they should all be glad he was allowing them to live in it.

"You have to forgive Calvin," Sabrina said. "Sometimes that's what comes with being privileged—ignorance and detachment."

"Oh yes. And mix that with idiot and moron. I wish you'd give me permission to beat the black off him."

Sabrina couldn't help but smile. "Calvin will be Calvin."

"Enough about Calvin. So glad God is providing a wonderful man for you."

Sabrina eyeballed her. "What I know is that God will bring me a saved, sanctified, Holy Ghost-filled man."

"Chandler can be all of that. You need to look beyond what you see in the physical. Extend yourself—"

52

Sabrina's eyebrows shot to her hairline, causing Amber to burst out laughing. She held up her hand before Sabrina could speak. "I don't mean it in that way. I say call him. You know, keep in touch and see where it leads."

"Yes, Mother," Sabrina answered sarcastically. "The mall is calling you."

"Ignoring!" Amber smiled at her. "What's up for today?" She was quick to answer her own question. "I know, Mother Rogers. Aunt Connie. Jenay."

Sabrina decided to ignore the unspoken—boring—in her voice. "Not going to Mother Rogers first today. Swinging by Aunt Connie and then I'll take her to Mother Rogers'."

"Swinging by Aunt Connie. You know you can't swing by Aunty. She'll have a meal prepared so you can show her how to use Google. Again."

Sabrina waved her away. "That's a good trade-off. I'll have dinner for today and tomorrow."

"I'd rather buy my food. Keep telling Aunty to write the stuff down, but no, she'd rather have you sit and watch her play with the mouse to find T.D. Jakes or T.B.N."

Sabrina grinned at her. "She's trying to be tech savvy."

"She's certainly taking her time. But then, time is what she has. Retirement looks good on her. The rest of us are trying to make it to retirement."

Sabrina laughed, moving her towards the front door. "Girl, bye! Go on and do your shopping."

"That's the plan," Amber replied, rushing out the door.

CHAPTER 7

Sabrina laughed, thinking this was what Amber always accused her of—'not being spontaneous.' She wasn't even sure why she was having an internal struggle.

She reached for her phone on the nightstand and pressed the call button beside Chandler's number. It rang and went to voice mail. She ended the call without leaving a message.

"That's that. I tried," she said, putting her phone back on the nightstand. He'd been gone for almost a week.

She reached for her portfolio on the bed, which held the notes from the summer production meeting for the Worship and Arts Ministry. She ran down the list of songs for the praise team, and found herself happily dancing around and belting out Michael W. Smith's "How Great is Our God."

Her phone started ringing and she sprang on the bed and reached for it on the nightstand. "Hi… Chandler!" she answered, trying to catch her breath.

"Hello. You're making me feel special with your breathlessness." He just couldn't resist.

Sabrina's mouth gaped as she stared at her phone. "Don't get it twisted." She held back the laughter bubbling up. "I don't even know you like that."

"Can't take a joke, I see."

She threw an eye-roll towards the ceiling. Now he was making her feel like his fun-loving friend had just become a stick in the mud. "Okay, Mr. Spontaneous. I'm not feeling you."

"I know." He chuckled softly as he stepped out of the elevator and made his way into his lavish Chicago home.

"Whatever," she responded. He was enjoying her a little too much for her comfort. "Any…way, I was checking on you."

54

"Okay, let this be the last conversation we have where you are checking on me." His voice sounded tight and strained. "I'm not your pet project."

"Don't get all bent out of shape. Lighten up."

"I don't want to be reminded of my... situation." He dropped his work bag on the floor and plopped down on the plush, blue sofa in the living room. "We are friends; you can call me whenever for whatever."

"We're friends?"

"I only give my phone number to my friends."

That silenced her.

"Look, I've had a rough day. I had to fire a member of my team. Human Resources was all over our department investigating and making sure the correct protocols were..." He wondered why he was telling her his business.

"I'm sorry to hear that," Sabrina jumped in. "Hope everything will be okay."

He let out a frustrated sigh. "Me, too. We have a lot to cover and that pushed the team back further."

She rolled on her side. "I'll be praying for your strength."

She was sure she heard him sigh again.

"Do you pray about everything?"

She could hear the smirk in his voice. "Yes. I try to be obedient to the Word of God."

"Oh boy! Here we go." *No doubt, queen of everything perfect.* He slumped back on the sofa. "Tell me where to find that Word you're referring to," he said sarcastically.

She was annoyed by his tone, but didn't respond in like manner. "First Thessalonians 5:17. It states, 'Pray without ceasing.' There are others, but that came to mind."

"Will check it out later."

"Do you have the Bible I gave to you?"

Displeasure rode him. "It's on my nightstand. You thought I threw it—"

55

"No," she answered quickly. "I didn't call to aggravate you. I wanted to know if you'd arrived safely... and if you're okay," she added quietly.

"I'm sorry, Sab. Please forgive me. I don't mean to be rude." *I'm on edge from so many things,* he wanted to add.

"It's okay, just breathe. God is with you."

"Thanks," he answered quietly. "And I appreciate you checking on me."

"No problem, glad to. Just remember, I'm on Team C.J."

"Okay. Thanks."

She could hear the smile in his voice. "Have a good night."

"Thanks. You, too."

Sabrina disconnected the call, shaking her head. *Men!*

She spread out on her bed and flipped on the television and channel-hopped until she landed on T.B.N. It was not long before a male preacher she'd not heard before started talking about deception.

A long, harsh sigh rushed from Sabrina's lips as a conversation she had had with Calvin almost a year ago, ran through her thoughts.

Why had she fallen in love with him?

Was it his charisma? Oh, no, it had to be his six-foot-two, coffee-colored, Adonis-like physique. Probably the way he expounded on the Scriptures. She was drawn to spiritual men.

After a year of friendship, and everyone assuming they were dating, she had decided to have that conversation with Calvin, and more so when Brandon had hinted that Calvin was seeing someone else. Frankly, she'd thought Brandon was joking, but the look in his eyes had told her otherwise. Even so, Sabrina had doubted him. How was that possible? Calvin visited her most evenings.

Turned out, truth is indeed stranger than fiction. Calvin, by his own confession told her he'd started dating Kayanna Boothe, an actuary who worked at a life insurance company in town.

Everything stopped as his words ripped Sabrina's hopes to pieces. She sat glued to the sofa in her living room, staring through him. He reached for her hand, but she swiftly pulled it away.

"Rina, I'm—"

She held up her hand, stopping him in mid-sentence. "Just don't."

"It's not…"

Don't say it. The look in her eyes warned him, but Calvin had to be Calvin.

"It's not you. It's me," he finished.

That foolishness from his lips was the last straw. Sabrina marched to the front door and flung it open. The silence was deafening as she waited for him to make his exit.

No sound.

She looked behind her and saw that he was standing behind the couch. Worse! He stood there looking fearful, like she'd suddenly morphed into the angry black woman. She all but hissed her teeth. He'd better be glad Jesus had taken up roots in her life many moons ago.

"You were leaving," she said impatiently, tamping down her mental screamfest.

He walked cautiously by her, stood on the patio, and opened his mouth to speak.

Her brows furrowed, indicating she was not about to take any more of his foolishness.

"Please don't let this ruin our friendship," Calvin begged. "I enjoy our—"

The look on her face stopped him. "Bye, Calvin." And with that, she closed the door.

57

The beeping of her cell phone broke into Sabrina's recollection. She reached for it and turned off the alarm that reminded her to take some of her red velvet muffins to Jenay.

She dropped the phone beside her and slumped on the pillows. *It's not you, it's me.* She pursed her lips, thinking, Amber had been right about Calvin all along. "Cal is waiting for the next best thing," Amber had told her, a disturbed expression on her face. "Don't settle for Cal. You deserve someone who will treat you like the queen you are."

Even after their little showdown, Calvin still wanted to visit. Eye-roll! Of course she'd told him he couldn't. The more she ignored Calvin at church, the more he attempted to be in her space. It took everything in her not to be rude to him.

But Calvin was not done yet.

One Sunday morning, he entered the sanctuary before church started with a woman who Sabrina assumed was Kayanna. Amber had told her what she'd heard from the rumor mill about Kayanna—'smokin' hot' with a striking resemblance to actress, Gabrielle Union.

Calvin, the showman, was on full display, greeting members of the congregation with much exuberance and introducing Kayanna, before they sat on the front row on the left side of the sanctuary.

Old hypocrite! Sabrina all but cut her eyes at him.

She was not assigned to sing with the Praise Team that morning. Strangely, she'd entered the sanctuary and decided not to sit in her regular spot, but instead she sat on the far right towards the back. Silently, she thanked God for that, because it could have been her imagination, but several members and friends in the congregation kept looking in the general direction where she usually sat.

58

After church, amidst the wagging tongues about Calvin and Kayanna, Jenay and Amber were her bodyguards, moving her out of the sanctuary as soon as time permitted.

"Are you okay?" Jenay's head swished from side-to-side, unraveling her huge, dramatic bun as she scanned the parking lot. Sabrina watched as Jenay gathered her long, jet-black hair and wrapped it on top of her head. She smiled apologetically at Sabrina. "Are you good?"

"Oh yes!" Sabrina opened her car door and placed her Bible and purse on the passenger seat. "Couldn't be better," she said, closing the door and facing Jenay.

"Are you—?" Jenay stopped mid-sentence as both she and Sabrina heard the ramblings of a hostile Amber.

"How dare Calvin Token come up in the church, acting like he's the man, when he was stringing you along all this time?" She threw her hands in the air. "Worse, he is protecting her like he thinks somebody is out to get her."

Sabrina tried to calm her. "It's okay. Seriously, it is."

"See. See." Amber began moving around, before stopping to say, "I told you, you should have dumped him. Up to a month ago, he was all up in your face. Chillaxing with you, while his eyes were elsewhere. If you had laid yourself careless, no doubt he would have taken what he wanted and left you hanging. Oh! He better be glad it's you and not me."

Jenay pulled her sturdy, coffee-colored frame closer to Amber, mortified by her behavior. "You're creating a scene. People are looking at us," she said, her round face stern.

Amber stared through Jenay, a crazy look in her eyes. "Rina, I'll call you later," Amber said, marching off.

Sabrina lifted her hand before Jenay could speak. "It's okay. Let her go."

"You sure, you're good?" Jenay asked, her dark-brown eyes laced with concern.

"Yes. Go find your family. I'm sure Brandon is wondering where you are." She smiled at Jenay. "Plus, the twins could be having a terrible six moment."

"Brandon can handle Ariel and Alina," Jenay told her. "I want to make sure you're okay."

"Don't worry. I'm fine. I'll call you later." Sabrina hugged her and slid behind the steering wheel.

Jenay smiled at her. "Yes, call me when you get a chance."

Still, Sabrina hadn't seen the last of Calvin Token.

Two weeks later, he popped by her home, telling her he needed to speak with her urgently. The seriousness in his gaze caused her to quickly let him through the front door. In any case, Brandon and Jenay were visiting so she felt adequately protected.

Calvin sat at the edge of the sofa, looking like he was about to give an important speech. He looked intently at Sabrina who was sitting across from him. "How is it going?" he asked.

Sabrina's brows slammed together. "Look, Calvin, I have several things to do this evening so if you don't mind, can you get to the point?"

"I wanted to let you know I appreciate your friendship. Please don't let the fact that I now have a fiancée ruin what we've had."

What on earth? Things could not be any stranger. Sabrina pursed her lips. "Okay," was all she could think of saying. Still, she knew there was more.

"We're getting married in December," he blurted. He placed the invitation on the coffee table between them.

Sabrina pulled to the edge of the sofa. "If that's it, thanks for letting me know."

She started to rise from the sofa, but his next statement caused her to sink deeper instead. No, she cringed. She couldn't have heard right. "What did you say?"

60

A salacious smile covered his face. "I'm extremely fond of you. Extremely fond of you. Maybe we could—"

Sabrina sprang up and marched to the front door. "Thanks for stopping by Calvin."

Calvin was on her heels. "Sabrina—"

She held up a hand and swung the door open.

"Are you throwing me out?" he dared to ask.

"Isn't it obvious?"

"Okay," he said, stepping on the patio.

Before he could turn around, Sabrina slammed the front door.

CHAPTER 8

Chandler pulled off the road to let the top of his red Ford Mustang convertible roll back. He intended to enjoy the relatively warm morning temperature and picturesque scenery. For the first time in a long while, he felt alive and on a new road to freedom.

Smiling, he continued his journey. He'd just left Marcie's apartment, and boy, oh boy, that Marcela Davidson sure knew how to delight his senses. He chuckled loudly, slapping the steering wheel. *That sister knows how to put it on a brother.* "Um!"

The two had been friends with benefits for the past two years, at each other's beck and call, with no strings attached. He didn't usually spend the night, but yesterday was special and he needed to celebrate.

He'd only been in Chicago for about two months when the Chairman, Rodner Calabazza, surprised him with the news that he would be promoted. He was aware that the position was up for grabs because of Rinauto's recent reorganization and expansion.

Rinauto Aeronautical and Design Corporation had held a long tradition of aerospace leadership and innovation in the United States and over sixty other countries. In a bid to reinvent itself, the company was being reorganized into two business units, namely, Commercial Airplanes and Defense, Space and Security.

In his last position, Chandler was Chief Aerospace Engineer over the Engineering, Operations and Technology Division. Truthfully, he was hoping he would be the one selected for the new position since he thoroughly enjoyed the design element it entailed.

He'd been at the company nearly all of his working life.

62

After that debacle of a wedding with Alana, he'd cut ties at home. He was always fascinated with airplanes, so when he moved from Washington, D.C. to Chicago, he got a job with a small aviation research firm. That job further fueled his interest in aeronautical science and he had eventually completed a master's degree in that field, which opened the door for him to work with Rinauto. Two years after starting at Rinauto, he was back in school pursuing further studies. On completion, he had been given a management position. Now, he would proudly hold the title of Vice President of Commercial Airplanes.

Woot! He pumped a fist in the air. *What do you know, dreams do come through... at least some of them.* But he wouldn't be concerned about Rozene now. She didn't know a good thing, even if it was before her.

At first, there was no communication between them after their hot-hot encounter in Chicago. But that didn't mean she wasn't always on his mind. He had dated a few other women to get her out of his system but that didn't work. He then literally became a recluse. His only desire— to get home from work and watch her on YouTube or TV. He was constantly on her website and her social media pages. He'd even taken to re-reading her books.

The unending silence between them was killing him slowly. He needed her and he needed her in a way that was foreign to him. He could hardly believe his own transformation into this supersensitive love machine. Oh, he was warm and fuzzy on the inside... all day... every day. *I carry her in my heart. I long to bask in her presence.* He'd found himself articulating sentimental phrases that he'd previously considered mindboggling, even stupid, when similar expressions were uttered by the women he'd dated.

At one point, he had glanced at Rozene's profile shot on her Facebook author page, and heard himself

63

breathlessly declaring, "She completes me." Yes, he was in love, hopelessly addicted to Rozene. That day, he had scampered through Don's defense and got her number after giving him a story.

Rozene took his call.

Hearing her voice almost sent him over the edge, but he calmed himself. At first, she was against him calling but he assured her he wouldn't call often. Soon, his weekly calls turned daily and they began to develop a relationship of sorts. They never met, but it was not for lack of trying on his part.

One day, he called her and played the sympathy card, crying when he told her he would spend Christmas alone. She promised they would meet up early in the New Year. She kept her promise when she had to do a book signing in West Palm Beach, Florida, a three-hour drive from Orlando.

On the last day of her book signing, he checked into the same hotel. The anticipation had his heart pounding all day. When he entered her suite, he had to lean against the door to catch his breath, even though his eyes flowed over her from head to toe. Moments later, he followed her to the sofa and they stood there drinking each other in.

He knew her desire for him was strong, for he saw her literally holding her breath before stepping slightly away as emotions she'd suppressed started to reemerge. She attempted a smile, "How are you?"

An unnecessary question, he thought. *Of course, you can see how I'm doing.* His eyes were raging with desire for her, and he was mentally commanding his hands to stay in place by his side. "I'm much better now," he said with a sensuous timbre.

"Great." She admired his lean muscles.

"No hug. No love for Chandler." He gazed at her in the way he always did—with the longings of his heart on display.

A heart-stopping smile lit her face, and whatever thread of control he was holding onto was forgotten, for in a second he lowered her on the sofa and they were doing exactly what they had pledged never to do again.

The beeping of his phone caught Chandler's attention and he looked at the dashboard to see who was calling.

It was Don.

His hands tightened on the steering wheel as silence covered him like a wet blanket. He did not take the call.

CHAPTER 9

Sabrina lifted her work bag from the sofa where she'd dropped it. She had been in a hurry to find food. She had helped two students during lunch, and before she knew it, lunchtime had passed and it was time for her next class. It was coming up to the end of the spring semester and it was all about the students.

A loud sigh escaped as she entered her bedroom and dropped the bag beside the nightstand before moving on to the bathroom. She still had a few papers to look at before retiring for the night.

Twenty minutes later, feeling oh-so-squeaky-clean, she slid under the bedcovers. Of course, the will to read the documents eluded her. She stared at the ceiling, knowing she should reach for her work bag yet having no real desire to do it. *I'll get it early morning.*

She prayed and called it a day.

Some time later, her cell phone rang and Sabrina bolted upright on the bed. She grabbed her phone from the nightstand, like a person possessed.

Chandler? She fell against the pillow. She hadn't heard from him in almost two months. *Need my wits about me to deal with him.* She glanced at the clock on the nightstand. *Oh wow!* She'd only been asleep for half an hour.

Chandler fingered the stem of his wine glass. He was about to disconnect the call when a soft, "Hello" filled his ear. Her voice was husky with sleep.

"Sab, in bed so early," he said. "Not yet the end of the semester and you're strung out."

A chuckle bubbled up and escaped. "You should see me at the end of the semester. No words, my friend. No words."

"Even so, I bet you wouldn't trade that experience for the world."

"I say true now, but catch me tomorrow when I'm operating on all cylinders; the answer might be different."

"So you say. What's up?"

She paused wondering if she heard him. "I-what…?"

"You rang?"

"No. I-I didn't."

"You didn't call me? Saw a missed call from you, around 7:00 p.m."

Her mouth slid to the side. "My phone must have dialed you."

"That's alright. I was going to call you anyway. Had a group lunch meeting today and they served red velvet muffins for dessert, and all I could think—"

"No, they didn't!" Sabrina squealed. "You should have sent me one over the phone."

He chuckled. "They sure did, and you ran across my mind. I could see you diving in."

She snickered. "Yep, I would be first in line."

"Hmm. I can't say I like any particular food that much. If it's good, I'll eat it."

"Well, when you eat from my mom's kitchen for most days of your life, then good food is a must. My mom can cooook."

He laughed.

"I can find my way around the kitchen," she told him, "but my mom, ohhh, my mom can cooook."

"Oh yeah?"

"Yes. My mom makes it happen in the kitchen."

"She sounds like a great chef. I'm always eating out or ordering in," he confessed.

"If you're nice to me, I'll let you taste her cooking."

"No worries there. I'm always nice to you."

"Hmmm, that's still under investigation."

67

"Really?"

"Yes, really. You're improving, though."

"That's great to know," he drawled.

She laughed softly. "I take it the situation at work with HR has cleared up."

"Yes. It worked out fine. In fact, things are better than I expected."

"That's great. Go on, Mr. Boss Man."

"If you insist." A strangled laugh broke free before he asked, "Where are your parents?"

"Mom and Dad live in Warner Robins, Georgia. Mom retired from teaching and now helps Dad with the fruits business."

"Sounds like a win-win to me. Are you more like your mom or dad?"

"I want to say a combination of both, even though some say I behave like Mom but look like Dad. Amber would tell you I look and behave like Aunt Lynn; that's her mom, who is my mom's sister."

"So you're like Aunt Lynn, huh?" he teased, causing her to giggle unconsciously.

She pursed her lips to suppress the giggles. "She may be right. Aunt Lynn is a gracious woman of God. I love her. I love both my aunts, Aunt Lynn and Aunt Connie. Like my mom, they both retired from teaching."

"So they had some amount of influence on you becoming a professor?"

"Yes," she admitted. "Strangely, though, I had said that I would never become a teacher. But even stranger, I'm at my best when I am teaching."

"It's innate. Great gift to have." A proud smile covered Chandler's face. *Just beautiful.* "I enjoy hearing you talk like that."

"Thanks. I love my job."

"Yes, you do," he chuckled.

"All my aunts are from my mother's side of the family," she mentioned. "Zilch—from my father's side."

"Zilch?" Chandler chuckled slightly. "I haven't heard that word in a long time."

"Yes, zilch. Naught. Nil. Dad's an only child, like I am. Amber is an only child, too, so we sort of grew up together. Aunt Connie has no children. Her husband died pretty early after they got married and she never remarried. There—I told you my family history in one go."

"You're a talker."

He seemed both amused and delighted, and for some strange reason, that thought made her smile. "Far from that."

"Thanks for sharing, though. For a long while I thought I was an only child. But that story is for another day. I have a half-brother, Don, on my father's side. We were great friends until…" He paused. *Why did I divulge that? How can I end the conversation without sounding rude?*

Sabrina jumped in. "I understand. Life happens."

"For the record, I don't have a great relationship with my parents."

"Okay."

"There you go again. Treating me like I'm frail," he accused.

"Chandler, stop. I didn't say a word for you to be thinking that way."

"You don't have to. I can sense it."

"Listen, Mr. Sensitive, what do you expect me to do? The last time I mentioned family, you pretty much shut down. I don't need that to happen again."

Chandler's eyebrows shot to the top of his head. "Well, give it to me straight, why don't you?"

"See, that's exactly what I'm talking about. That kind of attitude. Chandler, no family is perfect. We're all going through something."

"I know no family is perfect. Mine is far from it. I'm sorry for being sensitive about mine. I'm a private person. Not sure why I keep divulging stuff to you."

"No need to apologize. Thought you said that we are friends. Whatever you say to me will be held in the strictest confidence."

"Somehow, I don't doubt that. It's strange for me. I'm not accustomed to having close friends. Don was the closest person to me before…"

"I understand. Hopefully, you'll both be able to rebuild your relationship."

"I don't know if I want it back. When I needed his support most, it was not forthcoming."

"I'll keep both of you in my prayers."

"Yes. Please pray for us. Seems like it's the popular thing to do. My mother told me that she's now a Christian."

"That's awesome!" Sabrina wanted to dance around, but held herself together. "Can you tell I like that a lot?"

He chuckled softly. "I can tell."

"Would you be okay if I pray now?"

"Er…" She took him by surprise. *I can handle this.* "Okay, give me a second." Chandler placed his wine glass on the coffee table before him. "Ready."

Sabrina prayed. "Father, I thank You for the privilege of coming before You in prayer. Thank You for my friend, Chandler Peynard. Tonight, I specifically pray for his relationship with Don. Lord, I pray that You will move to create open communication and mutual acceptance between them. Father, I pray for peace between them so that the matter that caused their separation can be worked out. Lord, let reconciliation occur where there has been disaffection.

"I pray, Lord, that Chandler will have good, godly male friends—men of honor and great wisdom with whom he can share openly. Empower him, oh God, to be a person who forgives easily and does not hold things in his heart against others. Anoint him and rejuvenate him by Your Spirit. In the name of Jesus Christ, I pray. Amen."

"Amen." Chandler said quietly. He was unsure of how to react after such an inspirational prayer. "Thank you," issued softly from his lips, making him sound even more vulnerable than he felt.

Sabrina smiled at the gentleness of his tone. "You're welcome. Have a great night."

"I'll be back in town soon," he blurted without thinking. Not waiting for her to respond, he added a quick good night and disconnected the call.

CHAPTER 10

"I have to go," Sabrina hastily told Jenay on the phone, while stepping out of her car. "Remember to print the songs for production rehearsal. Space is tight, so everyone needs to stick to the rehearsal schedule."

"Will do," Jenay responded.

"If looks could kill, I'd be dead right now. Aunt Connie is looking like the three-headed beast, for no reason at all."

"Stop it!" Jenay laughed. "Before you go, what about the dancers?"

"I have all their songs on a CD. Will take it, too. Got to go. Do you want me dead? Smoke is coming from her eyes."

Sabrina disconnected the call amidst Jenay's raucous laughter.

"Three-headed beast? Smoke?" Aunt Connie stared at her, hands akimbo on her curvy hips, holding back a grin.

Sabrina grinned at her aunt. "Forgive me. I'm seeing things that are not so."

Aunt Connie marched her solid five-foot-five-inch frame to the door. "Is that what you call it? I hope it's not catching."

"I love you," Sabrina responded, holding back a chuckle. She grabbed a shopping bag from the back seat and slammed the car door. "Here I am!" She grinned at Aunt Connie. "I come armed with gifts of love."

"You'd better be glad I love you." Aunt Connie opened the door. "Been waiting for almost an hour."

"I'm sorry. Had to run to the mall to catch the sale with Amber."

"So you used up my time shopping?"

"Don't look at it that way." Sabrina smiled at her. "Got a few goodies for you."

Aunt Connie gave her the side-eye, before her face brightened with her usual heart-warming smile. "Let me see what you have there."

"There she is, my usually happy aunt."

"Show up an hour late again, and I'll be gone." Aunt Connie tried to pinch Sabrina's arm as she took the bag from her hand.

Sabrina escaped her. "Gosh, Aunty, you're so grouchy."

"Keep saying that," Aunt Connie threatened, lifting out an ivory paisley-printed georgette blouse from the bag. "This is gorgeous," she beamed. "You got the size right. I can tell." She hugged Sabrina. "Thank you. I'm beginning to like you again. Let me fit it."

"Ahhh, stop it," Sabrina said, following her to the bedroom.

She smiled inwardly at the pace at which Aunt Connie was moving. At fifty-six years old, her aunt looked more like she was in her late forties. She had dyed and cut her hair in a low, chic style that suited her round face. Not the typical mature woman, she was down-to-earth, and the life of every party. She loved life, and was generous to a fault, but she had limited patience for shenanigans. Better still, she was in great shape, and extremely proud that she had kept her weight below one hundred and fifty pounds.

"You certainly took long enough to get in here," Aunt Connie scolded Sabrina.

"Gosh, you're in a mood today. Do I need to call Brother Selvin?"

For the second time, Aunt Connie stood akimbo. "Don't start with that foolishness."

Sabrina couldn't help but laugh aloud.

Brother Nathaniel Selvin had moved into the neighborhood around six months ago and had started attending their church. Not long after, he had set his sights

73

on Aunt Connie and would do anything to have her in his corner.

"He's a nice man. I see him shooting you those loving looks," Sabrina remarked, taking the blouse from the bed and handing it to her. "You've been single for a loooong time."

"I'm not looking for company or trouble," Aunt Connie puffed out, before slipping out of her top. "What did I tell you about that man? I refuse to be anybody's number three."

Sabrina grinned at her. "It not his fault that his second wife died of cancer. He told you his first wife started seeing a younger man and asked for a divorce. At least, he's being honest. He could have been bitter, but no, he's trusting the Lord."

"Not interested." Aunt Connie prepared to put on her new blouse. "He's looking way too sure of himself. Anyway, I can tell he's been around the block a couple of times. And I know for sure leopards don't change their spots. What am I going to do? Rub off some of his spots and pretend he has changed? No, thank you, missy. I'm good." With that, she slipped the blouse over her head.

"But you don't know him. You should let him take you on the date he's been asking for."

"He can ask all he wants. I'm already singing 'Let It Go,' and I don't even have him."

She looked at a grinning Sabrina before walking to the full-length mirror to admire her blouse.

She turned to Sabrina. "Do you want more?"

Sabrina nodded, unsure what to expect.

Hands folded across her chest, Aunt Connie uttered, "Listen to this foolishness. I was driving out of the parking lot at church last Sunday. That man waved me down, running to my car like an Olympic sprinter. I rolled my window down to find him gaping at me." Aunt Connie

74

looked upward and shook her head. "He was breathless. Salivating, like I was a piece of meat. Not even my hard stare could take him out of that trance."

She shook her head again. "I couldn't take it anymore, so I said, 'How can I help you, Brother Selvin?'"

She looked pointedly at Sabrina. "You better sit down for his response."

Sabrina's eyes widened in anticipation as Aunt Connie shook her head from side to side.

"He said, 'I saw you in church, getting your praise on.'" A sigh escaped Aunt Connie's lips. "You know by now, my brows were meeting my hairline. Not that it mattered to him. He had to go there. He said, 'Your dance moves may show your age but looking at you, woman of God, I could never tell. The years have been gooood to you.'"

Sabrina was laughing so hard, she clutched the bedpost to stop from sliding to the floor. When she got her laughter under control, she was still looking into her aunt's unsmiling face. "No, he didn't."

"He sure did. I just can't with that man, Sabrina. He's cerebrally challenged. I want to be left in peace. All I did after that conversation was roll my window up and keep on moving."

Sabrina smiled inwardly. "He may be what you need to add more sparkles to your day."

Aunt Connie pursed her lips, before telling her, "Keep it up. You will join Nathaniel Selvin in the not-my-friend box. Anyway, enough about him. Check out this blouse. I'm totally rocking it." She strode back and forth like she was on a catwalk.

"It looks great." Sabrina admired the V-neckline with inverted front pleat.

"I love that it has long sleeves," Aunt Connie beamed. "It's very elegant. Thank you!"

75

Aunt Connie smiled at herself in the mirror, and then turned sideways to catch a glimpse of the one-button cuff at the end of the sleeve. "I'm absolutely rocking this."

"Yes, you are. I have two more for you." Sabrina pulled two blouses from the shopping bag, and laid them on the bed.

Aunt Connie gazed lovingly at her gifts. "I love them. Thank you. As always, you got my taste right. I'll fit them later."

She smiled at Sabrina. "Come on. Bring it in," she said, holding outstretched arms toward Sabrina, and then flapping them back and forth, encouraging her to take an embrace.

They hugged, and Aunt Connie moved them towards the bedroom door. "I have a surprise for you. I made your favorite."

Sabrina threw her hands in the air. "Yes!"

They made their way to the kitchen.

"Packed your food, too," Aunt Connie said. "I heard that you have a meeting with Jenay at church, and then you're off to see Mother Rogers."

Sabrina frowned, taking a seat at the island. "How did you know that?"

"Amber called to see if I could keep Kayla for the weekend, since Paul isn't well. She was going to ask you."

"Yes, she left the mall early because Paul wasn't feeling well, so she had to take Kayla to her dance classes." Sabrina smiled at Aunt Connie. "Where are my goodies?"

"In the bag on the counter."

Sabrina moved with haste to inspect her gifts. "Awww! Thank you," she squealed, salivating at the container of food. "Woo-hoo!" Red velvet muffins. She twirled before reloading the bag.

"You're welcome." Aunt Connie smiled lovingly. "Tea or juice?"

"Juice, please," Sabrina responded, moving to take a seat at the island. "You're really spoiling me," she said, gazing at the large treat on the small plate before her.

"Not at all." Aunt Connie's eyes twinkled, before she closed the fridge door, and walked toward her with two glasses of apple juice. She set one before Sabrina and the other one on the island before taking a seat next to her niece.

"No muffin for you?" Sabrina asked.

"Nope. Need to lay off the sugar. Doctor's order."

"Really? Are you okay?"

"Oh yes! I'm in great shape, but my doc recommended cutting back on my sugar intake."

Sabrina beamed. "So Brother Selvin was right. 'The years have been good to you.'"

"We're having a great time. Don't ruin it." *Gulp. Gulp.* Aunt Connie drank some of her juice, her crinkled eyebrows serving as a warning.

"You better be praying about that fine man, and see what the Lord is saying," Sabrina remarked. "Someone else may scoop him up."

"I wish they would."

"Oh no!" Sabrina covered her lips with her fingers to mask her laughter.

"Selvin will be okay. Soooo, I understand from a very reliable source that there's a new man in your life."

"Eh—" Sabrina almost choked on her muffin. She could feel the heat traveling up her face. She snatched a napkin from the stack on the island, and wiped her mouth.

Aunt Connie spluttered into laughter. "You have it that bad, eh?"

Sabrina focused on her glass of juice. Awkward didn't begin to describe how she felt. "Nothing could be further from the truth. Amber needs to get a life and leave mine alone."

77

"So this Chandler is not making any moves on you?"

Sabrina shrugged her shoulders, trying to appear as casual as possible. "Aunty, no. We're just—"

"So you've been in touch," Aunt Connie surmised. "Amber is not aware of that. She wants me to encourage you to call him. What's with the secrecy?"

Sabrina was sure her cheeks were flushed. *Amber! Ugh!* "No secrecy. I can't tell Amber we've been in touch because she's creating all kinds of stories in her head. Nothing is going on between me and Chandler."

"Nothing?" Aunt Connie's brows crammed together. "Amber is asking me to pray for both of you. Said you went on a date of sorts."

Sabrina shook her head. "Believe me, nothing is going on between us. You know the story of how we met. He was grateful for my help and offered to take me to lunch. He's away at his job in Chicago. He travels…" She stopped, wondering why she was saying all of that. "Not even sure when he'll be back," she concluded.

Aunt Connie watched the betraying glow on her niece's face. "But you like him."

"There's nothing to like." Sabrina blushed. "I don't know him. Amber needs to stop. I hope she hasn't told Aunt Lynn or Mom and Dad."

"No, right now, it's just between us. Don't worry, I know Amber is strong-willed but eventually she'll let it go."

Sabrina stifled a groan of frustration. "I love her, but sometimes I want to give her a good shake."

"She means well." Aunt Connie chuckled, thinking how different her two nieces were. Then, she had to ask, "You're not hiding your heart because of Calvin, right?"

"Noooo. I'm not even thinking about Calvin. He's history. But Chandler is not on my mind like that. Plus, I don't think he's a Christian."

"Did he say that?"

Sabrina looked sheepishly at her aunt. "No."

"Oh. Okay," Aunt Connie said, slowly.

But Sabrina did not back down. "I probably shouldn't say that; I never asked."

"Continue to pray for him. I'll add him to my prayer list."

"Thanks."

"What's his last name?"

"Peynard."

Aunt Connie nodded, then grinned at her.

"What?" she asked puzzled.

"Nothing to do with Chandler. I should tell you I'm getting more accustomed to using Google."

Sabrina clapped her hands. "Nice."

"Okay, I did get a little help from Amber this morning."

"Good for you." Sabrina high-fived her.

CHAPTER 11

Chandler stood in his living room, scowling at his cell phone. He'd told Marcie he was coming to see her, and she'd told him no. *That's like the hundredth time.*

The rain pelted against the window, matching his mood—hard and edgy. He began to pace in front of the sofa. Forward. Back. Forward. Back. Forward. Back. Finally, he threw himself on the sofa, still unable to comprehend why Marcie had said no.

He was dying to get laid. Now would be good. He was unaccustomed to putting his body under subjection but since he'd caught Chlamydia from God knows who, that caused him to be even more selective in his bed mates. Actually, these days he'd only been sleeping with Marcie.

Has she found someone? The question swirled in Chandler's ears. *Why else would she say no on a night like this?* An acidic tension rolled over his tongue. *Women!*

Letting out a frustrated sigh, he glanced at the aluminum and wood wall clock. It was 8:30 p.m. He decided he would review the documents for his Skype meeting in the morning with the directors on his staff. The last few months had been hectic, with traveling and meetings, but it was all worth it.

His phone rang and he found it on the sofa. He propped up on one elbow to inspect the caller ID, but before long, his head hit the sofa again.

It was his father.

It stopped ringing, only to start again.

It was Don.

His head hit the sofa again.

Since their big blow up, he'd taken a few calls from Don, but those calls became too toxic, so he'd decided to stop answering when he called.

Still, he couldn't believe his relationship with Don had not only ended, but ended the way it had. He marveled at the way they had met.

He had heard of Don through the conversations of relatives but had never met him until freshman year at MIT some twenty years ago. Don had graduated from MIT's Sloan School of Management with an MBA and apparently was a stellar student. He was asked to speak at a student forum about his overall MBA experience and its impact on his job.

Chandler was enrolled in the School of Engineering but attended the forum to score points with Varina, whom he wanted to date. He couldn't believe his eyes when he glanced up and saw Don speaking at the podium. Not only were they the spitting image of each other, but they sounded alike. Varina stared from Chandler to Don as if she'd seen a ghost.

After the forum, the line to speak with Don was long, so he and Varina waited before walking up to him. His face was priceless, before they all broke into senseless laughter.

Ever since that day, he and Don had been close, and remained close even though their lifestyles were like night and day.

Chandler exhaled deeply as he deliberated whether or not to return Don's call. He dialed Don's number.

"Hey, Little Bro," Don greeted him.

"Hey," Chandler responded, his tone careful.

"Can we talk?" Don asked.

"About what?"

Don decided to be upfront. "About what happened, and is happening between us. I miss you, man."

Chandler swung his legs off the sofa and reclined. "I don't know, man. Our conversations turn negative these days."

"That's why I need to talk with you."

"I'll let you know."

"Chandler—"

"I'll let you know, Don."

"Okay. 'Night."

Without responding, Chandler disconnected the call. *Should have thought about family ties when you showed up here to accost me the last time.*

That evening, prior to meeting Don, he was at Pa'Dada Restaurant and Lounge sipping his drink while sizing up the crowd in an attempt to get his mind off Rozene. He had discovered this upscale establishment, and loved it, because he got a chance to hobnob with the restaurant's affluent, impressive clientele.

After he'd left the restaurant, he was still in knots thinking about Rozene, so he'd stopped by the gym before heading home.

When he arrived home, Don's black Lincoln Navigator was parked in one of his two parking spaces. He mentally slapped himself when he glanced at the clock on the dashboard. It registered 8:37 p.m. He had forgotten, he was meeting Don at 7:00 p.m. Thankfully, Don had a key so he didn't have to wait outside.

When he walked into his home, Don was relaxing on the sofa.

"Sorry, man," he greeted Don with a fist bump. "Don't know where my mind went. I forgot I was meeting you, so I went to the gym. Habit. Why didn't you call me?"

"It's okay," Don told him, pulling to the edge of the sofa. "I needed the time to think."

"Sounds serious. But what do you always say? 'God is good all the time, and all the time God is good.'"

Don constantly told him about God's goodness and faithfulness in his life. He never missed an opportunity to thank God for just about everything. However, while he loved his brother, he didn't share his exuberance for this

82

God thing. The only time he'd attended church was when he was invited to a wedding or a funeral.

"You remembered that, Little Bro?" Don couldn't help the smile that popped on his face. "You're listening to me after all. I'm encouraged."

Chandler smiled at him. "Of course, I'm listening to you. Always have. Hope you made yourself at home. Back in a few. Need to change out of these clothes."

"Go ahead. I'm good."

"'Kay," Chandler said, walking towards the stairs.

Ten minutes later, Chandler re-entered the living room in army-green shorts and a red polo shirt. "It's about to rain," he mentioned, taking a seat on the sofa across from Don.

"Hope it holds up until I leave."

Chandler eyed him curiously. "What's troubling you? You don't look yourself."

He looked him straight in the eye. "Did you sleep with Rozene Kanate?"

Deny! Deny! Deny! An inner voice shrieked in his ears. He felt like he was about to pass out. "Yes," he confessed in a voice that he didn't recognize.

Before he knew it, Don had sprung off the sofa and grabbed him by the throat, pressing him into the seat. "Are you crazy?" Don hissed. "Why? Why did you have to sleep with her?"

He gasped for air, pushing at Don's hand. Don released him, but continued to glare at him while they both struggled to steady their breathing.

Don walked away to stare out the window. "I regret the day I introduced her to you, and allowed you to ..." Don paused. "You had it all planned. You became a volunteer on the book tour in Chicago for that very reason. Then you volunteered to take her back to the hotel. I thought it was odd that you had booked a hotel room. Now I see why."

83

Don walked back to the sofa and dropped on it. "How could you be so heartless?"

He didn't have a comeback so he'd remained quiet, feeling a strange and unfamiliar emotion...humiliation. When he was finally able to speak, he countered, "I tried to stay away from her, Don, but I couldn't. We only slept together twice. Now she won't take my calls."

"Listen to me, Chandler." Don pulled to the edge of the sofa. "She is married. She has a family. Leave her alone before you destroy her marriage and her ministry." He didn't see any reason to inform Chandler about the current state of Rozene's marriage. That may give him hope.

"I'm in love with her, Don."

Don sat motionless. Shocked. Dismayed. Speechless.

Man, say something. Anything, he willed Don.

"Chandler, have you lost your mind?" Don shouted, jumping to his feet. "She is married with kids." He paused, clearly tamping down his anxiety. "Chandler, listen to me," he began in an overly calm voice. "This is not a good situation, not for you or her. You need to go find a woman of your own. She's already taken."

"I don't expect you to understand, but I love her." Frustration made him throw his hands in the air. "She's always on my mind and I-I just can't have enough of her."

Don shook his head. "Of all the women in the world, why her? Is it because she's unavailable?"

"I wondered about that, too," he told Don, "but no. I genuinely love her and I can't see myself with anyone else."

Don walked over to him, the concern evident in his eyes.

"I was trying to help you, you know," Chandler hastily pointed out. "That's how it started."

His confession caused Don's head to snap upwards. "Help me out! How would that help me?"

84

"You'd said that she couldn't reach a certain group of people because she hadn't been on the other side of love—temptation, lust, unfaithfulness—she was clean."

He watched as Don's mouth opened, and then closed, and then opened again without him speaking.

"I thought I would seek her out," Chandler continued. "You know I have a way with the ladies. Anyway, one night, I was channel hopping and saw her. I couldn't believe all that she was saying, her words were beautiful and she is sooo beautiful herself. It was amazing to meet her," he gushed. "And, you know what else is amazing?" He clapped his hands together excitedly. "I'm even starting to believe some of the things she's preaching about."

His countenance fell as he saw the pain in Don's gaze. "I never expected to fall in love with her." His eyes begged for understanding. "I love her, Don."

"Little Bro," Don said like he was talking to a child, "you need to seek counseling for what's going on with you. I've always told you, you needed help to deal with your family situation. That is what's eating you up inside."

He did not respond, so Don continued, "Rozene is not going to leave her family and her ministry for you. She is deeply connected to her husband and he's a good man."

He exhaled deeply, listening yet not wanting to hear Don out. He hoped this situation wouldn't drive a wedge between them. What he and Rozene shared was different. It was nothing like what he'd experienced with the other women he'd dated, and slept with.

"You know I love you," Don told him, "but this, this situation will not end well. I'll be praying for you. Have a good night."

With that, Don walked out, but not before Chandler witnessed the look of disgust on his face.

Chandler snapped out of his musings, and decided to beat back his frustration at his home gym. An hour later, he showered and crawled under the bedcovers. He reached for his phone on the nightstand. Sabrina had called…again.

He rang her back. "You're sleeping, already?" he asked. "Those kids have you all stressed out, or are you just a morning person?"

"You got the morning person thing right. I'm not teaching for the summer semester. I'm doing research. But that's not the problem. I had praise team and dance rehearsals, and then Bible study. Phew! My body is talking to me." Sabrina rolled onto her back. "Anyway, enough about me. How are you?"

Chandler chuckled. "I hope you'll feel better soon. I'm okay. Sorry I've not returned your calls. Please don't give up on me."

"Never. Ouch!" She'd rolled on her side and a sharp pain hit her.

"You okay?" It was hard to miss the concern in his voice.

"I think so. Nothing a massage won't fix."

"Admit it," he teased.

"What are you talking about?" She grinned at his playful tone.

"I've been gone almost three months. You. Miss. Me."

Girlish giggles erupted from her lips before she could stop them. "Lord, help this man."

He lowered his voice. "Admit it, Sab, you miss your friend."

She turned the table. "Not until you admit you miss me."

"Of course, I miss you. Tell me."

"I miss you, Chandler John Peynard. Satisfied?"

"I want to say no, but I'll take that for now." Oh, he enjoyed her. "What else have you been up to?"

Sabrina laughed softly. "Crunched for time for our summer production. We have a little over a month to go, and we need more rehearsal space. Too many groups are trying to use the same space so our rehearsal schedule is tight, whether it's week day or weekend."

"Hope everything works out. It's the last Sunday in June, right?"

"Thanks. Yes, the last Sunday. Pastor Jackson mentioned the church board has a building plan. I'll certainly be contributing. Lord knows we need at least a dance studio and a music room."

"You'll be contributing?"

"Yes. I'm sowing into my ministry so I can have a place to use my talents in service for God."

"I love hearing you talk about God. It makes me feel happy."

"What's to be unhappy about?"

He remained silent, feeling annoyed for no reason. "Here we go again," he railed. "You're treating me like a pet project."

"Pet project? Chandler, please stop it. I'm on Team C.J., remember?"

"Stop using that tone with me."

"Don't be sensitive; I'm trying to hear your heart."

"Sorry."

She tried again. "Is it Don?"

Chandler huffed out a frustrated sigh. "Yes. He jumped to all sorts of conclusions before he heard my side of the story."

"Maybe he wants to apologize."

"I get that feeling but I'm still disappointed with him, even though I can see now that he was right."

Chandler rolled onto his side, in shock that he'd revealed that to her… and himself. "Yes, he was right," he confessed. "I shouldn't have done what I did."

"Don't beat yourself up," she said quietly. "It's going to work out."

"Thank you." Then he heard himself say, "Can you pray?" *What on earth?* He tried to fix it. "Er, that's what you did the last time." *I need rest.*

Sabrina was too surprised to delay. "Let us pray," she began.

CHAPTER 12

We have plenty to celebrate. Chandler beamed with pride as he glanced around the rectangular table at the group of thirty-five men and women—aircraft designers, aerospace engineers, scientists, mathematicians and computational specialists, to name some—all at the top of their game. These directors were the backbone of the new aircraft redesign project.

He'd treated his entire Chicago staff to lunch earlier in the day. Thanks to their hard work, the project was way ahead of schedule. At least, the revision phase was over. The long days and nights had paid off big time.

To continue the celebration, he'd decided to take his directors to dinner at the Rosebud on Rush, a traditional Italian Restaurant.

Chandler listened intently as Michael Inglewood, his second-in-command gushed about working on the project. A foot shorter than Chandler, Michael was sturdily built, and definitely more exuberant by nature.

They had shared a great working relationship for the past eight years, and now a budding personal friendship. Though Michael was ten years older, that had never affected their relationship. Chandler couldn't help the smile that crept up his face. Michael was zealous about even the minute details of the project.

"Thanks, man, for all your hard work," Chandler said, slapping him on his back. "Thanks, too, for having my back. It was tough going for a while, but we did it. Your leadership at the home base, while I roam the other bases, is well noted."

Michael smiled at him. "No problem. All in the line of duty." He watched Chandler for a moment before asking, "Are you going to do any extra celebrating tonight?"

Chandler chuckled. "You know not to go there."

89

Michael grinned back at him. "You're so secretive, bro. I know you have your eye on someone. I'm seeing changes in you and only a woman does that to a man."

"Is that so?"

"I've seen it a thousand times."

Michael knew that was the end of their conversation. His boss never mixed business with pleasure. He'd heard through the grapevine that Chandler was quite the ladies' man, but that had never interfered with their work relationship. He'd witnessed many of the women at work expressing their blatant interest, but Chandler had never been linked to any of them.

Truthfully, he admired Chandler, perhaps hero-worshiped him a little, because Chandler was super-smart and extremely creative. Chandler's brilliance and work ethics were always shining beacons at Rinauto. He was definitely not a quitter, and any negative response from the Board concerning the team's design project only drove him to work harder to prove the team's case or incorporate the Board's suggestions.

But this project was big.

Chandler had redesigned the shape of the company's airbus—all ground breaking and in keeping with the latest sophisticated aircraft structures that were not only safe, but could adapt to environmental conditions and perform with increased efficiency.

With environmental legislation tightening, the Board was adamant that the new concept should make the aircraft lighter and more efficient on fuel.

After several rounds of revision, the Board accepted the new design concept. The Board was also thrilled that this new design would lower manufacturing and operational costs.

At the last Board meeting, when the team had presented the project, one Board member asked, "Seriously, what inspired this new design?"

Chandler spoke up. "I was out jogging one morning and I'd stopped to catch my breath. Actually, I sat on a bench on the periphery of the park and I was so moved by all that was before me—the trees, the flowers, the early-morning sun peeking out—everything knew where it belonged. In that moment, I thought about building an aircraft that knew where it belonged, that blended in with nature." He chuckled. "You could say I got my inspiration directly from nature."

You could hear a pin drop before the Board members began clapping. The aerospace industry had found its beacon of hope.

"Will you be able to make the NASA run, tomorrow?" Chandler pulled Michael out of his reflections. "I know you're down two members from your team, so I understand if you can't."

"Man, I can't miss your presentation," Michael responded, handing Chandler an envelope.

"Great. What's this?"

Michael chuckled, glancing around the table, and observing team members happily chatting with each other. "Another spread of your face on a magazine."

Chandler took the envelope and rested it on the table, resisting the urge to sigh. After all, it was a good thing. "Thanks," he said quietly.

"Don't look so defeated. I would pay money to get on the cover of *Aerodynamics Magazine*. You're looking sharp, too."

"Sharp? Thought it was a group shot."

"The group shot is on the article page. You're on the cover with the caption, 'The Mastermind.'"

91

Chandler knitted his brows. "Thought it was the article unveiling the plans for the new hybrid-electric commercial aircraft?"

"No. That was for 'Aviation News,' with the title 'The Modern Aircraft.'"

Chandler let out a tiny smile. He'd written the article on behalf of Rinauto. "I enjoyed writing that piece."

"I can tell." Michael chuckled. "Great piece."

"Thanks." Chandler pushed off his seat. "I'm going to leave you guys to it."

"Calling it a night myself."

"Team!" Chandler signaled for attention. "It seems like I've said it a thousand times, but here I am again. Thanks for your hard work."

"Thanks for your hard work," Henny Thomas yelled, while several other members started to beat the table. Henny was Director over the Computational Specialists.

Chandler smiled broadly. "Thanks! This is a team effort, and I'd like for it to remain that way. Those of you who were sleeping on this project, it's your time to wake up and take the project forward."

Loud chuckles erupted as members playfully pointed fingers at each other.

Chandler couldn't help but laugh out, too. "You all have a great evening. See you tomorrow."

A chorus of goodbyes followed him out the door.

An hour later, Chandler stretched out on his bed staring at himself on the magazine cover. He wished they wouldn't. Not that he wasn't proud of his accomplishments, but he wished they'd used his professional headshot instead of having him sit on the edge of his desk like he was a male model. Thankfully, he was dressed in his navy suit.

His cell phone rang and he reached for it on the nightstand and looked at the screen before answering.

"Hello, Mother." Chandler almost gulped at how pleasant he sounded.

Veronica Peynard resisted the urge to comment on the sweetness of Chandler's tone. Albeit, he was still addressing her as Mother.

"Hello, son, how are you?"

"Good, Mother. I was about to retire to bed."

"I know, love, but I couldn't let the day finish and not tell you how proud your father and I are, of you and your accomplishments."

Chandler remained silent.

"We saw the magazines. Your father is showing it off to all…"

Chandler wondered why his parents thought they should have bragging rights. Pity, when he had needed them they hadn't been available.

"Yes, your father is very proud of you." She gave a little laugh. "He's saving all the magazines."

Father? Chandler sighed.

The closest Julius Peynard had ever come to being a father was around the time Chandler was preparing to wed Alana. He was home for about two weeks, and during that time he tried counseling Chandler about the beauty of being married. When the wedding day fell apart, Julius did not hang around to help him pick up the pieces. He had an emergency and had to hurry back to San Francisco to make sure the team of engineers was building the mall in cutting-edge fashion as he'd designed it. Chandler was thankful that his mother hadn't run off immediately to her world of fashion, but spent another two weeks with him.

"Chandler, I told you, your father didn't grow up with his father." Veronica explained. "He told me he called you a few days ago, but you did not answer."

Chandler remained silent.

"I know you heard me, Chandler."

93

"Yes, Mother. I heard you."

"Son, please don't get an attitude. We love you."

"Okay, Mother."

"Dad and I are praying for you," she said quietly.

Chandler had to bite back laughter. It was one thing for his mother to find Jesus, but his dad, too? *What is this?*

A chuckle must have escaped because his mother was silent. For what it was worth, he added, "Thanks, Mother."

She decided to leave it alone, and instead played her mother card. "I think I need to visit you, since you refuse to come home. I have to pick up a magazine to see my son."

Why? "Er, Mother, can I check my schedule and let you know?"

"I wasn't thinking about visiting anytime soon. Family is important, Chandler. It's God's way of telling us we're not alone."

Oh! Oh! Now you tell me!

At the silence, his mother added, "Alright, I won't keep you. Oh, I wanted to plan a surprise party for your father's birthday. I would like you to be there and I would appreciate it if you would say a few words."

Chandler's brows furrowed. *A few words?* "I won't be able to make it, Mother."

"Really, Chandler? Please consider attending. Have a good night."

"Good night, Mother."

Not too long after he hung up, his phone rang. Chandler eyed it thinking it was his father calling.

"Marcie?" He answered curtly when he saw the number. He was tired of her cat-and-mouse games so he hadn't been taking her calls.

"C.J., I'm worried about you. You haven't been responding to my calls." She let out a long, deliberate sigh of relief.

94

Chandler imagined her wiping her long well-manicured fingers across her forehead, and wanted to throw his phone down. "I'm fine. Was there something else?"

"What's with the attitude, baby? You can tell me you miss me. That's what that is." She giggled knowingly. "I have just what you need."

Displeasure creased Chandler's face. "See you around, Marcie."

"Are you mad at me?' she cooed.

"We've come to the end of our arrangement. Feel free to pursue your other interests."

"C.J., this sounds like goodbye. We need each other," she purred. "I'll catch up with you when you're not mad at me."

His heart hardened against her. "Goodbye," he said firmly, and disconnected the call.

CHAPTER 13

"I thought we were going to stop and eat." Aunt Connie grumbled from the back seat. "I know both of you heard my stomach growling. My stomach is thinking my mouth is on a vacation."

Amber snickered in the passenger seat, as she glanced furtively at Sabrina, motioning for her to respond.

Sabrina attempted to control her laughter. "We'll stop soon. I'm trying to cover as much ground as possible, before the rain starts."

They were on their way to Warner Robins.

"We've already driven over two hours," Aunt Connie complained. "Why are you taking me back to days I want to forget?"

Baffled, Sabrina took her eyes off the road to eye Amber.

"What are you talking about, Aunty?" Amber asked carefully.

"Back in the day when money wasn't flowing and I was cracking ice like it was a meal."

"What?" Sabrina and Amber asked in unison.

"These are my better days," Aunt Connie sang, throwing her a hand in the air.

Amber swung her head to the side to get a full view of her aunt. "You're kidding, right?"

Aunt Connie laughed aloud. "For me to know and for you to find out."

Sabrina and Amber looked at each other, then burst out into laughter.

"Here comes the rain," Sabrina announced.

"Then, I see food in the distance," Aunt Connie proclaimed.

"Soon. Very…" Sabrina paused, distracted by the ringing of her cell phone. Not taking her eyes off the road, she reached for her cell phone in the cup holder. She glanced at the screen and a low gasp issued from her lips.

Amber perked up, stretching her neck to see who was calling.

"Chand…" Amber paused as shock rushed in. She glanced at Sabrina and was met with guilty eyes. Amber pulled back towards the window. "Is that who I think it is?" she asked, her eyebrows almost colliding with her hairline.

Sabrina pursed her lip, before responding. "What? Are you monitoring my—?"

"You better get that," Amber said.

"Good morning," Sabrina answered her phone, wondering why she sounded so breathless.

"Good morning, my friend." Chandler's rich baritone rang out. "You're making me feel special again." He couldn't resist.

Sabrina stifled a snorting laugh. "Like I said, don't get it twisted."

From the corner of her eye, Sabrina saw a perplexed Amber watching her, but decided not to spare her another glance.

"I'm not the twisted one," Chandler said. "What if I answered my phone like that? I'm sure you'd think I was trying to hit on you."

"Oh no. I wouldn't be thinking that. I'd probably think you'd just returned from jogging."

He chuckled softly. "Sure."

"That's just the way my mind works."

"If you insist. I'll be back in town next week."

"Oh, great!" *Too much excitement.* She toned it down. "Good for you."

It was not lost on him. "Happy I'm returning, huh?"

She chuckled. "If you insist."

"I'll call you when I'm back."

Silence.

97

"Sab?"

"Sorry about that. It's raining hard and I'm driving. What were you saying?"

"It's raining hard and you're on the phone?" It was hard to miss that he'd gone into high alert mode. There was something else there, too, but she couldn't put a finger on it.

"Sab, I'm going to get off this phone. Call when you get to wherever you're going, okay?"

"Okay, I will."

"If it's raining too hard, stop somewhere. Promise?"

"Okay, I promise," she said softly, before disconnecting the call.

Sabrina pretended not to notice the deafening silence in the car. "Okay, another ten minutes and we'll stop for gas and food." She rambled on. "We shouldn't eat a lot because Mom is preparing dinner."

"Mom is preparing dinner?" Amber knitted her brows. "Is that your diversionary tactic? Well, it didn't work. What was all that about?"

Sabrina eyebrows crushed together. "What are you talking about?"

Amber put on a honeyed voice and imitated phrases from Sabrina's conversation with Chandler. "Good morning. Okay, I will. Okay, I promise."

Aunt Connie chuckled softly while Sabrina tried to burn Amber with her eyes.

"I didn't sound like that," Sabrina told her bluntly.

"Sneaky. That's what you are. First of all, you didn't tell me you were in touch with him," Amber accused. "Secondly, that conversation sounds like you've been seeing each other. Thirdly, you're sounding breathless, like you were about to drip honey all over that man. Fourthly, you—"

"Amber, I told you a thousand times, I'm not seeing Chandler, but you want to believe what you want to believe."

Amber stiffened. "Sure, Rina. Whatever you say."

Sabrina's eyes were on the road, but she could hear the sarcasm in Amber's tone.

"Alright," Sabrina relented, "so we spoke a few times, but that's it."

Amber remained quiet, turning her gaze out the window.

"Seriously, Amber, I don't know him all that well. Even if I did, I'm not interested in him. I need someone who has a deeper walk with the Lord. And, he's not interested in me."

"Okay, Rina, whatever you say."

Sabrina knew this was not the end of their conversation. She glanced in the rearview mirror and caught Aunt Connie's expression, but didn't know what to make of it.

"Can we stop, now?" Aunt Connie asked. "Food places are coming up. Hopefully, by the time we finish eating, the rain would have stopped."

An hour later, they were still anchored down at a table in Fylin Seafood Restaurant. It was still raining heavily, and as much as they wanted to be on their way, good sense prevailed. Few patrons were dining in the restaurant.

"It looks like it's going to rain all the way into the night," Amber pointed out. "We may have to camp out here.

Sabrina gave her a wry glance. "I hope not."

"I hope not," Aunt Connie echoed.

Just then Sabrina's phone rang.

Everyone glanced at the screen, where the phone lay on the table.

It was Chandler.

99

Amber laughed. "Do you need privacy?"

"Shush." Aunt Connie knitted her brows at Amber as Sabrina put the phone to her ear.

"Hello," Sabrina answered quietly.

Chandler pushed out a frustrated sigh before spinning his chair away from the window of the study and hoisting his feet on his Oxmoor traditional two-tone executive desk. He'd made no progress on his PowerPoint presentation to the Board. All because of a woman named Sabrina Abigail Benjamin who had taken up residence in his brain.

"Sab, I'm checking if you made it safely."

He was definitely questioning his rationality. Firstly, for being so edgy about Sabrina driving in the rain, and secondly, for his 'new-found faith' in God. Since he'd spoken to her, he'd prayed three times for her safety. He could hardly believe it.

"We stopped to eat and get gas," Sabrina told him. "We have finished eating, but we're waiting for the rain to stop, somewhat."

"Glad you stopped. Stay there until you're sure it's safe to move. Are you traveling alone?"

"No. I have Aunt Connie and Amber with me. We're going to visit our parents—me and Amber, that is. Aunt Connie is visiting her sisters."

"Warner Robins, Georgia, right?"

"Yes." Sabrina absentmindedly used her finger to trace the rim of her empty glass. "We're a little over an hour away."

"You started out early."

"Yes, before seven o'clock. Returning tomorrow."

Chandler's smile shone through his voice. "Sounds awesome. Around three years ago, I visited the Robins Air Force Base near Warner Robins."

"Are you serious?"

100

"Yes. You know I'm into aeronautics. A small team of us from work did a tour."

"Nice," she said. "Don't know if I told you my dad was in the Air Force. So this town is right up his street."

"I can see why. Call me when you get there, okay?"

"I will." She smiled. "Bye."

Sabrina placed her phone on the table. Unaware that she was still smiling, she glanced up to find Amber watching her. She could hear a pin drop.

Guilt flushed Sabrina's face. She swung her head toward Aunt Connie, who was seated on her right. No help was forthcoming. *Interesting*, was all Sabrina could read from her gaze.

"Nothing is going on," Sabrina declared, way too loudly in her estimation. "Seriously, nothing," she added.

Amber remained quiet, suddenly studying her well-manicured nails.

"Look, the rain stopped." Aunt Connie's enthusiastic voice rang out.

"Yes, we can leave," Sabrina said, giving her aunt a grateful look.

Still, she knew Aunt Connie simply made a note to self.

101

CHAPTER 14

Easy on the eyes, was all Sabrina could think when Chandler emerged from his car. *A strong, intelligent, magnificent leading man. Oh, and the kind of man your mother warned you about.*

Unsmiling, she stared at him as he strode closer. *Swagger!* He had plenty of that. And the air of confidence surrounding him was attractive. *Life has been kind to him.* At that thought, Sabrina let out a giggle.

"What a relief." Chandler spared her a tiny, heart-fluttering smile. "I was beginning to think I'm not welcome. Good evening."

She grinned up at him, taking in his chiseled jawlines and full, symmetrical lips. "Good evening. What gave you that idea? Of course you're welcome. Welcome back!"

"Thanks." He hugged her, careful not to overdo it. "How do you manage to make me feel like your beloved pup, all the time?"

She playfully slapped him on his shoulder. "Stop that nonsense."

"I know you're harboring those secret thoughts." He smiled, pulling his eyes from her beautiful face.

"Keep up that foolishness, and you'll find yourself with one less friend."

"Wouldn't want to risk that." He displayed his pearly whites. "Ready to go in?"

"Sure."

As if it was the most natural thing in the world, he held her hand, and they walked into Olive Garden Italian Restaurant.

Soon, they were seated and served their dinner. Chewing his salmon, Chandler scanned Sabrina's face as she spoke animatedly about her visit home last weekend.

Her jet-black hair was parted in the center and streamed behind her. He noticed it had grown longer.

Lost in thought, he hadn't realized she'd stopped talking. *What did I miss?*

Her wide, dark eyes stared intently at him. "Are you looking at my hair? It was kind of windy out front."

He smiled at her. "No. I was thinking your hair was shoulder-length the last time I saw you."

She seemed unconvinced and her eyebrows climbed further. "You're thinking it looks better shorter?"

"No. It looks nice." He tried to sound casual, adding, "It suits your face."

"Thanks." She took a sip of her apple juice.

A smile tugged at his lips. She wasn't sure how to take his compliment. "How are rehearsals going?" he asked, lifting a forkful of rice to his mouth.

"They are going very well, despite the space issues. Everyone is sticking to the rehearsal schedule, so that's good. My research is finished, and I'm handing in my article on Friday. That means I have more time to spend at rehearsals. And, I've decided to only sing in the production. No dancing since…"

Chandler took in her coral, long-sleeved silk blouse with its soft tie neckline. It brought out the perfection of her golden-brown complexion. He remembered her blouse flowing slightly above her curvy hips when he was walking towards her outside. *Lots of hips for a slender frame.* He had to drag his eyes from her shapely legs below the hem of her black pencil skirt. *No doubt her jacket is in her car.* Then it struck him, she was more conservative than he'd thought. *Was I even thinking about her that way?* Anyway, he liked her.

Her gaze bounced all over his face, watching him intently. "What's up with you staring at me? Is something wrong? One minute you're looking perplexed and the next minute you're smiling." She swirled pasta on her fork and placed it in her mouth.

"I've annoyed you." A chuckle almost burst from his lips. All the women he'd dated were busy trying to impress him; he hadn't seen this side of any woman.

Sabrina chuckled, too. "You need to come off what you're taking."

"Forgive me for staring. I'm trying to adjust to the I-am-about-the-business woman who's sitting across from me. You were so much nicer when I was your pet project."

She gave him the side-eye. "Thought you were resistant to that, but I can make it happen, if that's your desire."

"You're too nice for that kind of ugliness." He smiled at her—one of those smiles designed to melt any heart. Her eyes darkened and he knew he'd hit home. He let it slide. He wouldn't play with her.

Dropping her gaze, Sabrina moved her dinner plate away and reached for her dessert. *Careful*, she cautioned herself as she cut into the slice of red velvet cake. "Why were you so concerned about me driving in the rain?" she asked.

Chandler paused to collect his thoughts. "An associate of mine was in an accident last year. She didn't realize she was speeding, and it was raining. I'm grateful she made it out alive." He'd thought Rozene had died that day.

"I'm sorry to hear that. Is she okay?"

"Yes. She's good."

"Wonderful. How's work going?" she ventured. "Aeronautics, right? Is it the same type of work you do here as you do in Chicago?"

"Work is hectic, always hectic but good. When I'm in Orlando I get a breather. I focus on training here." He answered quickly, determined to change the subject. "Have they started on the new building at church?"

104

"Yes, they have actually begun to lay the foundation. It's behind the main building that houses the sanctuary. You can see it from the front when you drive in." She swallowed more of her cake with gusto.

"That's good news. At least, you can look forward to more rehearsal space in the future." He downed a piece of red velvet cake.

A smile played on her lips, for she was touched by his concern. "Yes. Glad for that. We'll have a dedicated room for the performing arts, but I was hoping we would get three rooms for dance, music, and drama."

"I see. The funds weren't enough to make that happen?"

"Pretty much. The church decided to go with a larger nursery, which I can understand, and they are also putting in a library. Children will be able to swing by and do their homework anytime. Happy about that."

He smiled perceptively. "I know you are, but you still wanted the rooms for the performing arts."

She nodded.

"What would these rooms look like?"

She wiped her mouth, smiled ecstatically, and launched off. "Ohhh! The music room would have a built-in sound system, a grand keyboard, and several other musical instruments. Nicely padded chairs and…"

Chandler listened as she spoke. All that vision locked up in one lithe, curvaceous frame. *Amazing.* "Haven't seen such zeal in a long time. Admirable." He smiled warmly at her, but she remained unmoved.

"Thanks," she murmured.

Chandler signaled to the waiter for the check. When he returned with it, Chandler handed him his credit card, and he left to process the payment.

"It's almost seven o'clock. Are you going to make it on time for Bible study?" Chandler asked.

105

Sabrina glanced at her watch. "Goodness! Time flew by."

He sent her a teasing wink. "Only when you're having fun."

"I know you were having fun."

"A tad bit."

"Are you coming with me?" Sabrina asked.

He eyed her keenly. "To church?"

She nodded.

"No, not my thing. I believe in God, though."

She chuckled. "Never heard it said like that. Afraid you might like it?"

An incredulous expression crossed his face. "What's to like? Church folks seem so fanatical. Well, let me not generalize. Don is okay and I know a few others. I would say they're exuberant."

"I hear you. Would you prefer to attend on Sunday?"

He tensed in his seat. "Er, no."

"Thought you wanted to see Pastor Jackson. You may stand a better chance of seeing him tonight than on Sunday morning."

Chandler deliberated. His thoughts were disturbed when the waiter returned for his signature on the receipt. He signed, included a tip, and sent the waiter on his way.

"Thanks for dinner," Sabrina said. "It was nice to catch up with you. Although I did most of the talking."

With an amused grin, he rose telling her, "I could say you're a chatterbox, but let me say, you had a lot on your heart."

"Smart of you." Sabrina smiled at him, rising and moving towards him.

Instinctively, he held out his hand and she took it and allowed him to lead her out of the restaurant.

"Where did you park?" Chandler asked when they'd exited the building.

"I'm two cars away from you," she muttered. His woodsy cologne was killing her. He smelled good. He'd released her hand but his light touch was now burning a hole through the small of her back.

As he ushered her across the parking lot, Chandler slowly removed his hand. He didn't realize he was touching her.

"Nice car," he told her as she unlocked the door of her Acura. He opened the driver's door for her, and peered inside the car. "Looks fully loaded."

"Yes. I got it last year. Your car is nice, too. All sporty."

"Thanks. I purchased it earlier this year."

"Good for you." She edged towards her driver's door.

"Aren't you forgetting something?" he asked.

"What?" Sabrina eyed him softly.

Simply beautiful. He loved her innocence and vulnerability. A smile washed up his face, and he opened his arms and embraced her lightly, lighter than he really wanted to. He didn't want to scare her.

She hugged him, too, feeling a vacuum when he released her. "Thanks again. See you soon," she said, not meeting his eyes.

Then, he heard himself say, "I'll attend church with you. I'll try to see Pastor Jackson tonight, or make an appointment to see him."

Her face blossomed into a smile. "That's great."

"Okay, after you, then."

107

CHAPTER 15

Smiling, Sabrina waved at the two ushers who were standing at the door leading to the sanctuary. She avoided their enquiring glances.

"Praise and worship has started, but we can go in," she said to Chandler.

"Okay."

Sabrina led him up the aisle to the middle row where she always sat. She nodded at Sister Susan, who was singing her heart out further down the row, before taking a seat at the end.

Chandler sat quietly beside her as she prayed. She was glad he had the good sense to not hang on to her hand or shoulder when they walked in. The last thing she wanted was the wagging tongues bringing up issues of impropriety, since she was in charge of a ministry.

She took her Bible, pen, and notepad from her purse. The congregation was in high praise, so she wrote a note to Chandler—*I'm going to stand. You can, too.*

He nodded, and as she stood he rose, as well.

Awkward, Chandler thought. He didn't know the song they were singing, even though the words were displayed on several projectors. He settled for clapping, hoping it would be over soon.

Sabrina tried not to pay too much attention to Chandler, but she was aware he was out of his comfort zone.

After praise and worship, Chandler recognized Deacon Walter Tucker, who said the opening prayer. He was the other man who was in Pastor Jackson's office that fateful night he'd rushed into the sanctuary.

Next, Pastor Jackson came to the podium. He looked well-groomed in a tan-colored suit over a white shirt that

108

opened at his neck, and complemented his skin. Strangely, he looked taller and thinner than Chandler had recollected.

"Welcome, brothers and sisters," he greeted the church in a deep voice.

Murmurs of "Thank you," and "Great to be here," bounced around the huge, half-filled sanctuary.

Pastor Jackson's gaze bounced around the large room. "I know we have visitors with us this evening. Stick a hand up if you're visiting." He paused, left the podium and walked from the altar towards the congregation.

Sabrina glanced at Chandler, noticing he'd already lifted his hand.

"Welcome, my sister! Welcome, my sister!" Pastor Jackson said, making his way across the front of the church. "Welcome, my brother! Welcome…" His eyes fell on Chandler and as recognition dawned, it was as if he'd received a gift he'd been praying about. "Welcome, my brother!" Pastor Jackson began dancing in circles. "Praise the Lord!"

Chandler smiled at the man of God who had come to his rescue. As Pastor Jackson moved on to greet the other visitors, a thought hit Chandler, *This is a moment I will always cherish.*

Sabrina could identify with Pastor Jackson's excitement at seeing Chandler. She'd indicated to him that she was in touch with Chandler.

A smile was plastered on Pastor Jackson's face as he made his way back to the podium. "God is good." His voice rang out happily. "This evening, I would like us to talk about, being loose and available for God. As is customary, put your hand up if you have a comment or question. Again, our topic is 'Loose and Available for God'. He turned the pages of his Bible, "Let's read Second Corinthians 5:17. Say amen, when you've found it."

109

A few seconds later, shouts of "Amen!" echoed in the sanctuary.

"Let's read together. 'Therefore if any man be in Christ, he is a new creature: old things are passed away; behold, all things are become new.'" Pastor Jackson moved away from the podium. "The scripture says if any man be in Christ, if you accept the Lord Jesus Christ as your personal savior, then that man is a new creature, meaning he has a new nature. Old things—old expectations, heathen philosophies, earthly standards—are all passed away. They are gone from that man, now that he has a new life in Jesus Christ.

Again, "Amens!" flared up all over the sanctuary.

"Now that you have the new life in Jesus Christ, the question is—are you loose and available for God? You are here to fulfill your portion of God's plan."

Pastor Jackson paused to take a question. "Yes, sir."

Chandler perked up. Sounded like some of what Rozene had taught in one of her YouTube videos.

A man on the second-to-last row spoke. "I am growing in grace and in my faith but I know I'm not completely transformed."

"Great point," Pastor Jackson said. "We are being transformed daily, if we allow God to do His work in us. Roman 12:2 states, 'And be not conformed to this world: but be ye transformed by the renewing of your mind, that ye may prove what is that good, and acceptable, and perfect, will of God.'"

A loud groan came from Sister Susan, followed by, "The process, though, Pastor. Ouch!"

That caused a few snickers.

"Sister, I feel you," Pastor Jackson said. "However, don't hate the process. The things that you go through are designed to get you into the presence of the Almighty God.

And in the presence of the Lord, there's fullness of joy and are pleasures forevermore."

Loud "Amens" erupted.

Pastor Jackson stared into the audience. "God has need of you and me. And, He calls us into service based on what He wants from each of us."

He walked back to the podium. "Let me make one final point then I'll open up for discussion. Here's what I say to you and me—when God calls you, He knows you—everything about you. Your past or your pedigree doesn't scare God. The grace of God rearranged my life...rearranged my capabilities. And He can do the same for you, to take you places you've never dreamed of."

Everyone clapped, and Chandler found himself clapping, too.

Half an hour later, Bible study ended. Sabrina greeted several church members, while warding off curiosity about Chandler. They were making their way to Pastor Jackson when Deacon Tucker intercepted them, a big smile covering his face, making his dark eyes smaller. He was a short, ruggedly handsome man around thirty years old. His sturdy, coffee-colored body indicated he'd spent much time in the gym.

"Sister Sabrina!" Deacon Tucker greeted her.

Sabrina extended her hand, and received a firm handshake. "Hi, Deacon Tucker. How are you?"

"I'm doing great, Sis. Are you doing okay?"

"Yes. I'm doing great." She turned towards Chandler. "You remember—"

"Hey, man! It's great to see you." He shook Chandler's hand, while patting his shoulder.

"It's great to see you, too, Deacon Tucker."

As Pastor Jackson joined them, Deacon Tucker bid them goodbye.

111

"Chandler, absolutely great to see you." Pastor Jackson shook Chandler's hand, his light-brown eyes gleaming with delight.

Up close, Chandler noticed the gray strands lacing his black hair and the gritty stubble on his chin.

"Thanks, Pastor Jackson," Chandler said, smiling. "Thought I would swing by to say hello and thank you."

"You're welcome, my brother. Always."

"How are you, Sabrina?" Pastor Jackson asked Sabrina.

"I'm doing great, Pastor," she responded.

Pastor Jackson looked at Chandler. "This young lady is such a hard worker. She makes it happen around here."

Sabrina smiled. "Pastor, you give me too much credit. You have many wonderful people running around here at full throttle. All willing vessels."

Pastor Jackson let out a healthy laugh. "And I'm super-grateful for all of you."

"Pastor, how do I get on your calendar?" Chandler asked.

"Helen Bass, my assistant, does my scheduling. Would you like to meet after church on Sunday?"

What? I'm a member now? Chandler relented. "Yes. Thanks. What time does church start?"

"Church starts at 10:00 a.m.," Pastor Jackson said. "We have Sunday school at 9:00 a.m. Usually, we're out by noon."

"Great. I'll be here."

"I'll see you then, my brother." Pastor Jackson shook Chandler's hand. "God bless you both. Drive safely."

"Thanks, Pastor," Chandler and Sabrina responded.

Again, Sabrina escorted Chandler out of the sanctuary amidst prying eyes.

It was not lost on him. "Am I a favorite?" he asked.

112

She smiled at his profile. "Just don't want to entertain any conversations about you."

"You mean the nature of our relationship?"

"Yes. But seriously, it's no one's business."

Chandler didn't like the nature of their conversation, so he changed it. "Weren't you supposed to be singing? Thought you said—"

"I'm a part of the praise and worship team but we have a schedule. I'll be singing on Sunday."

"Nice. I enjoyed Pastor Jackson's teaching." *'God has need of you'* kept reverberating in his mind.

"Me, too," she said as they came to a stop at their cars. "This is where we part. I'll see you on Sunday."

"I'll escort you home."

"Okay," was out of her mouth before she realized. *Lord, help me!* He looked delighted so she couldn't withdraw her response.

Fifteen minutes later, Sabrina pulled into her garage, still fuming with herself for having Chandler escort her home. *I don't know him like that.* True, too, she didn't hear any warning bells in her head.

She gathered her belongings and stepped out of the car.

Chandler had left the engine running in his car and was standing outside the garage. He chuckled softly as she moved towards him. "I'm going to church now?"

"Is that a bad thing? What do you have against the church?"

He let out a long sigh. "I have nothing against the church. I just wasn't brought up in church, like you."

"How do you know I was brought up in church?"

"Your conversation." But he also remembered Rozene sounding the same way.

"And that's a bad thing?"

"Not a bad thing. I like the teachings, at least, the ones I've heard."

113

"Are you going to make it on Sunday? No pressure," she added.

"We'll see." He smiled at her. "Have a good night." He reached for her, and then pulled back. "Wait, I have something for you."

He hurried to his car, opened the trunk and closed it, before walking back to her. "This is for you." He handed her a gift bag.

"Thank you!" She looked up at him and took the bag. Her heart started a happy dance. Some of the pain in his eyes was gone. That made her even happier, and a smile burst from her lips.

"Okay, what was that?" he asked, returning her smile. She had a way of looking at him, really looking at him, like he was under examination. He did not want to come up short.

"Feeling thankful," she told him, deliberating whether or not to hug him.

"Now, that's good. Have a good night."

"Night," she said, turning away from him.

"Aren't you forgetting something?" Chandler asked.

That was all the encouragement she needed, and she turned and gave him a hug.

CHAPTER 16

"Rina, where are you?" Amber asked in hushed, rushed tones on the phone.

"Heeey! Aunty Connie and I are at my car in the parking lot behind the church."

"Girrrl, your man pulled into the parking lot in the front. Dear God, he's fiiiiiine. I'm going to take him to you."

"No. No. Take him to the sanctuary."

"Are you crazy?" Amber hissed. "He'll be under attack, and I don't have my Taser. We'll come to you. Let him sit with Aunty. She can handle the folks."

"Amber, take him to the sanctuary, and I'll tell Aunt Connie—"

"Got to go. Don't want him to disappear on me." With that, Amber disconnected the call.

Sabrina scowled at her phone. She hadn't heard from Chandler since Wednesday. She knew he must be suffering from her slight rejection but she had to be careful with him. She was definitely a hugger, but if he couldn't handle it, she would have to pull back.

"Should I start praying?" Aunt Connie asked.

"No," Sabrina said hastily, dropping her Sunday school journal on the back seat of the car and closing the door. She eyed her aunt. "But, then maybe you should. Amber is at it again. Chandler is here and she wants to take him to me. Told her to take him to the sanctuary."

"Why didn't you let her take him to you?"

"He came to church. He didn't come here to see me. He didn't even tell me for sure that he was coming. Anyway, what were you saying about Brother Sel? He was looking rather dapper at Sunday school."

Aunt Connie gave her a penetrating look, letting the situation with Chandler slide. "Okay. I admit he was looking... okay. But then, he opened his mouth and ruined it."

A loud chuckle erupted from Sabrina as she locked her car. "Seriously, you need to give the man a break. He was simply saying hello. It's your fault he's attracted to you. Look at you! You're looking like a blushing bride in that white suit."

"This old thing," Aunt Connie glanced down her fabulous white fitted skirt suit, complemented by a chic pair of red Nine West pumps. Chunky gold jewelry added to her regal look. "I've had this outfit for two years now."

Sabrina grinned at her. "You're still rocking it, though."

"Sabrina," Aunt Connie said under breath. "We have company. Amber is taking a very fine gentleman to see you." Aunt Connie gazed at the vision of handsomeness striding towards them. He looked like he had stepped out of *GQ* in a stylish navy blue suit, yellow shirt, and red and yellow pin-striped tie.

"What man?" Then, it dawned on Sabrina, and her eyes popped.

Aunt Connie nodded at her, before letting out an exuberant, "Good morning!"

Chandler and Amber returned her greeting.

"Chandler, this is our Aunt Connie." Amber rushed in.

Aunt Connie extended her hand and Chandler took it. "So nice to meet you, Chandler."

He flashed a charming smile. "Likewise, Aunt Connie."

"Glad you made it," Sabrina told him.

"Me, too," he said, touching her arm. *We're at peace.* For that, he was thankful. He'd been agonizing over the way he'd held on to Sabrina when she'd given him a hug on Wednesday night. He felt as if he'd hugged her a little

116

too tight. *Way too exuberantly.* Which was confirmed when she pulled away from him, not all too subtly.

"I saw Chandler in the parking lot," Amber mentioned, "and decided to take him to see you since you'll be singing."

"Right. You did say you would be singing today," Chandler said.

"Yes, and on that note, I'll see you all after church. I am going through the back entrance, as usual," Sabrina said. She glanced at Amber. "Can you please show Chandler where the church office is? He has a meeting there after church."

"My pleasure," Amber said, in a tone that made everyone chuckle.

"Chandler, you can sit with me, if you don't mind," Aunt Connie volunteered.

Chandler flashed his megawatt smile. "Thank you. I would like that."

"We'll see you later, Sabrina," Aunt Connie said, moving away with a smiling Chandler.

"I'm right behind you all," Amber yelled.

As soon as they were out of earshot, Amber leaned against the car, "Oooh weeee!" she screeched under her breath. "If you let that man get away, I'm holding you responsible."

"Stop this nonsense." Sabrina all but rolled her eyes. "You need to be praying for his soul to be saved."

"He's at the right place. If that's your only concern, then that will be my prayer." Annoyed, Amber sashayed off.

"Sorry," Sabrina threw at her back.

Sabrina pulled herself together, then realized a tiny smile had popped at the corner of her mouth. Chandler was carrying the Bible she'd given him as a gift. Her smile widened when she remembered his gift of twelve extra-large red velvet cupcakes.

Almost half an hour later, praise and worship ended and Sabrina sat with five other praise team members on the front row on the left side of the sanctuary. The Spirit of the Lord moved from the first song to the last song. Even now shouts of praises were echoing all over the sanctuary.

Thankfully, she had the corner seat, so she slipped to her knees in reverence before God.

For the first time in his life, Chandler was glad to be in church. For sure, something new was happening in him, even though he couldn't put a finger on it.

A sniffle caught his ear and he leaned over and asked Aunt Connie if she was okay. She nodded, mopping her eyes to prevent tears from trickling down her cheeks.

Sabrina! Chandler's eyes flitted to where the praise team sat, but he couldn't see her. He had no idea she had such a powerful, yet beautiful soprano. His mouth twitched into a smile. She was in her element, too. *Totally at ease.*

"Pray for the person next to you," Pastor Jackson's voice rang out from the podium. "The Spirit of God is moving. Pray, church. Pray!"

Aunt Connie touched him, indicating that she wanted his hands. He grasped her hands and she began to quietly pray for him. Chandler closed his eyes because it felt like the right thing to do. In his heart, he thanked God for Aunt Connie and Sabrina.

"Amen," Pastor Jackson said, indicating that the congregation should finish their prayers.

"Amen," Aunt Connie said, smiling and releasing Chandler's hands.

"Amen," Chandler mumbled quietly, settling back on his chair.

"We're coming to a close. And, yes, I know we didn't follow the order of the program. We have to move as the

Spirit of God leads." He wiped his forehead with a towel. "This is the point I would like to make before we leave here. Many of you are leaving here with clear minds and so I am thankful to God for that. You see brethren, if you are disoriented, the House of the Lord is the best place to be." Pastor Jackson looked at the congregation. "In the House of the Lord, clarity is brought to our situations."

Chandler's breath hitched as Pastor Jackson's eyes caught his before moving on.

"In the house of the Lord, there is an answer for what you are going through. Now, as Sister Sabrina sings, there's room at the altar for those who want to come. If you need to be saved—come; if you need healing - come; if you're waiting for a breakthrough—come; whatever your need—come."

Chandler gazed ahead as several members of the congregation moved to the altar. *I need to be there.* But guilt held him in place.

CHAPTER 17

"Mighty man of God," Pastor Jackson greeted Chandler, moving from behind his brown wooden desk.

"Hi, Pastor Jackson." Chandler gave him a half smile. He'd been called many things, but that was a stretch. "Mighty man of God?" Chandler questioned.

Smiling, Pastor Jackson shook Chandler's hand. "My brother, that's how I see you. Let's sit on the sofa."

"Okay." Chandler walked to the brown leather sofa and sat. He noticed Pastor Jackson had changed out of his purple and white pastoral regalia, and was wearing a pair of black pants and a long-sleeved white shirt.

"Would you like something to drink?" Pastor Jackson asked.

"Water. Thanks."

"How have you been?" Pastor Jackson asked, taking a bottle of water from the refrigerator sitting in the corner of the room. He handed it to Chandler.

Chandler took a few sips. "Better. Much better than the first time you saw me." Chandler looked intently at him. "Thank you for saving me from destruction."

"You're welcome, but I can't take credit because God brought you here." Pastor Jackson took his cup of tea from his desk and sat on the sofa across from Chandler.

"I'm not accustomed to being in church," Chandler confessed. "But, I'm sure you already figured that out."

Pastor Jackson smiled at him. "The good thing is that you're here now."

Chandler cut straight to the chase, asking the question that had been on his mind since the service. "How does someone get saved? My mother told me she and my father got saved, so they're now Christians. You mentioned it in the worship service, too."

There was a quickening in Pastor Jackson's spirit. "Man of God, the Scripture tells us in Saint John 3:16 – 'For God so loved the world that He gave His only begotten Son, that whosoever believeth in Him should not perish, but have everlasting life.' God loves you and me so much that He made a way for us to be saved, through the shed blood of His son, Jesus Christ. Because of that, we will be able to spend eternity with Him."

Chandler knitted his brows.

"Let me explain further," Pastor Jackson said. "You see, man is a sinner and sin separates us from God. You may think you're a good person, and rightly so, but being good is not enough. The Bible tells us that every man has sinned, but there's hope. God provided His son, Jesus Christ to be the remedy for our sin. To be saved, you must confess with your mouth that Jesus is Lord, and give Him full control of your life."

"I can do that anywhere, right?" Chandler asked.

"Anywhere, you please." Pastor Jackson felt led by the Spirit of God to ask. "Would you like to do it now?"

Chandler squirmed. "I'll think about it."

"Don't look for any rolling thunder. It's simply a confession to let the Lord into your heart. It is a commitment of your heart."

"I don't want to be caught up in the moment and not make a genuine confession. Then, I'll be disappointed when I return to my regular behavior."

Pastor Jackson walked to his book-shelf and pulled out a book with the title, *Finding God*. "This book helped me and I believe it will help you." He handed it to Chandler. "After you accept the Lord as your Savior, a transformation process will take place in you as you read the Bible, pray, fast, and fellowship with other Christians. It takes time for us to be renewed, to lose all our bad ways and to walk in the Spirit."

121

"Okay."

"Man of God, let me tell you that God is real."

The seriousness in his tone caused Chandler to take his eyes off the book and look at him.

"I got saved when I was thirty years old. I turned sixty this year," Pastor Jackson said. "And my only regret is that I didn't get saved earlier in my life. At thirty years old, I had it all... or so I thought. I was at the height of my career, in charge of a huge financial institution." He pulled to the edge of the sofa and eyed Chandler. "I had all the women I wanted. None was out of bounds." He paused, beating back shame, but he needed to share, to bring another soul into the Kingdom of God. "I hate to tell you this—I had a wife."

Pastor Jackson watched the uneasiness spread across Chandler's face.

"Yes, I did. Sayata died of a broken heart. Haven't said that to anyone in a long time," Pastor Jackson humbly confessed. "She died before I became a Christian. And I tell you, guilt almost killed me. I asked the Lord to forgive me, and over time I allowed God to restore my soul. I can't change my past, but going forward I am committed to making better choices."

He smiled at Chandler, who was still trying to decide what facial expression to wear. "It took me a while to feel worthy of another woman's love. I got remarried at forty-eight. I love the very ground that Joy walks on. Her name says it all." His smile widened. "She helped to heal the wounds I was carrying around."

"Thanks for sharing," Chandler said, looking away at nothing in particular.

"God is good," Pastor Jackson rejoiced. "I have much to give thanks for, so, I do all I can to help bring people to the knowledge of God. A life in Jesus Christ is the best life."

Chandler was quiet for a moment. "It feels crazy, but I know I need a change. I don't want to keep living this way. What do I need to say to be saved?"

"Alleluia!" Pastor Jackson couldn't help the shout of praise that came from his lips. He placed his cup on the table before them. "Repeat after me. Lord Jesus, I am a sinner and need Your forgiveness. I understand that my sin has separated me from You and I am asking You to forgive me. I believe that Jesus Christ died on the cross for my sins and was resurrected, so that today I can live. Take control of my life and show me how to live for You. In the name of Jesus Christ, I pray, amen."

"Amen," Chandler concluded. He was feeling the same, but somehow relief washed him. "What's next?" he asked a smiling Pastor Jackson.

"Rely on the Spirit of God to lead you. Pray as often as you can for guidance. No situation is too large or small for you to talk with God about." Pastor Jackson pointed to the Bible on the table before them. "This is your instruction manual. Test your situations against the Word of God."

"Thank you."

"Call me any time. Now, remember you're a work in progress with God. Don't be too hard on yourself when you find yourself doing what you're accustomed to doing." Pastor Jackson lifted his hand skyward—and prayed.

"From this day forward, I declare that God's agenda will be your agenda. I dismantle every evil plan for your life. I declare that the Lord will fight your battles, and that by His strength, you will run through troops and leap over walls. I declare a hedge of protection will be around you and that God will birth ministry in your life so that His name will be glorified. In the name of Jesus Christ, I pray, amen."

"Amen," Chandler said quietly, trying to digest all that had been said. "Thank you."

"You're welcome. Sabrina told me you work in Chicago sometimes."

Chandler was surprised at the sudden shift, but he went with it.

"Yes, I work with Rinauto. The main office is in Chicago."

Pastor Jackson nodded. "We have a sister church there. Around fifteen to twenty minutes from Rinauto. I'll be heading there soon."

"Really?" Chandler couldn't hide his surprise.

Pastor Jackson smiled at him. "Pastor James J. McKinney is the lead pastor there. Huge congregation, over six thousand, that's about three times the size of ours. I have cards for him. Would you like one so you can visit?"

"Okay." *It sure won't hurt.*

He leaned sideways to get his wallet, then handed Chandler the card.

"Thanks!" Chandler looked at the street address. "Yes, I know where it is."

"Great."

"And speaking of Sabrina," Chandler said, "she tells me you are expanding the church facility and I saw it this morning. I understand the performing arts ministry will have a room, but her ideal would be to have three rooms for the three arms of the ministry."

"Yes, she heads the Worship and Arts Ministry. She gave a healthy contribution to the building fund, too."

"That's great." A smile lit Chandler's face. "I recognize there's space to accommodate the rooms she needs, so I'm asking if you could possibly modify the building plan. I'm willing to pay for the modification and the necessary materials to build the rooms. I will also pay for the equipment needed to outfit these rooms."

"Man of God, that's very generous of you!" Pastor Jackson's eyes seemed to pop wider. "I thank God for you and your desire to bless this church. We have the space but funds are limited. Sabrina has played an important role in your life, and I understand you feel the need to compensate her, but you really don't have to. She is a kind-hearted soul."

"Pastor Jackson, I hear you, but I wanted to do something tangible for her. She is very gifted. The least I can do is give her a place where she can hone her skills and talents, and also develop the skills and talents of others." Chandler decided to appeal to his philanthropic side. "This way, the church will have more to offer to the community."

Pastor Jackson was thoughtful. "I would need to take it to the Board. What would you gain from this?"

"Nothing. I want nothing. I don't want anyone to know that I gave the money. No one, not even Sabrina."

"You don't want Sabrina to know?" It was Pastor Jackson's turn to knit his brows.

"No. If the Board agrees, please make sure she's involved in deciding the layout of the rooms and the equipment that will be needed."

Chandler caught Pastor Jackson's enquiring gaze. "Don't worry. All my finances are legitimate. The money will come from my private foundation. If the Board says yes, then one of my lawyers will be in touch with you and the church's lawyer."

"I will be praying about it. As the Spirit of God leads me, I'll mention it to the Board. Actually, we have a meeting on Tuesday evening. I'll keep you posted."

Chandler took out his wallet and whipped out a card for his lawyer and another for his foundation. He handed them to Pastor Jackson. "If you don't mind, I'll call your cell number and you can save my number." He did, and then hung up.

"Got it," Pastor Jackson said.

"Pastor, I'll be grateful if you do not reveal my identity to the Board when you speak to them."

"Are you in trouble?"

"No," he hastily responded. "I like to keep my donations anonymous."

"Okay. I will be discreet. Don't you want to put a limit on the funds you're willing to donate?"

"I'll trust you with that."

"Thanks. I'll do my best."

Soon, Chandler made his exit and entered the foyer.

"You certainly took your time," Sabrina greeted him smiling.

"You're so demanding. Geez!" Chandler exclaimed playfully.

"You got that right, Mister." She grinned at him as they walked out of the foyer. "I drove around and parked next to you."

"That was smart."

"My best attribute."

He stopped and then held up his right hand. "High-five!"

She eyed him curiously. "What's that for?"

"Come on, high-five!"

She high-fived him.

"Sister, you sang those songs. You're a song-bird." His eyes twinkled. "You were great."

She was blushing all the way. "To God be the glory. Thank you."

"Where are we eating today, Food Dictator?" he asked.

Giggles erupted from her. "I can't believe you said that. Fine! It's not like you know the places around here anyway."

"Keep that up."

She laughed. "Let's do Olive Garden again."

CHAPTER 18

Chandler's breaths came out in short puffs. "Marcie, for God's sake, close your robe," he demanded.

Marcie's coffee-colored body was on full display on the huge, white sofa in her living room.

His body was in sprint mode, ready to partake and she knew it. She blew him a kiss. "Baby, one last time for the road."

His eyes traveled the length of her frame. Lord knows he hadn't gotten any action in a looooong time. He felt like a man, dying of thirst and seeing water nearby.

"Let me take care of you," she purred, smiling.

He shifted his body, turning slightly away to hide the evidence of his arousal. "Where are my things?" he puffed out.

Her sleek, long black hair streamed behind her as she sashayed towards him, the opening at the front of her gown displaying all he longed for. It was hard to drag his eyes away… so he didn't try.

She threw her arms around his waist and pressed herself against him from behind. "Forget your things. I need you, baby." Then, in a girlish voice she told him, "I thought you needed me too. We're a team."

A sliver of heat rushed through Chandler's core, rendering him speechless.

Marcie slipped in front of him, and circled his neck with her hands. Her seductive smile caused a moan to slip through his lips.

"I'm yours, you know. Always," she gushed.

He gripped her derriere with both hands, desperate for her lips.

She parted them, and he sampled her offering. Oh, the sweetness.

127

Lifting her slender frame, he laid her on the sofa, and began to unbutton his shirt with great haste.

"Hurry, baby," she groaned.

The longing in her voice stirred him even more. He drew closer. Ready was an understatement. Her vibrating phone distracted him and he hesitated. He tried to read the screen where the phone rested above her head on the small glass table.

"I'll get it later," she said impatiently.

Her phone started to vibrate again. He moved closer and glanced at the screen. *Gerald Murset.* He didn't know the name, but a warning bell went off in his head. He continued to stare at the phone until it stopped vibrating.

"Baby…" Marcie paused as her eyes met the suspicion in his.

"Gerald been good to you?" Chandler asked.

"No. What?" Marcie sat up on the sofa. "Gerald and I are not like that. He's just a-a friend."

Chandler began to button his shirt. "Where is my stuff?" That's what he'd come to collect, at her urging.

"C.J., Gerald is nobody."

"So you say." He spotted his sports bag near the entertainment stand and walked to retrieve it. Swinging the strap across his shoulders, he moved past her. "Have a good evening."

"C.J., please." Marcie attempted to block his path to the front door.

"Excuse me." Chandler slipped around her.

She ran near the door, and faced him humbly. "Gerald had my attention for a minute."

Chandler laughed aloud. "A minute. It has been weeks. I hope you find what you're looking for. See you around."

"I don't understand." She attempted to reason with him. "Our relationship benefited both of us, right? So I slept with someone else. It was just a passing fancy. Are

128

you saying you never slept with anyone else? I find that hard to believe. Last fall to early this year, you were taken up with someone. Very taken. You didn't return most of my calls, and when you did, you hastily got rid of me. I said nothing. I simply waited for you."

"Are you done? Step away from the door, please." He was annoyed. He didn't want to be reminded of his past failings. The Lord had rescued him. *The Lord! Oh God! I almost fornicated. Oh God!* He all but sprinted past her.

"Someone caught your eyes. I know it. If that falls through, I'll be here, okay. I'll wait—" The slamming of the door cut off her sentence.

Marcie's eyes brimmed because her little plan had failed. She had to go back to the drawing board.

She had not worked a day since she graduated college and became the sweetheart of her college president. However, Danny Melano had the gall to die three years ago, so she had to find a replacement. Six months later, she met Chandler at a charity ball that a friend was hosting, and quickly attached herself to him. After months of offering herself, he took the bait, and since then, they had a mutually beneficial relationship. He had been generous, but even so, she knew she never had him.

Chandler blasted music all the way home, but not even that could pull him out of the slump. Nausea churned in his stomach. Maybe he couldn't handle this walk with Jesus.

He pulled into his garage, snatched the bag from the back seat, and took the elevator up to his home. Soon, he dropped the bag in the passageway leading to the bathroom, took off his shoes, and threw himself on the bed. "Lord, have mercy," he murmured, curling on his side. *Don is right. I haven't changed.*

He and Don had had an argument last Wednesday night after he left Bible study. Determined to try again with

129

his relationship with Don, he'd called. True, too, he had been excited to share what he'd learned at Bible study.

"It's incredible," he had told Don with much fervor, "God loves us so much."

"Little Bro, I'm happy you're now a Christian. I've prayed and waited for this day. I've heard Pastor Jackson preach. You're in great hands."

Chandler's heart felt good. "I feel that way."

"How did you start attending the church?"

"Funny thing. Last August, after my debacle with Rozene, I..." Chandler had almost burst with excitement, telling Don how Sabrina had rescued him. "I thank God for her, man."

"God is good, Little Bro. God is good."

"Sabrina and I are fast becoming friends, too," Chandler mentioned. "I like hanging out with her."

Chandler stopped, hearing the silence at the other end of the line. "Don, you there?"

"Did you say Sabrina Benjamin?" Don asked in a quiet voice.

"Yes. Lovely lady. Beautiful inside and out," Chandler gushed.

"Chandler, don't hurt her."

Chandler was too shocked to respond immediately. "Why would I hurt her?"

"I know of her," Don told him earnestly. "People may not know her name but they sure remember her voice. All I'm saying is, don't play with her emotions."

"I'm not doing anything with her." Then, he was angry. "What are you really saying?"

Don would not back down. "You've hardly mentioned hanging out with a male friend, and now, you're hanging with a female friend. Sabrina is not that type of woman."

A hollow laugh left Chandler. "You know the funny thing, Don, I don't even see Sab that way. She's a friend."

130

"Sab? You're both on good terms, indeed."

"Not sure why I'm defending myself. Bye."

Chandler disconnected the call, and flew out of Orlando the following morning.

When he arrived home in Chicago, he'd called Sabrina. She sounded a little disappointed he'd left town so quickly, and disappointed that he would miss the production.

He smiled just thinking about her. He missed everything about her. She made him feel alive in a different way.

After Bible study, she was literally jumping up and down in the parking lot. Pastor Jackson had told her she would be getting the three rooms for her ministry.

"Thank You for her, Lord," Chandler whispered.

His heart was heavy, so he unclipped his cell phone from his belt. He needed to talk with Pastor Jackson.

CHAPTER 19

"Chandler!" Aunt Connie masked her low squeals of delight as Chandler sat beside her.

He hugged her.

"I've missed you," she whispered.

"I've missed you, too." Chandler flashed his pearly whites, settling in beside Aunt Connie to continue watching the production. He had camped out at the back of the sanctuary, but too many prying eyes and too much small talk made him feel uncomfortable, so during the intermission he'd decided to move.

An hour later, Sabrina took the podium to a standing ovation. The dancers gave her several gifts, and the church gave her a bouquet of beautiful red roses. The stage crew helped to hold the gifts as she introduced the cast to the joyful audience. Next, she thanked the cast, the church, and the attendees. Afterwards, Pastor Jackson prayed and it was over.

Aunt Connie managed to keep by Chandler's side as she greeted members of the audience. Amber and Paul greeted them, and while Amber practiced restraint at seeing Chandler, Kayla let it all hang out. She squealed with delight when her eyes landed on Chandler, and she wouldn't stop until Chandler picked her up. She looked into Chandler's eyes then hugged his neck, giggling. She repeated that a few times, much to the amusement of everyone.

"Okay, I believe my child is having her first crush," Amber said.

Everyone burst out laughing.

Chandler sat on the chair to put on Kayla's shoes, which she'd lost in her little hustle.

Sabrina walked up to them talking with Jenay, and almost swallowed her tongue when her eyes landed on

Chandler. Not even the deafening silence could break off the look that lingered between them.

Chandler recovered first. "I had to see your handiwork. Great job! You were awesome, as usual."

Sabrina's pulse pounded in her ears. "Thank you. To God be the glory," she replied, smiling self-consciously. "Thanks for attending."

"You're welcome," Chandler responded. "Wouldn't miss it for the world."

He stood with Kayla's tiny arms still wrapped around his neck. Oh yes, Kayla was hanging on for dear life, and she didn't like it one bit that she was not the center of his world. Her tiny hands caught Chandler's jaws and attempted to turn his head towards her, and when he continued to give Sabrina his attention, she all but slapped his face.

Everyone laughed at her antics.

Chandler smiled at her. "What were you saying, Kayla?"

That was all she needed. She hugged him tightly, causing laugher to erupt again.

"You are your mother's child," Aunt Connie teased drily.

Amber feigned shock. "I can hear you!"

"I bet you can," Aunt Connie joked, causing more laughter.

When the laughing frenzy died down, Jenay nudged Sabrina.

"Ah, Chandler," Sabrina said, "this is Jenay Pullier, my sister, my friend."

Jenay extended her hand, smiling. "Nice to meet you."

"Likewise, Jenay. Thanks for a great production," Chandler told her, smiling.

"I'm glad you enjoyed it," Jenay responded.

"Hi, I'm Sameria! How are you?"

133

Sameria Carter, Sister Susan's way too grown-up twenty-year-old daughter crashed the party and addressed Chandler.

When Chandler didn't respond, she continued. "You look so familiar. I couldn't help but try and get a closer look." She slurped Chandler through her teeth. "Yes, you look familiar, but your voice, though. Aaaamazing."

Aunt Connie almost choked.

But before anyone could comment, Sister Susan appeared. "Good evening, good people! We're just leaving." Not waiting for a response, she dragged a grumbling Sameria away.

"Okay," Aunt Connie said breaking the silence. "That's Sameria for you."

"She's here on summer break. Every time the university closes, she comes home to create drama." Amber shook her head. "You should have seen her when she came back after her internship with NASA," she chuckled, "you would have thought she headed the organization."

"Let's not ruin our evening," Aunt Connie jumped in. "Congrats, ladies. I'm proud of both of you." She hugged Sabrina, and then Jenay.

She wanted to hug Chandler but Kayla was already giving her the hand, while throwing daggers with her eyes. Aunt Connie patted her. "You're your mother's child."

There was chuckling all around.

Chandler looked at Sabrina. "Do you need help with anything?"

"Yes, thanks. I need to put a few things in my car."

"Okay. Let me walk Aunt Connie to her car and then I'll return."

Chandler attempted to hand Kayla to Paul, but she held on to his neck.

134

"Oh boy!" Amber rolled her eyes. "It's going to be that kind of night. Chandler, please don't go away again. Someone can't handle it."

Everyone laughed.

Ten minutes later, they all waved goodbye to Aunt Connie. Paul pulled a crying Kayla from Chandler's neck, and he was off to see Sabrina.

CHAPTER 20

Sabrina pulled into her garage, while Chandler pulled to her garage door, and turned off the ignition. Several trips later, they were standing in the living room. The gifts and boxes were now piled near the coffee table.

"Nice," Chandler complimented her on her décor. Her home smelled welcoming—fresh and floral.

"Thanks." She smiled at him. "Would you like something to eat?"

"I hate to say yes, but I'm tired as well as starving. I flew in today, dropped my carry-on, changed clothes, picked up an order, and headed to church."

Sabrina's eyes widened. "Goodness. Thank you! I appreciate you coming. Give me a minute," she said, walking towards the passageway.

She returned to the living room in sandals. "Let's go to the kitchen," she said to Chandler, who was standing where she'd left him.

"Sure." He followed her through the living room to the large kitchen.

"I'm surprised you're here. Seemed like work had you bound," Sabrina told him.

"It's the nature of the beast. Have to keep project timelines."

"I got you. You can sit at the island."

He was surprised at the size of the kitchen. "Do you cook a lot?"

"I enjoy cooking, but I need people to help me eat. Sometimes, I'll cook and invite my ministry members to partake."

A grin split his face as he took a seat. "Nice."

Sabrina piled rice and beans and baked chicken on a plate and placed it in the microwave. Taking a dinner mat from the kitchen counter along with utensils and a napkin, she placed them before him. While the food warmed, she served tossed salad into a small bowl and set it before him.

"Blue cheese, raspberry vinaigrette, or ranch?" she asked, peering into the fridge.

"Vinaigrette."

Smiling, she handed it to him. "You like that, huh?"

Chandler nodded.

"Do you need water?" Sabrina asked.

"No. I'm good. On second thought, can I have tea, please? Lipton tea, if you have it."

"Sure."

She took the food from the microwave, wiped around the edge with paper towel and set it before him. "All yours."

"Thanks. Looks good. Lots of milk, little sugar, please."

"You're welcome! Sure." Before too long, she was pouring hot water over the tea bag. She added milk and sugar, stirred it, and then placed it before him. "Just the way you like it."

"Thank you. Aren't you going to eat?"

"No. I'm not hungry." She sat across from him and watched as he ate.

"It's delicious." *Haven't had a home-cooked meal in a while*, he wanted to say.

"I'm glad you're enjoying it."

"I can see why you needed more space for rehearsal. The cast was huge." He chewed on a forkful of rice.

"Yes." She wondered who the mysterious donor was. She looked at Chandler and found him watching her. "What did I miss?"

"I gave my heart to the Lord," he confessed.

"Oh my God, Chandler! That's great!" She danced around then plopped down on the seat. "When did you do it?"

137

"When I met with Pastor Jackson." He smiled at her. "I'm a babe in Christ. Still drinking milk."

"Ahhhh, Bible talk from the babe. Love it."

He chuckled, then stopped and stared at her. "Do you know that you glow when you're happy?"

She smiled at him. "Really? Never been told that before."

He returned her smile. "Glad to be of service."

His smile warmed her heart. "Will you be here for the Fourth of July holiday?"

He took his time to answer. "Ummm, not sure."

"I usually visit my parents, and the rest of the family comes over and…" She paused, realizing his countenance had changed to one of sadness.

"It's so much fun," he finished her sentence. "Don't let me kill your joy."

"Er, no. You could spend the holiday with us," she heard herself say. *What on earth?*

He looked at her and chuckled. "Trying to save your pet project?" He silenced her protest with a question. "Why aren't you married?"

She shot him a look. That came out of nowhere and she was momentarily stunned.

He eyed her boldly, waiting.

"I could ask you the same question."

"I've asked you first."

She considered an appropriate response. "No one has asked. Well except Randy Walker, when I was in third grade."

His gaze penetrated her for a moment. "I find that hard to believe."

"They say I'm picky."

"Shouldn't you be? A lot of marriages end in divorce. You still have time."

"Thank you." She chuckled softly. "I am thirty-one years old, but Amber thinks I'm destined to die an old maid."

"I somehow doubt that. I'll have a word with her for you."

"Oh, to be a fly on the wall when you're having that conversation. What about you?"

"One more question before I answer yours. Are you dating?"

She decided to be honest. "Not at the moment. Calvin, the fellow whom I thought I was dating, had his eyes on a bigger catch. He's getting married soon. Yep, dropped off the invitation himself. "

"What a fool." It was out before Chandler could stop himself. He contemplated pulling her into his arms when he noticed she was looking nonchalant. "You've gotten over that fast."

"Oh, I sure did. I only want God's best for me. You'll meet Calvin and Kayanna at church sooner or later. He's off on a medical mission."

"I see." Chandler sipped his tea. "I'm not dating anyone."

"Married?"

"Would I be here if I was?"

"No," she hastened to say. "I'm surprised you're not."

"I'm not sure how to react when people say that. A good woman is hard to find. Plus, I don't even know if I want to be married." He held his hand up while he chewed on a piece of chicken.

Sabrina waited.

"Way back in the day, I thought I found someone." He sipped more of his tea. "She found someone, too—my best man."

Sabrina eyes popped.

139

Chandler howled with laughter. "You should see your face. I feel you, but I can confirm, it gets better with time. You can understand my apprehension about standing at the altar."

"Sorry to hear that," Sabrina said quietly.

"Which part? Being dumped at the altar or going to the altar a second time?"

She looked at him, trying to mask whatever expression was rising.

"You're not about to give me that poor thing look, are you?" he asked.

"No, no," she said, way too quickly.

He sighed, taking in a forkful of rice and chicken. "Good stuff. Thank you." He drank more of his tea, then moved the plates to the sink.

"I'll get them," Sabrina told him.

"Thanks, but I'll get them myself. You can dry, if you like."

A few minutes later, Sabrina put away the last plate, and turned to find him gazing at her.

She blushed, pulling on the sides of her dress. "What?" she asked softly, her eyes growing larger.

He swallowed... hard. "I have something for you," he let out a deep breath, "in my car." He pulled his car key from his pocket and they moved towards the living room.

Sabrina followed and they made their way to the front door.

Chandler opened the door. "Wait here."

She turned on the patio light and watched curiously as he descended the steps. *Oh boy!* She dragged her eyes from his tight rear, up his back, and to his broad shoulders. She covered her mouth as a tiny moan escaped.

When he finally returned, blood rushed to her cheeks. He was holding a huge bunch of yellow roses. She moved inside to allow him to enter and closed the door.

"Oh wow! They're beautiful." She clapped her hands together at her chest. "Thank you!"

"Where should I put them?"

"On the coffee table. Thank you!"

"Glad you like them. I have a vase, too." He set the flowers and vase on the coffee table, and then released a charming, thousand-megawatt smile.

Her heart raced and her pearly whites displayed themselves without reservation. Few people were born with full, symmetrical lips to create a perfect smile. Of course, he had to be one of them.

"You can hug me now," he said, noting her heartfelt appreciation.

Like a child, she flew into his arms, circling his waist with her hands.

He chuckled softly, lifting her to his chest, and turning around with her.

Giggles of happiness escaped and she clutched his shoulders as he set her on the ground.

He watched her, and in that moment, all was forgotten. His hand snaked around her waist. "I've missed you," he told her softly.

"I've missed you, too," she murmured, cupping his muscular shoulders.

He sighed above her head, and she buried her face in his chest.

Chandler couldn't quite let go of her, and instantaneously, he felt a delightful surge of emotion. An unexpected pleasure—like a burst of sunshine on a cloudy day.

"We need to let go," she told him softly.

He lowered his mouth to her ear, cradling her with both hands. "What if I don't want to?"

His voice had dropped an octave, causing heat to rush through her. She lifted her head to witness the determination and intensity in his gaze. Lowering her eyes to his chest, she attempted to arrest her conflicting emotions. It had been forever since she'd been held, not to mention touched. Lord knows, she wanted to be touched.

She pulled her hands to his expansive chest, feeling the strong beating of his heart. "Chandler..."

Everything faded as pleasurable sensations hit her stomach. He was rubbing circles with his fingers at the small of her back.

Stop, she almost yelled, but she couldn't. Didn't want to. She gazed up at him. Her rapid, deep breaths made it impossible to speak so her mouth hung open.

It took all the strength he possessed not to kiss her. Unable to help himself, Chandler nuzzled her neck, kissing the soft skin.

A strangled sound ripped from her throat, and he released her, desire sweeping through every part of him. His eyes roamed her quivering chest and he pushed his hands into his back pockets to prevent himself from reaching for her again.

"I-I'm leaving." His voice sounded hoarse and tight. "'Night."

Sabrina's chest constricted as unexpected desire seized her.

She wasn't moving, so Chandler repeated, "'Night."

That took her out of her stupor, and she moved robotically towards the door.

He walked in silence beside her.

"'Night," she said quietly.

His hand on the doorknob, he turned towards her and everything seemed to happen in slow motion. *God, I need her.* His eyes swept over her body, lingering on the rising and falling of her chest.

Her breath hitched, and then labored. *Oh! Oh!* An uncontrollable desire ran through her.

142

Their eyes locked and held.

Several seconds ticked by, but no words passed from their lips.

She shrank back and saw the flicker of hope die in his eyes, before he opened the door and closed it behind him.

CHAPTER 21

"Shhh. Shhh. It's going to be alright. Nothing happened." Jenay consoled Sabrina, who was crying her heart out.

Sabrina didn't attend Sunday service, so Jenay knew something was wrong. She'd decided to accept Sabrina's story that she was resting; however, when Wednesday came and Sabrina seemed bent on avoiding Bible study, she knew she had to stage an intervention.

"I-I'm so embarrassed. I-I…" Sabrina stopped as a bout of waterworks took over.

"Nothing happened. You should be thanking God, not crying."

Sabrina mopped her tears with Kleenex. "Of course, I thank God. But, I'm supposed to be a mature Christian. Jenay, he's a babe in Christ and I almost led him down the path of unrighteousness." She blew her nose in the tissue she was holding.

"Give yourself some credit. Almost, but you didn't. I hate to be the one to tell you this—you are human. You have needs and desires."

Sabrina cut her eyes at her. "Well, thanks for letting me know."

"Stop being annoyed with me. Have you spoken to him since?"

Sabrina knitted her brows. "No. What am I going to say? Sorry for leading you on?"

Jenay smiled at her. "Why would you say that? You're not sorry."

No, she didn't! Sabrina jerked upright on the sofa, ready to defend herself.

"Before you say anything," Jenay said quickly. "I think both you and Chandler are becoming attached to each other." She lifted a hand as Sabrina opened her mouth to speak. "I could be wrong, but after the production you two

144

were…let me say…a little more than happy to see each other."

Annoyance lined Sabrina's face. "Jenay, I don't know what you thought you saw, but you're wrong. I think we were both tired on Sunday night."

"Okay, Sabrina, but those yellow roses speak volumes to me. I'm not sure if you know that yellow roses represent joy and friendship. The number of roses in that vase is staggering." She chuckled. "That's more than a healthy dose of joy and friendship."

"Okay, so he's a little over the top. He's grateful."

Jenay relented. "Well, give yourself a break, since nothing happened."

"I have to be more careful though," Sabrina admitted.

"And nothing is wrong with friendship. You both enjoy each other. Just keep enjoying each other in public places."

Sabrina threw a small cushion at her. "Whatever."

"I've never seen you like this though," Jenay said. "Not even when Cal said goodbye."

"It's two different situations."

"You better protect him before Sameria steps in. I saw her after church on Sunday and she asked if I have a number for Chandler. That stopped me in my tracks."

"Oh boy! I can only pray for Sameria at this time."

"For real."

"He wasn't at church, either?" Sabrina asked.

"No. Like you, he didn't make it. You should call him, see if he's okay."

"No need. I'm sure he's fine."

Jenay threw a cushion at her. "Chicken."

"Whatever. He's fine."

Jenay chuckled. "You keep saying that. I agree, he's fine."

Half an hour later, Sabrina tried not to wince under Amber's glaring gaze as they sat at a table in Olive Garden.

Amber had asked—"Did you and Chandler have a late date on Saturday? Neither of you were in church. My poor baby was beside herself turning around to see if Chandler was seated by Aunty."

Sabrina grinned at that. "No. No late date. I can't account for him but I was home."

"You were home?" Amber eyed her with a disbelieving look and Sabrina tried her best not to squirm.

Jenay looked from one to the other with great curiosity.

Sabrina jutted out her chin. "Yes, home—the place where I live."

"I see," Amber responded. "Anything done in the dark will be brought out in the light."

Sabrina went quiet, before asking, "What's that supposed to mean?"

Amber was ready. "Exactly, what I said. I don't know you to be missing church. You would have to be near death's door to be absent from church, so make that never."

Sabrina's jaw twitched with annoyance, but before she could speak, Jenay jumped in. "All right. This is not the Great Inquisition. Our desserts are going to waste."

"You're right, Jenay. It's none of my business," Amber said, looking at her slice of chocolate cake, before cutting a piece, and dumping it in her mouth.

Jenay chuckled. "You can't help yourself, Amber."

"Oh, oh, I forgot to tell you. Calvin asked Paul to be his best man. And Paul said yes." She glared at nothing in particular. "I was so mad."

"Amber, I'm not sure why you would be surprised that Paul said yes," Sabrina scolded. "Those guys have been friends for a long while."

146

Calvin, Paul, and Brandon had met at medical school and had been friends ever since.

"But Paul knows that Calvin isn't right. He shouldn't be encouraging him to marry anybody."

"All this negativity." Jenay exhaled. "Let's get out of here."

"I'll get it," Amber called out as Sabrina signaled for the check.

"Didn't you get it the last time?" Jenay asked quizzically.

Amber cocked a brow. "That's alright."

"Just want to make sure you have enough savings for your other children," Jenay told her.

"Read my lips," Amber remarked. "One child. One child."

"Kayla would like a brother or sister, then she wouldn't have to be hanging on to other people's property," Jenay told her cheekily.

"Kayla will be alright. Anyway, Chandler wasn't looking too shabby with Kayla on his arm. I bet he'll make a great dad." She gazed deliberately at Sabrina. "He's going to spoil his baby girls—and wife—rotten."

Not willing to go there, Sabrina whipped out her credit card and gave it to the waiter.

"I said I'll get it," Amber scowled.

"You can get it next time when you're not so busy," Sabrina said, flashing her a fake smile.

Amber grabbed her head. "A smile. Thank You, Lord. She's smiling again."

"You better stop that," Sabrina responded.

Jenay chuckled loudly, looking from one to the other.

Shortly thereafter, Sabrina signed and handed the waiter the merchant copy of the credit card receipt, and they were on their way.

147

Some twenty minutes later, they were all parked in the church's front parking lot.

Help me, Lord! Sabrina gulped when she laid eyes on Chandler's car. She tried to hurry Amber and Jenay along. "Praise and worship already started."

"Oh, that's a heavenly sound," Jenay said, singing along with the praise team.

"Paul and Brandon are here," Amber announced, looking towards the row of cars on their right.

Jenay nodded, still singing.

Sabrina held her breath because Amber was still gazing at the cars. *Here we go.* She caught Amber's excitement from the corner of her eye.

"Ohh, Chandler is here, too. Yeah!" She started dancing alongside Jenay. "Our husbands and Sabrina's husband-to-be are in the house. Woo-hoo!"

Sabrina couldn't help a broad grin. "I'll be praying for you," she told Amber as they entered the foyer.

Amber and Jenay sat with their families, and Sabrina took a deep breath and headed to sit with Chandler, who was standing and singing. He stared at her for a second when she entered the row of chairs, then he took up his Bible so she could sit next to him.

"Hi," Sabrina said quietly, not looking at him. She sat and said a short prayer before standing beside him.

Chandler smiled at her. "Are you doing okay?"

She gave him a tentative smile, nodding, before singing along.

Ten minutes later, after Pastor Jackson welcomed the visitors, he launched into his topic for the evening—focus on Jesus.

Chandler could hardly wait until Bible study was over. He had hit a rough patch on Saturday night after he left Sabrina's house. He missed church on Sunday because he

148

didn't feel right to be in church, getting his praise on, when he'd almost led Sabrina astray.

He had recovered somewhat when Pastor Jackson called Sunday evening to enquire how he was doing. He had glimpsed Chandler at the production.

Without mentioning names, Chandler told him about his run-ins with Marcie and Sabrina. The question on Chandler's heart was how on earth he was going to remain celibate. On top of that, he was feeling guilty for wanting to have sex.

Pastor Jackson quickly reassured him the desire to have sex was normal but he reminded him that it belonged in the confines of marriage. He encouraged him not to be in settings with females alone, and to seek the Lord as to which ministry to join so that he would be actively engaged outside of work.

Chandler let out a sigh of relief when church was finally over. He leaned towards Sabrina. "I'll wait for you outside." With that, he moved out of the row, only to hear a girlish voice screaming his name.

Kayla was on her job.

Chandler scooped her up in his arms. "How is baby girl doing?" Chandler asked.

"You didn't come on Sunday," Kayla accused him. She looped an arm around his neck.

Chandler smiled at her. "I'm sorry. I'm here now."

Paul and Amber joined them and greeted Chandler.

"You created this monster, Chandler," Amber told him.

Chandler chuckled. "That's my bad."

Kayla turned his face towards them. "Uncle Chandler, will you have Fourth of July dinner with us, please?"

Chandler looked to Paul and Amber for help.

"Baby, remember we're going to Aunt Lorraine for dinner."

149

She reached for her father, and he took her from Chandler's arm. "Uncle Chandler, can come with us, right, Daddy?" She gave him a toothy smile.

Smiles popped on everyone's faces as they witnessed Kayla breaking down her father's defenses.

"He sure can. I'm sure Aunt Lorraine will have a plate for him," Paul said. He turned to Chandler. "Aunt Lorraine is Sabrina's mom."

"I heard Mom's name." Sabrina said, joining the group.

Amber's eyes gleamed. "Kayla was inviting her Uncle Chandler to Fourth of July dinner."

"Is that so?" Sabrina asked.

"Uncle, will you come?" Kayla asked again.

Chandler smiled at her. "I'll think about it, Kayla."

"Yeah!" Kayla clapped her little hands together, causing laughter to erupt.

"I think she heard a yes, somewhere in there," Amber interpreted.

"Let me get her out of here before she asks for your first-born," Paul teased, looking at Chandler. "Have a good night, you all."

"'Night," Amber said, following Paul.

"'Night," Chandler responded.

Sabrina gazed after them. *Oh, Lord, here we go.*

Chandler's mellow voice crashed her thoughts. "Are you ready?"

She looked at him, and then nodded.

Soon, Sabrina drove into her garage and Chandler pulled up nearby. He came out of his car and walked into the garage, then waited for her to join him.

She emerged and offered a nervous smile. "Thanks for making sure I got home early, I mean safely."

Nerves. He almost chuckled. "Look, Sabrina," he ran a hand over his head, "I'm sorry for—"

"No need to say it. We're fine. We were both tired."

"I don't want anything to ruin our friendship, okay?"

"Chandler, seriously, we're fine. I need to be more careful, too."

"Okay."

They both stood looking at each other before hysterical laughter broke out. Sabrina bent over, while Chandler clutched the back of her car for support. They laughed mostly because of the extra care they were taking not to be in physical contact with each other. And because of the relief they felt to be back in sync with each other.

"This is crazy," Chandler said, when he got his laughter under control. "Goodnight."

"'Night. Text me when you're home."

"I will."

He was walking towards his car when she yelled, "Wait!"

He stopped and turned to see half her body in her car and half out, before she scooted out.

"Here." She walked to him and handed him a Michael W. Smith worship CD. "I wanted to give you this."

"Thanks." He wanted to hug her, but exercised restraint. "Goodnight then. I'll wait until you close the garage door and I see lights on."

"Thanks. 'Night."

CHAPTER 22

Sabrina swung her front door open for Chandler. "Good morning! Happy Friday!" she greeted him, taking in his cool, casual attire.

His perfectly-fitted white shirt was tucked into a pair of dark blue Chino-style pants, showing off just the right amount of his well-defined abs. His sleeves were cuffed at the elbow, drawing attention to the soft hairs on his hands.

"Good morning to you, too." He entered, closed the door behind him and soaked up the attention she was giving him. "Do I look appropriate?"

She smiled at him, conscious of being caught. "Yes, you do."

He eyed her dark-blue jeans and baby pink off-the-shoulder top. "So do you. All cute."

"How do you manage to make me feel like your beloved pup?"

Chuckling, he followed her into the living room.

"Please make yourself comfortable while I grab my purse," she told him, moving towards her bedroom.

He glanced at his watch. "You said we're leaving at 7:00 a.m. sharp. It's 6:50."

She pivoted and gazed at him. "Are you going to be that kind of person?"

One side of his mouth curved into a smile. "Are you listening to yourself? If you give me a time, I'm going to make the time or call to say I'll be late."

"So you are that kind. Lord, help me."

"Lord, help me, too." He sat on the sofa, hearing her soft chuckles as she disappeared into the bedroom.

Ten minutes later, he closed the car trunk, and sent her an eyebrow lift. "Are you sure that's all?"

"Watch your tone, young man."

"Okay, ma'am." He chuckled, moving to open the car door for her. "Wait." He reached for the transparent container with Red Delicious apples that rested on the seat. "I washed them."

"You brought apples? I packed snacks for us, as I told you." She lifted the snack bag in her hand to show him.

"I know, but I forgot to mention I can't live without apples."

A smile lit her face. "I have a surprise for you when we arrive in Warner Robins."

"Sounds great."

He placed the container and the snack bag on the back seat and closed the door.

By the time he returned to her, she had already taken her seat. He closed the door and walked to the driver's door.

"Comfy?" he asked, after sliding behind the steering wheel and closing the door.

"Uhhh…"

He watched her keenly. "Would you like me to raise your seat a bit?"

"That would be nice, since we're traveling further than usual."

He was reaching across her to adjust her seat with the button on the side, when the faint scent of her flowery perfume filled his nostrils, wreaking havoc on his senses. He inhaled a lungful before his gaze traveled up her neck to rest on her mouth. "What fragrance are you wearing?" he asked, meeting her bewildered eyes.

She blushed, dropping her eyes to his lips, and all thoughts ceased. "Uhhh..."

"I like it," he told her, chuckling softly. He opened the driver's door and walked around and opened her door. Kneeling, he pushed a button to raise her seat. "How's that?"

She squirmed a bit. "Hmm, uhhh…"

He watched her curiously, trying to concentrate on the task at hand and not the sounds she was making. "A bit more clarity, please."

"A little bit lower."

He adjusted the seat again and watched her lean back and smile.

"A happy camper. Great."

She smiled sweetly at him. "Thanks for your patience."

"I heard that," he told her, closing the door and walking to the driver's door. For the second time, he slid behind the steering wheel and closed the door. "Can you please program the GPS with your parents' address?"

"Sure." She plugged in the address. "You do know I'm in the car, so I could supply directions, right?"

"It just makes sense."

She eyed him with knitted brows as they slipped on their seatbelts. "So you say, but you, my friend, are a control freak."

"Control is good," he said, hitting her with a rakish smile. "You make it sound like it's some kind of personality defect or character flaw."

Sabrina shook her head. "Your kind of control is."

He eyed her. "I'm going to ignore that. Now, freak, I'll take issue with. What kind of freak am I?"

She giggled. "At least you have jokes."

He studied her face momentarily before a lopsided smile appeared. "Please pray so we can be on our way."

He did not trust himself to pray out loud yet. He'd been learning a lot from his conversations and prayer times with Pastor Jackson. He was thankful that Pastor Jackson's assistant had emailed him the links to podcasts of his sermons.

Chandler's request took Sabrina by surprise, but she quickly gathered herself and prayed.

Slowly, Chandler pulled away, pressing the play button on the steering wheel. The voice of Michael W. Smith filled the air.

Sabrina flashed him an I-am-totally-impressed smile.

It warmed his heart. "I'm enjoying the CD. Thank you," he told her. "I ordered a few more of his albums, and a couple more CDs from other gospel artistes."

"That is awesome!" She smiled at his profile. "So you're no stranger to the Robins Air Force Base, huh?"

"Not at all." He omitted to tell her he'd done a presentation there.

"We're proud of the Base, in particular the Aviation Hall of Fame in the Museum of Aviation there. Would you want to visit the Base again?"

"No. Just want to take it easy this weekend. Thanks though."

"No problem. It's going to be a great weekend. Paul, Amber and Kayla will be here tomorrow, but of course they'll stay at Aunt Lynn, Amber's mother," she filled in. "Aunt Connie will be at my parents with us. Dinner tomorrow evening will be at my parents' home."

"Sounds like a plan."

Sabrina grinned. "Kayla will be the happiest camper."

Coming on Kayla's invitation, they'd taken time over the phone to firm up the details of Chandler's visit.

Chandler chuckled softly. "I love baby girl too."

Sabrina smiled. "You're very good with her. Do you have nieces?"

"Only Don's daughter. Anyway, right now, I'm alone in this world."

"Never. Hopefully, you guys will patch things up." She was still praying and trusting God for that.

"Hopefully," he said without an ounce of conviction.

"Have you decided about your parents visiting?" she asked. "It would be good if you could accommodate them,"

155

she pressed on. "Your mom seemed to be trying really hard to win your affection."

He looked at her briefly, then put his eyes back on the road, saying nothing. Somehow he was not annoyed by her line of reasoning; something about her centered him.

"Okay, then. Sooo, you don't want to talk about them, but at least tell me where they live and what they do for a living."

He let a sigh slip out. "They call Washington, D.C. home. Father is an engineer; he has a business. Mother is a fashion designer and she has a business, too. She claims she's trying to retire."

Sabrina noticed how his expression softened when he spoke about his mother. "Now, I can see where you get your sense of style."

"Sense of style?"

"You're a sharp dresser. Aunt Connie would say, you're dapper."

Chandler chuckled. "Thank you."

She settled back on the seat, smiling to herself.

Several hours later, Sabrina blinked a few times then woke from her slumber. "Wha-what?" She tried to focus, staring at the profile of Chandler's handsome face. His scent washed over her and she sighed. He was sporting sunglasses.

As if in a trance, she lifted a hand and softly touched his cheek.

"At least you've stopped snoring," he quipped.

Her eyes widened and her hand fell onto her lap. "Snoring? Was not."

"Yes, you were snoring. I'll let your husband-to-be know that sleeping with you will be like competitive sport. He'll be tossing and turning all night."

At his playful tone, she giggled girlishly.

"I bet you're the type who will hog the comforter in the middle of the night. Poor fellow. But he'll figure it out—it's every man for himself and God for us all."

Sabrina chuckled softly. "He'll be fine. I promise."

Glancing out the window, she realized they'd arrived at the gate. The last thing she remembered was chatting blissfully about her childhood days. Oh yes, and she did have the pleasure of watching him eat the apples.

She feigned hurt. "You made me sleep all the way."

"You were tired." He took off his sunglasses. "I wanted to make sure you were up before I drive in."

"Oh no! I must look a mess." She grabbed tissue and a small mirror from her purse.

"That's impossible."

"You're trying to make me feel good."

"No," he said in all seriousness. "Even on your worst day, you would still look good."

She smiled at him. "I'm going to take your word for it."

CHAPTER 23

Chandler drove the quarter-mile stretch and pulled up near the front of the sprawling, four-bedroom, Victorian-styled home. The traditional porch, tiled roof, and stunning blue and white house, made him smile. The pretty pink and yellow flowers blossoming in the front yard made the landscape lovely.

He'd opened Sabrina's door and was taking out their luggage, when a shriek sounded near the car.

"Riiiiiina! Glad you're home!"

"Miss Jenny!" A wide grin covered Sabrina's face as she exited the car and found herself in the usual bear-hug against Miss Jenny's plump body. "I'm so glad you're here," Sabrina told her. She had been on vacation leave the last time Sabrina visited.

Since high school days, Miss Jenny had been working with her parents as part of the house staff.

"You look wonderful," Miss Jenny told Sabrina, holding her at arm's length.

Sabrina smiled at her. "Thanks! So do you."

"I'm going to take your word for it." Miss Jenny made a face at her, smoothing her hair in place. Her brown cotton dress hugged her large breasts, but flared at the waist over her full figure.

Smiling, Miss Jenny glanced at Chandler, who was standing nearby, surrounded by luggage.

"And this is your handsome young man?" Miss Jenny asked.

"No," Sabrina hastily corrected her. "Chandler is a friend."

"Okay. Whatever you say." She held out a hand to Chandler. "Nice to meet you, Chandler."

"The pleasure is mine, Miss Jenny," Chandler said, smiling.

158

"Great." Miss Jenny giggled foolishly. "Just between me and you, if you need to know anything about Rina, just ask."

Chandler flashed her his megawatt smile, knowing he was in. "Thank you!"

"I can hear you both," Sabrina warned.

"No, you can't," Miss Jenny teased. "Let's get you inside before your mom starts tapping her feet." She grinned at Chandler, looking at the bags. "I can safely assume, anything not pink is yours."

"I can hear you," Sabrina warned again, causing everyone to chuckle.

Together they took up the luggage, climbed the patio step, and entered the living room door.

As soon as they dropped the luggage on the tiled floor, Chandler heard screams of delight, as Sabrina hugged her parents. Next, Sabrina made the introductions.

"Pleasure to meet you, sir," Chandler said, shaking her father's hand.

Lloyd Benjamin, a tall, medium-built man with a full head of gray hair and a winning smile, extended his hand. "You, too, son."

"Nice to meet you, too, Mrs. Benjamin," Chandler offered.

Lorraine Benjamin was about to offer her hand, but instead gave him a quick hug. She looked nothing like Chandler had anticipated. She was slightly heavy-set and a much shorter version of Sabrina. Her voice, very soft, conveyed compassion.

"It is so nice to finally meet you, Chandler," Lorraine said.

Chandler looked at Sabrina and then smiled at her mother. "Whatever you heard, it's not true."

Lorraine Benjamin smiled widely at him. "All great, I assure you. All great."

Chandler feigned relief, wiping his forehead. "Good to know."

That brought much laughter.

"I know it has been quite a journey," Lorraine said, "so why don't we meet for dinner in another forty-five minutes?"

The nodding of heads indicated consensus all around.

Some three hours later, after a fun-filled dinner, Sabrina and Chandler kicked back in the family room. Her parents had excused themselves, retiring to bed early.

"I can tell they like you."

Chandler smiled at her. "I like them, too. You are right, your mom cooks well. Dinner was excellent. She had me going for seconds."

She wriggled her eyebrows. "I could tell you liked her cooking."

Chuckles burst from him. "Didn't I tell you to stop having fun at my expense? I'm going to hit you with a check."

"Harmless banter." Her eyes caught his and she grinned good-naturedly, settling on the large army-green sofa next to him.

"Hallmark is my channel," she said, "but since you're here, what about an action-packed movie?"

"Now you're talking my language."

A few clicks and she found *Mission Impossible II*. She glanced at him and found him looking at her. "What? You watched it already?"

"I did, but that's not it. I prefer to sit lower, on the floor."

"That's okay." She pointed to two neon-green bean bags in the far corner. "You can haul one of the bean bags closer."

"Yessss," he said, moving towards them.

160

By the time he was back, she was lying on her side, with a yellow cushion under her head, and the matching one clutched to her stomach.

He leaned the bean bag on the sofa, and got comfortable on it. "Am I blocking you?"

"Nope, I'm good. Ready?"

"Yes, ready."

They were twenty minutes into the movie when Chandler heard soft snoring behind him. He chuckled softly as he turned and watched her curled around the cushion, her knees pulled into her chest. *She is a talker, alright.* She had chatted through the portion of the movie she had already seen.

Chandler decided not to wake her.

When the movie ended, she was still asleep so he turned off the TV, sat back on the bean bag, and gazed at her, wondering the best way to rouse her.

Touch her hand.

No. Touch her shoulder.

No touching. Too personal.

He placed his elbow on the sofa, rested his head on his hand, and gazed at her, resisting the urge to touch her face.

"Sab," he called out gently. When she didn't respond, he said her name again.

This time she looked at him but wasn't fully awake.

"The movie is finished," he told her, looking beyond her so he wouldn't drown in the tenderness of her eyes.

She cupped his jaw with her hand, pulled his face back to her, and gently traced his jawline with her fingers.

A wave of heat rushed up his spine, and he clutched her hand. "Sab, wake up."

The urgency in Chandler's voice jarred Sabrina. She stared at him wildly, wondering why he was holding her hand. She couldn't even remember hitting the sleep zone.

161

In an effort to calm his passion, Chandler released her hand and hastily moved to put the bean bag where he'd found it. When he returned, Sabrina was sitting on the sofa looking dazed.

He chuckled softly. "You look like something the cat dragged in."

"So you lied to me?" She stood up and smoothed her hair. "And I quote—'Even on your worst day, you'd still look good.'"

"Where have you read that a cat always drags in riff-raff?" Chandler lifted a hand and helped to smooth her hair in place. "There, now you're looking like yourself."

She chuckled at his attempt to get out of the mess he'd created. "Let's go."

He followed her out of the room, waiting as she turned off the lights.

They exited into a passageway, which led to a foyer with a staircase leading to the second-floor bedrooms. "That's my parents' quarters," Sabrina pointed to her right as they entered a circular landing at the top of the stairs.

Get it together, she reprimanded herself. *He already knows that.* For some strange reason, she felt jittery.

She moved on and he followed.

"This is my spot." She stopped, entering the small area leading to her room door. "I'll see you tomorrow. Breakfast is served around seven o'clock."

Chandler leaned against the wall and tucked his hands into his pants pockets as if he had all the time in the world. In reality, all he wanted to do was follow her into the room.

Sabrina knew she was babbling; she didn't want him to go, either. "I try to hit the breakfast table around seven-thirty. You know, middle it." He was still not moving, just looking at her. "Even if you come down after the hour, I'll make sure you get breakfast, okay?"

162

"Okay. Goodnight." He tore himself from the wall and mentally saw blood dripping from the rip. "Sleep tight." With that, he dragged himself down the passageway. *Lord, I need more prayer than I thought.*

CHAPTER 24

"Thanks for breakfast, Mrs. Benjamin." Chandler smiled at her across the table, before biting into his omelet. Well, his second omelet. "This is really good."

Lloyd leaned towards Chandler conspiratorially. "Be careful. Before you know it you'll start packing on the pounds like me." He smiled lovingly at his wife. "I can't resist her cooking. She had me going from day one."

"I can see how that happened. High school sweethearts?"

Lorraine chortled. "You got that right. But there were twists and turns before it all happened."

Chandler smiled, first at one and then the other. He was beginning to admire the love they shared and the ease with which they related.

"Lots of twist and turns," Lloyd agreed. "Thankfully, history will show me as the debonair choir boy I was."

Lorraine playfully smacked his hand, which was resting on the table. "Yes, it will, hon. Yes, it will."

"Do you have siblings?" Lorraine asked Chandler.

"No. I'm the only child from my mother. I have a half-brother, Don, on my father's side."

"Oh wow! Another only child. You do know Sabrina is an only child. My dear husband is an only child," Lorraine remarked.

"So Sabrina told me," Chandler said.

Lorraine cupped her hands on the table. She would be lying if she said she wasn't extremely curious about this eye-catching man that her daughter had brought home. She couldn't wait to pull Sabrina aside. Somewhere between her last conversation with Sabrina and this current situation, things clearly had changed.

Sabrina had indicated that they were just friends, but watching them, she sensed a growing mutual attraction.

164

Which was confirmed when she entered the family room last night, to witness Chandler gazing oh-so-tenderly at Sabrina. She'd backed out of the room as quietly as she'd entered.

"I'm sure glad Lorraine has two sisters," Lloyd said.

"Me, too." Lorraine smiled at her husband, before telling Chandler, "You met my sister, Connie. You'll meet my other sister, Lynn, at dinner later."

Chandler nodded. "I also met Amber, Paul, and the new-found apple of my eye, Kayla."

A hearty laugh burst from Lorraine. "Kay-Kay has all the men wrapped around her little finger. She has her father kissing her ring, and she gets my husband to do the most insane things."

"Guilty as charged," Lloyd said, before downing the rest of his coffee.

Chandler chuckled. "Sounds like love. Lots of love."

"That's what I'm talking about. Bam!" Lloyd pretended to high-five Chandler, and everyone started laughing.

"Your last name is Peynard, right?" Lloyd asked.

Chandler nodded, even though trepidation washed through him.

Lloyd eyed him keenly. "Any relationship to the Peynard who is the world-renowned—"

"Well, good morning! Happy Fourth of July!" Sabrina swept into the room and headed straight for the buffet table.

A chorus of "Good morning! Happy Fourth of July," followed her.

She slowed her strides, and her eyes burned into Chandler. "Why didn't anyone wake me?"

Chandler smiled at her, grateful for her timely entrance. "Thought you wanted to rest."

"You thought so?" She raised an eyebrow and looked at her parents.

165

"Thought you wanted to rest, too," her mother volunteered.

"Did I look that tired?" Sabrina complained.

"No!" they all said in unison.

She looked suspiciously at them before continuing to the buffet table.

"Need help?" Chandler asked, putting the last piece of his omelet into his mouth.

"No, thanks."

"I wandered to the top of the stairs," Chandler told her, "and was greeted by the wonderful aroma of your mom's cooking, so I followed my nose. Breakfast wasn't ready so we had devotion and then your dad took me horseback riding."

Sabrina had been reaching for a slice of bread, but her hand froze mid-air. Her father got out of bed early and it wasn't a work day? Wasn't Chandler a city boy? "Oh, I see." She turned to look from Chandler to her father, before picking up the bread.

Chandler was busy taking in her red, sleeveless summer dress, when he remembered her parents were in the room. *Oh boy!* "Please sit by me," he said as Sabrina walked towards the table. He pretended not to see her parents raising their eyebrows at each other.

Sabrina hesitated then moved towards him. She was still annoyed about being left to rest.

Chandler moved as if he was about to stand.

"Don't get up," she told him. "I have to get a cup of tea." She placed her breakfast on the table mat and another smaller plate with fruits next to it, before leaving to make her tea.

Her parents and Chandler looked on curiously.

Sabrina turned and faced Chandler. "Would you like tea, too? We've got Lipton."

She'd noticed he didn't have a tea cup.

166

Lorraine's eyes met Lloyd's again and they both held the same question. *What is going on with these two?*

"Thank you," Chandler said. "Remember, lots of milk and—"

"Little sugar," Sabrina interjected.

"You've got it." Chandler smiled broadly, pleased she'd remembered. *Oh boy!* He'd forgotten her parents... again.

Sabrina walked towards Chandler with two cups of tea in her hands. She almost laughed aloud when she saw Chandler making eye movements towards her parents. She arrived at his side and put the cups on the table before taking her seat beside him.

She prayed, before sending a brilliant smile towards her parents, going into damage control mode. "Thanks for breakfast, Mom."

"You're welcome, dear." *But, we need to talk.* Lorraine made sure to send that message to her.

"And Dad, thanks for taking Chandler horseback riding. He clearly enjoyed it."

Her father nodded.

"Mr. and Mrs. Benjamin, did you get a DVD of Sabrina's summer production? It was wonderful, and the turnout was great, too."

Lorraine beamed proudly. "Not yet, but looking forward to it."

"The DVDs aren't ready," Sabrina filled in, looking bashful. "I usually send my parents a copy."

"Great," Chandler said. "You're in for a treat. This daughter of yours sure can sing."

Lorraine landed him an ear-to-ear smile. "Oh yes! We're proud of her."

"Indeed," Lloyd agreed, glancing at a blushing Sabrina.

"Do you enjoy music, Chandler?" Lorraine asked.

167

"Yes, I do." Chandler looked at Sabrina. "I was a part of a band during high school. Even did a bit of voice training."

"Is that so? Nice," Lorraine said.

Sabrina gazed at him. "I didn't know you can sing."

He chuckled. "I said no such thing. Still, Aunt Connie and I do hold up the middle at church. Happily so."

Her parents chuckled loudly.

"What are the plans for today?" Lorraine asked.

"I wanted to show Chandler our specialty," Sabrina said, looking at Chandler. "Remember I told you I had a surprise for you."

He smiled at her. "Yes. Can't wait. I'm in."

That smile almost unglued her girlish giggles. She bit her lips in an effort to hold them back, knowing her parents were in the room. "Today is that day."

"Okay, we leave you to it then," Lorraine piped in, as she and Lloyd rose from their seats.

"Excuse us," Lloyd added.

"Okay, Dad. Mom, we'll catch up later," Sabrina said, while Chandler nodded.

Sabrina watched her parents leave, then turned her attention to Chandler, only to find him gazing at her.

"You're wrong for that," she chuckled softly.

He met her eyes unflinchingly. "I have no idea what you're talking about."

"You're good," she chuckled loudly, and then he found himself under her usual scrutiny. *Oh God!* He loved it. He wished she wouldn't stop looking. Her eyes would go from inquisition, to assessment, then a gentle, pleasing look...at least, these days. In earlier days, her final look was one of deep worry, like she'd found a bird with a damaged wing.

She drank the rest of her tea, letting it warm her insides.

168

"I did not sleep well last night," he told her. "I read most of the night. I finished reading about Joseph."

She sent him an eyebrow lift. "Joseph?"

He spat out a laugh. "You know, Joseph in the Bible."

She grinned at him. "That's what I thought you said." She almost wanted to kick her tactless, high-minded self. She attempted to fix it. "Did anything stand out from your reading?"

Chandler laughed again. He knew she was trying to fix her insensitive comment, but he had to go there. "Is this a test?

Her mouth dropped open. "Noooo!" Then, she cut her eyes when she saw the amusement in his.

"Yes," he said, like he'd come to some kind of major decision.

She eyed him with knitted brows. "Yes, what?"

"Yes, several things stood out from my reading, but what amazed me is that Joseph was operating in his gifting even though he was constantly going through disastrous situations. I liked that."

She smiled, gazing at him with new appreciation.

"But, this is the kicker," he said with intensity. "God was with him. God was working out everything for Joseph's advancement. I loved it."

"Yes," she agreed. "Sometimes we can't see our way, but God is working it out for our good. God is a way-maker."

"God is a way-maker," Chandler agreed, leaning toward her and lifting a hand. "High-five."

She high-fived him. "I'm surprised to find any apples left at the table."

"I had a few." He pushed his chair back and rose.

"Good for you." She took in his well-defined legs. "You're in shorts. You may want to put on a pair of jeans and sneakers for our little trip."

169

"Can do." He noticed her fixation with his legs and watched the range of emotions cross her face. He let it slide.

"Let's meet on the front patio in fifteen minutes," she said, slowly dragging her eyes from his legs.

"See you shortly." Pushing his chair back in place, he headed to the door. Knowing she was watching, he deliberately added extra swagger to his walk.

He heard her soft chuckles as he moved through the door.

CHAPTER 25

Sabrina's stomach quivered as she scanned the sight before her. Chandler was leaning against the wooden beam on the patio, staring outside with the phone against his ear. His hand rested easily above his head which was covered in a grey Oasis cap, his gym-honed physique on display. He'd swapped out his shorts for a pair of black jeans, and his gray Polo shirt was almost clinging for dear life across his chest.

She swallowed dryly and raised a hand to signal she was nearby but he didn't look up from what seemed to be an intense conversation. She inched closer, admiring the way he subtly exposed the black leather belt, where the front of his shirt was slightly tucked into his jeans.

He shifted his head, and her eyes fell on the scowl that formed on his lips, before it disappeared in his smile.

"You look nice." He eyed her approvingly, and then placed his phone in the clip on his belt.

"Thank you," she said, resisting the urge to look down her body at her navy jeans, yellow Polo shirt, and blue and white sneakers.

Chandler gazed at her, surprised she was not wearing any makeup. He'd noticed that, too, when she'd entered the breakfast nook. But what surprised him most was that he liked it. All the women he knew, including his mom, wore makeup. Not that he was against women wearing makeup, but Sabrina certainly did not need it. She was radiant.

Sabrina lifted her eyebrows, sending him a questioning look. His intense gaze was unnerving her. "You're staring."

"I like your hair in a ponytail," Chandler said.

She looked at him quizzically, not sure how to respond. "Thanks, I guess." *It's just a ponytail.*

171

He rocked back on his heels, a hint of a smile playing on his lips. "It's not just a ponytail. It makes you look womanly and girlish, in one."

A surge of excitement stole through her, and she looked away. "Thank you."

"You're welcome."

She managed a smile. "Everything alright? You looked rather intense minutes ago."

Chandler shrugged. "It's work. They need me to resolve an issue."

"Oh." She sounded deflated. "Do you need to do it now?"

"Noooo. Later, I'll work on it from my laptop."

"Oh, great. Let's go."

"Yes, ma'am." He fell in step beside her, looking curiously at the medium-size bowl she was carrying. "A bowl? The plot thickens," Chandler said. "Where are we going?"

"You'll see in ten minutes." She walked towards a four-seater electric cart that was parked on the driveway. "Hop in."

He stalled, all kinds of emotions running through him. On top of his list—he hadn't been driven by a woman in forever. He glanced at her and found her piercing him with her gaze.

"I know you're not deliberating if I can drive this thing," she argued. "I've been driving things like this since my teenage years."

"Let me drive," he said.

"Why? Stop being silly and hop in." She turned on the ignition.

Oh God! This is weird. His feet refused to move.

"Are you coming?"

He dragged himself over to the cart and slid in beside her.

172

A grin covered her face. "You're such a control freak."

"I'm not," he mumbled, as she drove off. "I'm just not accustomed to being driven by a woman."

"Is that so? Don't you worry, I'm a very careful driver."

She drove through a small gate to the left of the house, and onto a narrow, paved road that led up-hill.

As the warm air whipped around them, Chandler remarked, "Nice to be outdoors."

She gave him a brief smile. "Yes, it is."

He chuckled, wanting to pull on her dangling ponytail. "You're really driving this thing."

"Oh yes!" She stopped on an incline and looked at him. "Are you ready?"

"Can't wait."

"Here we go!"

She drove all the way up the incline, and then began to descend on the other side.

Chandler's eyes popped, and he shouted, "Yeah!" A massive Dorsett Golden apple orchard.

"What? Oh man!" He hopped out as soon as she stopped, and walked quickly to get a close-up.

Sabrina turned off the ignition and joined him.

He looked at her, holding his head with both hands. "I can't believe you didn't tell me."

"My dad has been doing this forever. Harvesting is happening soon."

"These apples are huge." He reached for one. "Thank you."

She chuckled, holding out the bowl. "We can fill it."

"Yeah!"

She walked behind him as he picked apples.

Soon they hopped back in the cart with Chandler clutching the bowl on his knees. Sabrina drove five minutes

173

to a large building with a huge, open patio with brass metal tables and chairs.

"We can wash some here if you want to snack on a few."

"Definitely," he was now clutching the bowl to his chest.

She chuckled, leading the way. Before long, she pushed open the door and they entered the room. Huge glass windows provided light for the room.

Chandler rushed to the sink at the bottom of the hall, poured the apples in, and began to wash them with a bit of dishwashing liquid. "I need a paper towel, please," Chandler told her.

"Sure." Sabrina pulled out sheets of paper towel from the cupboard nearby, and returned to Chandler's side.

He took some of the paper towels and dried the apples and put them back in the bowl.

They made their way outside.

Chandler waited until Sabrina closed the door, then they moved to a table in the middle of the patio.

Chandler grinned at her as they took their seats. "I could totally live outdoors."

"I'm down." She grinned back at him.

Chandler chewed on an apple, looking like he was in heaven.

Sabrina smiled at him. "I'm proud of you for reading about Joseph."

"Here we go again," he chuckled. "You're making me feel like your beloved pup."

She lifted a hand. "Okay earthling, I come in peace," she said, biting into her apple.

His eyes widened as she drooled. They both reached for the paper towel, but she beat him to it.

"Sorry," she mumbled, mopping her mouth. "Forgot they're juicy." She lifted her chin to him, still chewing. "Did I get it all?"

Chandler stared at Sabrina's soft lips and swallowed hard. Her innocent question was triggering all kinds of crazy emotions in him. *It has been too long.* His body was definitely reminding him.

He pushed his chair back and rose, if only to hide his frustration. "Yes," he stared down at her. "You got it all."

He lifted a huge apple. "Look at it. It's saying hello."

As he stared at the apple with deep devotion, she rose and snatched it.

"Victory is mine," she yelled, lifting the juicy trophy above her head.

He reached for her. "Give it back."

She was sprinting towards the entrance when he caught her from behind, bringing her to a standstill.

"No!" she yelled.

He squeezed her tightly against him. "Give it back." He wrapped both hands around her waist and lifted her off the ground.

Surprised, Sabrina let out a yelp, clutching his hands. "Okay! Put me down."

"Will not."

Her feet were dangling. "You're killing me… and the apple," she begged. Strands of hair that had escaped her ponytail were tickling her neck.

"I will for the sake of the apple." He lowered her to the ground and relaxed his hold. "Let me see it."

She held it out, only now aware that she was in his arms.

"Turn around so I can see it."

She did, while tucking strands of her hair behind her ear.

His light-brown eyes watched her intently.

175

"Here," she said, handing the apple to him.

Their eyes collided.

His piercing, hooded gaze made her squirm, and she attempted to control the thundering of her heart. She failed miserably.

Silence stretched between them for several seconds.

The urge to kiss her landed with a thud in Chandler's heart before splattering into endless ripples. *Lord, help me,* he pleaded as their bodies leaned in on their own accord.

As if heaven had heard his cry, a huge flash of lightning lit the sky, followed by the rolling of thunder. He released her and they both stared as drops of rain started.

"The rain came out of nowhere!" Sabrina exclaimed.

"It's going to pour."

"Oh no! The cart." Sabrina ran towards the cart with Chandler in tow. "We need to put down the cover or it will be soaked."

The rain began pouring, but they managed to quickly roll the hard plastic cover over the cart and ran back to the patio.

Breathing heavily, they faced each other.

Chandler's breath halted and he shivered. Sabrina's soaked clothes clung to her hourglass shape. Next came the insane thought—*Rip her clothes off.* He perished the thought as quickly as it came. Stepping away from her, he leaned against one of the wooden beams with his back to her. *Oh God, help me!*

Awareness tingled through Sabrina as her eyes wandered over his tempting rain-drenched physique. She moved towards him. "Chandler…" and before long, she touched the small of his back.

Her simple touch caused him to shudder. "I can't do this with you, Sab," he said hoarsely.

Overwhelmed with raw need, she hugged him from behind, pressing her damp body against his.

176

He all but moaned out loud, repositioning himself. "Sabrina, stop." And against his will, he turned and put her away from him.

Her heart dropped at his rejection, but shock held her in place, her gaze dropping to the floor.

"You don't want to do anything you'll regret," he said quietly.

Her embarrassment came to a screeching halt. His words stung. Now she was angry… at herself.

A burst of thunder disturbed her contemplation, and the rain drenched the earth.

Not looking in his direction, she marched in a rather unladylike fashion to the door and flung it open. *A moment of insanity.* Later, self-examination would definitely be in order.

Once inside, she wiped water from her face with her hands, then tugged her Polo shirt back in place, before moving quickly to the back of the room. Leaning against the sink, she watched the rain through the window, wishing there was a way to escape.

Bizarre! I can't believe I did that. She shivered as lightning flashed across the darkened sky, and a clap of thunder shook the windowpanes. Just as she decided to back away from the window, Chandler called out her name.

Please God, make him go away, she cried silently.

"I know you heard me," Chandler said loudly, behind her.

A helpless sigh escaped her. "Wha-what is it?"

"Are you going to turn around? You're not making it easy for me back here."

Hands stiff at her sides, she turned. "Yes?"

He gazed at her for a while, even though she was looking everywhere but at him.

"Why are you being so stiff? I'm only trying to help us both." *Me, more than you.*

177

"Okay," was all she could think of saying. She turned slightly away from him.

Without warning, he crowded her and pulled her to him.

"Cha-Chandler…" Her voice trailed off as his hand wrapped around her waist. His fingers tangled in her ponytail, then pulled her head back so his mouth lingered above hers.

Heart thumping, she arched against him as pleasurable sensations rocked her body. "Chandler." She breathlessly murmured, her fingers digging into his biceps.

He said nothing, his gaze remaining on her mouth. He loved how she called out his name, like her life depended on him. His hand tightened around her waist as his other hand massaged the small of her back.

His body perked. She was bathing his face with warm puffs of air. He liked that. He trailed soft kisses up the bare skin of her throat, lingering satisfyingly at spots that delighted his senses.

Spiraling into sweet oblivion, Sabrina moaned loudly, desperate fingers clawing his shoulders.

His hand grazed down her back, resting just above her derriere as he forced her body into his.

She groaned deep in her throat, goose bumps cascading up her arms.

He eased away from her neck and studied her mouth, and instinctively, she opened her lips eager to meet his.

So responsive. A burst of anticipation hummed through him as his hand behind her head guided her mouth towards his. But before he could enjoy the sweetness of her, Pop! Pop! Pop! Bam! reverberated through the air, accompanied by flashes of brilliant blue light.

He pulled on her so they both ducked to the ground.

"What was that?" Sabrina asked, her voice shaky.

178

"Sounded like a transformer went up in flames," he puffed out.

They both rose and peered through the window.

He was right. A transformer nearby had exploded.

As he leaned forward to get a wider view, Sabrina swiftly edged away from him.

"Thank God, it's not burning the whole place down," Chandler said.

"Um-hum!" Sabrina responded, speed-walking away from him, and hoping to disappear before he turned around.

"Sab!" he called out.

Panic rushed through her. "The rain stopped. We can leave now," she told him, moving towards the middle of the room.

"Sabrina, stop."

The slight edge in his voice made her stop, but she didn't turn around. *Lord, please. I can't. Slay me now before shame kills me,* she groaned inwardly.

"Where are you going in such a hurry?" he asked.

She looked towards the door. "We need to get back."

"Why?" His brows shot up. "You weren't in a hurry a few minutes ago."

Her head snapped back as she addressed him. "No. You did not just say that."

He didn't back down, even with flashes of anger burning in her eyes. "Are you mad at me... or yourself?"

She turned her back to him. "I like you right now. So please, don't talk crazy to me."

"Stop being angry, Sab," he said without missing a beat. "This will not turn into a friends-with-benefits situation."

Aghast, Sabrina closed her eyes. *Jesus, please get this man away from me.*

"I'm kidding. Stop being so uptight. So you're disappointed with yourself. You found out you're human."

179

Her eyes cut him in two. "You better stop talking."

He cocked a brow. "I'm not doing this thing between us. I—"

A gasp escaped her. "Look, Chandler—" Warning voices buzzed in her head telling her to stop, so she marched towards the door.

He beat her to the door and stood before it.

She puffed out her chest, her expression steely. "Excuse me."

"Listen," he said in all seriousness, "we were thrown together by circumstances, and that always provides the breeding ground for passion to kick in. You're having a chemical reaction. You don't need me; you need a mature Christian man, as Don would say. I don't want to set myself up for disappointment."

Swallowing hard, she stared at his chest, willing him to move so she could run all the way home. When he wouldn't comply with her silent request, moisture blurred her vision and she blinked rapidly in an effort to dry them.

"You know it's the truth," he told her quietly. "And believe me when I tell you, you need someone else... not me. You deserve someone else, so please help me to help you."

It killed something inside him to say that, but he had to face reality.

While they had never discussed sex, he knew she was a virgin. She'd kept herself, and she deserved someone who did the same.

The more he got to know the Lord, the more he realized how much he'd taken advantage of the women who had been part of his life. Yes, he'd made their status in his life plain to them, but he was still ashamed of how he treated them when they became cling-ons. He had 'loved' and left too many of them. *Dear God!* He remembered the hurt in their eyes when he reminded some of them of their arrangements. No, he didn't deserve Sabrina.

A frustrated sigh left him and he pledged in his heart never to touch her like that again. "I'm sorry," he offered.

Sabrina rubbed her eyes with her finger. "Me, too."

For the first time in her life, she felt her heart hurting. She lifted a hand and rubbed her chest. She needed something. Her heart was crying, for too many reasons.

"Sabrina, we were just caught up in the moment," he pleaded. "I have enough regret in life and I don't want you on that list. I need you... need you to be my friend."

Sabrina straightened herself, and gave him what she hoped was her bravest look. "Okay."

His eyes pierced hers, searching. "Are you okay?"

She lifted her chin. "Yes. Let's get back."

He allowed himself a long sigh. "Okay."

CHAPTER 26

"I'll be in shortly. Please save a seat for me," Chandler told Aunt Connie. "I need to see Sabrina."

Sabrina had just driven past them in the church yard, barely lifting a hand to greet them. She was still mad at him.

Since their return from her parents', he'd been avoiding her. Not because of anything she'd done, but mainly because he'd been trying to save himself, and because he'd felt bad about touching her.

After their little episode, they'd gone back to the house, and he had spent most of the evening working. When he eventually came to dinner, he catered to Kayla's every need.

He was grateful Sabrina's mother had taken the time to make apple shortcake, and he thoroughly enjoyed it. Since he had to work after dinner, Sabrina escaped to see a few childhood friends.

They'd decided to leave early the next morning, to avoid more searching glances from her parents and relatives. It was all too obvious that things were not right on their side of the kingdom. It didn't help, either that her mother knew she was avoiding a conversation with her.

Still, the memories of having her in his arms came at him day and night, but he'd been pushing them away. The only other person he'd ever thought about like that was Rozene, and that had not ended well. *That did not end well, at all.* And he had the battle scars to prove it.

He didn't want to feel that way again... like his life depended on anyone. Longing for someone he couldn't have. He remembered the tearful, sleepless nights that left him haggard and drained. Dog-tired, one morning he'd worn sunglasses to a leadership meeting at work.

He shook his head. Another reminder he had no business wanting Sabrina. *She's completely off-limits. The forbidden fruit.*

Anyway, he preferred relationships that were more like connections.

Simple.

Uncomplicated.

No commitment.

Those relationships worked for him… as long as a wedding ring was not involved.

He smiled inwardly. It had worked for him, back in the day.

He was now a man of God, Pastor Jackson's word.

He had to keep it holy as the church folks say. *That had to count for something, right?* At that thought, a smile lit his face.

"Good to see you, too." Sameria caught him by the arm, and grinned up at him.

He was so absorbed in his thoughts he'd almost ran into her. He quickly pulled away and grunted out a few acknowledgements, before subtly stepping away.

He rounded the corner of the church with a determined stride, and spotted Sabrina straightening her form-fitting red dress.

A stab of guilt set him on edge as she looked up and did not acknowledge him.

Sabrina hesitated. The ground seemed to tilt under her feet at the sight of Chandler approaching. She leaned against the car to steady herself, before reaching in to pull out a red jacket from the back seat and slip into it.

She was surprised to see Chandler.

Stilted. That's how she remembered their conversation after leaving her parents' home to journey back to Orlando. Even so, she'd made two—not one, two—calls to him during the week, and their conversations had been short and overly formal.

She stared at him as he neared. He'd lit her body on fire like no one ever had. *No one ever had.* No one had ever been that close to her. Indignant, she grabbed her small purse and Bible that rested on top of the trunk.

Chandler's smile faltered. "Good morning."

Sabrina spared him a glance. "Good morning."

"I wanted to say hello before going into the sanctuary."

She tried not to look cross-eyed. "Okay," she mumbled, shifting from one foot to the other, mostly because she was uncomfortable with the way he was studying her.

She tried again. "Good to see you."

"Good to see you, too." He edged closer, lessening the distance between them. "I'm looking forward to worshiping with you. Have you been praying for me?"

Her eyebrows rose and she swallowed a retort. "No."

He eyed her for a few seconds. "Thanks for your honesty. I've been praying for you."

Looking past him, she swallowed the lump in her throat. "Thanks."

"Sab, please look at me."

She shifted her purse on her Bible in an effort to fix her expression before looking at him. "I'll continue praying for you," she told him.

"Thank you. I apologize for my behavior with you at your parents' home."

She let out a sigh of relief, her expression softening.

A small victory. Chandler wanted to lift his hands in praise. "You look beautiful."

A tiny smile appeared on her face. "Thank you. You look beautiful, too." Her eyes floated over his trendy, fitted black suit covering a red shirt, paired with a red, black, and white striped tie.

His heart raced as always as he watched her enjoying his appearance before her gaze shifted to his.

"I need to go," Sabrina told him, checking her watch. "You and Aunty had better do the usual—keep the singing going in the middle of the sanctuary."

"We've got it covered." A thankful smile covered his face at her attempt to be civil. "Talk with you later," he told her, moving away.

Forty-five minutes later, after what Chandler mentally described as a healthy praise and worship session, Pastor Jackson made his way to the podium.

The room quieted.

Chandler glanced around the sanctuary. Standing room only. People of all colors, shapes, and sizes crowded the large room.

"Good morning, church!"

Spontaneous cheers rose from the congregation, followed by a thunderous applause.

Pastor Jackson continued, "Philippians 3:13-14 says, 'Brethren, I count not myself to have apprehended: but this one thing I do, forgetting those things which are behind, and reaching forth unto those things which are before, I press toward the mark for the prize of the high calling of God in Christ Jesus.'"

He moved to stand beside the podium, and was quiet for a moment.

"I have a past—some of you know it—and there are things in my past that I am not particularly proud of. No sir! No ma'am! Not proud at all. But when we don't know who we are in Jesus Christ, we do crazy, shameful, and abominable things. But here's the thing," he hollered. "I met Jesus and He's making something beautiful out of my life. I am a work-in-progress. You are a work-in-progress. God is at work in our lives."

Pastor Jackson moved to stand before the podium.

185

"Here's the key: don't be so connected to your past that you can't see your future. The Scripture says, lean not church, lean not on your own understanding. 'In all thy ways acknowledge Him, and He shall direct thy paths.'"

Chandler shifted his position as Pastor Jackson's words hit home. *God help me*, was all he kept saying.

"Your storms give you a good indication of who you are," Pastor Jackson encouraged. "All you need is for God to speak over your storm. Do not! Do not let the Red Sea intimidate you. Like Moses, lift your hand over your Red Sea, and declare the Word of the Lord, and watch God at work. Church, it's time to activate your faith. It may be dark but don't stop praying. Have faith in God."

The congregation cheered. Some members stood and began worshipping. For the rest of the service, Chandler was deep in thought, meditating on the Word.

After church, Chandler walked Aunt Connie to her car, then pulled his car up to Sabrina's vehicle. She was nowhere in sight so he pulled his iPad from the glove compartment and powered it on. He typed "Moses and the Red Sea" in the Google search bar and scrolled through until he came to a link detailing the Biblical narrative. He clicked the link and began reading about the escape of the Israelites from Egypt under Moses' leadership. *Hmm, this is good*, Chandler declared to himself fifteen minutes later.

He hopped out of his car, looking around for any sign of Sabrina. A few people were still moving about.

"Have a great week, Brother Chandler," Sister Susan, greeted him.

Chandler smiled at her. "Thanks, Sister Susan. You, too." He was thankful Sameria was nowhere in sight. The thought made his smile widen.

Sister Susan's smile widened, too. "I sure will." She hesitated, and then spoke. "I'm sorry for my daughter's behavior towards you. I saw her at it again this morning

186

before church. She's growing up, and I hate to say I was not a good example for her." She lifted a hand as Chandler was about to speak. "I know, I can't change the past, but I'm doing everything to make sure Sameria and my boys will have a bright future."

"You are a wise mother."

"Thanks, my brother." She smiled appreciatively. "I needed to hear that."

Chandler smiled at her. "You are welcome."

"Keep on loving the Lord," she encouraged. "I can't help but feel He has mighty things for you to do."

"Now, that's a good thing to say."

Sister Susan grinned at him. "I try to keep it positive and straight. By the way, Sameria insists that she knows you. Only, she can't put her finger on it." She shook her head. "She'll be back in college in a few days."

"Good for her." Chandler refused to comment otherwise.

"Alright then, off and running."

"Drive carefully."

"I will," Sister Susan said, walking away.

Chandler looked at his watch. As if on cue, Sabrina stepped out the back door. Lost in her thoughts, she didn't see him. As she came closer, Chandler cleared his throat.

She paused, stared at him in bewilderment, then moved closer.

"I've been waiting for you," he said.

Why? A scream of protest clawed its way up her throat. "Is everything okay?" She hoped she sounded natural and, of course, concerned.

"Yes. Can we talk at your house?"

Throat tight, Sabrina tilted her head and nodded.

With that, they got into their vehicles and pulled out of the church yard.

187

Soon, Sabrina pulled into her garage and turned off the ignition.

Chandler parked nearby, then hopped out of his car. He wondered what on earth he had to say to her. Truthfully, he just wanted to be near her.

"Come in," Sabrina told him, clutching her purse and Bible.

He hesitated.

"Chandler, I'm not going to stand in the garage and have a conversation with you."

"Okay," he said, locking his car door and moving toward her.

Masking her annoyance, she turned away from him, walked to the door and pushed the button to close the garage door. When she looked at him again, he was watching her, but did not speak. "Let's go inside," she said, unlocking the door.

He followed her to the living room and she motioned for him to sit. He took a seat on the large sofa as she placed her Bible and purse on the coffee table.

"Would you like something to drink?" she asked.

"No, thank you."

"What did you want to say?" Sabrina asked, sitting away from him at the other end of the sofa.

"How's the building going? Rooms going according to your liking?"

Surprise lit her eyes. *The building? The rooms? Wasn't he just at church?* She held back a sigh that was dying to pop out. "It's going well. The building is going up fast. You should take a looksie. I understand that painting should begin in another few months."

A smile popped on her face. "Sister Zena, who is responsible for the décor, called to say she'll be giving me catalogs this week. I need to make selections for the three rooms. I'll talk with Jenay and the other members as soon as I get the catalogs."

"Sounds like a plan." Chandler watched her. He couldn't get enough of the joy that always lit her face when she was passionate about anything.

Sabrina linked her fingers. "Honestly, I'm surprised at how involved they want me to be. I mean every time I get a call from the building committee, I get the feeling that my suggestions and recommendations are of great importance."

She eyed him keenly.

That one look caused him to almost squirm in his seat.

"You know," she told him confidentially, "they even wanted to put my name on the door of each room." Her brows furrowed. "I told them no. I'm doing God's business. I'll even help them to come up with appropriate names."

"Sounds good."

Once again, she looked at him. *That look!* She was waiting for that special thing he wanted to talk with her about. Well, he had nothing.

"What did you want to say to me?"

"I wanted to catch up."

He made movements to rise and panic spiked her pulse. "Do you want something to eat?" she offered.

"I would love to, but I have to work from home, and I better get to it."

"Would you like a to-go box?"

He smiled at her. "Yes. Thank you."

She smiled as she moved away. "Let me get it for you."

A few minutes later, she returned to find him gazing at a huge photo of her on the wall.

"My graduation photo," she told him. "That was a particularly wonderful day."

"Awesome, Dr. B. I can tell. Look at that beautiful smile."

189

She waved him away, smiling. "Stop. Just stop."

"It's the truth."

She didn't make eye contact, but instead handed him the bag with the food.

"Thanks." He restrained himself from hugging her. "I'll be sure to return your container. Let me get out of here."

The walk to the front door was a silent one… way too silent, each absorbed in their own thoughts.

"I'm still looking at my work schedule, but I'll be leaving for Chicago soon."

Sabrina counted to ten as her anxiety level raced up several notches. "Okay."

"Pastor Jackson mentioned a sister church in Chicago. I intend to check it out."

She tried to inject enthusiasm in her voice. "That would be great." *Lord, please, reveal to me what it is with me and this man.* She recalled Pastor Jackson's words, 'If you need a revelation from God—pray'.

Chandler paused at the door for a moment before quietly asking, "May I hug you?"

Sabrina looked away, hoping she hadn't just witnessed the hint of desire in his eyes. Yet—she had to admit, she wanted his touch. "Sure," she told him softly.

He closed the gap between them and pulled her against him, careful not to hug her too tightly, but just enough to breathe in her essence.

She wrapped her arms around his waist, and allowed him to hold her.

Before he could give himself another opportunity to think, Chandler released her.

Blissfully smitten, Sabrina stared at him.

Chandler watched her for a second, before tenderly kissing the top of her head. He pulled back to gaze at her a final time.

Lost in the moment, Sabrina heard the door close with a soft thud behind him.

CHAPTER 27

Chandler dropped the book he was reading on the bed. "Mother, I'll let you know." He felt like banging his head against the top of his sleigh bed.

"Son, you told me the same thing weeks ago," Veronica Peynard replied. "Why do I get the feeling you're trying to avoid us."

"Mother, I told you, it doesn't make sense for you to come here. I'm leaving for Chicago tomorrow. When I'm in Chicago, I'll prepare for a visit from you and Father."

"Prepare? The last time we visited everything was in order, as I suspect they still are."

"That was moons ago," he told her. "Things were different."

She winced. "Did you get married?"

"No, Mother."

"Are you dating anyone?"

He paused... way too long.

"Son, if it's serious, please do a background check. I'm a Christian and I trust the Lord, but we need to be careful with what He has blessed us with."

Chandler refused to go there. "Mother, that's not necessary. I'm not seeing anyone."

"But you're interested in someone. I suggest a background check before you go deeper. Do I know her?"

He avoided the question. "Don't worry about that, Mother."

"I'll leave that alone for now. I miss you, son, and your father misses you, too."

Chandler resisted the urge to laugh aloud. "Mother, you do you realize I'm grown?"

Veronica gasped. "Chandler John Peynard, I spent eighteen hours in labor to bring you into this world. Didn't even know I could have children. So do not use that tone with me. I know I have not been a good mother but I'm really trying, so give me a break."

Chandler remained silent, annoyed with himself for having empathy for his mother. It was the first time she'd confessed that she didn't know she could have children.

"Chandler, we know we have not been good to you, especially on an emotional level," Veronica conceded. "We were wrong for offering you things instead of our love and time. We want a relationship with you, and we're praying it's not too late."

Chandler was silent. *We were wrong*, became an echo that bounced all over his bedroom and he was saddened by it. A single tear slipped down the side of his face. He had been disappointed with his parents, and now, he was disappointed with himself because he could not find it in his heart to forgive them.

"Are you there?" his mother asked.

Chandler wiped the tear away. "Yes, Mother."

"Please give us a chance to make it up to you. We won't overstep our bounds."

"I'm not good at relationships," he admitted quietly.

"That's okay, son. We'll take it slowly."

Chandler released a pent-up sigh.

"I canceled your father's birthday party. It would have been too much to explain your absence."

"Are you trying to make me feel guilty, Mother?"

"No. Just information. I'm planning a getaway for us."

"Okay."

"Son, please don't let the breakdown in your relationship with me and your father hinder you from forming a close relationship."

"I'm not interested in a close relationship."

Veronica grabbed her chest. "Are you going to rob me of the chance of having grandchildren? Marriage is a great institution."

193

Chandler chuckled softly at the shock in her voice. "Not planning to get married."

"Don't let your past dictate your future, son."

"Mother if you are speaking of Alana Hobart, I'm long past that."

"Yes, but will you allow that situation to ruin what God has planned for your future?"

"Of course not, Mother."

His mother sighed loudly. "I hear you. Speaking of Alana, I have been in touch with her. I'm looking for another person to join my management team. Well, her parents begged me to at least give her an interview."

"Mother, I've got to run. I'll catch up with you soon."

"Okay, son. Just remember, the altar is not a bad place."

"I'm aware of that. Sometimes, I go to the altar when I'm at church." He decided to let that cat out of the bag.

Veronica's spirit soared. "You've been attending church? That's just wonderful."

"It's more than that," Chandler proudly told her. "I'm a Christian."

His mother rejoiced. "That's the best news I've heard in a long time." Overcome with emotion and the need to spend the next few minutes—maybe even hours—thanking God for a modern-day miracle, she decided to end the call. "Enjoy the rest of your day, son. We'll talk soon."

"Bye, Mother."

Half an hour later, Chandler glanced at the time on the dashboard. He would make it on time to see Sabrina. Shifting gears, he bobbed to "Grace Wins" by gospel artiste, Matthew West, as he weaved in and out of the early afternoon traffic. Before long, he pulled into a parking space at the church. He stepped out of his car and greeted Jenay who was in her car with the engine running.

"Where's Sab?" he asked her. "Thought she was meeting you here?"

"Yes, we met," Jenay told him smiling. "She's talking with Cal in the sanctuary."

"Cal?" Chandler questioned with an eyebrow lift.

"Calvin," she explained, her eyes urging him to remember. Sabrina had mentioned that she'd shared that much with Chandler. "He came back from his medical mission."

How could I forget? Chandler stared back at Jenay, trying not to grit his teeth.

As if sensing his mental deliberations, Jenay said, "I'm guessing Sabrina is sympathizing with him. One of his cheeks is a bit swollen. He said he had a fight with an umbrella and the umbrella won."

Chandler chuckled. "Thanks. Let me go rescue her." Something about Sabrina talking with Calvin brought out his territorial and protective instincts.

"Okay. I was giving her a few minutes before checking on her, myself, but I'll leave her in your capable hands. Have a great evening," Jenay said.

"You, too. And thanks for taking Sabrina here."

"You're welcome."

As Sabrina exited the foyer with Calvin, she laid eyes on Chandler chatting with Jenay in the distance.

"Chandler," a grin lit Sabrina's face.

"I thought you were going to the movie with a girlfriend?" Calvin said.

His voice had taken on an accusatory tone but Sabrina was not looking in his direction. Her gaze was fixed on Chandler, who was striding purposefully towards them.

"Is that him?" Calvin's cutting tone caused her head to whip towards him.

"Him who?"

195

Calvin had already climbed on his soap box. "You have to be careful. You know the role you play in this church. Everyone is talking about you and this man."

Annoyed, Sabrina attempted to cut off the rumor mill at the knees. "I beg your pardon. You all need to mind your own business."

A scowl creased Calvin's face. "You certainly fell out of love with me quickly."

Sabrina fought the urge to cut her eyes. "Love? Don't run ahead of yourself." She moved gracefully towards Chandler, leaving a mumbling Calvin behind.

Someone's happy to see me. Sabrina's breathtaking smile caused Chandler's heart rate to spike. He loved her stunning red floor-length halter bodice dress, which was fitted at her tiny waist to show off her feminine curves. Once again he marveled how such a slender frame could carry such curves. He admired her barely-there makeup, highlighted by lip gloss with a hint of red. Her ponytail was now curly, giving her a dramatic appeal.

Chandler whipped out his drop-dead, eat-your-heart-out smile, quickened his pace, and gave her a light hug. Still smiling, he released her. "You look absolutely amazing."

"Tha-thank you." The warmth in Chandler's voice caused her to stutter a little, but the man filling her eyes almost took her breath away. His snugly-fitted, button-down, blue short-sleeved shirt and his trendy, navy jeans showed off his ripped physique. She noticed he was sporting a more rugged beard than the last time she'd seen him.

Chandler saw her approving look, and beamed.

At Calvin's "A-ahem" behind Sabrina, Chandler didn't bat an eyelash.

"Chandler, this is Calvin," Sabrina encouraged.

"Hey, brother." Chandler extended a hand, and the two shook hands briefly. Chandler felt the way Calvin squeezed his hand in what must have been an attempt to show his strength, and quickly returned the favor. He didn't spend all those hours at the gym for nothing. Two could play that game.

Calvin mumbled, "Hey," and Chandler couldn't help but notice the way the other man flexed his hand as if it hurt.

They sized up each other, the tension between them thick as ever.

Chandler lightly touched Sabrina's arm, offering his hand. "Let's go."

She took it. "See you later, Calvin," she said, while Chandler nodded.

They walked in silence to his car, and Chandler reached for the door handle, then paused. "Let's take a selfie."

"A selfie?" she grinned at him.

"Yep."

He unclipped his cell phone from his belt. After unlocking it, he hugged her shoulder, and held up his phone.

"Smile," Chandler said, clicking away with his index finger.

"I look a mess," Sabrina said, self-consciously.

"What? You look great. I love the curls."

Her heart kicked up. "Thank you," she managed to say, before offering a tiny smile and turning to look at the camera. He knew that would be his favorite pic.

He gently held her hand, then opened the door for her to enter. Once she was settled, he closed the door and walked around to the driver's side.

As he switched on the ignition, Calvin's car zipped by, kicking dust in the air. Chandler coughed out a laugh, and

Sabrina leaned back and chuckled softly, causing him to laugh even harder.

"There are nine Fruit of the Spirit. I think I'm down to three, with that little performance," Chandler told her as he drove out of the church yard. "Pray for me, please."

An avalanche of giggles erupted from Sabrina. Still, a part of her was thrilled he wanted to save her.

A little over two hours later, Chandler eyeballed Sabrina who was sitting across from him on Aunt Connie's plush, multi-colored sofa. He'd been waiting for this opportunity, so when Aunt Connie left for the kitchen, he seized the moment.

"I don't think I'll watch another movie with you," he told her. "You're a talker. Aunt Connie will not invite us to dinner again."

She clutched her chest. "You're hurting my feelings."

He chuckled softly at her antics. "You talked through the entire movie. Geeeeez!" he exaggerated.

She patted his shoulder. "You'll be alright. Aunty is used to me by now, so she's definitely alright."

"Guess we'll live," he grumbled.

"I heard that."

Before he could respond, Aunt Connie walked in. "I have your bags packed," she told them.

Chandler looked puzzled, since he was included in the sweep of Aunt Connie's hand.

Aunt Connie came to his rescue, pointing to a small table nearby. "Pink bag for the lady and blue bag for the gent."

Chandler smiled at her. "Thanks, Aunty. Olive Garden is going to miss me."

"Ahh, it's nothing. Glad to help. You're planning to get out of Dodge and I know how that can be."

"You're right," Chandler confirmed. "Let me get the bags."

Fifteen minutes later, Chandler set Sabrina's pink food bag and a blue food container on the island in Sabrina's kitchen. He had placed the food container in his car to return it to her.

Disbelief made Sabrina look twice. "You're probably the only one who returns my container. You're going to be the poster child for returning Tupperware products."

"Ahh-ahh. I'm being smart. This way, I'll get more food."

She took a moment to think. "Smart, indeed."

They made their way in silence to the front door, and her heart sank.

"Stop looking like that," he told her as they came to a stop at the door. "I'm a phone call away. Call me any time, okay?"

She nodded, not looking at him.

His heart twisted. That was the very reason he'd decided to hang out with her today... because he anticipated that she would be saddened by his imminent departure.

He gently lifted her hand and brought it to rest on his chest.

Sabrina's jaw dropped. She couldn't help it.

"I'm going to miss you," he said tenderly. "Thanks for everything." His eyes lingered on hers, warming her heart.

She nodded, unable to speak.

He willed her to look at him.

And when she bravely did, she saw the hint of desire in his eyes. Against her screaming, unyielding will, she told him goodnight, her voice barely above a whisper.

"Have a good night, too," he responded.

Letting go of her hand was the hardest thing he'd ever done, but he did, tenderly caressing it before releasing it.

Sabrina mentally told herself to stay in place when Chandler opened the door and closed it behind him. But her emotions refused to be trapped, her body shuddered uncontrollably. *Oh Lord! Oh Lord!* Her heart cried out, causing her to clutch the door.

Out came a single sob.

Then another.

And the dam broke.

CHAPTER 28

Finding God, Chandler stared at the light streaming through the tall trees on the cover of the book that Pastor Jackson had given him. He needed the comforting arms of Jesus... right now would be good. The book had been of great help and comfort, opening him up to the Lord of all creation.

He flipped to where he'd stopped reading, removed the marker and read the three sentences in italics—*Repentance demands a change. Your heart and appetite must be changed. There must be a shift in your mindset.*

He allowed the book to slip from his hand and curled around a pillow. He prayed for courage.

When he opened his eyes, the clock on the nightstand indicated 9:00 a.m. He rolled on his back, wishing he didn't have to leave. He'd barely slept a wink last night. After he'd left Sabrina with the hole in his heart, he'd come to a stop halfway on his journey home, after receiving her text—*I'm going to miss you.*

His finger moved automatically to respond: *I miss you already.*

In torment, he'd called Pastor Jackson who prayed with him, and urged him to get home safely.

Determined to get out of the slump, Chandler reached for the TV remote on the bed and began channel-hopping. His eyes popped open when he saw Rozene smiling on T.B.N. He watched, not feeling any one emotion.

The female moderator was enthusiastically yelling out congratulations, but for what? *Had Rozene written another bestseller?*

He didn't have to wonder for long. The moderator clapped her hands and hollered, "Twins! I can't believe it. Look at God."

201

Rozene grinned back at her. "Look at God, indeed. Surprised. Shocked. Unexpected. You name it, but now, we're happy." She looked into the audience and the camera showed a beaming Larry. His clean-shaven face, highlighted by miniature dimples from a drop-dead gorgeous smile, reflected his bold personality and freedom of spirit. His naturally sun-kissed complexion glowed with vitality. He was all male—physically appealing, tall, and lean.

Chandler switched off the TV, rolled out of bed, and dropped to his knees. Guilt was not an emotion he needed to entertain. After a while, he rose. He didn't exchange an audible word with God but it was enough to be in His presence. It had successfully crowded out the weariness attempting to take over his soul. A thankful sigh left his body; he was grateful for so many things.

An hour later, Chandler greeted Pastor Jackson and took a seat in front of his desk. Thankfully, the road was almost traffic-free, which was odd for a Friday, but he was not about to complain. He arrived at the church with a good fifteen minutes to spare, and went to check out the new building.

"The building is going up fast," Chandler mentioned.

"Yes. We're hoping for a grand opening later in the year."

"That's great." Chandler settled deeper in the seat. "Thanks for seeing me."

"No problem. I'm always here for you."

Chandler eyed him. "For all my life, most people liked me for my possessions. I don't feel like that here."

"I'm glad for that," Pastor Jackson smiled at him. "What's on your heart?"

Chandler pursed his lips for a moment. "Love seems to elude me every time I try a relationship. After college, I decided to get married. I waited at the altar but my bride,

202

how should I say this?" A hollow chuckle left him. "She found herself another man—my best man."

Chandler looked into Pastor Jackson's sympathetic eyes. "Since then, I have stayed away from any serious relationship, until over a year ago. I saw her and wanted her. It had to be her. I'm not even sure why. Maybe no one ever said no, and I liked the challenge. But, aside from that, there was something about her presence that I liked. It felt like peace. We got into a brief relationship, but in the end, she decided to stay with her husband and family."

As reality hit like icy water, Chandler paused. This time, he hadn't been floored by the reality of Rozene leaving him; it was the reality that he had used and left many women.

"It's okay," Pastor Jackson encouraged. "We have all done things we're not proud of. You know my story. Remember the Scripture, 'As far as the east is from the west, so far hath He removed our transgressions from us.'"

Chandler nodded his thanks.

"Have you gotten over your relationship with her?"

"Yes. It took me a while, but since I'm developing my relationship with the Lord, I'm even better. I struggle, mostly with the guilt that I-I," he paused to gather himself, "almost broke up her marriage."

"I'm sorry it happened to both of you. You need to lay that guilt down in prayer. I'll add her to my prayer list." He held up a hand. "No, I don't need her name."

"I surprised myself," Chandler said quietly. "I've never been in a relationship with a married woman. Even as an unsaved person, I shouldn't have crossed that line."

"The good thing is that you've realized your mistake."

"I'm grateful to God for His grace on my life. I'm depending on Him to fix the situation with my parents. They gave me everything I wanted when I was growing up. I have to give them that. But turning blind eyes toward my emotional stability..." he paused for a moment, "that's hard to forgive."

Blinking rapidly against the moisture that was forming, Chandler spoke, "I feel they are the reason I can't have a stable relationship or settle down into anything remotely called a friendship."

Pastor Jackson listened intently, trusting the Lord to give him the right words.

With a metallic tension on his tongue, Chandler rattled on. "My mother and father never discussed it with me, but I understand through my aunt on my mother's side that my father was married to another lady, and he left her, then married my mother."

Suddenly, Chandler flew out of the chair, his back to Pastor Jackson.

"Are you alright?"

Pastor Jackson rushed towards him just as Chandler swung around, and started to pace. "No, not possible," Chandler reasoned, looking at Pastor Jackson. "Do you think with Rozene, subconsciously, I was perpetrating a kind of mirror experience to what had occurred between my parents?" His brows slammed together as he dropped in the chair before Pastor Jackson.

"Possibly." Pastor Jackson perched at the edge of his desk. "You'd be surprised what is buried in our psyche."

Chandler shook his head, trying to come to terms with his discovery.

Pastor Jackson watched him, praying silently. "Chandler, as you are aware, many things will happen during the course of your life. The good thing is you have discovered Jesus Christ. He will not let you go in plenty or in scarcity, in happiness or sorrow, in peace or in war. Nothing will ever separate you from the love of God."

Chandler piped up, filled with renewed hope.

"This morning," Pastor Jackson continued, "the Lord put it in my spirit to fast and pray for you. He reminded me of your full name, Chandler John Peynard. Your middle name jumped out at me. Your middle name, John, is Hebrew, and it means 'Jehovah has been gracious. God has shown favor.'"

He looked at Chandler's surprised expression.

"Yes. You can Google it. I'm saying that to say, the favor of the Lord is upon your life. Don't be afraid of what's in your DNA, for you are a child of God. You were created to do good work, which God has ordained for you to walk in."

Chandler became still.

Pastor Jackson moved closer to him, laid a hand on his shoulder, and prayed for him.

CHAPTER 29

Sabrina drew in a deep, calming breath as she stared out her kitchen window into the warm glow of the afternoon sun. She closed her eyes, thinking how the world had continued turning on its axis and no one had a clue how much help she needed. *If it wasn't for the Lord on my side, I would have fainted in the land of the living.*

The problem—she missed Chandler.

Her body craved to be free of the torment...

She was encountering feelings that she couldn't express, yet couldn't suppress.

Chandler had been gone for three weeks, and the fact that he'd only called twice petrified her. Their conversations were short. He'd told her he was busy attending to work matters. *As if that had ever stopped him from calling.*

Still, she had no right to infringe on his time. He did say that he only wanted her as a friend, but the feelings he'd evoked in her were not how she rolled with her other friends.

She sighed, thinking she needed to go back to Jenay, who was reclining on the sofa. Jenay had showed up earlier as prearranged and they had modified the annual action plan for the Ministry of Worship and Arts. They'd also discussed activities for the opening of the new community center later on in the year.

Amber wasn't a part of the ministry but she'd indicated she would visit a little later and together they could watch a movie. However, while they were in the throes of planning, Amber called to say she wasn't feeling well. She was down with 'the bug or something.'

"Sabrina!" Jenay called out over her shoulder.

Oh God! Sabrina's eye popped open.

206

Jenay was standing with her hand akimbo. "Thought you went to get a glass of water, but nooo—"

Don't say it! Sabrina flashed her a glance she knew was as guilty as ever.

"—here you are, daydreaming again," Jenay concluded.

"I did get and drink the water. I was admiring the backyard."

"The same backyard you've had for years. Bestie, don't let me shake my head in here." With that, Jenay walked away.

Sabrina entered the living room feeling like she was walking the plank, and took up her position at the other end of the sofa, away from Jenay. Pointing at the notebooks and papers piled on the coffee table, Sabrina asked, "Do you want us to put these away and catch a movie?"

"No."

"Oh, I thought that's what we said we would—"

"What I would like for us to do is talk about what's troubling you." She eyed a dumbstruck Sabrina. "I see you. And I'm tired of repeating myself when I'm talking to you. Your mind is all over the place."

Sabrina squirmed. Sharing her bizarre situation with someone else, even Jenay, was a no-no. "There's nothing—"

"Don't forget I know you, Sabrina. Why can't you even admit that you miss him?"

Sabrina's gaze hit the floor. "I feel like such an idiot. My brain is hurting right now."

"It can't be because you miss him. You've fallen in love with him."

"Love? Oh good Lord! Don't be throwing that in the atmosphere. Recall it now."

Jenay knitted her brow. "We've always been straight with each other."

207

Sabrina balled her hands at her chest. "I can't fall in love with him, Jenay."

"Please don't do the semantics thing with me. It's a little too late for that. You're in love with him. And let's get this out of the way, too—everyone knows if you Google "hot" you'd find his picture." She paused for effect. "That you can't help. My beef with you is—why is it so difficult for you to talk about him?"

Sabrina's bottom lip quivered and she blinked a few times, assessing the situation, before taking the plunge. "Because he looks like my next mistake."

"I hear you. Now give me the truth."

She let it out. "Because I feel connected to him. It's like a violation if I do." She pulled on her ponytail. "He drives me crazy sometimes, but I like him a lot. And I absolutely love what God is doing in him."

Jenay grinned at her. "Ahhh, the sparkle has returned."

"Stop it. I'm so mad at myself. I'm feeling like one of those silly women who fall for a guy she knows she can't have."

"How does he feel?"

"He's not admitting it, but I know he has feelings for me. I think he's afraid because he has been through stuff. He would prefer for us to be friends."

"And what are you going to do about it?"

Sabrina sulked. "Nothing. What can I do? Force him to love me?"

"You and I know you can't force anybody to love you. Have you called him since he left?"

"No. He called twice." Her eyebrows slammed together. "Twice in three weeks."

"I bet during those calls you were stiff and brooding."

Sabrina knitted her brows. "You expect me to be accommodating? I'm not about to have my heart broken."

208

"You're not much different from him. Hiding your heart."

"I'm not, but I can't just lay myself carelessly out there. I could get run over."

Jenay shook her head. "Lord, intervene, please. Sabrina, if you continue like that, you're just giving him more ammunition to hide his heart. For if he can't trust you—you who rescued him from the darkness—to be his friend, who else can he trust?"

Sabrina bit hard on her lower lip. "I get what you're saying, but it's very hard to walk the friend line."

"He probably has things to sort out. Things he can't share with you just yet, Ms. Perfect."

"Stop saying that. I'm not."

Jenay lifted a hand. "Your persona says, 'Don't even think of coming over here if you don't have your ducks in a row.' Remember that's what Terrence said."

Sabrina was quiet as she remembered Terrence and their one date. She remembered, too, when Chandler had said, "I don't want to set myself up for disappointment."

Jenay watched Sabrina, knowing she'd hit home. "So what are you going to do about it?"

"Why do you keep asking that?"

"A Scripture just came to mind—'The king's heart is in the hand of the Lord.'"

Sabrina looked at her as if she'd grown an extra head.

Jenay smiled at her. "Take it easy. I'm only pointing you in the right direction. God knows the beginning and the end, so let us ask for His divine guidance."

A sigh left Sabrina. "You're right. I forgot God will only give me good gifts."

"No problem. Chandler is a great guy. Let's take the matter to the Lord. Whatsoever God does is well done. We need to be praying as we would about any other situation. And I don't have to tell you, you need to guard your heart."

Sabrina nodded.

Jenay's eyes twinkled. "The man had you gaping like a fish, huh? Made you want to do baaaad things to his body." She waggled a finger at Sabrina. "Naughty girl, not time for that."

Sabrina's jaws dropped and she quickly slammed her mouth shut, threatening a chuckling Jenay with her eyes. "Keep up that foolishness, and you're going to lose your friend."

"Har-har! Friends for life."

Sabrina grinned at her. "Good to know because I'm not giving you up, either."

Jenay clutched Sabrina's hand. "That's what I'm talking about. Let's talk to our Father."

CHAPTER 30

"You can choose not to live there—in the mess you've created in your life or in the mess others have created in your life." Pastor McKinney's words from this morning's church service kept rolling through Chandler's thoughts.

He had been at the altar praying, when Bishop McKinney started to prophesy over his life. "Your words will be filled with the power and the anointing of the Lord," Bishop McKinney had said. "Your voice will be filled with force and charisma. Only make sure the words that come from your mouth, come from the Spirit of God. God will put words in your spirit that will break yokes, break chains from people's lives. Chains of rejection, chains of depression, chains of guilt, chains of condemnation."

Chandler could hardly believe he was going to church on a regular basis. He wanted to pinch himself sometimes. He was thankful for his growing relationship with both Pastors Jackson and McKinney.

Pastor Jackson was visiting Pastor McKinney for a week, and even though he was booked solid, Pastor Jackson told Chandler he would swing by later in the evening.

After church, he'd warmed up and eaten the mouthwatering food that Connard Connelly, his private chef, had prepared, then decided to relax on the sofa. Unconsciously, Chandler stretched himself, his mind still on all that had occurred during the church service.

Everything seemed to be in place, except...

Then it hit him, like a light being switched on... *Sabrina!* He hadn't seen her in almost a month. He picked up his cell phone and looked at the selfies they'd taken. He smiled widely even though he'd seen them a thousand times.

Before he knew it, he was calling her.

"Hello," she answered quietly.

His brows furrowed. *Where did the youthful exuberance go?* "I'm going to hang up and call again." And he did just that.

"Well, hello again," she chuckled softly. "What was that about?"

"Oh, there she is. Thought I'd lost you forever."

"Why?"

She sounded curt, but he ignored it. "I was waiting for my adrenalin rush. I didn't get my high when you answered the phone."

"Didn't know about all that," she said dryly.

"I haven't called often because work and church activities were going at such a pace that I needed to schedule my sleep time. I know you'll be happy that I joined the Men's Ministry at church."

"Sounds great."

"What's up with you, Sab? We're way past the days of offering lip service to each other."

Sabrina toed off her stilettos and plopped down on the sofa. She'd just entered her home, after spending time with Aunt Connie after church. *Let me see. You haven't called, sent a text or emailed in forever, and now I should be on the same page with you?* "What exactly are you getting at, Chandler?"

"Are you mad at me?"

"Why would I be mad at you?" Her voice was anything but calm.

"Sab, you only get this stiff when you're annoyed with me."

Shucks! Sabrina pursed her lips, knowing she couldn't say what was on her heart.

"You miss me," he stated quietly.

Good Lord! She closed her eyes as her heart hammered. *He must enjoy doing that for the shock value.*

212

Chandler wasted no time. "I miss you."

Words failed Sabrina. Utterly. Her eyes darted all over the living room as she attempted to come up with her next words.

"Are you there?" Chandler asked.

The warmth in his voice sent shivers up and down her spine, and her eyes stretched with apprehension. She leaned deeply into the back of the sofa, hoping to relax somewhat.

"Yes, I'm here," she admitted in a tiny voice. *Oh, sweet Jesus!*

He encouraged her along. "You can tell me you miss me."

Unable to resist the appeal in his voice, she murmured, "Yes. I miss you."

Her breathy voice warmed his heart. Smiling widely, he said, "I miss you, too. More than I care to admit."

She heard the smile in his voice, and that caused her to smile, too. "So what else have you been up to?" she asked, attempting to regain some sense of normalcy.

Chandler chuckled at her need to control the situation. "Apart from work and church activities, reading the Word mostly. Pastor Jackson is visiting me shortly."

"Really? Is he your bestie?" she teased. "How does he get to visit and I don't?"

"Bestie?" Chandler chuckled. "Isn't that a girl thing? No visits for you. You'll boss me around."

"Me? Never!"

"Yes, you. Strange how I allow it."

"Boss you around? You—the control freak?"

"I told you I don't like the word freak."

"Yeah. Yeah."

"See, with that kind of attitude, I can't invite you here. Plus, you would be fixing everything." He mimicked her voice. "Too much brown in the place, Chandler. Oh, all this blue. Too much man-caving going on here."

213

Sabrina laughed loudly. "Stop pretending you don't need help."

"I'll take your help as long as I don't become your pet project again."

"Again? You keep saying that."

"You keep denying it."

"We've exhausted that subject, so I have no comments. And what of your parents? Have you decided when they can visit?"

Chandler wanted to laugh out. In true Sabrina fashion, she'd moved the conversation along. "Yes. They'll be here next Wednesday."

He said it as if it was the most natural thing in the world, but she knew he was dreading it.

"I'm proud of you." Sabrina resisted the urge to cheer. She had been praying in that regard. "Absolutely proud of you," Sabrina reiterated.

His heart leaped, and he quietly told her. "I want to obey the Scriptures."

"Glad you are. By the way, Jenay, Amber, and I are going on a three-day cruise for my birthday next month."

"Great! When is your birthday?"

"The last Saturday in October."

"You must feel proud, all of thirty-two."

She chuckled at his playful tone. "I'm a big girl now."

"I beat you by almost seven years, so stop bossing me around. Dictating where I eat and all."

Sabrina snickered. "Trying to help a brother out, but I can pull back."

"I'm going to put in a prayer request for wisdom. I'm a sucker for punishment."

"You'll be alright." She comforted him. "When is your birthday?"

"Not saying."

"This doesn't make any sense. I can understand if you didn't want to say your age, but you did. So what's up with hiding your birthday?"

"I'm not saying."

"There you go. Secrets destroy friendships."

It was his turn to chuckle. "You should have been a psychologist. All these mind games."

"I think you enjoy them, that's why you keep coming for more."

"Oh, that's what that is?"

"Um-hmm."

"I'll take your word for it. What would you do if you came into a lot of money, Sabrina Benjamin?"

Without blinking, she said, "I would open an arts academy and teach part-time. The reverse of what I'm doing now."

No surprise there. "I can see you doing that."

"Thanks." Her heart warmed. "Why did you ask?"

"Just curious."

"What would you do?"

"I would establish an aeronautical school for under-privileged kids."

"I love it! I can see you doing that. You would be a great role model for the kids. You're heading your department now, right?"

"Yes. Gladly so." He sidetracked her. "I'm expecting Pastor Jackson in a few minutes, so I'll call you later."

"I would like that. Later then," she said, smiling. "Enjoy your bro-fest."

"I will." He smiled at the joy in her voice. "Talk with you later."

CHAPTER 31

What is going on? Chandler's jaws clenched. It had been two weeks since he'd returned to Orlando, and he had yet to see Sabrina outside of church settings. This was the second time she had called and canceled their "date." She had great reasons. School was back in session. She was helping Amber out. Amber was pregnant and having a hard time. In light of that, Sabrina had postponed her birthday cruise. He loved Amber, too, but he was feeling left out of Sabrina's pet project department.

He crushed the thought of going to the gym, and decided to go to his home office to plan Sabrina's birthday party.

"Hmmm! What can I do to rock her world?" He drummed his fingers on the desk, picked up one of the bite-size peanut butter apple bars from the glass jar next to his desktop, then popped it into his mouth. Absentmindedly, he crushed it between his teeth. *Rock her world*, echoed in his mind as he stared at the computer screen, which was waiting for his password.

Uneasiness draped itself around him. Was Sabrina trying to avoid him? He remembered only too well how Rozene had backed away at break-neck speed, and how he'd chased her like a man possessed. *Oh God! A total nut job.*

Self-loathing swirled inside him; he could hardly believe the level he'd stooped to win her affection. *Borderline stalking. That chapter of my life will be my secret shame.*

His eyes drifted closed to blot out the many scenes from his mind. He needed to free himself of this emotional baggage, and the others he'd been carrying.

His parents.

Alana.

216

Don.

His parents' visit had been good, but not smooth by any stretch of the imagination. His mother was overly accommodating towards him, but his father remained reserved. They were all content to let their relationship be a work-in-progress. He'd also noticed that his parents were still very much in love with each other—with his mother fawning over his father and his father gushing over her. Secretly, a part of him liked that.

A deep sigh left Chandler's mouth and he began to pray. "Lord, thank You for Your constant love and grace. Open the eyes of my heart, Lord, so I will see You and Your plans for me. Let Your will be done in my life on earth as it is established in heaven.

"Lord, I humbly ask for Your forgiveness for the manner in which I have treated my parents, Alana, Rozene, Don, and the women in my life. Help me to have peace in my heart concerning them. God, for those whom I need to talk with, inspire me to do so and open the doors for those conversations to take place.

"I declare that I have been redeemed by the blood of Jesus Christ, and I will not be held captive. Order my steps in Your Word, Lord, so that I'll no longer be a slave to my sinful ways. In the name of Jesus Christ, I pray, amen."

At the end of the prayer, he picked up his cell phone, scrolled through his contact list, and pressed Rozene's number.

"Hello!" she answered quietly, enjoying the cool weather where she was reclining on the sofa on the balcony outside her bedroom.

"Ro…" Chandler paused briefly, deciding not to use his special name for her. "Rozene, how are you?"

"I'm doing well, Chandler." Her tone carefully asked, *Why are you calling?* Nevertheless, she took the time to ask, "How are you?"

"Glad you're doing well. I'm doing well, too. I was calling to see if we could meet."

"Chandler, don't start that again." Her voice was filled with anxiety. "I'm—"

"I'm aware you're pregnant. I wanted to apologize to you face-to-face."

She was silent.

"Seriously, I only want to apologize."

"I-I don't think that's a good idea. Larry and I have made significant progress in rebuilding our marriage and I don't want to do anything to jeopardize that."

"I understand. I'm sorry for enticing you to commit adultery. Please forgive—"

"I'm sorry, too," she said quietly. "I had to say yes, you know."

"I'm sorry, nonetheless. God has been good to me, and I'm glad for His grace on my life."

"You've given your heart to the Lord? Oh my Lord! That's wonderful news."

"Thanks. I'm still learning."

"That's wonderful. Take care of yourself, Chandler."

"Thanks. Take good care of yourself. All the best with the twins."

She laughed softly. "How do you know I'm having twins?"

"I saw you on T.B.N. the other day."

"Oh. Okay."

"Rozene…"

"What is it?"

"Do you think I could talk with Larry? I wanted to apologize."

"That's not a good idea," she pleaded. "Larry won't…" She sucked in her breath as Larry sat beside her on the sofa.

"What won't I do?" he asked, rubbing her growing belly.

"Is that Larry?" Chandler asked.

"Yes…," Rozene said cautiously, aware that Larry was awaiting a response. "I have to go," she added tensely.

By now Larry had stopped rubbing her belly and was staring at her. "Who's that, Roz?" He did not wait for a response. "Is that who I think it is? Is that him?"

She nodded slowly and watched as Larry jumped off the sofa. He swung around to face her, hands clenched at his side.

"He called to apologize," Rozene said quickly. "He wanted to speak with you."

Larry stretched out his hand for the phone.

"Larry, no," Rozene told him. "It's okay, really."

"Give me the phone, Roz."

She handed it to him.

"Don't you ever call my wife, again," Larry told Chandler. "Ever. Do you read me?" Without waiting for a response, Larry disconnected the call.

Chandler stared at his phone as heat climbed up his face. *Lord, that did not go well.* He could only hope Rozene would be okay.

Half an hour later, Chandler greeted Marianna, Don's wife, and their children before he and Don withdrew to the study.

"I'm glad you've decided to come over," Don told Chandler, who was sitting on a cream-colored leather sofa across from him.

Chandler ran his hand over his head. "I should have come way before now."

"No time like the right time," Don said.

"I saw Rozene on T.B.N. the other day."

"She's pregnant," Don mentioned.

"Yes. I'd noticed." Chandler eyed him. "I spoke with her before I came here."

Don was careful not to show alarm. "You spoke with her?"

"I called her to apologize."

Don smiled. "That's good."

"Don't smile too much. We had a great conversation, but Larry burst in."

Don eyes widened. "Did he know that you were on the phone?"

Chandler puffed out a harsh breath. "Yes, and he went ballistic. He told me not to ever call his wife again." He eyed Don. "That, I understand. But could you please make sure that Rozene is okay?"

A stab of sympathy hit Don. "Okay, I can do that. I'm sorry for not hearing you out about Sabrina. I was seeing red. Sorry, I broke your trust, Little Bro, and our friendship."

"No problem. We're good. And I apologize for my response, too."

"You're now a Christian, huh? We need to celebrate when you get a moment."

Chandler chuckled. "Sure. Let me clear Sabrina's birthday party first."

"What? Sabrina is still in the picture?" Don teased.

"Yes. She was supposed to be on a cruise for her birthday with her friend, Jenay, and her cousin, Amber. Amber is pregnant and not doing well—whatever that means—so Sab has been spending time with her."

"I'm still at Sabrina. Are you guys dating now?"

"No. I like her very much, but we're just friends."

Don watched him closely. "I hope you realize you've fallen in love with this woman."

"Love? No. We're friends."

"What's going to happen if she starts dating?"

Chandler's heart skipped several beats and before he could respond, Don jumped in.

"Exactly! Does she make you want to stop and smell the roses?" Don teased.

Chandler chuckled loudly. "She does, but love... I doubt it. She's my friend."

"She'll soon be frustrated with your shenanigans, so I would humbly suggest you start pulling away if you're not planning to go down the aisle."

"An unexpected bond has developed between us, but trust me, we're only friends."

"I'm taking your word for it."

Don couldn't help but smile, too. *A chance at love and life.* Little Bro was finally drinking from the well of love.

CHAPTER 32

"Did I tell you, you're my favorite aunt?" Sabrina wrapped an arm around Aunt Connie's shoulder before taking a seat across from her at the island. They had just eaten red velvet cupcakes in Aunt Connie's kitchen.

Aunt Connie smiled at her. "Yes, you did."

"Did I also tell you I saw your knight in shining armor watching you walk across the parking lot on Wednesday?" Sabrina said.

Aunt Connie gave her a blank stare. "I hope you told him to keep it moving. He and that horse he rode in on."

Laughter bubbled in Sabrina's chest. "How could I? You looked like you were on the catwalk before you entered the foyer. You knew he was watching, didn't you?"

Aunt Connie's dark-brown eyes twinkled. "For me to know and for you to find out."

"He's a God-fearing man, Aunty. Why don't you go on a date with him?"

Aunt Connie scowled. "Are you having the same hearing issue he's having?"

"You say that now, but we'll see."

Aunt Connie shot her a look. "Nathaniel Selvin insists on being a fixture in my life, but if he doesn't quit, I'm going to hold up my pinky, lower my head, and excuse myself from the church. Permanently."

"I hear you, Aunty."

"I hear you, too," Aunt Connie said in a no-nonsense tone. "You're wrong." She fixed Sabrina with a look. "Shouldn't you be helping yourself, first?"

The anxiety that had laid dormant twisted in Sabrina's stomach and reared its ugly head. "What do you mean?"

"'What do you mean?'" Aunt Connie mimicked. "When are you going to stop hiding from Chandler? He told me he has been trying to hang out with you since he

222

came back, but you've been taking care of Amber. Now I know Amber ain't that sick. And, if she needs twenty-four-hour care, she needs to be in the hospital. In fact, she looked quite healthy when she dropped you off this morning. Paul will soon be asking if you've moved in."

Flustered, Sabrina took a deep breath. "I'm not hiding. I'm trying to save myself."

Aunt Connie interrupted Sabrina's internal struggles. "Is falling in love a crime?"

"It is, if it's not reciprocated."

"Hiding is not the way to go. You know that poor baby came up the rough side of the mountain. Give him a chance to sort himself out."

"I can't handle my heart being crushed every time he leaves. He'd rather be friends than risk what we have going on."

Aunt Connie shook her head. "I can just imagine the fear surrounding you two when you're alone."

"We get on very well. Fabulously. As long as we don't touch that subject."

"Are you seriously praying for him? And you need to be praying for yourself, too. You need to make sure that the Spirit of the Lord is guiding your decisions. Chandler is fine and all, but fine will not help you if you two are not spiritually and emotionally connected. If I were you, I would get to know more about him."

Sabrina released a sigh. "I am praying, and Jenay is, too." Sabrina was nervous, but she had to ask. "Have you been receiving anything from the Lord concerning him?"

"Yes, and only this will I divulge: if you marry Chandler, it will open up new doors, new playing fields for you, so you need to remain solid in your faith." Aunt Connie watched her carefully. "What have you been receiving?"

223

"This one Scripture has been on my heart every day for the last few weeks. Psalm 138:8 – 'The Lord will perfect that which concerns me; Your mercy, O Lord, endures forever; Do not forsake the works of Your hands.'"

"Well, continue to allow the Lord to lead you." Aunt Connie looked at Sabrina, and for a moment Sabrina thought she was going to say something else. She didn't.

"You'll see Chandler in half an hour," Sabrina said. "He's taking me to an early lunch."

Aunt Connie chuckled. "He managed to yank you out of hiding. He's got skills."

"Really, Aunty. Try to be nice."

"It is you who need to be nice. After all, he's handling your birthday activities."

Sabrina grinned at her. "Ahhh, yes. A whole day of activities."

Ten minutes later, Aunt Connie opened the door to welcome Chandler while Sabrina rushed to freshen up, and change her clothes. Chandler had arrived early.

"Aunt Connie, good morning!" Chandler greeted her warmly. "How's it going in your neck of the woods?"

"Happy Saturday! It's wonderful to see you, as usual. I'm doing great. Sabrina is getting ready."

She led the way to the living room, and Chandler followed.

Smiling, he sat across from her noticing her pensive expression. "Is everything, alright?" he asked.

"Yes…" Aunt Connie weighed her next words. "Last night, I Googled your name."

Chandler was initially stunned. He pulled to the edge of the sofa. "Does—?"

"No. I didn't mention it to Sabrina."

He became apologetic. "I never meant to—"

224

"I know. Secrets are comforting but they destroy lives. You probably have good reasons not to tell Sabrina, but you should."

"Okay. I will."

"Great." Aunt Connie smiled at him. "I packed you some food. I want Olive Garden to miss you for a while."

"Thank you," Chandler responded, his mind reeling.

Aunt Connie rose from the sofa. "Let me get it for you."

As Aunt Connie made her exit, Chandler let out a deep sigh.

"Everything okay?" Sabrina greeted him. "I love your hat." It had gotten cooler so Chandler was wearing a black, knitted beanie hat.

"Thank you, Miss Hide-and-Seek!"

"Stop it." Sabrina chuckled, plopping down on the seat recently vacated by Aunt Connie.

He eyed her jeans and white, long-sleeved, button down shirt. "You're looking great. All that hiding did wonders for your countenance."

She chuckled. "You better stop."

He was about to respond when Aunt Connie re-entered the living room. He rose, took the bag, and hugged her. "Thanks for looking out for me."

"I heard that." Sabrina stood, resisting the urge to roll her eyes. "Thanks for looking out for me, too."

She hugged Aunt Connie and they headed out the door.

"Grateful you've managed to carve out time for me," Chandler said, putting on his seatbelt.

"Here we go again." Sabrina poked his side, and he jumped. "What? You're ticklish?" She poked him again, causing a chuckle to burst from his lips.

"Aunt Connie is still at the door," he said between his teeth.

225

She grinned mischievously. "I can't believe you're ticklish."

"Believe it."

He waved at Aunt Connie and pulled away.

CHAPTER 33

Sabrina and Jenay quietly admired the painting in the huge hotel foyer as they waited on Brandon.

"It's over," Jenay remarked. "The ballroom setting was ideal, too."

"Yes, it was nice," Sabrina agreed.

Calvin and Kayanna had outdone themselves with creating the Cinderella-themed wedding. No doubt, Calvin's parents had a hand in it.

Sabrina's phone vibrated and a text message popped up. A smile blossomed on her face.

Chandler: *How is it going? Do I need to rescue you?*

"It's Chandler, isn't it?" Jenay asked.

Sabrina nodded, then texted back: *Going well and yes.*

"I'll be back," Jenay told her.

Again, Sabrina nodded, her eyes fixed on her phone.

Chandler: ☺ *You sound bored.*

Sabrina: *It is what it is.*

There was no response from Chandler, so she turned her attention back to the paintings. Less than five minutes later, her phone vibrated, displaying another text.

Chandler: *We need to fix the situation then.*

Sabrina: *We? It would help if you were here.*

Chandler: *Who says I'm not?*

Surprised, Sabrina swung her gaze towards the door.

Her heart kicked into a gallop as Chandler walked towards her. *Debonair.* His black tuxedo, white shirt, and bowtie looked like they were custom-made for him.

"Red is your color," he told her. "You look unbelievably gorgeous."

His eyes raked over her, and her halter neckline, fitted-bodice gown felt two sizes too small. *Staring. You're staring, Sabrina.* Her senses returned. "Tha-thank you."

227

She stuttered, slightly overwhelmed by the intensity of his gaze.

"Do I look gorgeous, too?" he teased.

She cocked her head to the side, allowing a tiny smile to reduce the pressure bubbling inside her. "Yes, you do," she said, after returning a similarly candid appraisal.

"This calls for a hug then."

At her nod, he wrapped an arm lightly around her waist, resisting the urge to mold their bodies together.

Help me, Lord! Sabrina yelled silently. He'd broken the synchronized rhythm of her heart by more than a few beats.

Chandler released her just as Jenay joined them.

"Hey, bro," Jenay greeted Chandler. "Great to see you."

He hugged her. "Likewise, Jenay. Likewise."

Sabrina's eyes darted to Jenay, then back Chandler. "I'll be ready in a moment."

"Sure."

Sabrina pulled Jenay towards the restroom.

"Listen, my sister," Jenay said, "you need to be praying, but girrrl you also need to be fasting. Let me know when, because from what I'm seeing, that man will not let you go."

"Oh boy." Sabrina released a deep sigh. She didn't want him to. "I didn't need to use the bathroom, I just needed a breather."

"I understand. It would help though if you would stop clinging to him like he's a life saver," Jenay teased.

"You're so wrong for that." Sabrina offered a weak smile as they exited the restroom.

Soon, she and Chandler were on their way in silence. Sabrina attempted to lighten the moment. "Did you enjoy your event? I didn't know it was a black-tie affair."

228

"Yes, it was good. It was an award ceremony. I left near the end."

"You left?"

"Yes. I came to rescue you. Plus, I prefer to be with you." *Be with you?* Chandler almost closed his eyes. He'd really said that.

"That's nice," Sabrina said softly. She wanted to sing a love song. *The way you make me feel...*

Forty minutes later, Chandler parked in Sabrina's driveway, and oh, the silence that descended between them.

She noticed the engine was still running, and fought the smile that wanted to sprout. "Are you coming in for a little while?"

That was all the encouragement he needed. He quickly switched off the ignition, slipped out of his jacket, and escorted her inside.

"Make yourself at home," she told him, moving deeper into the living room to drop her purse on the sofa, and kick off her red stilettos.

He didn't respond, but when she turned around he was right behind her… smiling and leaning towards her, his bowtie undone and dangling.

Her eyes widened as her heart flipped. To make things worse, her stomach flipped, right on cue.

"I feel right at home," he said straightening himself, unbuttoning one cuff, and rolling up his sleeve to the crook of his elbow. Then, he turned up the other sleeve.

"That's…" She lost her train of thought, distracted by the way his athletic body flexed beneath his white shirt. *Oh wow!* She spoke to his chest. "Would you like something to drink?"

"My eyes are up here," he told her playfully.

Trepidation spiraled in her heart and she didn't look at him, afraid of what her eyes might reveal. "I-I take it that's a no."

229

He reached for her, but she hastily stepped away towards the kitchen. "I'll get something for myself."

He followed closely, and as she neared the island, he pulled her to him, wrapping his hands around her waist.

Her pulse kicked. "Chandler," she puffed out.

"I want to hold you," he murmured, raining soft kisses on top of her head.

She closed her eyes and allowed herself to relax in his embrace, her back against his broad chest. He needed comfort. How could she not accommodate him?

After a long moment, she placed her hands on top of his. "You need to let me go."

"Hmm." He sighed in her hair, but still held her.

She rushed on. "Chandler, you can't—" She could hardly think straight with him holding her like that.

He turned her around to face him, and tilted her face with his hand, igniting fire in her.

Her heart stopped. She was sure of it.

A smile touched his lips. "You're so beautiful," he told her, gently kissing her forehead.

Oh no! Do-don't do that. She could barely hear him over the sound of blood rushing through her ears. "Chandler..." she murmured his name, and to her delight, he lightly kissed the corner of her mouth. Twice.

She was certain her brain short-circuited, for of their own volition, her arms flew around his neck and she was on tip-toes, craning her neck just high enough for more of his delightful pecks.

Chandler wavered between keeping the promise he'd made not to touch her, and wanting to satisfy her. With his whole body on fire, he pecked her lips sweetly, keeping her close.

They both started breathing rapidly.

Release her, sounded in his brain, and he did, trying valiantly to keep his libido in check. Only she didn't move

230

away. For a long, charged moment, they gaped at each other.

Temptation overwhelming, Sabrina leaned closer so their lips were almost touching. *Oh my!* She was pulsating everywhere.

Seconds ticked by as their warm breaths mingled.

When she opened her mouth, he took it in a wild rush, groaning as he melted into its softness. He relished her passionate cries, his mouth demanding more of her— tasting deeply.

His brain sent out several warning messages, but when he attempted to put her away, her breathless murmurs kept him bound. With his mouth hot on hers, he gave her what she wanted— kissing her long, kissing her into oblivion.

Her hands dug into his shoulders as he drove her to the edge—hungrily and urgently.

A loud groan ripped from his throat and he pulled away from her, thankful for the support of the island behind him. He'd fought their attraction for months, but tonight the desire for her had overwhelmed him. He glanced at her beside him as she gripped the edge of the island like she'd run a marathon.

Heavy silence stretched between them for what seemed like hours.

Sabrina's face flamed and a deep sense of panic rose within her, tightening her chest. With trembling fingers, she pressed her hands to her chest, attempting to breathe slowly from her now dry mouth.

Chandler's face twisted as emotions rolled across it. "I told you, I'm not doing that with you."

His words ran around in her brain before she shifted back to reality. Tears pooled, but she refused to acknowledge them. "You are already doing that with me, Chandler," she snapped. His desire to protect her from himself angered her even more.

Chandler gazed into her angry eyes, having no idea what the correct response was.

Sabrina's mouth was set in a hard line. "Okay, if that's what you want." With that, she stormed out of the kitchen, her feet hitting the hardwood floor in the living room.

He followed closely on her heels. "I just did you a favor. You're welcome."

She halted, and he almost slammed into her.

Her head tilted left as she glared at him. "Don't get it twisted. You did yourself a favor."

Chandler gazed at her helplessly. This was not their first quarrel, but he had no idea how to approach it.

"You know you did," Sabrina accused, before moving on.

She plopped down on the large sofa, grabbed a cushion and hugged it to her chest. Tears threatened once again, but she refused to cry.

Chandler eliminated the distance between them and sat next to her.

"Sabrina," he called out softly. When no response came, he circled her waist with both hands and pulled her into an embrace. He kissed the top of her head. "Please don't be upset with me."

"Let me go," she hissed, tossing a glance sideway. "Just don't touch me."

He flushed. This was not the reaction he was accustomed to getting. However, the seriousness in her tone caused him to release her, and he moved slightly away from her.

"What is it with you?" he asked.

She pushed back on the sofa and gave him her undivided attention. "You really have to ask?"

"Sabrina, please—"

"Please, what, Chandler?" Her eyes flashed with anger. "You wake up my emotions, constantly. Then—"

232

"Don't say that." He frowned.

"But you do! You wake up my emotions, then run away to clear your head, and when you think the coast is clear, you come back."

His frown deepened and he didn't speak for a while.

"Sabrina, I'm not good at relationships. I leave a trail of broken dreams whenever I get involved. I've tried the relationship thing," he claimed. "Trust me, I'm not good at it."

Her gaze flitted all over the room, before she felt settled enough to respond. "Okay, Chandler. If that's it, then…"

He read her loud and clear.

He rose abruptly from the sofa.

"Yes, go ahead. Do what you always do," she accused, her voice taunting. "Run. Run away from it all."

That stopped him in his tracks.

He swung around. His face twisted in pain. "That hurts."

"It was meant to."

His eyes narrowed. "You're not that kind of person, Sab."

She remained silent.

"You've never asked me why I was crying on the night we met." Chandler quipped. "Don't you want to know?"

Sensing they were on dangerous ground, she appealed to his reasoning. "I hoped you would tell me when you were ready."

He bought it.

"I thought I was in love." His voice was a hoarse whisper, so he gathered himself. "She ripped out my heart and left me for dead." He stared beyond her. "Dead!"

Dead! Dead! Echoed in Sabrina's head. "I'm sorry to hear that," she empathized. "I'm really sorry."

233

"Me, too, but that didn't make it any less painful," he choked out, scrubbing his hands over his face. "My heart… my heart was broken in a way that I didn't think I could ever recover. I don't ever want to put myself in that position again."

Sabrina braced herself as something cut into her belly. She didn't know who was in a more sorry state—him or her.

"The relationship was doomed from the get-go," Chandler admitted quietly, "but I didn't want to face the truth. Nothing about it was of God."

Sabrina rose and stood before him. Putting herself aside, she spoke softly. "I'm really sorry that happened to you. I'm glad the Lord rescued you and set your feet on solid ground."

His frustrated gaze met hers for a moment, and then he nodded.

There was nothing else to say.

He ran a hand over his head. "'Night then," he said, moving towards the door.

She followed quietly behind him.

With his hand on the door knob, Chandler paused. Something else needed to be said, but what? Turning to look at her, he was unprepared to witnesses her unshed tears. It was like a blow to his stomach. He'd done the very thing he'd pledged not to do from the very start. He'd hurt her.

He stretched a hand to touch her shoulder but she shifted, and his hand fell by his side. "I'm sorry. I crossed the line with you. Please forgive me."

The swift nod of her head told him he could disappear—now would be good. He quickly pulled the door open, and closed it behind him.

In a daze, Sabrina turned the knob on the door and stood staring at it. Her gut twisted and the urge to throw herself on the ground was overwhelming. She was still standing there when she heard Chandler pulling away... dragging her heart behind him.

CHAPTER 34

Sabrina hummed as she made her way from her car into her home. For the first time in three weeks she was feeling herself. The entire October would have been sad except for this last Saturday in the month.

Today was her birthday.

She'd spent the entire morning listening to prayers and words of encouragement from her family, friends, co-workers, and church members. Between the calls and text messages, she'd managed to open all her gifts and then headed to the hairdresser.

Chandler had called in the morning, too, but conversation between them had been stilted and uncomfortable, as it was these days. He was always filled with apologies. That was expected. After all, he was the reason she'd spent time grieving.

Grieving? No one had died, but it sure felt like it. She remembered all too clearly, the moment the crack in her heart had widened on the night he'd left her, and she had fallen to the floor.

Getting up in the mornings was a chore, however, taking a day off from work was a no-no, so she tried to maintain a positive front before her students.

Anyone would think she was a flower fanatic, because she spent most of her evenings by her bedroom window staring at the Orange Marmalade Crossandra flowerbed outside her window, in a bid to ease her mind.

That did not work. Her mind had no room for scenery. Thoughts that she'd bundled in her heart and mind since the blow up with Chandler rushed in at every opportunity. She felt like she was losing her faith slowly… drip by drip.

By the following weekend, although she didn't want to, it was time to ask God to examine her heart concerning Chandler. She spent more time in her prayer closet, and that

236

gave her a chance to lay down her fears and open her eyes. She was in love with him.

Tears flowed, but in the end, she had to put on her big girl's hat and survive... one day at a time. Her go-to Scripture was Psalm 84:11, "For the Lord God is a sun and shield: the Lord will give grace and glory: no good thing will he withhold from them that walk uprightly."

By the second week of Bible study, she bravely greeted Chandler and sat beside him. After all, he was the one who had joined her in the spot she'd occupied for years. She wasn't going to move just because of him.

His joy at having her back was evident, even though his smile still held an apology. That Wednesday night, he'd opened Bible study with prayer and read the main scripture before Pastor Jackson took over. Later, he did the usual—drove behind her to ensure she reached home safely before driving away.

In the kitchen, Sabrina whispered a prayer for strength as she took a plate from the cupboard then opened a small drawer to retrieve a knife and fork. Heading to the island, she opened the cake box and cut a slice of the red velvet cake that Jenay and Amber had given her when they had celebrated her birthday last night.

Tears brimmed as she swallowed a piece of the cake. Jenay and Amber had been nothing but supportive. They had done everything possible to make sure she had a fun-filled evening. Still, they held high hopes for a relationship between her and Chandler. Truth be told, she expected nothing less from them.

She finished eating and was about to cut herself another slice when her phone rang. She picked it up from the island.

"Yes," she answered, then in a kinder tone, she added, "Happy Saturday."

237

"Happy Saturday." Chandler got anxious at Sabrina's first response. Nevertheless, he pressed on. "How is the birthday lady doing?"

"Doing well. Thirty-two and counting."

"You are wearing it gracefully," he drawled.

"Thank you," she said dryly, unable to hide the displeasure radiating in her.

He pushed past her tone. "Is four o'clock a good time to pick you up?"

She paused, wondering if she could handle being around him. With all that had transpired between them, she'd asked him to cancel all of the plans for her birthday. He had literally begged her to come to dinner with him. Feeling a bit guilty, she had given in. Okay, she was still soft on him.

"Sab?" Chandler urged. "Is four o'clock still good?"

She pushed away her creeping annoyance. "Yes. Four is good. See you then."

"I'm looking forward to it."

Almost two hours later, the doorbell rang. Chandler was fifteen minutes early, but this time she was ready. She looked through the peep hole and did a double-take, butterflies taking flight in her stomach. *It is so unfair for anyone to look that great.* Taking a moment to gather herself, she swung the door open.

A smile tugged at the corners of his mouth as his eyes lazily swept over her.

Too strong to resist, her heartbeat accelerated. "Please come in."

His smile widened, as he stepped in. "Thanks. Good to see you."

He followed her hips as she sashayed to the living room. "You look beautiful," he told her, admiring her red, hi-low taffeta dress, completed with silver ankle-strap dress

238

sandals with rhinestone detail. Her cubic zirconia earrings sparkled when she moved.

She made a face at him. "You said dress up."

He chuckled softly. "And that you did."

Her tension melted. "You don't look so shabby yourself." He made a lasting impression in a sleek, fitted, black suit, which was highlighted by a sky-blue shirt and black bow tie.

He flexed his biceps. "Are you saying I am handsome and edgy in this outfit?"

"Umm, I could give you that." A smile climbed her face and she hid it as she bent to retrieve her purse and a sterling silver bracelet from the coffee table.

"Let me get that for you," he told her, reaching for the bracelet.

She handed it to him and all but passed out from holding her breath as he clasped it on her wrist. In an effort to cool herself down, she used the back of her hand to push her hair over her shoulder.

Chandler admired her sleek hair, which was parted from front to center. "Haven't seen you with your hair out in a while. I love it. Hmm, red is your color. I already said that, right?"

Sabrina avoided his eyes, slowly dropping her keys in her purse. "Yes, sir, you did."

He smiled momentarily, before saying, "Ready?"

She nodded and led the way.

"I'll get the door," he told her.

When they stepped onto the patio and closed the door, he turned, only to find Sabrina watching him curiously.

"Yes, that's my car." He offered his arm. "Please don't be cliché and mention midlife crisis."

She didn't. Speechless was how she felt as he opened the door of his red BMW convertible. *A thing of beauty*, she thought as she settled in.

As he walked to the driver's side, she quickly took in the eye-catching details—a darker shade of red on its seats with woven red stitching, the headrest with the embossed BMW logo...

"Very nice, sir. Six series, right?"

"Thanks. Yes, six series." He strapped himself in and started the engine. Sensing she was looking at him, he turned to look at her.

She had her usual deep gaze, the one she gave him when she wanted the truth and nothing but the truth. "What do you do for a living, again?" she playfully asked.

"What kind of question is that? You know where I work." His lips curled in a smile. "Can we go now or are we going to spend your birthday talking about my car?"

"Take it away," she motioned with her hand.

CHAPTER 35

Forty minutes later, ignoring all her questions about their destination, Chandler waved at the gate attendant at Baladere Estate. He approached another gate and it opened automatically.

"Is this where you live?" Sabrina asked, with a frown creating wrinkles on her forehead.

"Yes. Why are we talking about me… again? I can show you my employment contract."

"I'm good for now, but I might need to see it later."

She gazed at the magnificent dwellings as Chandler pulled up to his townhouse, opened the garage door, and drove into the space beside his black BMW. It cost a small fortune to live anywhere on this side of Orlando. Chandler closed the garage door, then looked at her. "Are you going to be alright? You only turn thirty-two once."

"Yes, I'm good," she offered quietly.

His eyebrow lift told her he was not convinced.

She chuckled softly. "I am. Let's get this party started."

"That's my girl," he said, alighting from the car.

He opened the door for her and led her to the house door. "What I'm going to ask you to do will require you to trust me, okay?"

"Huh?" She looked at him quizzically.

"I won't harm a strand of hair on your head. I just don't want to kill the surprise, so I'm going to ask you to close your eyes and let me lead you."

"Er…"

"Let me lead you, Sab," he said coolly.

"Okay." She gave in, clutching her purse to her chest.

"Good girl." He opened the door. "You are not going to the gallows, so relax. I'm going to step in first."

"Okay," she responded breathlessly.

241

"Okay, take your time and step in."

"Good girl," he encouraged. "Stay there." He reached around her and closed the door. He chuckled softly. "Now don't break my fingers."

She nodded, hastily.

"All right. Let's go. It's flat, we are in the passageway, leading to the living room.

"Okay."

He ushered her along. "You're doing great. Almost there."

A few more steps and he stopped her. "Stay there."

Roses, she thought, smiling. The sweet scent drifted into her nostrils.

"These are for you," he told her.

She blinked to clear the haze from her eyes, and found a smiling Chandler handing her a beautiful bouquet of white roses, tied by a huge red bow. She took the flowers from his hand feeling like she was in a fairytale. It was surreal.

She smelled the roses and all but gasped when she lifted her head to take in her new environment. A huge sign marked *Happy Birthday, Sabrina* in red hung from the ceiling with dangling, tiny, red velvet cupcakes made from paper. Two huge bunches of balloon helped to make the place festive. Of course, single balloons on top of each bunch boasted red velvet cupcakes designed from paper. A huge picture of her stood on an easel near the door leading to the terrace.

Her heart pounded as her brain asked, *What does this mean?* Immediately, her mind started singing, *I won't go back.* She broke out of her thoughts, realizing he was speaking to her.

"Are you pleased?"

"Very," she admitted softly. "You out did yourself."

242

He chuckled softly. "Glad, you're pleased. Let me put these in water for you. Make yourself at home." He walked away with her flowers.

She stared after him and was still standing in the same position when he returned.

He placed the flowers, which were now in a vase, on the huge, glass coffee table beside her. At least she'd moved, he thought, noticing her purse on the coffee table. He was wondering what to do next when she spoke.

"Can you please give me a tour?" She needed to settle the many thoughts that ran to and fro in her head.

"A tour? You sound like you're at the museum."

"Oh no, far from it. How long have you lived here?" she asked glancing around his massive home.

"Around four years. I bought it when I realized I had to be here extendedly."

"It's beautiful. No man-caving going on here," she concluded chuckling softly.

He chuckled, too. "Thanks! Only in my bedroom."

Turning, she observed the setup, taking in all the details. It was designed with contemporary living in mind. Soaring, vaulted ceilings and distinctive wood detailed his home. Shades of yellow, along with tasteful green and white accents, decorated the furniture and walls.

He led her across the grand, spacious living room which expanded into a terrace.

"Oh my. What a view!" she gushed. "And this picture, it's lovely."

"I love it, too. You know it's one of the selfies."

"So I realize."

"You can check it out later. Let's roll."

He took her down a passageway nearby, then halted. "You are only allowed to glance in here. You can check it out later."

243

"Secrets again." She peeped in to see the huge kitchen. A chef's dream, the kitchen offered sleek state-of-the-art, high-tech appliances and tools. "Oh my. Gorgeous!" she told him.

"Uh-huh."

He pulled her away to show her the additional room near the kitchen, which served as a gym. Next, he took her upstairs where he raced her through two bedrooms and his larger-than-life master suite with two huge walk-in closets. The bathrooms were equipped with Jacuzzi tubs and other delightful amenities. Large, brown bean bags were positioned before the TV. *Ahem!* She didn't have the courage to ask about the silk sheets. *Extravagant*, was all she thought as they hastily moved through.

"A bit of man-caving going on in your bedroom, but I couldn't see everything properly with you rushing me." Her eyes bored holes at his back as they headed through the passageway. "That was a huge bed. What's the size of that thing?"

Their eyes met and for a second, she caught the heat in his gaze. She pushed out a breath, thinking, *Change the subject now.*

"Never mind. I got it," she managed to squeeze out.

"This is my home office." He opened the door and flicked on a switch.

She followed him inside. "Nice set up." She knitted her brows when her eyes caught sight of a keyboard in the corner near the balcony door. "Do you play?"

"I can, but I'm a bit rusty. Took lessons back in the day."

"You've never mentioned it."

"I had mentioned at your parents' home that I used to be in a high school band."

"Yes. You did say that."

244

"That area is my prayer closet." He pointed towards a space with a plush, blue sofa and several cushions on the floor. A Bible rested on one of the cushions.

"That's awesome!" Truth be told, she was a bit surprised.

"This is a temporary one. I'm creating the real one in my bedroom. Construction is in progress. Speaking of prayer closets, I would like to pray for you."

She raised an eyebrow in surprise, but her only response was an almost imperceptible nod.

They walked to the prayer closet, and held hands among the cushions.

"Lord, thank You that we can call You Savior and Lord. This evening, I bring before You, Sabrina Abigail Benjamin, my sister and my friend. Thank you for the role she has played, and is playing, in my life. Lord, You know how grateful I am that You have brought us together, even though the circumstances under which it happened were far less exciting; nevertheless, I'm thankful for our connection.

"Help me to celebrate her, Lord, so she truly understands how precious and valuable she is to me, her family, and others around her. Lord, I pray that You continue to bless the works of her hand. Mold and shape her into the woman of God that You want her to be.

"Lord, may she always feel Your wall of protection around her. Empower her with great skills and understanding, so that Your anointing on her life will continue to destroy yokes and set captives free. I declare that Your divine favor will always be upon her life. Thank you for many more birthdays for her. We bless You and we honor You. In the name of Jesus Christ, I pray, amen."

"Amen!" Sabrina agreed quietly, her head bowed. "Thanks so much."

"Anytime," he responded, returning her smile, and releasing her hands.

245

CHAPTER 36

Dinner passed in a haze of succulent entrées and an array of mouthwatering desserts. Chandler refused to tell Sabrina where he'd ordered the food while they ate in companionable chatter. Several times, she caught the twinkle of admiration in his eyes as she spoke. Still, she couldn't help but wonder, *Why can't we just be at peace like this all the time?*

The silence caused her to gaze at him, and again, she broke out of her thoughts, realizing he'd spoken. *This is happening way too often*, she warned herself. Placing a hand on her heart, she batted her eyelids. "What were you saying?"

Chandler chuckled as he walked around the table towards her. "Come," he stretched out his hand and she took it. *No questions.* He had to stop the smile threatening to visit his face. He led her to a small table away from the dining room table. "Close your eyes," he told her.

She did.

He lifted the white table cloth that had covered the table and rested it on a chair nearby. "Okay, open your eyes."

"Wooo-hooo! No, you didn't!" she hollered, gazing at the stunning, two-tier cake with white frosting. She danced around after reading the small card beside the cake, which indicated that it was red velvet with the layers infused with buttermilk and cocoa. Unable to help herself, she hugged him, then released him to clap her hands.

He chuckled softly. "I'll take a pic of you cutting it." He unclipped his cell phone from his belt.

"Oh no! I haven't taken one photo all evening," she lamented. "Hey, wait a minute, let me get my phone. I'm still waiting for you to send those selfies."

"Not to worry. I'll send them along with these."

246

"Okay, if you say so."

He chuckled softly. "Don't be ugly on your birthday."

"You're wrong for that. You're the reason I'm being ugly."

"Now you tell me. Camera is ready. Should I count you down?"

"Yes, please."

"Okay, smile."

She did, and he took a few shots.

"I don't hear any counting," she sang between shots, as if he was taking forever.

"Didn't I say stop being ugly?"

She flashed him a huge smile, batting her lashes. "This is me playing, Ms. Nice."

"Love it. Counting down."

"Yeah, finally!" She pushed the stainless-steel cake slicer into the cake.

"Here we go," he said joyfully, clicking away. "Three... two... one! And she cuts the cake, ladies and gentlemen."

Smiling, she placed a slice on each of two plates and took them back to the dining table. Chandler returned to his seat across from her and they both dived in.

"It's wooonderful. Thank you," she moaned, stuffing another piece into her mouth. Her eyes lit up with the glow he loved.

"You are welcome," he said, before tasting the cake.

Sabrina cut another chunk. "You've got to tell me when is your birthday, so I can celebrate you."

"You may have to plan for next year."

Her eyes darted from her cake to his. "And why would you say that?"

"My birthday is tomorrow."

Silence stretched between them as she gazed at him.

"It's no big deal," he told her quietly. "I plan to start the day in my prayer closet, then church, and I'll probably end it in my prayer closet."

"Really, Chandler? Really?"

"Seriously, Sab, it's not a big deal. I usually spend my birthdays alone, anyway. If I'm here, Don and his family throw a dinner for me."

"I can't imagine why you would spend your birthdays alone."

"It's not that I wanted to spend them alone; it just happened that way. I'm not accustomed to having people in my space. But enough about me. Let me put your cake in the box so you can take it home."

How can it be? Celebrating birthdays was a big thing in her family. Sabrina watched him walk over to the table and pack the cake into a box that had been resting under the cake table. He also put confectioneries into another box.

He walked towards her with the boxes. "I'll put them on the coffee table so we won't forget." He chuckled softly. "As if you would."

"I still want to celebrate your birthday," she told him.

"Okay. Tomorrow is off the table, though. But, I'll keep you posted."

"See. That's what I'm talking about. It's that control freak thing rearing its ugly head."

"Stop talking smack before I spank you."

"Wouldn't you like that?" she said sarcastically.

"Quite the contrary." With a sense of triumph, he whipped out a drop-dead gorgeous smile. "I'll spank you and make sure you like it."

Heat rushed up her face. "So now we know what kind of freak you are."

He flashed her a wicked smile before moving on.

She dabbed her mouth with a napkin, resisting the tiny smile that wanted to curl her lips. *Bad to the bones!* She was glad he'd disappeared to put the boxes down. She placed the last bit of cake into her mouth and rose to clear the dishes.

"No, that's okay," she heard Chandler say. "They'll be cleared up by the team I hired once we leave."

"You're making me feel pretty special.'

His pearly whites flashed. "You are."

She walked towards him, noticing he'd taken off his jacket and bowtie.

"Thanks for a great evening," she told him as they walked back to the living room. "I enjoyed every minute of it. Your place is great, too."

"Thanks. You're welcome." Then with much fanfare, he added with a wink, "Always, and anytime."

That caused an avalanche of giggles to burst from her lips. "You've got jokes."

"A natural part of my make-up," he drawled.

"Yes, it is," she teased. "Oh, can I see the view from the terrace? And don't let me leave my photo. I'm taking the easel, too."

"Sure. Please take it away."

He walked over, turned on a switch that provided intimate lighting on the terrace, and pushed open the sliding door. "There you go." He smiled at her.

That smile almost turned her insides to butter. "Thanks," she managed to say, before stepping onto the terrace to witness the spectacular view—lush greenery in a lighted garden below, stars twinkling in the night sky, and a stunning cobweb of city lights. It would be a perfect spot to snap a selfie.

"It's beautiful," she said, bending to get a closer look.

Chandler remained silent. He was distracted, staring at her body.

Something squeezed Sabrina's heart and she knew what was coming, as she turned to face him. *Lord, help…*

He was watching her from the doorway, his long-sleeved shirt showing off his muscular arms and pecs. His eyes met hers and she sensed a challenge of sorts.

Mesmerized, she watched him walk towards her. She had to do something, so she turned to look at the stars.

Chandler stopped behind her and trapped her with his hands on the rail. "There's a falling star," he pointed out.

His warm breath tickled her neck, and she wished she had the courage to step away. She didn't have to wish for too long, because he soon wrapped his arm around her waist. "Would you like to see the stars from my telescope?" he asked.

Her skin pebbled. "Ye-yes," she stuttered.

He took her hand and led her to the right side of the terrace. Releasing her, he uncovered the telescope, twiddled with a few buttons, then tilted it.

"All yours," he said with a swipe of his hand.

She moved towards the telescope, then bent to look through it.

"Step slightly to the right," he told her, his hands on her waist, helping her along.

She did as he requested. "Oh wow! Beautiful!" she blurted. "I'm stargazing!"

"Yes, it is," he murmured, watching her.

When his body began to acknowledge how close she was, he stepped away, but that didn't stop him from admiring the view as he leaned against the wall opposite to her.

Soon the dead silence caused Sabrina to pause. She'd been caught up in the excitement of being an amateur astronomer. She looked around and caught Chandler studying her closely, and practically jumped to full height.

Neither spoke.

Heat washed through her as he moved towards her, and she mentally visualized what would happen next.

A slight coughing sound made her open her eyes. She hadn't even realized she'd closed them from the rush of anticipation. Embarrassment heated her face and she mumbled something incoherent about the telescope.

"I'll get that later," he said, while invading her personal space. He breathed in her essence before softly pressing his lips against her cheeks.

The warmth of his lips caused her heart to kick against her rib cage. Thankfully, strength came from on high, because she turned and pierced him with a sharp stare, telling him, "I'm ready to go."

"O…" His throat constricted and he struggled to clear it. "Okay."

He didn't move, so she stepped away from him.

It was the longest ride she'd ever taken to get home. The silence in the car bordered on being oppressive. Both caught up in their emotions. Both caught up with feverish desire.

Soon, Chandler placed the boxes on the island, then walked out to get her balloons, flowers, photo, and easel. She watched as he slowly pulled the balloons from the car. He'd driven the black BMW, which allowed her to take all her presents.

Her eyes followed him each time he returned to the living room, and she silently asked the Lord for help.

When he was finished, he faced her. "This is for you." He handed her a small, pink gift bag with a white bow stuck to it.

"Chandler, you've done—"

"Please take it. It's my gift to you."

"Thank you." She took the bag from his hand, and tried to smile, but it didn't materialize so she settled for more words. "I enjoyed everything."

"My pleasure. I'm off to catch some Z's. Enjoy the rest of your night." He headed towards the front door.

251

"You, too," Sabrina murmured, feeling an urgent need to hold him, to touch him… to breathe him in. She was sure he needed it, too, but could she risk it? On top of all her needs, she sensed, too, that he didn't want to leave, and if she was being honest with herself, she didn't want him to. That last thought twisted her stomach in knots.

"Chandler," she heard herself call out.

"Yes." He didn't stop, long strides taking him nearer to the front door.

She rushed after him, desperation urging her on.

His hand on the door knob, Chandler swallowed hard, attempting to tame his desire. She was now standing behind him… *way too close.* "You were saying?" he asked, hoping his tone would not betray him.

"I want to-to…" Sabrina pushed out a frustrated sigh as she searched for the right words. "I want to hug you but I can't. I mean, it's best that we don't." She paused, and then anguish filled her voice. "Could you at least look at me?"

Chandler pushed his hands in his pants pockets and turned to look directly into her eyes, a look he'd perfected for professional settings. "You have my attention."

She fought hard not to fidget under his gaze. "Don't make this any more difficult than it is."

He did not respond, but his eyes dropped to her lips, and he leaned in.

No-no-no, don't do that. Then, heat flushed her face. It was she who was on tip-toes.

She lowered herself and dropped her head on his chest.

His stomach clenched, but he did not hold her.

"Chandler, I ca-can't." She cleared the lump from her throat, and her words rushed out. "I can't do this. This, this thing between…" She lifted her head from his chest, and leaned against the wall near the door. "We-I need to set some boundaries for our friendship."

"Don't worry about it."

252

Every word was painful. His response caused her to straighten her body. "What is that supposed to mean?" She nailed him with her eyes. "Do you think it's okay for us to relate this way? You're playing with my emotions."

He flinched. "No, I don't. I get it. You don't want me to touch you, so I won't."

Her mouth hung open, and all the air seemed to trickle from her lungs. It became clearer. He would rather take the easy way out. His heart was permanently locked away.

"Good night," he choked out, yanking the door open, and closing it behind him in a move that had become all-too-familiar.

CHAPTER 37

"God is your refuge and your strength, a very present help in times of trouble, so fear not. His attention is one hundred percent focused on you. Pray the Scriptures instead of your emotions."

Chandler sank deeper on the chair and stared out the window of his study as he listened to Pastor Jackson's words of encouragement, the phone pressed to his ear.

"Thanks," he pushed out. Peace had eluded him since he had left Sabrina almost two weeks ago. Her birthday evening hadn't ended like he'd hoped. Since then, he'd worked from home half the time, and then taken time off to sort himself out.

Minutes ago, he'd confessed he was in love with Sabrina.

"Being in love is wonderful," Pastor Jackson encouraged. "It's one of the most amazing experiences you will ever have."

"It feels strange to be so connected to someone," Chandler claimed. "The last time I felt drawn to someone, I ended up at the church's door. I cannot, will not go through that again." He had to be brutally honest.

"Go on," Pastor Jackson encouraged.

"Plus, I feel like I can't trust myself with Sabrina. If I hurt her, I don't know what I'd do. I'd rather keep her as a friend. Running away when the fire gets hot and going back when it has cooled off."

"How is that strategy working for you?"

A hollow laugh burst from Chandler's lips. "It's not. I'm frustrating both of us. I think she's on the brink of sending me packing."

"Let's keep it real," Pastor Jackson insisted. "The first time you thought you were in love, you were young and maybe you didn't see all the signs that something was wrong, or maybe you saw them and chose to ignore them."

He allowed Chandler to chew on that.

"The next time, you thought you were in love with a married woman. She wasn't separated from her husband, nor did she pretend to be. A fling presented itself and she took the bait."

Chandler said nothing, but Pastor Jackson knew he was listening.

"I'm saying all that to say, you never had a chance at love," Pastor Jackson concluded. "I'm talking about emotional, physical, spiritual, healthy love. Love that makes you sing, and dance, and laugh at nothing. Love that makes you think about her and how to please her. Love that makes you rush home from work because you can't wait to be in her presence." Pastor Jackson chuckled. "And yes, love that makes you do stupid things like drive three hours to purchase an antique chair, just because she likes it."

Chandler chuckled. "No, you didn't."

"I sure did. A happy wife makes a happy home."

Chandler exhaled, and a smile crept over his face. He could identify. He barely got any sleep preparing for Sabrina's birthday party.

"Chandler, it's not every day you'll find someone whose spirit bears witness with your spirit. It's like trying to find a needle in a hay stack." He chuckled with understanding. "The Bible states, 'Who can find a virtuous woman? For her price is far above rubies.'"

"Amen to that." Chandler's head bobbed up and down.

"What is it that you like about Sister Sabrina?"

A smile lit Chandler's face. "I enjoy being in her presence. She's like a breath of fresh air every time I see her. I'm my true, authentic self when I'm with her. She keeps me grounded—mentally, emotionally, spiritually, and physically."

"Go on," Pastor Jackson encouraged.

"She feels like home. Yet, I struggle with not deserving her. I feel like I need to wash, purge, and punish myself before I even hold her hand. I love her." Suddenly, he wanted to laugh for no reason at all. He was off-kilter.

"You do sound like a man in love." Pastor Jackson smiled. "And don't be afraid of something that hasn't happened. Instead, trust God that something great will happen. We have already prayed, and I will continue praying, but I need you to pray when you get a moment. Ask the Lord to reveal to you what the real problem is, for I suspect it may be deeper than what you have revealed."

"Pastor—"

"Come on, man—Anthony or Tony. We've had that conversation."

"Yes, we did, Tony. I appreciate your counsel."

"As the Lord gives it to me, I give to you. We'll talk again."

After Chandler disconnected the call, he placed his cell phone on the desk and walked into his prayer closet. He sat on the cushions on the floor.

"I love You, Lord. You have given me something that's greater than my earthly possessions—Your love and grace. I am forever grateful.

"Lord, I place before you my relationship with Sabrina. I love her, Lord, and I know deep down that she loves me, but Lord, all I can see is my heart being ripped into shreds. And if that happens again, I don't think I would survive. Help me, Lord. I don't want to lose her friendship and her love."

He slid to the floor and curled into a ball.

"Father, I am staying here until I get what I need. I need a greater anointing. Increase my faith, oh God, so that I will not be afraid, but move as Your Spirit leads. Father, I need less of me, and more of You. Lord, grant me wisdom, courage…"

An hour later, Chandler rolled onto his back and stared at the ceiling, emotions choking him up, for he realized he had unfinished business to take care of or he would lose Sabrina. Now that would be torture. His anxiety level hit full blast, as he thought about it.

He moved with great haste. Perched on the edge of the desk, he called her.

Sabrina picked up on the second ring. "Are you okay?" she asked without greeting him. She hadn't heard from him since he left her home the night of her birthday. True, too, she hadn't called. She had to set boundaries between them, for she had no intention of having her heart further crushed by him. Nevertheless, she'd taken to praying for him instead. Aunt Connie, Amber, and Jenay were also praying.

"Yes, I'm doing okay," Chandler responded. "How are you?"

"I'm doing well." She spoke quietly, hoping he would get to the point.

"I'm going away for—"

"You keep doing this, Chandler." Her tone was harsh. "Anyway, okay."

"It's not like that," he explained. "I'll only be gone for a few days. I'll probably leave tonight. I need to take care of a few things. Will you have dinner with me on Sunday?"

For a moment, Sabrina's brain short-circuited. *You've got to be kidding.*

"Please," Chandler pleaded.

Sabrina huffed out a long-suffering breath. "Chandler, it's best we only interact at church. It's too much, emotionally, to be in the same space with you."

Her words landed like a slap. "Okay, then," he said quietly. "I'll talk with you when I get back. Please pray for me."

257

"I will. And thanks for my gift. They are beautiful." She was stunned that he'd given her a pair of solitaire diamond earrings.

Exuberant. That was Amber's and Jenay's reaction when she told them about her birthday dinner. But his gift had left them speechless. Amber was the first to recover. Immediately, she pulled out her smartphone and started searching for bridesmaid's dresses.

"My pleasure," Chandler said affectionately. "Beautiful and radiant as the owner."

Her skin grew warm. "Flattery will get you nowhere."

"And here I was thinking it would. Anyway, that's not flattery," he said quietly. "It's the truth."

She had no air to respond, and on top of that her body was expressing great satisfaction. Nevertheless, she was unwavering in her decision. "Have a safe trip."

Tough cookie. Chandler smiled. "Thanks. See you soon."

CHAPTER 38

Early the following afternoon, Chandler found himself being smothered by a seriously grateful mother. The house staff was a sea of smiling faces when he greeted them, some of whom he hadn't seen in six years.

Soon, he was selecting from the assortment of food that had been prepared for him. He preferred to eat on one of the balconies, but it was a nippy November day so he opted to eat in the dining room nearest to the kitchen.

His mother chatted animatedly with him while he ate. She'd screamed with delight when he called to say he was coming home for a few days. She didn't care why he was coming, she was simply grateful he would be home. It had been too long.

Almost two hours later, shades of blues and gray filled Chandler's eyes when he entered a place that held thousands of memories—his luxurious suite. The huge oasis had been refurbished several times to his liking as he moved through the various stages of his life. It had its own living room, study, and a private balcony.

He sat on the blue love seat at the foot of the bed, exhaustion weighing him down. He sent a text to Sabrina. *Hello! Thinking about you. How are you?*

A few minutes later, she text back: *Hello to you, too! Thanks. Doing well. You made it safely, I see.*

Hint. Hint.

He should have contacted her sooner. Chandler chuckled softly before texting back: *Yes. Thanks. Got in early afternoon. I'm at my parents in D.C. Can I see you Sunday after church?*

Sabrina: *Remember our conversation.*

Chandler: *It's important.*

Sabrina: *Okay. I'll be at church.*

Chandler: *I will see you soon.*

259

Sabrina: *See you.*

Smiling, Chandler texted her the selfies and some of her birthday photos. *That should remind her of how great we are together.* When he'd done that, he walked towards the bathroom, deciding to take a shower then a nap.

Later that evening, he dined with his mother in the master dining room. His mother asked the servers to leave the room, and close the door.

"I need alone time with you," she told Chandler, smiling.

Really, Mother. "Okay."

"Now stop sounding like that. You'll be gone in no time, and who knows when I'll be seeing you again."

He smiled at her. "I promise, it won't be so long, and you can let me know when you'd like to visit me."

His response warmed her heart and she stared at her plate, thanking God.

Chandler sensed her deliberations and, strangely, his heart was glad. "Would you like me to pray over the food?"

"Yes, son." And for the second time, Veronica's heart warmed.

Chandler prayed and they partook of a sumptuous dinner—starting with Caesar salad with creamy garlic dressing, croutons and Parmigiano-Reggiano cheese, followed by roasted organic salmon filled with black olives and oven-dried tomatoes, and ending with caramel apple chocolate mousse cake.

When it was all over, Chandler couldn't resist eating more of the cake, which tasted like perfection. He chose not to drink wine, but instead selected the strawberry orange sunrise smoothie.

"Dinner was great, as usual, Mother."

"Thanks, son." She smiled at him. "I made sure an apple flavored dish was in the mix for you."

"I see. Thank you."

260

Veronica cleared her throat, then wiped her mouth with a napkin. "Are you still playing the keyboard? I remember how you loved music."

A smile flitted across his lips at her ice-breaker. *Strange.* His mother had discouraged him from playing when he was a part of his high school band. Her issue—she didn't think it was appropriate for him to be playing in a jazz band, with all his classical music training. After being punished too many times for stealing away to play with the group, he eventually quit the band.

"I've been playing again, at home in Orlando, since Sa..." He paused, realizing he'd almost said Sabrina. The first time he'd heard her sing, he was so inspired he'd purchased a keyboard that same week, and started playing again.

"I'm glad. You come alive when you play. Since we knew you were coming, your father bought a new keyboard for the music room, or you can use the grand piano. It's still in the living room. No one has used it since you… left," she said quietly.

Here we go, Chandler thought. "Thanks, Mother. I'm committed to building a relationship with you and Father. It's difficult sometimes, especially with Father, but I'm trusting God."

"I've been meaning to talk with you about the relationship between your father and me," his mother admitted quietly. "Your father and I were attracted to each other from the first day we met. That day, he came into my boutique. He told me he saw me go into the store and so he came to seek me out. We courted for a short while, and it felt like I was in heaven."

She paused, smiling, and then her expression turned to one of pain. "Believe me, when I found out he was married, I tried to get rid of him, but he refused to leave me alone. He wanted what he wanted."

261

Chandler opened his mouth to say something, but thought better of it.

"He pursued me, relentlessly. He told me Nadine had tricked him into marrying her, telling him she was pregnant. He'd been married for almost two years when we met. Before I knew what was happening, he'd divorced her."

Her eyes filled with anguish. "For a while, I was ashamed of myself because I'd broken up a marriage. He wasn't in love with Nadine, but clearly they were making love. We didn't find out Nadine was pregnant until after we got married. I was devastated, and it did cause our marriage to go through a very rough period."

She sighed loudly. "Your father insisted the child was not his and after a while, Nadine cut off communication with him, and your father didn't try to contact her. True, too, he was busy running around establishing his business."

Chandler listened carefully.

"Years later, I found out I was pregnant. Shocking, because my doctor had told me with my endometriosis issue, I could never get pregnant. Your father knew about my condition before we got married, and he was okay with it.

"For a few years after you were born, we tried to have another child. I even went through a round of In Vitro Fertilization, with no positive results. We decided to stop because during the process I was experiencing severe pelvic pain and bloating.

"After that period, without your father's knowledge, I decided to see if Nadine's child looked anything like your father. I tracked her down through a private investigator, and I was surprised to see that Don had some of your father's features. I showed the photos to your father, and that night he wept in my arms. He had two sons, yet he had none."

Chandler sighed.

His mother continued nonetheless. "I think that caused your father to bury himself further in his work," she explained. "He contacted Nadine, but she refused to give us access to Don, and she returned all the checks your father had sent to assist with Don's well-being. After a while, we got creative and paid for all of his education."

Chandler's eyes widened. "You did?"

Veronica smiled at him. "Yes. It's the least we could do. We were happy that you and Don discovered each other, and have a growing relationship."

Chandler exhaled deeply, grateful that Don hadn't given up on their friendship, even when he had.

His mother broke into his thoughts. "I have to tell you this—your father tracks the progress both of you are making. He's absolutely proud of his boys. He has photos of you both in his office here and at work. I told you he keeps all the magazines that you appear in."

Chandler twitched in his seat intrigued by his mother's words. "Yes, you did say something about that."

"In fact, he reminded me earlier this week that your annual work conference is coming up in a few weeks."

He smiled widely. "Yes. I'm looking forward to it."

His mother was quiet for a moment. "Do you need to know anything else?" she asked.

"Did Father try again recently to make contact with Don?"

"No. He's afraid of rejection."

Chandler was quiet.

"I'm hoping…" His mother clasped her hands at her chest. "I'm hoping you can help your father with his relationship with Don."

"Mother—"

263

"I know you have to work on your relationship with your father, but if there's anything you can do to help his relationship with Don, please do."

"Okay," Chandler responded quietly.

"God has been good to us, son, and as I grow older, I recognize how important it is for us to stick together as a family. Honestly, your father and I knew you needed a brother, so we tried to help you build a relationship with Clive." She eyed Chandler. "It was going well for a while until you didn't want to be his friend anymore. It broke his mother's heart that you two couldn't get along. You know how much Clara loves you."

Chandler offered no explanation. "How is Aunt Clara doing? She still has those high-end boutiques?"

"Clara is doing great on a personal and business level. I'm even beginning to think she has recovered from James' death."

Veronica and Clara, her only sister, shared a great relationship. They had been there for each other through thick and thin, but when her husband had died in a car accident some six years ago, it was the hardest Veronica had ever fought for the recovery of her sister. True, too, that was the last time Chandler had been home.

"Glad for that. She took Uncle James' death really hard, which is understandable."

"Tell me about this young lady who caught your eyes. Don't keep your mother in suspense. When do I get to meet her?"

A pensive expression shrouded Chandler's face. "There's nothing to tell. We're not in a relationship."

"But you love her. What's her name?"

He flushed. "Sab, Sabrina Benjamin."

A bright smile lit Veronica's face. "What's the hold-up? You don't think she feels the same way?"

264

Chandler considered it for a moment. "I haven't asked but I'm hoping when I do, she'll have me."

"Of course, she'll have you, son. Have you been praying about this?"

"Yes. She really loves the Lord," he gushed. "You should hear her sing. She's a beautiful soul."

His mother laughed softly. "I take it she loves God more than she loves you."

Chandler chuckled. "She sure does."

"That's a good thing, son." His mother smiled warmly at him. "That's a good thing."

CHAPTER 39

Sabrina! A grin curved Chandler's lips before he chuckled softly. *How ironic!* He was on the brink of getting his walking papers. Any fantasy he held about having anything resembling a platonic friendship with her was not happening.

He gazed through the windshield, not thinking about the gray sky or the light sleet stinging the windows of his parents' black Explorer. He was slowly eating up the miles to get back home to have lunch with his parents. His father had arrived late last night from London, and was still asleep when Chandler left after breakfast with his mother.

He'd happily made his rounds that morning, stopping by Aunt Clara and Clive. They were elated to see him, and made him promise to visit more often. In the excitement, Clive insisted he had to Facetime Chloe, his sister, so she could be in on the action.

As Chandler expected, Chloe gently chided him, for she'd reached out to him several times, since they both lived in Chicago. They hadn't seen each other for over three years. Chandler promised to pay her a visit when he was back in the Windy City.

Once he was home, Chandler made his way to his quarters and a huge grin popped on his face. He dialed Sabrina.

"Happy Saturday," Sabrina answered, even though there was no "happy" in her voice.

"Good morning, Sab. I can definitely hear the happy in your voice," he teased.

"Right." She adopted a friendlier tone. "How is it going?"

"Going great. I can't wait to tell you about it."

"When are you flying back?"

"I have an early-bird flight tomorrow."

"Oh, okay."

"Do you miss me?"

She fidgeted. *Well that came out of nowhere.* "Chandler—"

"Sab, why is it so hard to say you miss me? I know you do, because I miss you."

She sighed loudly. *Lord, have mercy! What am I going to do with this man?* "Yes, I miss you, but how is that going to help any of us?" she countered.

"Testy, are we, on this happy Saturday morning."

"Chandler, I care about your well-being, but I won't allow you to play with my emotions."

"I'm not playing with your emotions, Sab. Seriously, I'm not."

She was silent.

"I'll see you tomorrow," he said.

"Okay," she said quietly before disconnecting the call.

Chandler sighed, wishing he was with her.

A glance at his cell phone reminded him it was almost time to have lunch with his parents. He freshened up and made his way downstairs.

As he approached the living room, he heard female voices; one he recognized as his mother and the other sounded vaguely familiar. Curious, he entered the living room and came to a complete stop. *This is unexpected.* Alana Hobart was staring him down.

Her slender, five-foot-eight frame was wrapped in an elegant white jumpsuit, showing off her assets in all the right places. A tiny gold belt at her waist emphasized her Barbie look.

A heartthrob! Alana felt herself drooling… like she would have back in the day. Chandler looked even more handsome in person than his photos on the magazine covers. Caught, she clutched her gold purse and fidgeted under his cold stare.

Chandler relaxed his face. *No need for hostility.* "Good afternoon."

Alana was too shocked to respond to his greeting.

His mother rushed to the rescue. "We'd scheduled this meeting before I knew you were coming here."

Chandler ignored her statement. "Mom, where are we having lunch?"

"In the dining room adjacent to the grand ballroom."

"Okay, I'll see you there." Chandler was turning to leave when Alana called his name. He kept walking.

"Chandler!" Alana called out again, running after him.

He stopped, and turned to face her, but did not speak.

Silence stretched between them.

His mother passed by. "I'll wait outside."

"I'm sorry," Alana told him slowly, distracted by how incredible he looked.

Chandler looked into the face of the woman who had disgraced him at the altar and suddenly felt sorry for her. That surprised him, for back in the day, he'd played their meeting in his head and it did not go down well.

"I'm sorry," Alana repeated, admiring his face. "I was young and foolish. My marriage to Andrew didn't even last a year. I'm sorry for what I did to you."

"Okay." *If that's all…*

"Chandler, I really need this job with your mother. She didn't want to interview me because of the history between you and me. I had to pull many strings to get a meeting. Anyway, you look great," she murmured.

"What did you say?" he questioned in a harsh tone.

She flushed, but did not back down. "I was saying, you look incredible."

"Please excuse me."

Chandler walked away. It was the natural high he'd anticipated. God, it felt great.

268

Soon, his stomach was in bliss. The main course was over and the servers brought in the dessert—lemon blueberry cake for his father, mixed berry cheesecake for his mother and apple baklava for him.

Lightheartedly, he said to his parents, "You're spoiling me, I feel like moving back home."

His mother smiled at him. "You can, but I doubt Sabrina would like that."

Chandler toyed with his dessert. "I suppose you are right."

Julius Peynard, seated at the head of the table, had thought it best not to say much during lunch, but now he had to jump in. "Sabrina?" His father looked from his wife to his son.

"I'll leave that to Chandler to explain."

Heat rose up Chandler's neck and he gazed around the room, glad the servers had left. He felt like a young boy telling his parents about the girl he'd fallen in love with.

"Son?" His father was excited. "When do we meet her?"

Seated across from his mother, Chandler stared at the painting on the wall beyond her. "I haven't asked her into a relationship."

Silence swarmed them.

His parents waited.

"I feel like I don't deserve her." Chandler lifted his hand to ward off anything his mother had to say. He had to get it out. "Feel like, I'm not good enough…" His voice trailed off.

"Son, don't think like that." His mother mopped her eyes with a napkin.

"Why would you think that?" His father usual strong voice was now softer.

Chandler swallowed hard, wishing he could run out of the room, but it had to be said. A tear slipped down his face as he opened his mouth. "I battle feelings of isolation, which cause me to feel unlovable. I know Sabrina cares, but what if when she gets to know me better, she's disappointed?"

He cleared his throat and his mother tried to come to his aid. Yet, he was determined to press on. "I work constantly, even when I don't have to, for in the back of my mind, people love you when you are up, and on top. It's like I'm always trying to prove myself... to you both."

His mother's shocked, tear-stained eyes met his. "Why?" she asked, quickly glancing at his father.

Chandler rested his elbows on the table and placed his forehead in his hands. He'd never said this to anyone. He fidgeted, and then clasped his hands tightly between his legs.

His parents were attentive.

"You will recall, I was sl-slow... a slow learner." His words stumbled out. "When I was around seven years old, we went to Clive's graduation from Karate class. I wasn't hungry when we returned home so Mom told me I could go to bed. I did, but then I changed my mind and came back to the dining room and both of you were laughing and talking."

Disappointment flickered in Chandler's eyes as he gazed into his parents' puzzled eyes.

"You were going on about how brilliant Clive was," Chandler continued. "True, back then, Clive excelled at everything... and I-I didn't. I did poorly at everything— school work, piano, swimming, tennis. Everything."

He paused to catch a breath, but kept his gaze steady.

"It was hard enough to be around Clive, and feel bad about myself, but Father, I heard you say, 'How is it possible that we could have such a dumb kid? There will be no one to leave our legacy to.'"

270

His mother's eyes welled up with even more tears as Chandler's words tore into her, but it was his father who spoke. "Son, I'm sorry," he choked out.

But Chandler was not listening. "And Mom, you said, 'We don't even know if he'll make anything of himself. Still, God has blessed us with him. That ought to mean something. He could be a genius.'"

Chandler's eyes were filled with unshed tears. He'd died that day. "You made me sound like-like I was an anomaly, some kind of frea-freak accident."

Those words caused him to shudder, and he pushed his plate away and wept on the table.

His mother was the first to his side, hugging, and crying with him. His father swallowed emotions that rose within and stood by them misty-eyed. He had to fix this.

CHAPTER 40

"Heey, Sab!" A wide smile spread across Chandler's face as he stepped through the front door.

Sabrina blinked, momentarily distracted by the playfulness in his tone. "Hello to you, too."

Again, he'd broken down all her defenses so they could meet at her home. He had all kinds of excuses—He'd just come back from D.C. He was tired. He was hungry. He didn't want to sit in a restaurant. What he had to say couldn't be said in the church yard. But, she had to chuckle when he said he was willing to be her pet project.

She let out a sigh that was dying to escape as they walked in silence to the living room.

"Did you miss me?" he asked.

She stopped to face him near the coffee table. "Didn't we have that conversation yesterday?"

He edged closer to her, taking in her fitted, baby-pink dress. "That was yesterday." Brushing loose hair from her face, he smiled, tenderness in his gaze.

Her heart fluttered from his touch. "Yes, I missed you."

In one swift movement, his strong arms circled her waist. "Good, because I missed you, too."

The burst of anticipation made her heart pound. "Chandler—"

He leaned in and lightly brushed his lips across her forehead. "What's for dinner?" Releasing her, he ushered her towards the kitchen.

Relief washed over her. "Er, nothing too fancy—baked teriyaki chicken or marinated grilled shrimp, with rice and tossed salad."

"Sounds fancy to me. I'll have both."

"Everything is warm." She moved towards the refrigerator and took out a dish with tossed salad. He was right behind her, taking out the raspberry vinaigrette.

"Water, tea, juice?" she asked.

"Tea, please."

"Should have known." She gave him a half smile then turned the knob on the stove to heat the kettle.

"It's strange but this is pretty much where I drink all my tea, excepting when I was at your parents' home."

"Hmm, interesting."

"That's what I say, too."

He put the table mats on the island and placed a knife and a fork on each napkin. Then sitting at the island, his eyes followed her as she moved about the kitchen.

She set his plate and a cup of tea before him. "Just the way you like it."

He smiled at her. "Thank you."

Next, she gave him a bowl of salad and prepared one for herself. She sat across from him and he blessed the food.

"How was church?" he asked. "I really wanted to be there, but my body said no." He chewed on the chicken.

"Church was good. Pastor spoke about hitting the mark of excellence."

"Aren't you going to eat dinner?" he asked.

"No. Not hungry."

"This is becoming a habit—you watching me eat."

Sabrina melted. She did enjoy watching him eat. "I'm about to eat my salad."

"That's a relief. This food is delicious."

"Thank you." She placed a forkful of salad into her mouth.

He smiled at her, then sipped his tea. "I was praying about a few things and after that I felt the Holy Spirit impress on my heart the need to go to D.C. to visit my

273

parents. I didn't know what to expect, but I wanted to be obedient."

He stopped to eat more of his food and she waited patiently, eating more of her salad.

"I'm glad I went," he remarked. He told her about the conversations with his parents. Of course, he didn't mention the part about him being in love.

Sabrina's heart warmed as he spoke, and she silently thanked God for his breakthrough.

"Now that I know Jesus as my personal savior, I've realized I have never given my heart, all of my heart to anyone." He gazed intently at her. "I have always taken the easy way out when it comes to relationships, but that was because I was busy hiding behind my emotional walls. Trapped by the lies of the enemy."

Her gaze flicked over his face, taking in all he was saying.

He smiled at her. "God created us to be relational beings. I have asked God to help me to love my wife as much as He loves the church."

Her heart warmed, content to listen to him share his heart.

"Since I spoke with my parents, it became clearer that I have to let go of my mantra—Don't trust my heart to anyone." He paused and zeroed in on her, before flashing her a toothy grin.

She glowed with pride. "I'm happy you're mending your fences. Very proud of you, and the man of God you've become."

His heart warmed, because she'd referred to him as a man of God. He wanted to cartwheel across the table and hug her. "Thanks."

Together they stacked the dishwasher, and then he stood at the island watching her wipe the stove. He smiled, thinking that for the first time in his life, a poor choice had led him to the right place. The need to be close to her escalated and he trapped her with his hands on the counter. "I have really missed you," he moaned, his hot breath grazing the soft skin at the nape of her neck.

She jumped, instinctively leaning into him.

His arms circled her waist and a growl rose from deep in his throat. He released her, his chest heaving.

"Sorry," she pushed out, not looking at him.

He didn't speak, but when she was finished with the stove, he was sitting at the island.

He looked at her boldly. "Your body keeps calling mine, and I keep answering."

She witnessed the flames in his eyes, and decided to set him straight. "You need to stop answering."

"I'm trying," he shot back, grumbling, "Stop being so mean."

She held out her hand to him. "You have been spoiled, that's what that is."

"Yeah, yeah." He made a face at her before taking her hand.

They walked to the living room, and Sabrina took a seat on the sofa and he sat next to her. He draped an arm behind her on the sofa and turned towards her. "I love you."

She flushed, unable to meet his eyes.

He paused so she could absorb that, but when she still didn't look at him, he gently lifted her chin to help her meet his gaze. He was surprised to see unshed tears.

He laughed softly, kissed her forehead, and got up to retrieve a napkin from the kitchen. He dabbed her eyes, and then kissed them one at a time. Again, her eyes brimmed, and he dabbed them.

"This is a happy moment," he told her tenderly. "I love you with all of my heart." He pulled her into his arms and rained light kisses on the top of her head. "I love you, more than you can ever imagine."

Happiness ran through her and she clung to him, wrapping her arms around his waist. Her breath rushed out. "I love you, too."

Moments later, she lifted her head and smiled at him.

It was all over for him.

He slid to the floor, on his knees before her. His light-brown eyes darkened with a glint of amazement. "I'm in love with you. I admire your intellect, wisdom, intuition, and the grace with which you handle your life. I love that you're dependable, and that you're committed to always doing the right thing. I enjoy talking with you. You are not afraid to let me know how you feel and I'm glad you're not afraid to stand out, and to share your perspective on issues."

He held onto her hands, tickling one of her palms.

"Stop it." She giggled softly, slipping her hands from his.

He chuckled softly. "Your laughter warms my soul. I love so many things about you, but most of all, I love the heart of you—your genuine compassion and care for those around you."

She blushed beautifully, looked at her hands on her lap, then slowly raised her gaze to meet his.

"There it is. The glow about you that I love so much. It tells me that you're in a happy place. It's pretty clear, huh? I am in love with you, beautiful, talented, woman of God." He took a breath. "I love you and I would be honored if you would be in an exclusive relationship with me, and marry me, when the time is right."

Sabrina had to remind herself to breathe. Her prayers were being answered. She smiled at the man she'd come to love. Leaning forward, she cupped his face with her hands. "Yes, and yes," she told him sweetly.

Before Chandler could catch his next breath, she'd kissed one of his eyes, and had moved on to the next. He felt her warm, gentle breath, and closed his eyes, enjoying the soft touch of her lips. She dropped butterfly kisses from his forehead to the tip of his nose, working her way to his mouth. Everything in him was screaming, *stop her*, but his body was begging for more. Now, his arms circled her waist.

"I love you," she whispered against his mouth, before kissing him.

He groaned out her name, breaking the kiss and all but passing out on the floor. He lay on his back, inhaling and exhaling deeply. "Our chemistry is on point," he puffed out before pulling himself into a sitting position. "We don't need to test it any further."

"Got it." Her face was flushed from the adrenalin rush, and she pulled herself together.

He joined her on the sofa. "Time for prayer."

CHAPTER 41

"I'm good." Sabrina smiled as she spoke on her phone. "Everything is wonderful. I got a taste of the wintry mix of rain and sleet, but that's okay. I'm going to shower and then take a nap until you get here."

She was glad Chandler had persuaded her into coming to the Windy City. The final day of his work conference was tomorrow, so they would be spending a few days checking out the sights before returning to Orlando on Monday morning. She still had a class to teach Monday afternoon.

"Order room service, and don't worry about the bill," Chandler told her.

"Got it. Stop worrying." She toed off her shoes and spread out on the huge bed. "Did you get back to the conference on time?"

"Yes," he chuckled softly, "I slipped out to call you."

She laughed. "But you just got back."

"I looked in and then slipped out." His tone was conspiratorial. "I should be able to get away by four o'clock, so I'll come to get you around half past four."

"Great. See you soon. I love you."

"I love you, more. Later, babes."

"Okay, honey."

Sabrina grinned absent-mindedly as she disconnected the call and dropped the phone on the bed. She glanced around the grand suite, attempting to fully digest the elegance of the Waldorf Astoria Hotel, overlooking the Windy City's esteemed Gold Coast District.

She walked across the room and pulled the drapes aside to get more of the natural light, and admired the awe-inspiring view. She was feeling extremely comfortable in this extravagant setting—a huge bedroom with gorgeous marble master bath, powder room, living room, dining area, and a private terrace.

She had been surprised when she'd been escorted into her suite through a private external foyer door that connected to Chandler's suite.

It had been two weeks since they had begun their relationship. *What a man!* She loved God's gift to her. She smiled inwardly, something she seemed to be doing a lot of these days.

Last Saturday, Chandler had taken her to meet Don. It took her a moment to get over how they resembled each other, however, a fangirl moment happened when she later found out that Don worked for the Rozene Kanate Ministry. She admired the globe-trotting, bestselling author and had been at one of her book signings.

But, it was Chandler's birthday party that had been the kicker. She'd planned it in secret with Don. *Yikes!* She was glad she'd kept it small as recommended by Don. Chandler looked like he had been caught in some kind of dubious act when he arrived at Don's house and the spotlight was on him. She had managed to settle him with her love, but she realized then, that as much as he liked to surprise her, he did not like surprises himself. He had loved and appreciated his gift from her—a brown leather-bound, Thompson Chain Reference Bible, with his name engraved in gold on the cover.

The ringing of Sabrina's cell phone brought her out of her deliberations.

"Hello, my favorite aunt!" Sabrina answered.

"Are you alone?" Aunt Connie asked in a hushed voice.

Sabrina resisted the urge to giggle. "Yes, I am."

"Sabrina, you didn't call," Aunt Connie scolded.

"I'm sorry. I was caught up with everything."

279

"I called twice. I was just about to call Chandler, then I decided to call one last time. I'm not trying to be in your business, but I need to know you're okay."

"Aunty, I know. I didn't realize you'd called. My phone was in my purse."

Aunt Connie sighed. "We're here wondering what's going on."

Sabrina knitted her brows. "We?"

"Amber and Jenay are here." Aunt Connie chuckled softly. "They just happened to be in the neighborhood. I'm putting you on speaker."

She did, and after their screamfest, Sabrina told them. "Feeling mighty special. Reporting live from Chicago. I arrived a few hours ago, picked up by a limo. Now lying around in a huge suite. This man is simply spoiling me."

"Oh, I like that! Way to go, Mr. Chandler." Amber's happy voice filled the room.

"Um-hmm. That's what I'm talking about," Jenay agreed.

"Where is he?" Aunt Connie asked.

"He's at the conference. He'll be back in a few hours, but he whipped by for a few minutes, with a bunch of red roses."

"Lookie here!" Amber exclaimed. "You've given new meaning to happy Thursday. You go! Are you going out later?"

"Yes, but our agenda is pretty flexible. He mentioned taking me to see The Magnificent Mile. I'm excited just saying the name. Of course, we'll go to church on Sunday. Oh, oh, I'm hanging out with his cousin, Chloe, tomorrow during the day."

They all cooed happily.

"Glad you're meeting more of the family," Jenay said.

"I'll meet his mom and dad, soon."

280

"You'll love The Magnificent Mile," Aunt Connie chimed in, not liking where the conversation was heading. "It's Chicago's largest shopping district. Look out for the tall buildings like the John Hancock Center."

Sabrina couldn't help but smile. "I sure will."

"Did he mention taking you to his home in Chicago?" Jenay asked.

"Hmm, no," Sabrina responded. "I didn't even think about that. He must not live in the area."

"Rinauto Aeronautical Corporation is near your hotel," Jenay informed her. "He couldn't live that far, but who knows."

"Stand down, Jenay. You're killing the joy," Amber chimed in.

"Well, at least ask him, Sabrina," Jenay insisted. "Tactfully."

"Rina, no, don't ask," Amber jumped in.

Sabrina remained quiet.

"What do you mean, Amber?" Jenay argued. "Are you expecting her to marry Chandler and not know where he lives?"

"Whoa!" Amber exclaimed. "Don't jump the gun."

Jenay was relentless. "Sabrina, you should at least ask him to take you to his office."

"No. Don't—" Amber yelled.

"Sabrina is a big girl," Aunt Connie said. "I'm sure she knows what to do."

"Yes. I'm good," Sabrina said quietly. "Thanks for watching over me, you all."

"Rina," Amber said in a serious voice, "keep us posted if anything exciting happens."

Sabrina smiled. "Thought you reserved that tone for Paul, when you're trying to keep him in line. As if you can," she teased.

"I sure can," Amber quipped.

281

Aunt Connie struggled to maintain a straight face. "Okay, ladies, let's keep it happy. We're going to leave you to take your beauty nap. Enjoy the Windy City. We're all praying for you and Chandler. Bye-bye, now."

"Byeeee," Jenay sang. "See you soon."

Amber couldn't hold it in any longer. "Rina, if he proposes, say yes."

Sabrina laughed. "Amber, I'll try not to restrain myself. See you all soon." She hung up, in the midst of Amber's protest.

Almost two hours later, Sabrina had taken a relaxing bath, dressed and created an upsweep hair do. Turning several times in front of the full-length mirror, she tugged her dress into place and adjusted her gold necklace. A knock at the door told her he was ready.

She opened the door and grinned back at Mr. Always-on-time, wondering if she could do anything dress-wise to disappoint him. She gave him a moment to take in the sheer beauty of her royal-blue, chiffon dress with a surplice bodice framed by sheer long sleeves. The billowing maxi skirt created a stunning finish.

Chandler embraced her. "You look beautiful."

"Thanks. Please come in," Sabrina told him, holding back a happy grin, for he'd confessed that her embrace had been a source of comfort when he'd first become her pet project.

Chandler locked the door and followed Sabrina to the living room. "You look happy," he remarked. "I must have something to do with that."

"Of course." Sabrina twirled. "This is a direct result of all the love you've poured on this fair maiden."

Chandler's heart rate quickened. "Happy looks good on you. I could do more, but it's going to cost you."

A smile spread across her face. "How much?"

"Just another hug."

She chuckled softly, hugging him, and kissing his cheek. "Phew! You're a serious negotiator. I'm glad that's settled."

"More happy coming your way." He smiled at her as she slipped into her cream-colored, wool-cashmere-blend dress coat. "You're bringing glamour to a very gray winter evening."

"Glad to." She flashed him a quick smile.

Soon, they exited the elevator and walked amidst admiring glances across the foyer. Chandler had eyes only for Sabrina, until a familiar voice called his name. Unconsciously, his hands tightened over hers.

Sensing the slight change in his demeanor, Sabrina edged closer to him, and witnessed a slender woman strutting, oh yes, strutting towards them. *Tall and glamourous*, was all she could think… and very pregnant.

Chandler didn't need to look to recognize Marcie's honeyed voice. She arrived before them and struck a model pose before pouting deliciously at Chandler.

"C.J.," she cooed seductively, "so good to see you."

Chandler's mouth almost fell to the ground. *Marcie, pregnant?* She wasn't wearing a wedding band. *For sure, God saved me from something.*

It was Sabrina's turn to stiffen. *What on earth?*

"Hi, Marcie," Chandler responded. "We—"

"I almost dropped dead." She gaped at him with her hand pressed to her throat. "I couldn't believe it was you and your fine self." She gave up a hearty laugh. "You handsome creature, you."

"Marcie," Chandler said slowly, "we are on our way out."

Marcie's tone changed from seductive to annoyance. "Aren't you going to introduce me to your," She gave Sabrina a bored glance, "little friend?"

283

Chandler's brows twisted in disbelief. He stepped away from Marcie, and moved Sabrina along. "Have a great evening, Marcie."

"He'll soon get bored with you, too," Marcie scoffed, as they passed her.

Marcie's exaggerated effort to label him almost made Chandler laugh. Now everything he used to do in his life 'back then' seemed so ridiculous.

Sabrina saw the tension in Chandler's jaw as they moved from the foyer to the waiting limo. *Interesting.* She whispered a quick prayer as they waited for the limo driver to open the door for her to get in. When she did, he closed it. Chandler walked around and slid in.

"Doc, is it okay to pull away?" the limo driver asked through the intercom.

Doc? Sabrina knitted her brows but didn't look at Chandler.

"Yes. Go ahead, Mike," Chandler responded.

Sabrina reached for Chandler's hand. "Are you okay?"

The warmth of her finger seemed to have encouraged him. He muted the intercom, and gazed at her. "I'm okay. I'm sorry about that. All that happened before I started walking in the Spirit."

Sabrina was glad he felt comfortable enough to share. She squeezed his hand. "That's okay."

Half an hour later, Sabrina looked around the semi-private room at the Palavala Restaurant and Lounge. *Fine dining, indeed.* She chewed on a bit of her shrimp scampi with linguini. *Delicious.* Her eyes landed on a smiling Chandler, admiring her.

She couldn't help but return that favor. He had traded in the power suit and tie for a more trendy attire—a navy, two-button, wool sport coat and navy pants. The vest and jacket appeared to be all in one, only the vest had a waist to chest zipper. His stark white shirt opened slightly at his chest and gleamed against the neck of his jacket.

He observed her taking him in and his smile widened, causing her eyes to twinkle. *That smile*, she thought. *Ohhh! You better stop doing that.*

"I take it the Food Dictator is happy," he remarked.

"Yes, my tummy stopped yelling at me."

Chandler laughed. "I told you to order room service."

"I didn't. Had to fit in this dress," she teased, chewing on another piece of shrimp.

"Mission accomplished." His voice dropped an octave.

Heat flushed her face. "You need to stop doing that."

He shot her a wide-eyed, what-now look.

She fixed him. "You know what I'm talking about. Gazing at me and talking to me in low seductive tones. I'm trying to keep it holy over here."

He feigned a look of shock and disbelief. "I wasn't aware I was gaaazing. Did I look star-struck, too? I'm trying hard to keep my emotions in check."

Sabrina exploded with laughter. "No words."

He eyed her over the rim of his glass as he sipped. "Delightful."

"What?"

"Your laughter."

Now she was blushing beautifully. He loved it.

285

CHAPTER 42

"You don't think this is too much?" Sabrina stared anxiously into the eyes of the woman she'd met after a late breakfast that morning.

"No. You look great." Chloe's dark brown eyes twinkled, as she looked up from where she was kneeling on the floor, making sure Sabrina's red gown fell appropriately in place. Smiling, Chloe stood and admired her handiwork. "He didn't say, but I have an idea where he's taking you. This red gown is perfect."

"I can't repay you." Sabrina smiled at her. They had hit it off from the get-go, when Chandler introduced them before he left for the conference. To her surprise, Chloe had taken her shopping in her high-fashion boutique.

Indeed, Chandler had decided this occasion was an ideal time to replace her dress… the one he'd thought he ruined with his tears when they first met.

She sighed.

Epic Failure. That's how she would define her efforts to wriggle out of his plans to buy her a dress.

Now, she was preparing for what was shaping up to be another spectacular evening. Last night was great. The hard part—he had left her at the door, telling her he didn't think it was wise to come in. Her knitted brows didn't faze him either. For just like that, he'd confessed, he didn't think he could handle it.

Later that night, he'd called asking if she was thinking about their wedding date. He didn't think he could wait an entire year, as she'd been hinting. Her mouth had fallen open at his line of reasoning. They had prayed before ending the call, but that conversation made sleep come later rather than sooner.

"I think you'll make his eyes pop. You look beautiful." Chloe clasped her hands under her chin, emphasizing her

286

heart-shaped face. "You're what we in the fashion industry would call an angelic beauty."

"Thanks, Chloe!" Sabrina grinned at her. "That is a huge compliment coming from someone who looks like a Victoria's Secret model."

Chloe returned her smile. "Stop it. I look nothing of the sort."

Sabrina admired her five-foot-nine frame. "You look great, and so trendy."

"Thank you! It was great hanging out with you. I'm going to slip away before Chandler gets here. Have fun! Lots of fun!"

Sabrina hugged her. "Thanks so much. Don't be a stranger, okay? And remember to pray for us."

"I sure won't. Yes, I'll be praying."

Sabrina walked with her to the door and waved goodbye before locking it behind her.

Back in the bedroom, Sabrina took a last look at her reflection in the mirror. The Valentino crepe halter, crossover bodice evening gown clung to her in all the right places without begging for unwanted attention. The fit-and-flare silhouette and illusion waist made her stand out. Her hair was styled in a loose, super-curly updo with tendrils at the back for extra oomph. A beautiful gold bracelet was clasped on her right wrist, highlighting her French manicure.

Ten minutes later, a gaping Chandler followed Sabrina back to the living room. His heart rejoiced. *God has been good to me.*

A tiny gold purse in hand, Sabrina turned and smiled at him. "I hope that's not a permanent look?" she teased.

Caught in the act, he smiled widely. "You are beautiful. I love everything."

"Glad you approve." She gave his black tuxedo a once-over. "You're looking great. Quite dashing, I would say."

287

"Thank you, my lady."

When they'd slipped into their coats, he held out his hand and she took it.

Half an hour later, Sabrina placed her spoon in the soup bowl. They were seated around a table in a private room at the award-winning, exclusive Babarra Restaurant, one of the two hundred and seventy five restaurants along The Magnificent Mile.

Surreal! She glanced again at the expansive views of the city from grand windows before smiling at Chandler. He looked comfortable, way too comfortable in this environment. In fact... he looked like this was where he belonged.

"You're so quiet," Chandler said to her. "Are you okay?"

Before Sabrina could respond, the waiters entered to clear their bowls. They laid out the rest of their meal to create what she knew would be nothing short of the ultimate fine-dining experience. *Delectable.* She found herself smiling as the servers presented each dish with pride before bowing and taking their leave.

She couldn't wait to dive into the delicacies. She picked up her knife and fork and cut a piece of the enticing veal strip loin, and placed it into her mouth. The *"Hmm"*, came out before she could stop herself.

"I'm glad you're enjoying it," Chandler observed.

"Yes, I'm loving this mouthwatering experience."

He smiled at her and then placed a forkful of rice in his mouth.

They ate in companionable silence for a couple of minutes until Sabrina decided she had to ask, "Are you going to let me break your bank account?" She grinned at him, playfully. "We'll need money for retirement. You may want to cut back."

"Rest assured, you're not breaking my bank account," he said confidently, stuffing down a piece of pistachio crusted rack of lamb.

She sent him an eyebrow lift. "I run the risk of sounding crazy, but where do you get all this money?"

He looked away for a moment then back at her, and quietly said, "I need to talk with you about several matters when we return to Orlando." He watched carefully for her reaction, but she continued to gaze at him, curiously. "That would include visiting my parents, my finances and," he smiled at her, "whatever else you need to know. You can relax, I'm not working for the mob."

"Oh, I have no doubt about that."

"Can we spend the time enjoying each other and our vacation?"

She exhaled, and then looked at him seriously. "I would love to, but it's going to cost you."

He straightened, intrigued.

"How much?" he asked, reaching inside his jacket.

"Just one little kiss."

He sighed loudly. "Gosh, you drive a haaard bargain." With that, he rose, walked to her, and sweetly pecked her cheek.

In the joy of the moment, she closed her eyes, opening them only when he'd stopped. "It's a done deal, then," she told him as he sat down and continued eating.

"This is really good," he told her, chewing. "You've got to taste this." Using his fork, Chandler picked up a piece of the lamb from his plate and placed it near Sabrina's mouth.

She opened her mouth and took it in.

"Hmm-umm," she murmured, chewing away. "That was really good."

He gazed at her and she stared back, before smiling at him. "What are you looking at?"

289

A slow smile rode his face as he rose and walked towards her. "Not sure what you're looking at, but I'm looking at you."

Her eyes fluttered up at him, but he expertly stuffed down his emotions.

"Come with me," he said, moving to pull out her chair.

She was reluctant to leave her entrée half-finished, especially when it was so good, but curiosity made her follow his instructions.

He held her hand and led her past the waterfall in the center of the room, towards the lounge area with pretty pastel-yellow sofas.

Thinking they were about to stop, she slowed to admire the tall floral arrangement on the mahogany coffee table. He moved her towards the glass wall, and the red and yellow sheer drapes parted.

"Oh, wow!" She clutched his jacket in amazement. The innovative designs of the spectacular skyscrapers decorated the skyline, but it was the cluster of ballerinas in pretty, floor-length red dresses on the white rooftop below that almost floored her.

Chandler's heart warmed and he watched as Sabrina clapped her hands in delight.

Amazing! "I wish I could hear the music," she murmured, as the dancers took up positions to start dancing.

Chandler signaled to the server and the room filled with music—"God Made You Special" by gospel recording artiste, Deniece Williams. He hugged Sabrina's waist, soaking in her excitement while she watched the dancers. When the dance ended with the dancers in a cluster pointing towards them, she tried to hide in his chest. That made him chuckle softly.

"They can see us," she whispered.

290

"You're busted," he said through closed teeth. "Wave or something."

Her gentle wave set off a flurry of activities, and the dancers separated and got in a formation.

"Oh my…" Sabrina couldn't wait for them to complete the design. "Ohhh… oh, that's beautiful. Two hearts." She clasped her hands in delight.

"Very creative," Chandler said.

To the count of steady drum beats, five tall, sturdy male dancers dressed in foil-stripe spandex pants, white shirts, suspenders and black hats and shoes, walked to the center of the two hearts and formed a vertical line.

"Wow!" erupted from Sabrina's lips. Jazz music filled the air as the five dancers were hoisted on transparent steps, each one higher than the next.

In unison, they turned smiling faces towards Chandler and Sabrina as if they were putting on a show for them. Sabrina was beside herself with excitement as the dancers, maintaining their vertical formation, pointed towards them.

Pop! Pop! Pop! Pop! sounded and four of the dancers held four signs.

"Woo-hoo, that's just beautiful. Someone is being proposed to." Sabrina read the signs, starting at the first dancer. "Will. You. Marry. Me. Her voice faded as an even louder *Pop* sounded.

The dancer at the top of the stairs held a sign—SABRINA?

A loud gasp came from Sabrina and she clutched Chandler's jacket, trying to grapple with what was happening. She turned her head out of his chest in time to see the huge screen covering the wall behind the dancers, displaying a photo of her and Chandler, and then went blank, before showing them at their current location.

291

"I love you," Chandler told her, hugging her waist, for her head was again buried in his chest. He kissed the top of her head, murmuring sweet nothings in a bid to calm her.

Sabrina's heart hammered as she lifted her head from his chest and witnessed him going down on one knee. Tears spilled down her cheeks. "I'm sorry," she told him, wiping her eyes with her fingers. "These are happy tears."

He waited.

That was okay.

She'd broken down the barriers he'd erected around his heart with the strength of her love.

When she was ready, he signaled for the photographers, then reached into his breast pocket.

Sabrina's tear-stained face glowed as he'd anticipated. He smiled, opening the black, velvet Tiffany ring box, and displayed the eighteen-carat diamond engagement ring.

"I'm in love with your spirit and the originality of you. Every time I picture my future, I see you beside me. I love you. Sabrina Abigail Benjamin, will you marry me?"

His voice was like a sweet caress as she tried to absorb all he was saying. "I love you, too! Yes! Yes!" She said it twice because once didn't seem enough.

Smiling, Chandler removed the radiant band from the box and slipped it on her finger, as the photographers clicked away.

"It's beautiful," Sabrina beamed, gazing at the crown of diamonds surrounding a striking center stone.

Chandler stood and gently kissed her before wrapping her in a warm embrace.

Forty minutes later, Sabrina was still gazing at Chandler like he'd found the solution for world peace. *Euphoric!* Her brain kept freezing and going back to the moment when he'd proposed.

Chandler indicated that their ride had arrived, and she resisted the urge to take another glance at the rock on her finger as they left the restaurant and moved towards the waiting limo.

"Congratulations, Doc and Miss Sabrina," a smiling Mike greeted them.

"Thanks, Mike!" Sabrina joyfully responded,

"Thanks, man," Chandler told him, looking pleased with himself.

Soon they were on their way. Sabrina glanced out the window, unable to help the smile that climbed her face and remained there. Everything seemed to be dancing as the limo zipped along The Magnificent Mile.

She was glad, too, that Chandler was happy. Even now his body was pulsing with excitement, where she rested at his side. She eased away from him and attempted to see his expression through the flashes of light from the street. He was gazing at her. She cupped his head and drew it down, and pressed her lips to his. "Thank you," she whispered against his mouth before leaning back.

He gently touched her face with his finger, then pulled her closely to his side.

"Why does Mike call you, 'Doc'?" she asked.

She felt him tense, before he quickly relaxed. "That's a long story. I'll add it to the list of things to talk about."

"That list is growing rather long."

"And I'm sure you'll have your list, too."

Busted. She chuckled softly, melting into his side.

CHAPTER 43

Back at the hotel, Chandler held Sabrina's hand and led her through the revolving doors. Still overjoyed, Sabrina's face held a permanent smile. Sleeping would be difficult tonight... for good reasons. She had to call her parents, Aunt Connie, the girls...

She was brought out of her contemplation when she felt Chandler's hand gripping her. *What now?* She glanced around, thinking Marcie might be on hand, but she was not in sight. She wriggled her fingers and Chandler relaxed his grip, pushing out a breathy, "Sorry."

The source of his discomfort burst on the scene. A short, Caucasian man in a dark-gray suit. Smiling, he gripped Chandler's outstretched hand. "Doc, good to see you."

"You, too, Mr. Chairman," Chandler said, while strategizing.

The man turned and bowed before Sabrina with a sweep of his hand. "You must be Sabrina. A pleasure to meet you."

Sabrina extended her hand and Chandler made the introductions.

"Sab, this is Rodner Calabazza, Chairman of the Board at Rinauto Aeronautical and Design Corporation."

"Nice to meet you, Mr. Calabazza."

"No. It's Rodner. You're a part of the family now."

She managed to whip out an effortless smile. "Rodner, it will be."

Sabrina felt slight pressure on her fingers, Chandler was trying to get away... but from what. *Doc?* That was coming up way too often. As the thought left her, Rodner spoke.

"Looking forward to getting to know you, Sabrina. Doc told me you're a professor."

294

"Yes, that is so," Sabrina responded.

"Glad that you're in Doc's life," Rodner said. "I couldn't wait to meet the fair maiden who stole his heart." He chuckled to himself. "I was beginning to think you were a figment of his imagination until he showed me a photo of you."

Sabrina lifted a hand to her chest and allowed her eyes to flash wide. "This is me, in the flesh."

Chandler seized the moment. "Good to see you, Mr. Chairman. We—"

"Glad to see you taking time out for fun, Doc." Rodner clapped him on the shoulder and then turned to Sabrina. "His mind is always working. That's what happens when you come from two creative people."

"Indeed." Sabrina played along, well aware of Chandler's discomfort. She tipped her head and glanced at him.

His gut sank instantly.

"Mr. Chairman, no talking about work today," Chandler scolded him in what he hoped came out as a playful tone.

Rodner sent him an eyebrow lift, before chuckling loudly. "No work! I can hear you, Doc. Isn't that your middle name?" He focused his attention on Sabrina. "I once heard a member of his team say that Doc's inventions felt like such a blow to his intelligence."

"Noooo," Sabrina smiled.

"He sure did, but I wish you could have seen him in action at the conference. Told him he should have taken you. His keynote address was one of the best I've heard. Sure reminded us of what a class act looks like."

"Thanks." Chandler smiled, but he still had a death grip on Sabrina's hand.

"Let me leave you two lovebirds. Julia," he looked at Sabrina, "my wife, must be wondering where I am.

295

Hopefully, we'll see you both soon. I'm sure Julia can't wait to meet you. Enjoy the rest of your night."

"We will," Chandler said, while Sabrina told him, "Thank you."

As soon as Rodner turned his back, Sabrina wriggled her hand from Chandler's.

"Sab—"

"Please save it, Chandler," she told him through clenched teeth.

Just then a bellhop approached them. "Dr. Benjamin. Please see one of our receptionists."

"Thank you," Sabrina told him.

Two quick steps placed Chandler beside her. She was mad and he knew it. "Sab, I'll explain."

She flashed him a sweet smile as they approached the large, circular desk. "I'm sure you will."

"Dr. Peynard," a male receptionist greeted Chandler. "Great to see you again, sir."

"Hi, Colin, great to see you, too," Chandler responded on automatic pilot, edging closer to Sabrina.

"One moment, Dr. Benjamin," Colin said.

Sabrina resisted the urge to step away from Chandler. She hated to create a scene but he was making it really difficult. In desperation, her eyes began to roam, landing on a magazine that rested on a table across from the front desk.

She did a double-take. The image looked familiar. She mentally shook herself, as the receptionist handed her an envelope. "Thank you."

"You're welcome, Dr. Benjamin," Colin responded, smiling. "We omitted to leave your discount packet in your room. Sorry about that."

"That's okay, Colin. May I have a look at the magazine behind you?" Sabrina asked.

Colin looked behind him. "Sure."

296

Chandler looked on curiously as Colin turned, picked up the magazine, and placed it before Sabrina.

Oh God! Chandler stared at the cover of *Aeronautical News Magazine.* He was laid out on the cover—gray suit, white shirt and red tie—perched at the edge of his work desk, pearly whites on display.

"Thanks, Colin," Sabrina managed to say with a blasé expression as she pulled her eyes from the bold caption on the cover of the magazine—"Dr. C.J. Peynard, Reinventing the Airplane. A man on the move."

Chandler's breath came out in gentle spurts and sweat beaded his back. *Why is the magazine sitting there?*

His answer came as Colin proudly told Sabrina. "My son and I are fans of Dr. Peynard. My son attends Dr. Peynard's Aeronautical Academy."

Sabrina pulled herself together. "That is wonderful, Colin. I'll return your magazine later, if I don't, I'm sure Dr. Peynard will have his office send one over." She couldn't help herself.

"Colin, I'll do that," Chandler chipped in, trying to cover the slight sarcasm in Sabrina's voice.

"Thanks, Colin," Sabrina said, moving away.

Once again, with a few steps, Chandler caught up with her. He slipped a hand around her waist as they waited on the elevator.

She cocked an eyebrow. "Please don't do that."

Chandler slowly let his hand drop back to his side.

The tension between them hit a new high as they stepped into the elevator. He punched the number to their floor.

"Sab, I'm sorry. I'll—"

His heart twisted when he saw her tears. *Oh God, please!*

297

The elevator stopped and they walked out in silence. At the door, he swiped his card, entered the code, and at the sound of the click, pushed the door in.

Without a word, Sabrina marched to her room door, swiped and pushed it open.

He was right behind her.

"You're bent on invading my space," she argued, wiping her eyes with the back of her hand. She moved to the living room just as a hollow laugh left her. "Oh, I forgot, you're paying."

"Sab, that's a very unkind thing to say. That is not you."

She glared at him, her heart racing with anger. "Wasn't it unkind of you to have lied to me?"

"I did not lie to you, Sab."

She could feel herself growing hotter. "You lied to me, Chandler. You lied by omission." Then, she counted on her fingers. "One: you made it seem like you were a regular employee. Okay... a bit more than regular. Two: you made it seem as if you were a regular attendee at the conference, not the keynote speaker. Three: your aeronautical academy—the one you told me you'd like to open if you had the money—is in full swing. Do I need to continue?"

Every muscle in his body tensed. He placed a hand to his chest and rubbed it. "Sab, let's talk about this."

"What's the point?" she argued, walking towards the coffee table. She dropped the magazine on it and took up her tablet.

"Of course we need to talk."

"See, you want to talk, and I don't." She entered the name C.J. Peynard in the Google search bar, and felt her heart thrashing about as she scrolled through the millions of results—discoveries, innovations, education, qualification, training, skills, projected net worth, family fortune, endless magazine articles...

298

She clicked on the images link, and her heart plummeted. The women on his arm looked nothing like her—super models.

Overwhelmed, she let the tablet fall from her limp fingers and bounce on the sofa. She raced out of the living room and into the bedroom as if creatures from the dark were on her heels.

By the time Chandler got there, she was racing around the room, throwing her clothes and other personal items into her suitcase.

"Sab, what are you doing?" His voice shook. "Please stop."

"Stop?" She eyeballed him. "Chandler, I don't belong in your universe."

From his sharp intake of breath, she knew she had struck a nerve. "You did not just say that, Sabrina."

Without responding, she continued to pack.

He rushed over to her and wrapped his arms around her waist, held her closely and begged. "Sab, please don't go."

She pushed at his chest. "Let. Me. Go."

He released her. "Please give me a chance to explain."

"There's no need." She walked away to pick up a small pouch from the dresser and on her way back to her suitcase, she stopped abruptly. "I don't know who you are," she choked out. "I fell in love with someone else."

"I'm the same person," he cried out. "Please don't do this to us. Does having money make such a difference?"

"It's not just the money, Chandler." She wrapped her hands around her middle in a protective manner. "You deliberately withheld information about yourself from me. I suppose you had to, though, because I would only want you for your money."

"Sab, don't say that. You know that's not true. None of it is true."

She stepped further away from him. "I need to go. I can't do this."

His heart cried out, he was sure of it. He closed his eyes as a shiver ran through his body. He had been in this position one too many times. *Lord, please help me!*

He moved closer to Sabrina and touched her shoulder, but she jerked away from him. They sized each other up, the ticking of the clock on the nightstand loud in the silence. Sabrina was the first to move—walking towards the dresser and stacking her jewellery into a blue velvet box.

Chandler's stomach lurched. "Sab, can we at least talk about this?"

Gazing at him with troubled eyes, she drew herself up, steel in her spine. "I can't right now. Please understand I don't mean to hurt you."

A sound rumbled in his throat and he took deep breaths, willing himself not to cry. He had to try again. "Sab, I…" In his mind, he saw himself falling at her feet, but he felt a hand behind him pulling him back, reminding him…

You bow to no one. You bow only at the name of Jesus Christ. I love you. I freely love you. I freely died for you, because I love you. Love cannot be forced, cannot be taken, it has to be given freely. Rise up! Rise up, oh mighty man of God…

Sabrina stared at Chandler, he was looking at her, but she couldn't read his expression. "I'll be leaving on the first flight that's available," she told him, carefully. "I'll pay you back for my expenses."

Sabrina's voice jolted Chandler back to the present. "No, it's all covered," he pushed out quietly. "Please let Mike know when you are ready for the airport."

She ignored the turmoil on his face. "Thanks."

300

And there it was... another moment when he knew his life was over. His chest on fire, Chandler stared at Sabrina before gathering what was left of his heart, and walking out of the room. He was hardly out the door before his heart stopped beating, then shattered into pieces.

CHAPTER 44

I can't believe I left the comfort of my home to be subjected to this kind of treatment, but love makes you push borders. Aunt Connie consoled herself as she walked behind the security officer to the bank of elevators. She sighed and the officer gave her an apologetic glance.

The last two days had been nothing but difficult. She knew Chandler had an important job, but this... this process to get access to him was one for the books. For the last two days, she'd been at Rinauto Aeronautical and Design Corporation, hoping to see him. She'd visited morning and afternoon, on both days, and no one could say when Chandler would be available. She put on a brave front when Ray Millon introduced himself as head of security, and told her she was not on the list of Dr. Peynard's family members. Still, she'd told him she would continue visiting until she was able to see him. His expression told her, *Have it your own way.*

Today, she was resolute. She had to see Chandler. She'd even packed lunch for she refused to leave this huge, off-white, marble lobby, with photographs of Rinauto's hallmark innovations and designs hanging everywhere. Silently, she'd started praying more fervently, because she had an hour to go before the building was closed to the public. She secretly rejoiced when one of the security officers approached and told her Dr. Peynard would see her.

The security officer took her to a room where she walked through a body scanner and the contents of her purse were examined. She almost stomped her feet, because she'd already had to pass through a metal detector before entering the lobby.

Before long, she entered the glass elevator along with the security guard and they journeyed to the twentieth floor.

302

As the elevator door opened, Aunt Connie was taken by the sea of red, white and blue in the carpet and décor. The officer led her through another foyer and into a huge office to a smiling older woman, who was dressed in a navy-blue tailored suit.

"Good afternoon, Mrs. Lanny, this is Connie Harper. She's here to see Dr. Peynard," the security officer said before taking his leave.

"Mrs. Harper, welcome!" She motioned to a set of plush blue chairs away from the desk. "Please have a seat. Dr. Peynard will see you shortly."

"Thank you." Aunt Connie smiled at the woman and then took a seat.

Almost ten minutes later, Mrs. Lanny walked over to Aunt Connie. "Dr. Peynard is now available. Please follow me."

"Thank you!" Relief washed over Aunt Connie as she followed Mrs. Lanny from her office into another large waiting area, lined with plush blue and white striped sofas, and a magazine table at the center.

Mrs. Lanny approached a double door, and knocked.

"Come in," Chandler said, his voice quietly powerful.

Mrs. Lanny opened the door. "Dr. Peynard, Mrs. Connie Harper is here to see you." She stepped aside and allowed Aunt Connie to enter before closing the door.

Aunt Connie's eyes struggled to take in the huge office—a twelve-seater conference table to the right, huge TV screen on the wall near the table, a set of plush blue and white striped sofas, and his desk—a mahogany monster bearing two huge computer screens on each side.

Her eyes shifted to a smiling Chandler who was on his feet and heading towards her. "Aunt Connie, it's great to see you."

"Great to see you, too, Chandler. I could do with a hug right now. I have been through the storm to get to you. I

303

just know they were planning to call the police if I returned tomorrow."

Laughing softly, Chandler hugged her. "I'm sorry. My assistant told me you've been trying to see me since Tuesday."

She eyed him as she pulled out of his embrace. "And I'm sure she didn't use those kind words."

A chuckle burst from his lips. "Come, let's sit," he pointed to the sofas. "Would you like something to drink?"

"No. I need to leave by five before they throw me out."

"You'll be fine. In that case, would you like something to drink?"

She smiled at him. "I'll have water."

"Okay." Chandler walked towards the conference table, took up a remote and pressed a button. A mahogany door on the wall slid back to reveal a stainless steel refrigerator and shelves with glassware, plates, and silverware. He took out a bottled water. "Would you like a glass for it?"

"No. I'll have it from the bottle," Aunt Connie responded.

Chandler grabbed two napkins before making his way towards her. He handed Aunt Connie the water and napkins, and then sat some distance from her.

She gave him what was her sternness look. "I've been calling you. And I left messages. I'm on your side, you know."

"I know... but I couldn't handle what was going on between me and Sabrina. I thought it was best to let it all go."

She clutched her heart. "You mean wipe the slate clean."

"Something like that. It has been difficult, but God is still God. I wanted to be bitter but I remembered that I haven't been perfect. Honestly, I think my heart was crushed in such a way that there were no more tears left."

"I understand," Aunt Connie said quietly. "Believe me, I do. But, I would like to speak to you as an older woman. I sensed that you've spent years carefully crafting out who you should be, but God has released you from yourself and set you on a path to the real you. I'm hoping that you'll stay the course."

Chandler sighed. "True, and I have no intention of going back. I'll be the first to tell you, I was hiding behind my emotional walls. But now, I'm leaving the affairs of my heart to the Lord. It's the third time I've been crushed in this way, and believe me when I tell you, the shock has not worn off. I remembered you told me to let Sabrina know, but I had no idea she would have taken the news that way. I was ready to put down roots." He paused to gather himself.

Right before his face, he'd witnessed his nightmare come true, and had been totally powerless to do anything to stop it. Sabrina, of all people, had knocked him off balance. Literally, kicked him off his axis. She was supposed to be a point of peace in this wonderful, but chaotic life. A place to rest his heart.

Seeing the storm darkening the horizon of his life was dreadful. He was ready to start anew, to totally get away from his old lifestyle. And, he'd done everything, everything to make sure God was with him, and that his new life with Sabrina was a part of God's plan. But once again, his joy had been snuffed out and he had found himself going through the seven stages of grief.

"I'm sorry, Chandler." Aunt Connie touched his arm. "Still, I'm hoping you haven't given up on love. Sabrina loves you. I think she was a little overwhelmed with the magnitude of who you are."

His eyebrows climbed. "Sabrina and I had gotten to know each other without the fluff and I liked that." He

305

pushed out a frustrated sigh. "Anyway, that's in the past. It was bad enough that I was emotionally disturbed, but I was embarrassed, too, because I had to pay to keep our engagement pictures out of the press."

"Oh no," Aunt Connie winced. "I'm sorry you had to go through all of that."

Chandler gazed past her as memories he didn't want came rushing back. Thanks to Chloe, his parents had heard and had been anxious to offer their support. They had used their influence on a few media houses that insisted on publishing the pictures.

Yet, in his moments of despair, Chandler was extremely thankful he'd given his life to the Lord Jesus Christ. In doing so, God had a permanent place in his heart. Thankful, too, that God had provided Pastor Jackson, who had been a tower of strength—visiting, calling, praying, fasting—making sure he stayed the course, and didn't fall into depression.

"If a thing doesn't break you, it will make you," Pastor Jackson had told him. "You decide. In fact, you can make the situation take you for all it can or you can decide that you will not only survive but you will strive."

Aunt Connie reached for Chandler's hand and squeezed it before letting go. "I know you love each other, and I'm asking you to give her another chance."

"She made her intentions very clear when she left Chicago. Right now, all I need to remember is that Jesus is my first and forever love." Trying to gain control of his scattered emotions, Chandler found himself asking, "How is she doing?"

Aunt Connie's woebegone expression had him bound. "Honestly, these days, she looks like she's working three shifts."

Chandler's eyebrows furrowed in surprise, but he said nothing.

306

"Chandler, all I'm asking is that you give her another chance. I'll talk with her and ask her to come here to see you. Please make sure they allow her to see you." Aunt Connie chuckled knowingly. "She's tender right now, so she won't have my patience."

A spasm of worry tightened Chandler's stomach. He was not ready to put his heart on the line again. Not ready at all. With all he'd been through, he was in a good place, right now. For, he had to believe God knew how much pressure he could bear. Strange but true, the breakup had fueled his faith... and his athletic drive. He was in his prayer closet and the gym more often than he could recall.

"At least give her a chance to explain, Chandler. You would have wanted that. Wouldn't you?"

What answer should I give this persistent woman. "I'll think about it," he told her.

She smiled at him, watching his face soften. "Thank you! It has been two weeks too long since you've seen each other. I'll make sure she's here tomorrow afternoon. Hope that's enough time for you to think about it. If she can't get in, then I'll take it for what it is."

He nodded just as the intercom beeped, stealing his attention. "Please excuse me," he said, moving towards his desk. He lifted the receiver. "Yes, Mrs. Lanny."

He waited a moment. "Okay. Thank you."

He hung up and turned to Aunt Connie who was already on her feet. "The Chairman has arrived and we have a meeting."

"No problem. I need to get out of here anyway. No matter what happens, promise you'll stay in touch."

"I promise." He hugged her and kissed her cheek.

CHAPTER 45

Two hours later, Aunt Connie was relaxing on Sabrina's sofa sipping fruit punch. Sabrina sat across from her, still awaiting the news of what had caused her aunt to show up at her doorstep, exhausted but seemingly excited.

"I can't wait anymore. Did you say yes to Brother Sel? Don't think I haven't noticed you're getting soft on him."

Aunt Connie chuckled loudly and pointed at Sabrina. "You've got to get your head out of the clouds."

"So you say," Sabrina quipped. "I've been watching you two."

"Okay, I'll admit, I was a little taken on Sunday when he shared his testimony. He looked dapper in that black suit, too. But, once again, he had to kill the joy." She pushed out a sigh, shaking her head. "After church, I saw him heading to his car, only this time he was rocking something looking like a Walkman." She laughed loudly. "Who does that? I keep telling you, that man is living in his own alternate universe."

Sabrina chuckled. "But you like that. He's bold and unashamedly so. You need a strong man, Aunty, and Brother Selvin might just be the one."

Aunt Connie looked at her. For all she intended to say to Sabrina, it might help if she told her she was going on a date with Nathaniel Selvin. "You know what? You could be right. Selvin invited me to the movie, I should probably go."

"Praise the Lord. A breakthrough at last!" Sabrina clapped her hands ecstatically.

Aunt Connie smiled at her. "I knew you would like that."

Sabrina returned her smile. "Oh yes! And, you'll have a great time, too."

"I'm going to take your word for it."

308

Aunt Connie looked at her and despite the joy of the moment, Sabrina's eyes held the same sadness that had shrouded her since two weeks ago, when they'd wept together, after her break up with Chandler. She'd encouraged Sabrina to make contact with him and sort out the affairs of their hearts, but to date Sabrina had not acted on her suggestion.

"How have you been holding up?" Aunt Connie asked, and then decided to lighten the moment. "No, don't answer that."

A burst of hollow laughter spilled from Sabrina. "No, you did not say that. Amber popped by today with her plump self and told me I was no fun. She and her baby were leaving because, and I quote, 'You're like a huge energy zapper, and that's the reason my baby and I are reluctant to visit you.'"

"Trust Amber to say what's on her heart."

"How is that supposed to cheer me up?" Sabrina asked. "And let's not forget, she was all over Chandler." She mimicked Amber. "'Smart and compassionate, hot and fine are great combinations, but all of that, plus man of God and rich—no words. You know what I'd do? I would marry him and not let him out of the house. And if he left, I would have a special app to track his every move.'"

Aunt Connie was laughing so hard, her stomach hurt. "Amber is right," she teased.

Sabrina's mouth gaped. "I know you're not supporting foolishness."

"Gosh, no, but you have to admit Amber is right in some respect." She chuckled. "Not the part about not letting him leave home."

Sabrina sighed. "Today, I realized why Sameria knows Chandler. She's studying aeronautics and she was an intern at NASA." Her lips thinned and she continued without waiting for input. "I should have Googled Chandler's name

309

like I'd planned. But of course, I had changed my mind since he only wanted to be friends."

Aunt Connie remained silent, knowing all Sabrina was doing was continuing to build her case against Chandler. Experience had taught her time was fleeting, as Chandler seemed bound on letting Sabrina go. She needed to nudge Sabrina in the right direction.

Sabrina watched as Aunt Connie drank the rest of the fruit punch and placed the glass on the coffee table. "I knew about Chandler and his family," Aunt Connie admitted.

Sabrina's jaw dropped. "Wha-what?"

"Yes, I Googled his name. I told Chandler, and he said he would talk with you about it. I also told your parents. We agreed it was Chandler's story to tell, since he'd already asked your parents for your hand in marriage."

Sabrina gazed away from her aunt as anger blazed through her. "Mom and Dad knew? So, I was the only one who didn't know?"

"Technically, your father knew first. He connected Chandler to his father. As you now know, the Peynard name is global."

"So you all decided, huh?" She couldn't keep the bitterness out of her voice.

"Watch yourself, young lady," Aunt Connie eyed her. "Remember now, a relationship is between the two people in it. We didn't discover anything bad about him. If we did, we would have found a way to let you know. Why does it matter so much that he has money? At first, you were only concerned about his well-being and the saving of his soul."

"It's not just-just the money." Her eyes brimmed. "He lied to me. Deliberately. He withheld information because he thought it would influence how I felt about him."

"You have to admit, you are the exception rather than the rule in that regard. Many women will marry a man for

310

what he can provide, and that may have been Chandler's experience."

"You're on his side now?" Sabrina's shoulders shuddered as she held back the tears.

Aunt Connie rushed to her feet and sat beside her, pulling Sabrina in her arms.

Sabrina gripped her aunt around her waist and sobbed quietly.

"There, there. Let it out," Aunt Connie comforted her. "It's going to be okay. God is going to take care of it for you." Aunt Connie began to pray for her.

Ten minutes later, Sabrina lifted tear-stained cheeks to look at her aunt. "Thank you," she managed to say.

"I love you, and don't you forget it."

That brought a gentle smile to Sabrina's lips, and she nodded.

"I could say a lot of things right now," Aunt Connie told her, touching her hand, "but I will say what is important and leave the rest for later. I have known you all your life. I only want the best for you. Baby girl, you're making a mistake in not taking a chance at life with Chandler. I know you love each other. But love is not just a feeling. 'Love suffers long and is kind; love does not envy; love does not parade itself, is not puffed up; does not behave rudely, does not seek its own, is not provoked, thinks no evil; does not rejoice in iniquity, but rejoices in the truth…'"

Aunt Connie paused to let that sink in.

"I see how you and Chandler balance each other, and I'm pretty sure you keep him grounded. I'm encouraging you to color outside the lines of your emotions, and take a leap of faith with him."

Her mind reeling, Sabrina chewed the inside of her lip. She'd tried to wake up several times from this nightmare since she had left the hotel in Chicago in the wee hours wearing sunglasses. The days had gone by in a blur as she had immersed herself in end-of-semester work and church activities, while attempting to erase her memories of a man named Chandler John Peynard.

Aunt Connie, Amber, and Jenay visited and called as often as they could. And by the look on their faces, she could tell she'd sprouted a third eye on her forehead...the one they were trying to get rid of, so they could talk with the real Sabrina.

"Sabrina,"Aunt Connie's voice brought her back to the present. "You owe it to yourself to at least try."

"I don't know if I can," Sabrina countered. "He's a lot to handle."

"You were doing fine before you knew about his wealth. Oh, I see what is the real problem. You feel like you have to measure up to some kind of standard you think he's accustomed to, or the women he has dated. You're not beautiful enough, sophisticated enough, well-spoken enough, knowledgeable enough... and the list goes on."

Sabrina looked at her hands.

"Lies. All lies you keep telling yourself. You don't have to be anything but you, Sabrina. You have all that Chandler needs. I'm sure if he wanted someone else he would have chosen another woman, but he loves you. What you need to do as a matter of urgency is sort out your little self-esteem issue and then go and see him at his office. Tomorrow."

"See him?" Surprise lit Sabrina's face, and she wrung her hands. "Oh no. Not ready for that."

"Sabrina, listen to me," Aunt Connie said, "you need to go and see Chandler by tomorrow afternoon. Please don't delay. I'm going to head home now. I can't begin to tell you what I've been through for the last three days; that's for another time. I'll call and pray with you before bedtime, okay?"

312

"Okay," was all Sabrina could muster as Aunt Connie rose.

She eyed Sabrina, her forehead wrinkling deeply. "And for heaven sake, please go to the hairdresser. Not sure why you insist on looking like the Lion King."

Sabrina could not help the snort that came from her lips.

CHAPTER 46

Color outside the lines. Leap of faith. Sabrina had heard expressions such as these, but she'd never faced anything like this before. *Help me, Lord.* She squinted in the afternoon sunlight as she pulled out of her driveway. The stillness in the air made the pounding of her heart sound too loud in her ears.

She rolled up the windows and attempted to collect her thoughts, but that was proving difficult; she'd barely slept a wink since praying with Aunt Connie.

Aunt Connie was right. She'd felt like a grasshopper in comparison to Chandler. *Grossly inadequate.* On top of that, she realized she was still carrying feelings of rejection from her relationship with Calvin. All brought to light when she'd looked at the photos of the glamourous supermodels hanging on to Chandler's arm. They reminded her of Kayanna, whom Calvin had chosen over her.

During her prayer time that morning, she confessed it all to the Lord. Her confession made her face burn, partly because she couldn't understand how she'd allowed herself to think those thoughts. With all of her accomplishments, she'd allowed fear and apprehension to corner her. This was a testimony she would give one day.

All things considered, she was now up and running on 'all cylinders' as Amber would say. With the Lord's help, she'd prayerfully let go of fear and anxiety, and was now up to the task of getting back the love of her life.

Almost an hour later, breathing fresh resolve, Sabrina pulled up at a busy intersection, and waited for the traffic light to flash green. Soon, she pulled off and caught sight of the state-of-the-art blue glass building, with huge gold letters announcing its name—Rinauto Aeronautical and Design Corporation.

She drove through the scanner at the entrance of the parking lot, collected her ticket, and parked. Her heart sped up as she walked towards the building. Pushing back a lock of hair off her forehead, Sabrina shivered as a blast of cool December air pushed against her body. She halted on the steps, to take a deep breath, before she pushed through the revolving door.

After passing through a metal detector, Sabrina swept into the splendid lobby. Her red stilettos clacking in perfect rhythm as she crossed the tiled lobby to the male security officer.

"Good afternoon. How can I help?" he asked from the circular desk.

"Good afternoon." Sabrina attempted a sweet smile. "I'm Sabrina Benjamin, and I'm-I'm here to see Chandler Peynard." Her voice sounded strange in her own ears.

"Dr. Chandler Peynard?"

Sabrina gazed at him, unsure whether he was reprimanding her for not using Chandler's title or trying to make sure he was the one she really wanted to see. She decided to maintain her cool.

"Yes. Dr. Chandler Peynard."

"Do you have an appointment?" he asked.

Her nails bit into her palms. "No, but he's expecting me."

He gazed at the revolving door, then back at her. "Please call his office for an appointment."

Sabrina nodded, pivoted, and headed straight for the door. She was halfway across the lobby when someone called out her name. Her legs shaking, she fought for a breath, as she turned and saw another male security officer approaching.

"Dr. Benjamin, I apologize for the mix-up. Dr. Peynard is expecting you. Please follow me."

315

Sabrina clutched her black purse tightly and followed him.

When she'd completed the relevant security checks, another security officer escorted her to Mrs. Lanny.

Phew! Relief filled her body as she sat in the waiting area. *Now to collect my thoughts.*

"Dr. Benjamin," a voice called out.

Sabrina jolted, staring wide-eyed at Mrs. Lanny. She hadn't even been aware that the woman had walked up to her.

"Dr. Peynard will see you now."

Sabrina's stomach clenched. *So much for collecting my thoughts.* "Thank you," she responded, standing and clutching her purse.

Chandler waited for Mrs. Lanny to close the door, before taking up the position of power in the room. He swiveled slighty in his black leather chair as Sabrina walked towards him.

Beautiful. He took in her chic, red, round-neck skater dress. *Leave your emotions right where they are—buried,* an inner voice warned him.

Sabrina summoned the courage to look at him. His white shirt and red and white striped tie complemented his navy-blue jacket, which sat well on his broad shoulders. Everything about him seemed as impeccably sculpted as she recalled. She smiled inwardly, but almost recoiled when she looked into his solemn eyes.

They regarded each other in silence, before she politely said, "Hi." *That came out way too breathless.*

Chandler's Adam's apple bobbed. "Hi." He motioned towards the set of blue chairs before his desk. "Please have a seat. How are you?"

"I-I'm…" A sigh stuck in her throat and she swallowed it down, "doing okay," she continued, taking her time to sit. She opened her mouth to speak, just as his phone rang.

316

"I need to get this," he told her, picking up the receiver. "Mrs. Lanny?" His voice was filled with authority. He paused to listen, then said, "Yes, thank you."

He paused for a second time, leaning back confidently in his chair. "Mr. Chairman, I'll be delayed, about fifteen minutes. I've asked Michael Inglewood to do the preliminaries, and by then I should be there." He paused to listen again. "Yes… yes." Then, Chandler almost laughed out. "I cannot answer that, but I will see you shortly."

He hung up, beating back a smile that found its way to his lips.

Mr. Chairman had asked him three questions.

Is Sabrina sitting before you?

Are you going to give her a chance to explain?

Did your heart rate go from zero to a hundred?

Chandler had told him what happened between them. Needless to say, the Chairman was very apologetic for his role in the breakdown of the relationship. He had not ceased to encourage Chandler to try again. When Chandler told him that perhaps Sabrina would stop by, he was on board.

Got to love that man. Chandler turned his attention to Sabrina. "Sorry about that. I have a meeting, so I'll have to leave shortly."

"No problem. Thanks for taking the time to see me. I've missed you." She paused for his response.

Silence greeted her.

Nervous energy filled her, but she pressed on. "Chandler, I'm sorry for dismantling our relationship." She paused again, hoping he would say something, but his silence persisted. She smoothed the skirt of her wrinkle-free dress then gazed at him. "Please say something."

"Like what, Sabrina?" His lips thinned before his words stumbled out. "Like you left me for dead." He pulled forward in the chair, a bitter smile twisting his lips. "You

317

didn't even give me a chance to explain, even though I told you I wanted to talk with you when we returned to Orlando. Instead, you took the easy way out. Which is crazy, at least in my mind."

He felt himself growing hotter by the second. "The only reason I didn't tell you, Sabrina, was because for once—just once—I enjoyed being appreciated for who I am. For being me, with my good, bad, and quirks, and not my bank balance. I wasn't trying to be deceitful. All my life, everyone wanted to be in my circle, for so many reasons. You have no idea. You should have known I wouldn't do anything to harm you."

Guilt pinched her insides. "I'm sorry." She bit her lips, trying to find a way to express her feelings. She had to get the truth out. "I-I was overwhelmed by the situation. The truth is, I felt inadequate…to handle your lifestyle," she said softly. "And, I didn't feel beautiful enough to be by your side after seeing the women you had dated."

Surprise lit his eyes. He would have laughed if she didn't look so serious. "Sabrina, you're the most beautiful, most intelligent woman I have ever met. If I wanted someone else, I wouldn't have proposed to you. You have everything that I ever needed in a…" He paused, realizing he was becoming emotional.

She jumped in. "I get that now. Everything was happening so fast. I couldn't breathe."

He stared at her, fighting off myriad of emotions that swirled in his stomach. "If that's it, then—"

"Chandler, please." Pressure built in her chest. "Let's try again."

Her soft tone sounded like velvet in his ears. God, he missed her, but he wouldn't be sucked in.

Sabrina's bravado chipped in. "I love you. I pray for you with gladness in my heart. When I am with you, I know that's where I belong because you make me come

318

alive in ways I have never experienced. And when I look into your eyes," her eyes brimmed, "I see the depths of your heart and I love you even more." She leaned forward and pleaded, her voice a mere whisper. "Let's try again. I don't have a lot of regrets in life, but I think this would be my biggest."

Lacing his hands on his desk, Chandler summoned a confident voice. "I don't know if I want to, Sabrina. You might run away again, and that might kill me." His forehead bunched. "No, let me not confess that. That will set me back."

She clutched her hands to her chest and looked at him. "So you'd rather give up on what we shared? I love you. You know I do."

Denial died on his tongue, and he searched his mind for words that wouldn't betray his feelings. "By the looks of things, apparently, it takes more than saying I love you to keep a healthy relationship." Then, with extreme force of will, he tried for a casual shrug as he looked at her. "Clearly."

"I'm sorry." Regret swamped her and she sagged against the back of the chair.

Praying.

Waiting.

Hoping.

Minutes ticked by without Chandler speaking, and Sabrina prayed silently, again.

Keeping his features schooled, he finally broke the silence. "I'm sorry, too."

Shell-shocked, Sabrina pulled her resistant body forward on the chair, and then reached into her purse. "This… this…," she choked back a cry, "is yours." She placed her engagement ring on his desk and raced from his office.

Oh God! Chandler gripped the arms of his chair so he wouldn't leap across the desk. That exchange had told him his heart was in deeper trouble than he'd thought.

He sat there staring at the door, long after it had slammed shut.

Over an hour later, Sabrina returned home, a feeling of defeat threatening to weigh her down. Tears spilled down her cheeks, once again. She'd embarrassed herself for nothing. Pulling a piece of tissue from the box on the sofa next to her, she mopped her now swollen eyes, and discarded the tissue on the floor where several other pieces were scattered. *Lord, please ease the pain in my heart,* she cried out silently.

The ringing of the doorbell stole her attention and she sat up, but didn't move. She remained quiet, hoping that whoever was there would go away. No such luck. This time, the beeps came in rapid succession. She hoped it was Aunt Connie, because she needed a good cry.

She balled up the sodden tissues and placed them on the coffee table. Clearing her throat, she approached the door and looked through the peep-hole. *Oh God!* She backed away, stunned, her eyes widening as her breath caught.

It was Chandler.

Quickly, she determined her approach. "Who is it?"

"You know it's me, Sab. Open the door," he encouraged.

During his meeting after Sabrina had left his office, he had not ceased thinking about her and her petrified expression.

Sabrina, Sabrina, Sabrina. His gut knotted as reality hit him hard. And, in the middle of his meeting, his love for her blossomed. Intensified. And that equated to one thing— "I still love her."

320

Sudden silence greeted him, and his heart lodged in his throat for the many smiles that had met his wide-eyed expression told him he'd verbalized his thoughts in the middle of the meeting.

Smiling, the Chairman had told Chandler that Michael Inglewood would take over the meeting. "Bring us back good news," he said, smiling.

He didn't need to persuade Chandler to take off; he was out of his seat like he was being chased by hungry wolves.

"Open the door, Sab," Chandler said gently.

"I look a mess." She rolled her eyes inward. *I did not just say that.* "I mean, I can't see you right now."

"I miss you, too," he told her.

With trembling fingers, she pulled the door open.

"Hi," Chandler said, stepping in and locking the door. "What have you...?" His heart accelerated as her blood-shot eyes met his. He'd caused her tears—again—and he couldn't stand it. Before she could blink, he effortlessly scooped her up in his arms and began raining feathery kisses on her forehead.

Sobbing loudly, Sabrina buried herself deeply in his arms.

He sat on the sofa and cradled her on his lap. "Don't cry. It's going to be okay."

She clung to him even more.

Chandler glanced at the tissue box on the sofa and the balled tissue on the coffee table and his heart broke. His velvety voice filled with longing, he comforted her. "I love you. I love you so much." He felt her trembling against him and held her tighter.

When her cries subsided, he mopped her eyes and wiped her face with tissue from the box. A contented purr came from her lips before they curved in a smile.

"There you are." He gazed unblinkingly into her swollen eyes, before his lips opened to expose perfect teeth as he smiled. "You had me worried for a moment."

Sabrina snaked a hand around his neck and tugged his head closer. "I love you." Then, without hesitation, she kissed him—soft, sweet, yet tentative.

"Hmm!" Chandler groaned softly, caught by surprise, before masterfully leading the way.

Darts of electricity fired through Sabrina and she arched against him, shuddering and squirming softly as he transported her into another dimension.

Fiery passion blazed between them. Each making up for the time lost during their separation.

Stop! seemed to be bouncing everywhere in Chandler's head. Sabrina's scent was dizzying and the softness of her body against his was driving him wild. He was fighting for self-control. Breathless, he lifted his head, against her soft cries of protest, knowing they were heading for trouble.

Her chest heaving with desire, her breath came out in small, whispering puffs as she stared up at him with longing, yet understanding.

His body pulsing, Chandler pulled in a deep breath and smiled at her, his expression thankful. In pulling back, they both understood what they were doing. They were choosing to honor Him.

CHAPTER 47

"Praise the Lord, Church!" Chandler said, smiling at the podium, with a beaming Sabrina by his side. "I am glad to be in the house of the Lord this morning. I am expecting God to do exceedingly abundantly above all I can think or ask."

A proud Pastor Jackson looked on as if his 'child' had turned out to be all he'd ever wanted him to be. He'd just announced Chandler and Sabrina's engagement, and the congregation had gone wild. He had to stop the celebration in order to pray for Chandler and Sabrina.

"As you all know, this is a special day for us, but more so for me. I want to say thank you to Pastor Jackson and by extension, Elder Joy. Pastor Jackson, I couldn't have asked for a better spiritual..." He paused to collect himself and Sabrina squeezed his hand reassuringly. "I couldn't have asked for a better spiritual father, leader, brother, and friend. You have prayed for me, counselled me, and lifted me during a crucial time in my life. Thank you."

Chandler turned and gazed at Sabrina. "My fiancée, you are God's gift to me. All my life, I've wanted a place for my restless heart and I thank God that you pointed the way to Jesus Christ. I love you with all of my heart."

At that, the congregation roared with joy, and Sabrina smiled and patted his shoulder, mouthing, "I love you, too."

Chandler smiled at Sabrina before continuing. "Mr. and Mrs. Benjamin," he looked at them in the congregation, "thank you for the gift of Sabrina. Thanks, too, for accepting me in the family. Truthfully, I felt accepted from day one. And, thanks for an unforgettable Christmas dinner." He glanced around. "Where is my Aunt Connie?" She was not in her usual spot. He smiled as she waved from the back right side of the sanctuary.

"My dear lady, you are my she-ro," Chandler said to her.

Pockets of bubbly snickering were heard all over the congregation.

"Thank you. I love you." He paused to embrace Aunt Connie who had walked forward.

"And, lest I forget," Chandler said, "thank you, my church family, for helping me to walk in the Spirit."

The congregation clapped loudly.

"At this point in my life," Chandler told them, "I only want what God has for me. I have discovered that it is not about how small or great I am in this world; it is about discovering my God-given purpose and walking in it. I have done many great things, but let me confess not all my actions were great. But I've placed my shame, my guilt, my pain, my fears, and my hurt, at the foot of the cross.

Today, I stand here as a witness to the grace and delivering power of the Almighty God. I am a witness that God can save you and keep you. If you ask me who I am, I will gladly tell you I am a witness. A witness to what God can do in your life, if you let Him. I am living proof that God's grace wins every time."

The congregation cheered, but Chandler held up his left hand. "God has liberated me so I am not ashamed of the gospel of Jesus Christ. "For it is the power of God unto salvation to everyone that believeth."

"Amen! Amen! Amen!" the congregation roared in response.

"I will conclude my testimony with a song." Chandler heard Sabrina's gasp, but did not look around. "It's called 'Grace Wins' by Matthew West."

He looked at Sabrina and smiled. "I'm going to ask my fiancée to help me sing. Please continue to pray for us."

With that, Chandler handed the microphone to Sabrina. "You can stand next to the keyboard," he murmured. "I wanted to surprise you."

"Consider me surprised," she said, smiling, before walking to her spot.

Her level of curiosity ramped up. She had no idea he'd been practicing the song, even though he'd been to some of the rehearsals when she was practicing her songs for the opening of the center. Thankfully, she was always bobbing her head and singing loudly, when he played the song in his car.

Oh my! Her mouth hung open as the chief musician got up and Chandler sat behind the keyboard. *Good surprise,* she told herself, just as she had last week before the opening ceremony for the center, when he'd told her that he had paid the extra money to do the state-of-the-art rooms she had yearned for. She had pardoned him; after all, his heart was in the right place. True, too, she had to hold ugly back when he mentioned that he hadn't done a background check on her, but most likely his parents had.

Chandler's voice snapped Sabrina back to the present. She smiled encouragingly at him, as he spoke.

"Grace!" Chandler said. "Let me introduce you to God's amazing grace."

He began to sing, and before long the congregation was singing along, some on their feet dancing. The praise dancers danced all over the sanctuary, helping to create a celebratory atmosphere. Sabrina could hardly believe her fiancé had such a great voice, and had the swagger of a rock star—high-spirited, yet soulful as he testified in song.

Shouts of joy and praises filled the sanctuary as Chandler sang the last line of the song—"But I'm living proof, grace wins every time." The congregation wanted more and he gave them more, repeating the song, after a firm nod from Pastor Jackson, who celebrated with his hands in the air.

Chandler wrapped up the song, testifying, "God has a sacred place in my heart. God saved me and if you are not saved, He can save you, too."

With that, he headed for the baptismal pool.

He was baptized by Pastor Jackson.

CHAPTER 48

"Are you okay?" Chandler's concerned eyes met Sabrina's as the limo driver pulled away from the Ronald Reagan Washington National Airport in Washington, D.C.

Bubbles of joy welled up within her and she smiled into his eyes. "I'm fine."

For a long minute, Chandler gazed at her, his eyes searching the face of the woman he'd grown to love deeply. Her feminine presence seeped through his senses, and he continued to look at her and was satisfied.

They were on their way to his parents' home.

Sabrina was thrilled about meeting them, and from conversations, it appeared his parents were equally delighted. Chandler's parents had sent their private plane to pick them up in Chicago, and now they were being chauffeur-driven to the mansion.

For the last two days, they had been in Chicago at Chandler's home. Oh, he insisted—no more secrets. They'd travelled on a private jet, along with her parents and Aunt Connie. Mike, who Sabrina now realized was Chandler's personal chauffeur, had picked them up at the airport and transported them to Chandler's home.

She'd anticipated Chandler's home would be luxurious, but wow, it was spectacular—a penthouse suite that took up the entire floor.

Everything was impressive. From the Bond-like private elevator to the incredible view from the wrap-around balcony overlooking the city. Shades of blues, gray, and silver dominated the twelve-foot ceiling home—four bedrooms including master bedroom, kitchen, formal dining and living rooms, family room, bathrooms, study and gym. Still, its design, furniture and decorative accessories made her feel at home.

After they'd completed the tour of his home, Chandler had dared to ask, "Is it to your liking?"

What's not to like? She'd smiled at him. "It's gorgeous."

They had agreed that after they were married, they would make Chicago their permanent home, because Chandler's job was about to ground him there; however, when they were in Orlando, they would live at Chandler's townhouse. Sabrina had decided to put her home up for rent, but Chandler convinced her to sell it to him, insisting that he would pay her the value for it. He wanted to purchase it for Sister Susan—another secret mission he was undertaking with Pastor Jackson.

She eased away from Chandler and gazed at him as he read from his tablet. She'd come to realize how hard he worked, and oftentimes wondered how he'd found time to spend with her, back in the day.

Last night at Chandler's home, she had peeked out several times and saw the light still on in the study. Before breakfast that morning, she had asked him if he'd slept, and he told her he got in a few hours.

Breakfast. *Oh boy!* That had been an extravagant affair—spinach and cheddar mini frittatas, cheesy sausage croissant casserole, onion flavored york-style bagels, freshly baked treats, fruits, and an assortment of hot beverages. All prepared by Chandler's private chef who believed in starting the day right, with a fancy breakfast.

According to Chandler, all this, so they could get some well-deserved rest.

Rest! Heat rushed up Sabrina's face when she recalled Chandler teasing her at breakfast.

"You were snoring loudly when I entered the living room last night," Chandler said. "I don't think your parents and Aunt Connie got any rest."

Sabrina tilted her head and challenged him. "Weren't you working all night?"

"I took a break and that's when I discovered you snoring in a new language."

Belly-laughs echoed in the dining room and Sabrina burst out laughing, too.

How could I not snore? Sabrina thought. Fatigue had set in and she was at rest in a soothing sanctuary with cozy bedding, that shouted *Relax and escape everyday life!* The pleasant warmth in the home helped, too, for it was all snowy on the outside. "The usual in Chicago, at this time of the year," Chandler had told them.

Wish I was in that bed right now. Sabrina chuckled softly, then realized Chandler had stopped reading and was watching her.

She grinned at him.

His eyebrows climbed his forehead. "This is awkward."

She waggled her eyebrows. "What?"

He poked her side. "You know what."

"You did not just poke me, knowing you're ticklish."

He chuckled softly. "It won't happen again."

"Yes, right after I…" She jabbed a finger in his side several times and he doubled over laughing. His tablet fell to the floor of the car.

"Stop!" He grabbed her hands. "You'll stop, right?" he whispered against her lips.

The woodsy scent of his cologne filled her nostrils, and she fought the urge to kiss him. They hadn't kissed in forever… thanks to him. They were 'keeping it holy.'

Her heart stuttered as his gaze dropped to her lips.

His mind begged him to reconsider.

He didn't. His head swooped and he captured her lips in an intense kiss. When he felt like she'd had enough, he pulled back, releasing her hands, but stayed in place.

329

Breathless, Sabrina spread her hands on his chest, itching to kiss him again. It wouldn't take much; he was so close.

Chandler smiled at her, enjoying the rise and fall of her chest. "Couldn't help myself," he confessed quietly. "But that," he touched her cheek with his index finger, "that is a bad idea." He didn't want to but he slowly turned back to his reading.

She grinned at his profile, knowing he'd read her mind.

Tugging on her green dress, she set it back in place, and then sank into the warmth of his side.

In three months' time, she would be a married woman.

Married! A grin climbed her face.

There was a lot of planning to be done. Thankfully, her team—Jenay, Amber, Aunt Connie, her mom, and Chandler's mom—was competent. Things were shaping up for an unforgettable day.

Sabrina was glad her mother-in-law had made herself available. Veronica Peynard had pulled off an amazing feat—booking the elegant indoor Grand Ballroom at the Waldorf Astoria in Orlando. It was booked out every Saturday in March, but after pulling a few strings, Veronica had made it happen. They had to schedule their wedding an hour later than they had originally planned, but that was alright.

Life is good. Exhausting right now, but good, Sabrina thought.

"We're here," Chandler broke into her thoughts.

"Oh. Great!" Sabrina glanced ahead. *Oh. Wow.* The opulent Mediterranean-style, three-story mansion was impressive up close. Its beige, stone roof stood out.

From what Chandler had told her, the twelve-bedroom, fourteen-bathroom property had undergone three renovation processes to ensure that it remained a modern masterpiece.

330

The limos pulled near the circular driveway, edged with lawn and plants, to enter the massive garage.

"Ready?" Chandler searched her face for a moment and then offered a hand.

Smiling, she nodded and took his hand. Before long, she stepped out of the vehicle.

Several attendants dressed in black slacks and white shirts greeted them politely, and began taking their luggage from the limousines.

Chandler escorted Sabrina, along with her parents and Aunt Connie through a beautifully decorated foyer and into a huge entryway with two marble staircases on the right and left. They greeted a male attendant in the entryway as he opened a mahogany double door. Chandler ushered the party into a formal dining room where his parents greeted them.

Hugs all-around.

Sabrina was glad to meet the incredible pair who would be her in-laws.

Veronica Peynard's face lit up, mirroring a smile just as delightful as Sabrina's when they embraced. Her eyes were the same light brown as Chandler's. And as Sabrina anticipated, she was tall and slender, towering a little over her. Her soft skin was the color of honey and her sleek, brown hair hung down her back. Her laughter was infectious, expressing what Sabrina thought was her eclectic style.

Sabrina glanced at Julius Peynard as he greeted her parents. He'd accepted her hug, even though at first, it seemed he would have been content with a hand shake.

Standing around six-foot-four, Julius' frame looked like someone who had recently lost weight but Sabrina could see where Chandler got his more muscular build. True, too, Julius was not as handsome as Chandler, but his charisma and influence would be hard to overlook in a

331

crowd. And, there was something about him that drew the eyes, perhaps his rugged handsomeness.

After pleasantries were exchanged, Chandler insisted he would escort everyone to their rooms. Tired as they were, the magnificent setting energized them, and before they knew it, they were on a mini-tour.

Oh, what a tour! Sabrina thought.

The mansion's amenities included a library, theater, wine room, heated pool, sauna, gallery, media room, gym, roof garden, and wraparound marble terrace.

Rich, yet warm, earthy colors welcomed them along the stairways and corridors. Everything about the home was vibrant…everything in place, and perfectly fitted to convey the wealth and personality of its owners.

On the first floor, softer shades of greens created a tranquil ambiance in the bedrooms that would be occupied by her parents and Aunt Connie, however, when Chandler escorted Sabrina to her bedroom on the second floor, a sea of white greeted her. Gold accentuated the room to brighten up the space.

An hour and half later, Sabrina sat at the dining table in the sunken dining room, listening to happy banter. It was surreal to see Chandler in his childhood environment. A natural fit. She'd noticed that Chandler looked like a combination of his parents. She'd observed, too, that Chandler's mother was happily accommodating him, but his father was more reserved.

Sabrina glanced up at the fabulous crystal chandelier that hung from the thirty-foot domed ceiling and refracted the light. She could stare at it forever.

Service was also top-notch. They were treated royally, every step of the way.

After dinner, while the others retired to the family room, Chandler decided to snatch his fiancée away. He held Sabrina's hand as they walked along the corridors on the ground floor towards the gallery. She slowed their pace to admire the details of the beautiful family portraits framing the wall along the lengthy hallway.

"Ohhh, look at baby you!" she exclaimed.

"Yeah. Yeah." Chandler barely stopped, gently tugging her along.

She bumped him with her hip, and chuckles erupted from him.

As soon as they entered the gallery, Sabrina barely got a chance to notice the expensive paintings. Chandler closed the door with a thud, then halted. When she swung around, his eyes were glued to hers.

"Are you doing okay?" he asked, concern evident in his expression.

"Yes. Everything is great."

He cocked a brow. "My parents weren't too much?"

"No. They were super-cool. It was wonderful meeting them."

The warmth in her gaze melted his lingering doubts, and before Sabrina realized what was happening, he hoisted her into his arms and began to twirl.

She hugged his shoulders, girlish giggles erupting from her lips.

Chandler carried her to one of the stylish, red leather benches in the room. He straddled the bench, and pulled her into his arms, crushing her in a fierce hug.

He released her, but his lips were tantalizingly close.

She couldn't look away.

Energy gushed through her, blotting out all the reasons kissing him would be a bad idea. Before he could object, Sabrina hooked her arms around his neck and kissed him— savoring slowly.

He caressed her back, not wanting their kiss to end.

Sabrina released his lips. "I love you," she whispered, desire darkening her eyes.

A moan jumped from his throat, before he dropped his head in the crook of her neck. He wanted her, and he wanted her bad.

She held him in her arms, until their sparks of desire slowly drifted away.

CHAPTER 49

The following day, Sabrina woke up in a glorious mood. She couldn't stop singing praises unto God. She was blissfully surprised that Mr. and Mrs. Peynard asked them to gather for devotion, along with the staff.

"Way to run a household," she told a smiling Chandler while they were heading to breakfast.

Half an hour later, they were eating to their hearts' content—smoked salmon eggs Benedict, tomato-herb frittatas, toast, baked goodies, fresh fruits, and a variety of hot beverages.

Sabrina grimaced. *Weight gain is inevitable.*

Chandler smiled warmly at her, and she returned his smile. He'd been kind and attentive, making sure her new environment didn't overwhelm her.

"I need to snatch you away for some us-time," Chandler said.

"Can't wait." Sabrina grinned at him, and he almost snatched her up. They were still gazing at each other when he noticed the silence around the table. He prepared himself, and glanced up. Yes, everyone was looking at them.

"I can't wait for this wedding to happen." Aunt Connie came to their rescue or so they thought. "But somehow I doubt anything will change."

Everyone started laughing.

"I hope not," Chandler piped up.

When the laughter died down, Veronica spoke. "Chandler, please don't run off with the bride-to-be, I need to speak with her."

"Mom, I thought you were all going out in another few hours to do women's stuff." He knew they'd made a schedule of activities for the entire time they would spend with his parents.

"Yes, dear," Veronica answered, "but I need to see Sabrina to run through a few things."

"Honey, that's alright," Sabrina said. "We'll get together after."

"Thanks, Sabrina!" Veronica flashed Sabrina a grateful glance. "Chandler, you can have her in another hour. Unless our girl talk goes on forever," she teased.

Chandler opened his mouth to speak, but his father beat him to it.

"Chandler, I need to see you, if you don't mind. Perhaps, this would be a good time."

Chandler reined himself in. "Okay, Father."

Half an hour later, Chandler followed his father into the study. Their relationship had been anything but vibrant. It didn't help that his mother was constantly trying to get them to have a conversation. Chandler absolutely hated when he called and his mother would ask, 'Do you want to speak with your father?' How could he say no? His father was in the same room with her. He'd spoken with his mother about her interference but she'd feigned shock, claiming she was 'doing nothing of the sort'.

Chandler closed the study door, and sat on a brown leather chair in front of the desk. He watched his father gazing out the window with his hand stuffed in his pockets. Chandler swallowed the emotion that was building inside him. He hadn't noticed his father had grown a bit thin.

His whole body tense, Julius stepped away from the window, and sat behind the desk. He rested his elbows on top of the desk. "It was nice to finally meet Sabrina and her family," Julius began. "I can tell you love her, and she definitely loves you."

Chandler nodded and waited. Well, he was trying to process where the conversation was going.

"I'm happy you're happy, son, and I'm very proud of you and your accomplishments. I-I know..." Julius Peynard

336

struggled to find the right words. "I know I haven't been a good father to you. I'm sorry."

Chandler remained silent, his gaze darting between the trees and the buildings outside. He could hardly believe his father was apologizing.

"I'm sorry," his father repeated. "I allowed everything in my life to take precedence over raising you."

"Father, I hear you, but I'm a little too old for this. I'm about to have a family of my own, and trust me, I intend to be a great dad to my children." Hurt laced his eyes as he spared his father a glance.

"Chandler, all I'm asking for is another—"

"Another opportunity? Another chance?" Chandler's voice went up an octave. "Where were you when I needed you, Father?"

Julius' heart fell. "I'm sorry, son. I wish I could change the past."

"But, you can't." The memories had cut way too deep for Chandler. The harshness in his eyes fought against the melancholy in his father's eyes.

Their conversation was over.

Chandler walked out the door. Aggravated, he paused to collect himself before moving on. He hoped Sabrina was finished with whatsoever she was doing with his mother.

Laughter rose as he approached the family room and he paused to listen. He attempted a pleasant expression before knocking. Both ladies smiled as he entered. "I was checking if you're done," he said looking at Sabrina, who sat next to his mother on the circular, blue leather sofa.

"I need another fifteen minutes," Sabrina told him. She examined his face. Something wasn't right. "I'll make it less."

"Call me and I'll meet you in the gallery."

"Okay. I will." She watched him until he left the room.

337

Veronica remained quiet for she realized Chandler's conversation with his father had not gone well. *Oh Lord, I'm back on my knees.*

"Where did two hundred and fifty guests come from?" Sabrina asked.

"You would be surprised," Veronica responded. "Jenay told me she included only the parents of the dancers who are close to you, and some of the senior dancers."

Sabrina ran over the guest list on her tablet. "Jenay will lose her position as matron of honor for this."

"And Amber will gladly fill in," Veronica told her. "I can't wait to meet her. She has such a colorful personality."

Sabrina chuckled. "That's Amber for you. I'm surprised she bowed out of being on the bridal party. Never thought her plump belly would stop her. Although that hasn't stopped her from hauling herself on her soapbox to have her Oprah moment about me and Chandler."

"Yes, considering she—," Veronica smiled and air quoted—"brought you and Chandler together. Anyway, Chloe was more than happy to fill in."

"Glad she was able to. I know we're all tired of Amber and her soapbox," Sabrina said, with a blank expression. "I assigned her to read the Scripture."

"I'm glad you found something for her to do."

"Oh, she would have it no other way." Sabrina couldn't stop the scowl that crept up her face, causing Veronica to chuckle.

"Accent pieces. Bouquets. Cake. All checked," Veronica said. "Bridal Party? Has Chandler decided on his—?"

"Yes. Had to drag it out of him. Don will be his bestman, and Michael Inglewood will be the groomsman."

"Okay, great. That takes care of the program, too." Veronica glanced at the checklist, then looked at Sabrina.

338

"I have to admit I didn't see you all using red, but I love it. So timeless."

"I agree." Sabrina said, even though her thoughts were resting heavily on Chandler. "Everything looks great."

Veronica placed her tablet on the sofa beside her.

Sabrina watched as her lips parted, but Veronica hesitated, then looked at Sabrina.

"Please say what's on your heart, Mrs. Peynard," Sabrina encouraged.

A wordless moment passed between them as Veronica considered her words. "Thank you for loving our son, and for giving him what he needs to continue the next leg of his journey. I'm so glad he found you. You have touched his life in so many ways. Your love has saved him, changed him, and healed him. Thank you so much. I can only see the blessings of the Lord following you both."

She paused, and Sabrina waited.

"I don't know how much Chandler has divulged about me and his father. Julius and I were not the best parents. Frankly speaking, we would not be getting any award for parenting. Now that we've found the Lord, we see the folly of our ways back then. We love our son. He's all we have, and we're trying hard to build our relationship with him. Even more so now…" She paused and her eyes welled up with tears.

Sabrina moved closer and squeezed her hands reassuringly.

Veronica wiped her eyes with her finger tips. "Especially now that Julius is ill. He's very sick, Sabrina. The doctor diagnosed him with lung cancer."

Sabrina clutched her hands. "Mrs. Peynard, I'm so sorry to hear. We will be praying and helping in whatever capacity you need."

"Thanks, dear. By the time we discovered it months ago, it had already progressed to stage two. Meaning, the

339

cancer is present in the underlying lung tissues and nearby lymph nodes. He has done surgery and is now going through chemotheraphy. It's not spreading into his chest wall, so we're grateful to God for His healing power."

"I'm glad you caught it," Sabrina rejoiced. "Thank God."

"Sabrina, my relationship with Chandler has been improving, and I would like for his relationship with his father to get off the ground. It would be good for Chandler and I know it would be great for Julius' health." She breathed a sigh of relief, glad to get all that off her chest.

"Mrs. Peynard, I understand. As you know, I have a great relationship with my parents. I'll do everything in my power to encourage Chandler along in his relationship with you and Mr. Peynard."

"I'm grateful for you, Sabrina." Veronica hugged her tightly. "Thanks for accommodating me."

Sabrina squeezed her tightly, too, before letting her go.

God is good, Veronica confessed as she watched Sabrina leave the room.

She was glad she didn't break from her decision not to hire Alana, even though she was the most suitable candidate for the job. She wouldn't do anything to jeopardize her relationship with Chandler. Anyway, she'd only given Alana a chance to interview because of the relationship she shared with Alana's parents.

Ten minutes later, Sabrina sat beside Chandler on one of the red benches in the gallery. She listened while he recounted his conversation with his father.

Shoulders hunched, Chandler confessed. "Babes, I thought I had forgiven him." He gazed at her for a moment.

Her heart went soft, but she allowed him to continue.

"But when he starts talking, all I hear is him telling Mom how dumb I was as a child."

The knots in Sabrina's stomach kept tightening as she saw the anguish in his eyes. "Honey, your dad has recognized he was not a good father to you." She rubbed his back. "Now, he's telling you how proud he is of you and your accomplishments. Can you try and flip the switch and hear his heart? Instead of hearing him saying, you're dumb, can you replace it with, I'm proud of you?"

He sighed deeply, knowing what she was trying to do. "I'll try."

She hugged his shoulder. "That's great."

"Father was looking rather thin," Chandler mentioned. "I wonder if he's not feeling well. He was looking a bit shaky in his office. For a second, I was concerned."

When she didn't respond, he eyed her. "What is it now?"

"Your mom just told me your dad was diagnosed with stage two lung cancer."

Stunned, Chandler gripped her hand.

And that grip told Sabrina things would never be the same between Chandler and his father. He needed his father as much as his father needed him.

CHAPTER 50

"Happy New Year, everyone!" Julius Peynard said, walking towards his wife and kissing her cheek.

A chorus of "Happy New Year!" rang out.

"Sabrina, I hope you left enough breakfast for me," Julius teased, taking a seat at the head of the table.

"I sure did. Plenty, too." Sabrina smiled at him. "If you had delayed a bit, then who knows?"

Julius laughed. "I thought you had my back."

"I do. I would have given you a bit of Chandler's. And speaking of my beloved—where is he? He's really enjoying his swim."

"Saw him heading to his room," Julius remarked. "Said he wasn't hungry."

"Oh boy!" *That's a first.* Sabrina glanced across the table and found Aunt Connie giving her the side-eye. *What did I miss?*

"I need to speak with you," Aunt Connie mouthed to her.

Sabrina's eyes popped, and she nodded, cramming the last piece of her cheddar eggs Benedict in her mouth.

Aunt Connie motioned towards the door and they excused themselves. Together, she and Sabrina walked in silence to the gallery.

Aunt Connie! Just the thought of her caused a tiny smile to curve Sabrina's lips. Her aunt had eventually confessed that in an effort to help love along, she'd visited Chandler's office. Three times. She didn't divulge their conversation but despite all she'd been through to see him, she felt it was well worth it.

Still, Sabrina realized she wasn't the only one in a happy place.

Nothing shocked her more than when her aunt had confessed she would be attending the wedding on the arm of Brother Nathaniel Selvin. According to her, "He made me an offer she couldn't refuse."

Dumbfounded, Sabrina had stared at her, questions about to roll off her tongue, but Aunt Connie had lifted a hand and cut the conversation before it got started. Stunned, she had tried again, but her aunt had told her she had to run, murmuring, "Why didn't anyone tell me Nat had turned over a new leaf?" That day, she had sauntered from Sabrina's home, looking like the world was at her feet.

Aunt Connie had been tight lipped about the nature of her relationship with Brother Sel; however, Sabrina had overheard a telephone conversation that confirmed things were syrupy between them.

Sabrina opened the door to the gallery and allowed Aunt Connie to enter first. As soon as they were seated on one of the red benches, Sabrina asked, "What's going on?"

"I'm not trying to meddle in your affairs, but I think Chandler needs your attention. We've been busy planning but I sensed that he misses you."

"Really?"

"Yes. He was rather reserved at dinner last night, while we were fussing about wedding stuff, and he didn't make it to breakfast this morning. I think you should spend some time with him today. I can't recall what's on the agenda, but you should make him your agenda."

"Okay," Sabrina said quietly. "Thanks. Let me try and find him."

"Okay. See you later," Aunt Connie said, making her exit.

Lord, have mercy! Sabrina let out a sigh, deciding to text Chandler.

Sabrina: *Hi honey! Where are you?*
Chandler: *Why?*
Sabrina: *I miss you.*

343

Chandler: *Why?*

Sabrina: *That's not the response, I was anticipating.* ☺

Chandler: *What answer were you expecting?*

Sabrina: *Can we meet somewhere? Please don't ask why.*

Chandler: *Meet you in the gallery.*

Sabrina: *Wonderful. (Beating-hearts emoji)*

No response from Chandler.

He's not in a sparkling mood, Sabrina thought. She began to pray silently.

Since Chandler's baptism around two weeks ago, she realized that added to his many credentials, her husband-to-be was a rock star evangelist. She'd had many flashbacks of his magnetic appeal when he'd sung at church.

After church, many in the congregation had wanted him to sing again. He belted out "This Is Amazing Grace" by gospel recording artiste, Phil Wickham. Each time he sang the chorus, "This is amazing grace; this is unfailing love...," it seemed like a jam session was happening in the sanctuary.

Even more amazing, when it was over, several of the younger members of the congregation flocked him, asking if he could help them form a junior band. Chandler had looked surprised but told them yes, as long as Pastor Jackson agreed.

Pastor Jackson was thrilled with the idea. They'd brought up the subject at the end of their premarital counselling session that week.

Sabrina was brought back to reality when the gallery door gave way to Chandler's touch. He entered with long strides and lowered himself on the sofa beside her.

"What's up?" he asked dryly, not making eye contact.

A man-pout? No way! Sabrina hugged his shoulder, but released him when he didn't warm to her embrace. "You look like you've lost your best friend."

344

He shrank back, rubbing the back of his head, and then resting his hands on his thighs.

Sabrina moved closer to him, and rested her hand on his back. "Honey, what's wrong?" She had realized from day one that he had issues expressing himself when he felt emotionally hurt. She waited patiently.

He exhaled, still not looking at her.

She moved to kneel between his legs. "Are you missing me?"

His gaze grew soft, and he nodded, his shoulders drooping. Clearly, feeling bad for reacting the way he did.

She moved in closer to him. "I'm sorry. I was caught up with everything. We'll spend the day together."

"It's not just that," he added slowly, "the wedding seems to be getting out of hand. Why is the guest list so long? I thought we agreed to only close family and friends."

Her mind raced. She didn't want to disappoint the Peynards and her parents. She took a deep breath. She had to figure out her priorities, and from now until forever, Chandler was always going to be more important than the rest of them. "Okay, I'll take care of it. Keep it intimate like we agreed. What else?"

He was quiet for a moment. "I like how we are when we're in Orlando. Feel like I'm losing you... like we're drifting apart. I know you're planning, but I still want to be your... pet project."

Sabrina wrapped her hands around his neck and kissed his cheek. She loosened her hands to rub his head. "Thanks for telling me. I know that was hard." She kissed his forehead. "Always let me know how you feel. I want to know so I can fix it." She gazed at him, tenderly. "You make me so happy. I want you to know that your happiness is very important to me. I love you."

He pulled her closer, wrapping his arms around her. They held each other for a while, as tightly as they could, saying nothing.

Minutes later, Chandler kissed the top of her head, and told her what had been on his heart. "You have seen me on the worst day of my life, yet you were not daunted, you stuck by me day after day. I don't think I can adequately express how much I appreciate you for saving me that day. Thank you." He kissed the top of her head again, choking out, "I love you. I will always love you."

Her heart melted, and she held him closer, telling him softly, "I love you. I will always love you." Then, she began to pray. "My Lord and my God, You are worthy to be praised. Thank You for Chandler John Peynard, my beloved, my husband-to-be. Help me to be a good wife, a companion and friend to him. Oh God, I realize that I cannot do it without Your help. Work in me whatsoever it takes to accomplish this so he'll be proud to say, This is my wife.

"Show me, oh, Lord, how to love him unconditionally and to communicate my love in a way that he'll understand. Help me to create a home that he'll be happy to enter. And Lord, as he rises to a place of leadership in our home, help me to be engaged in our decision-making and to support and respect his decisions.

"Make us a team, Lord, working together to achieve that which You have planned for us. May we be committed to each other, 'perfectly joined together in the same mind and in the same judgment.'

"Lord, teach me how to pray for him. Grant me wisdom to understand his dreams and aspirations. Help me see him with new appreciation daily. Thank You for giving him to me. In the name of Jesus Christ, I pray, amen."

"Thank you." Chandler used the back of his hand to wipe his tears, before he prayed.

"Father, thank You for Your presence. Help me to grow more in love with You daily so that I'll grow more in love with my wife-to-be, Sabrina Abigail Benjamin.

"Lord, You are the giver of all good and perfect gifts, and I'm grateful that You have entrusted her into my care. I celebrate and love the grace and beauty that You have bestowed upon her. Help me to love her, Lord, in ways that she will appreciate. Help me not to disappoint her, fail her, or make her sad. May I always be in awe of the love we share.

"Give her a heart that will always long to do Your will. May she respond to You with increasing love. I pray that she will continue to be an ambassador of Your love so that others will see You in her.

"Help us in this in-between place to continue to honor You. I pray that our love for each other will grow stronger each day. May we take pleasure in fulfilling each other's desires in our marriage. Unite us, by Your Holy Spirit and give us revelation knowledge so we'll know what You want us to do daily. In the name of Jesus Christ, I pray, amen."

They squeezed each other before moving apart.

"Thank you," Sabrina said as she returned to where she'd been sitting on the sofa. She looked at Chandler and giggled happily. He was looking at her with a goo-goo-ga-ga expression—full of love.

"I decided to work on my relationship with my father," he told her.

Sabrina's eyes filled with tears and she grasped his hand. "I'm sorry. These are happy tears. That's wonderful. Thank You, Jesus."

"We're taking it slowly," he told her. "Please continue to pray for us."

"I sure will."

"Thanks." He smiled at her. "I'm really happy that my parents have decided to reach out to Don and his family… again."

She returned his smile. "Yes, me, too. I'm amazed at what God is doing."

"Indeed." Chandler beamed. "On another note, I would love for us to minister together in song. I enjoy worshipping with you."

Her eyebrows rose and she gave up a wide grin. "You are rocking my world right now. I would absolutely love that."

He quirked his eyebrows. "In that case, I want to show you something," Chandler said, rising and reaching for her hand.

She took it, allowing him to lead her out of the gallery. Three doors down, they stopped. Her eyes flashed wide as she waited for him to open the door and when he did she gasped.

Inside was a music room equipped with several instruments.

"Oh. My. Goodness!" Sabrina exclaimed, sweeping the room with her hand. "This is now my favorite spot in the house."

"Mine and yours." Chandler chuckled, moving to turn on the keyboard, before walking across the room to the sound board and pushing buttons on it. He glanced at Sabrina who was standing next to him. "Please test two of those microphones on the table."

"Sure!"

Sabrina was only too happy to test the cordless microphones, which she took out of a case. She walked towards Chandler, who now sat touching buttons on the keyboard. Then, she placed one of the microphones on the stand near the keyboard.

He glanced up, smiled at her, and positioned the microphone closer to his mouth. "We will bless the Lord at all times," he declared, hitting a few keys on the keyboard. "His praise shall continually be in our mouths."

"Amen," Sabrina responded on her microphone. She watched Chandler as he caressed the keys with passion. She smiled inwardly, knowing they would no doubt be setting up a studio in their own home.

Chandler began the introduction to the song "Flawless" by the gospel recording group, MercyMe, and it struck Sabrina how much he seemed to enjoy contemporary Christian music.

"There's got to be more than going back and forth…" Chandler sang the first lines of the lively song, swaying with a glorious expression on his face.

Sabrina joined him in the chorus, "No matter the bumps, no matter the bruises…"

They were in full-blown praise by the time they sang the last line of the chorus—"The cross has made you flawless."

Suddenly, the doorway was filled with their exuberant parents and Aunt Connie. With a sweep of her hand, Sabrina joyfully encouraged them into the room.

EPILOGUE

"The heavens declare the glory of God..." Chandler thought, as he star-gazed on the balcony of Sandals Royal Caribbean Hotel, in Montego Bay, Jamaica. He had originally had Paris in mind, but he was glad Sabrina had suggested this hotel for their honeymoon. They'd struck a compromise—a week in Jamaica and a week in France.

"An absolute island paradise!" was Sabrina's description two hours ago when they'd walked the white, sandy beach and admired the clear blue water that stretched to meet the horizon.

There were many options at this stunning utopia, with great amenities, and friendly yet respectful staff. After their walk, they'd happily settled for a sunset dinner, in an appealing gazebo perched on a pier overlooking azure waters.

The service had been impeccable. A private waiter served their four-course gourmet meal at a table covered with crisp white linens and decorated with a tropical floral arrangement and candle light.

A smile curved Chandler's lips as he thought about the happiness that had shrouded the face of his little food dictator while they ate. He didn't have to ask if she was enjoying herself; Sabrina had been glowing all over. He liked to think he'd contributed to her radiant countenance.

He recalled how she'd blushed when he had asked her to dance after dinner. There was no music in the gazebo, but they had danced. He'd given her his undivided attention... in preparation for what was to come later. A smile climbed his face for even now, he was consumed by that single thought, and he couldn't wait.

The wait to have her had been downright painful. Absolutely so. Anyway, he felt he'd worked for the rite of passage. He'd worked through praying and fasting... more

350

praying and fasting, reaching out for help from Pastor Jackson, who had become his accountability partner. Against his will, he'd even put in extra measures—keeping away on days when seeing her was too much to handle, telling her on other occasions it wouldn't be wise to visit, and he'd put in some serious time at the gym.

Tonight, he was ready to dine with his wife in a new way.

Wife! He could hardly believe he was saying that word.

He smiled, glad the Lord was now writing the story of his life. He'd stepped into the light of grace and God had taken him out of his comfort zone, stretched him and set him on a path that was sure to bring many victories. Above all, God's love had awakened his heart, and made him a suitable husband for Sabrina. She stirred something deep inside him that he couldn't remember feeling… ever.

To that end, he hadn't even tried to contain the tears flowing down his face when she'd entered the church that morning. She had looked stunning in an exquisite, white Oscar de la Renta wedding gown. The A-line gown had a scoop-neck, cap-sleeves, and an incredibly long train. Pretty elbow-length white gloves complemented her gown. She looked every bit like a queen with the silver sequin crown on top of her head.

Hanging onto her father's arm, Sabrina seemed to have floated up the aisle to him. Her face had glowed with a smile reserved just for him. God, he had felt special. His joy was now complete, for he was not only marrying the love of his life, but he was also marrying his best friend.

Just then, Sabrina walked to the balcony door and jerked to a stop when she saw her husband resting on his elbows against the balcony rail. His back to her, he was stirring her most primitive instincts. No shirt. A pair of jeans hugging his muscular thighs. She couldn't resist ogling her husband's athletic build.

351

Her heart leapt, recalling their wedding day. *A day of beauty and elegance. A day filled with love.* She distinctly remembered standing at the entrance to the church, while Amber adjusted her veil, but all she wanted to do was sprint up the aisle to Chandler.

Soon, she had latched onto her father's arm, and when the pianist started to play, they took the walk. Yet while she had smiled at the attendees, her heart was set on getting to her beloved, and with good reason.

Looking sharp from head to toe, Chandler owned the day, even with his tears. He was as handsome as ever, suave in a black tuxedo that was made for his body. A white wing-collar shirt was the perfect companion for his suit, along with a black bowtie and highly polished black shoes. A dash of character was added with a red pocket square.

She would always remember when Chandler took her off her father's arm. He'd flashed a heart-stopping smile like she was the only one in the room. She'd had to remind her heart to beat again. Lovingly, he waited for her to regain her composure before moving her forward towards a smiling Pastor Jackson.

Tonight, as nervous as she felt, she was looking forward to the consummation of their marriage. The waiting period had been extremely hard for Chandler. Truthfully, it was hard for her, too. Whosoever said, 'what you never had, you'll never miss' was lying through his or her teeth. There were days when she desperately wanted to jump Chandler and do unimaginable things to him. She could hardly believe her thoughts. Oh, the struggle had been real!

Adrenalin surged through her and she called out his name.

He turned at the sound of her voice. *Oh! Oh my!* His heart slammed against his ribcage. Nothing could have prepared him for her flirty white chiffon, baby doll lingerie, which was made transparent by the light streaming from behind her.

He scooted away from the balcony, his eyes fastened on the eye-catching lace details where her twin mounds were begging to be released from the white silk bow that held them in place. He stopped in front of her, commanding his hands to stand down.

Sweet Jesus! Sabrina gaped. Barefooted. Bare-chested. Every muscle prominent. Chandler's jeans were open at the waist, exposing his ripped lower abs. "Ho-honey," she stuttered softly.

"Yes." His eyes sparkled with mischief. Oh, he wanted to play.

Sabrina's eye lashes fluttered as she gazed up at him, swallowing hard.

He almost chuckled aloud, but for the vulnerability in her gaze. She had his attention and didn't know what to do with it. He came to her rescue. "You're finished with the bathroom, I take it. My turn?"

She grinned self-consciously realizing what he'd done. "Yes. Hurry back."

Hurry? His jaw felt slack. He was sure his tongue had hung out of his mouth, for he had wanted to consume this woman who had become his wife. Before Sabrina realized his intention, Chandler scooped her up in his arms, walked to the bed, and gently laid her on it. Smiling, he told her, "I'll be back before you know it. You. Look. Yummy."

A hot flicker appeared in her eyes. "Hurry," she told him breathlessly, her eyes not leaving his.

The intensity of her gaze caused something delightful to stir within him—something delightful and oh-so-familiar. He rushed from the room to the bathroom. *Hurry! That I can do.*

353

Fifteen minutes later, Chandler slid under the bedcovers, braced himself for the impact of touching her, and then pulled her into his arms. His eyes wandered over her face taking in her beauty, and then settled tenderly on her eyes as if they held the answers to all the mysteries of life. He had wanted nothing at all, until he'd found her. His Sabrina. His *"everything."*

"Chandler." Sabrina's voice was appealing, yet filled with uncertainty.

"You're not supposed to be calling out my name yet," he teased, looking down at her. "You've got to wait for that part."

Nervous laughter erupted from her lips and her body ignited, ready to embark on a new adventure.

A surge of tenderness rode Chandler and he caressed her face with his fingers. "You're absolutely beautiful, my wife." His tone all velvet. "So beautiful. Don't be nervous. We'll take it slowly. I love you." He was glad that came out calmly, because every nerve in his body was on full alert.

A delightful expression filled her face. "Okay, I won't." Eager to make herself available, she looped an arm around his neck, brought his face within inches of hers and pecked his lips.

Surprise flashed in his eyes and his whole body reacted. He accepted her invitation, pressing an open kiss to the sweet hollow of her neck, once, twice, thrice...

Barely breathing, Sabrina gripped his shoulders, moaning softly as his lips seared her skin, before traveling along her jawline towards her mouth.

Savoring her delightful feminine sounds, Chandler claimed her lips, kissing her softly at first, and then exploring her mouth—deeply, fiercely. Oh, the rush, the thrill that went on and on.

Pressing her body flush against him, Sabrina responded with equal passion, her hands roaming his body,

354

everywhere. *Closer. Closer.* She maneuvered her body, trying to attach herself to him, begging for relief. She almost screamed aloud when he pulled his lips away. *No! Please! Not now!*

Adoringly, Chandler gazed at her face. He loved her more with each passing day. Now all he could imagine were extraordinary days and unforgettable nights with her.

But he couldn't gaze at her for long. Her chin was tilted, desperate for more of him, and he dared not disappoint his wife. He leaned in and allowed his lips to duel and dance with hers, unleashing emotions that would not be held in check.

Tantalizing.

Intoxicating.

All-consuming.

She melted into him wherever their bodies touched.

Hungry for every ounce of her, his hand slipped under her lingerie—slowly, teasingly—blazing a path upward.

Tonight, her pleasure would be his pleasure.

Not a moment would be wasted.

Every touch connecting their bodies.

Every kiss connecting their souls.

There was an understanding between them, an understanding far beyond words. Thousands of tomorrows later, their love, faith, and friendship would remain strong. All because they had discovered the most secure place for their hearts—Jesus Christ. For in Jesus Christ, they would always be satisfied.

READING GROUP GUIDE

01. Which of the characters in *A Place For My Heart* did you identify with most, and why?

02. Why was it so difficult for Chandler to acknowledge his love for Sabrina?

03. What do you like and dislike about Chandler's character?

04. Why do you think Sabrina was not immediately attracted to Chandler?

05. Why was it so difficult for Sabrina to talk about Chandler with Jenay?

06. Was it strange that Sabrina found herself with self-esteem issues?

07. How did you think Sabrina handled Chandler's commitment issues?

08. Veronica Peynard asked for Sabrina's help with building her relationship with Chandler. What are your thoughts about that?

09. Brother Nathaniel Selvin made Aunt Connie an offer she couldn't refuse. What do you think that offer entailed?

10. How would you explain Amber's colorful personality?

11. What are your thoughts on the role that Pastor Anthony Jackson played in the story?

12. Was there any advice that you could relate to?

13. Did you understand why Chandler felt he was a recipient of God's grace?

14. How well are you guarding your heart?

CHANDLER'S SONGS

Grace Wins
By Matthew West

YouTube Link:
www.youtube.com/watch?v=tZ9dvAWNvsw

This Is Amazing Grace
By Phil Wickham

YouTube Link: www.youtube.com/watch?v=rjXjkbODrro

Flawless
By MercyMe

YouTube Link: www.youtube.com/watch?v=wjLILPZderk

A NOTE FROM THE AUTHOR

I am delighted to continue the *Encounters of the Heart* series, with *A Place For My Heart,* a compelling account of a most unexpected love. As always, I am glad to share what God has placed on my heart.

A Place For My Heart is Book 3 in the *Encounters of the Heart* series. This series is based on Proverbs 4:23 –"Keep your heart with all diligence, for out of it spring the issues of life." Although the books are in a series, they are also stand-alone novels. Book 1 - *Shades of the Heart* (www.amazon.com/dp/B00T512KQ2) is a novel about the courage to love in the midst of broken promises, and ultimately about the healing power of forgiveness. Book 2 – *Mirrored Hearts: Sealed by Fire* (www.amazon.com/dp/B01AKUA4UK) is a deeply stirring and satisfying novel that recounts the struggles of two broken hearts, mended by enduring love, and sealed by fire.

Thank you for taking the time to read *A Place For My Heart,* and for your continued support. I pray that the story of Chandler Peynard touched your heart in a meaningful way, and that you experienced the amazing grace of God as you read. Remember, "Love suffers long and is kind; love does not envy; love does not parade itself, is not puffed up; does not behave rudely, does not seek its own, is not provoked, thinks no evil; does not rejoice in iniquity, but rejoices in the truth;" (1 Corinthians 13:4-6)

May God continue to bless you on your journey. Stay victorious!

With love,
Ann Marie

359

ABOUT THE AUTHOR

Ann Marie Bryan is a dedicated, graceful, multi-talented leader with a passion for excellence. She is the CEO & Founder of Victorious By Design, an organization committed to providing top quality professional writing services, comprehensive personal and professional development programs and exceptional performing arts services to meet the unique needs of individuals and organizations.

A Christian Fiction author, Ann Marie writes to educate, inspire and empower others. She desires to tell great stories with fascinating characters to show the awesome power of God in the lives of people and places.

Ann Marie's greatest passion is to empower others to succeed by tapping into their God-given potential. She enjoys writing, reading, dancing, teaching, meeting people and traveling.

CONNECT WITH THE AUTHOR

I would love to hear from you. Please let me how *A Place For My Heart* may have spoken to you. As always, I would like to hear your testimonies about God's faithfulness. Let's stay connected!

Email: abryan@victoriousbydesign.com
Website: www.annmariebryan.com
Twitter: www.twitter.com/authorabryan
Pinterest: www.pinterest.com/authorabryan
Instagram: www.instagram.com/authorabryan
Newsletter: http://eepurl.com/bOw6sr
Facebook: www.facebook.com/authorannmariebryan

JOIN MY FACEBOOK READERS' GROUP
Ann Marie Bryan's Reader's Café
www.facebook.com/groups/authorannmariebryan

PLEASE WRITE A REVIEW
A Place For My Heart

Amazon
www.amazon.com/Ann-Marie-Bryan/e/B008VTK62O

Goodreads
www.goodreads.com/author/show/6448888

AVAILABLE TITLES
BY ANN MARIE BRYAN

Unforgettable, My Love Has Come Along
A Circle of Love Novel

Two paths, destined to cross. Friendship, faith and love are intertwined in ways neither could have imagined. Can love conquer all things? Find out in the heartwarming and humorous pages of Unforgettable, My Love Has Come Along.
Amazon: www.amazon.com/dp/B0091NR6XQ

Mirrored Heart
A Short Story

He is determined to keep his secret close to his heart. She is living under the crushing weight of her own secret. Will their marriage survive when mirrored secrets are exposed? Find out in the page-turner, *Mirrored Hearts*, a fascinating story about faith and love in the face of crushing secrets.
Amazon: www.amazon.com/dp/B0109R2380 (FREE)

ENCOUNTERS OF THE HEART SERIES

Book 1 - Shades of the Heart
A Novel

A riveting story about the courage to love in the midst of broken promises, and ultimately about the healing power of forgiveness.
Amazon: www.amazon.com/dp/B00T512KQ2

Book 2 - Mirrored Heart: Sealed by Fire
A Novel

When life takes unexpected twists and secrets are laid bare - remember to breathe. Two hearts. Mirrored secrets. The ultimate solution – A marriage sealed by fire.
Amazon: www.amazon.com/dp/B01AKUA4UK (Kindle Unlimited)

COMING NEXT

Encounters of the Heart Series - Book 4
(The story of Madison & Tyler)

VICTORIOUS BY DESIGN

Lighting the path to your next level

You are one of a kind.

You are fearfully and wonderfully made.

Embrace your uniqueness, talents, and abilities.

You are designed for your purpose.

You are perfect for your purpose.

You are Victorious By Design.

Visit www.victoriousbydesign.com for more information